BONDS
of
COURAGE

A NOVEL

SANDY HILL

"Tangled Threads"
"Bonds of Courage"
"Deadline for Death"
"The Blue Car"

This book is a work of fiction. Although some of the people mentioned, including my ancestors the Stropes, really existed, and some events are real, my interpretations of characters, actions, events and motivations are fictional. Any resemblance to living persons or current events is coincidental.

ISBN: 978-1477581834

tangledthreadsbook.com
tangledthreadsbook@gmail.com

Cover photo: The Susquehanna River above Tioga Point, Pa.

For my daughter, Heather Hill

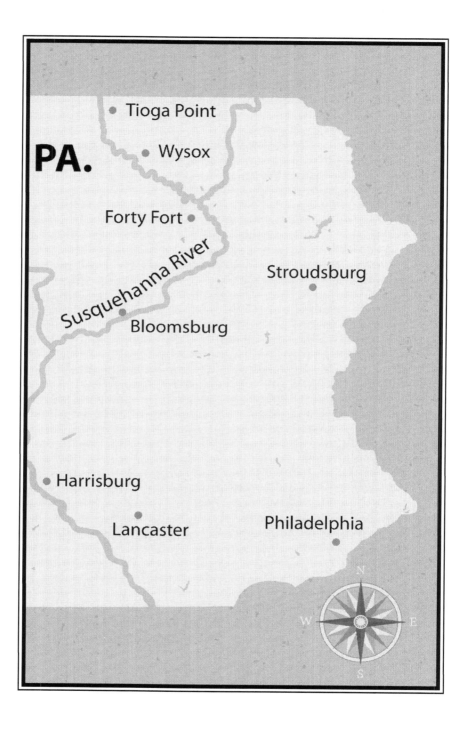

Chapter One

May 1778, Wysox, Pennsylvania

Sebastian Strope lay in bed listening to the sounds of his family settling in for the night. It was a practice he'd drifted into a year ago after Gideon died, a coda to the day, a reassurance his family was still safe, untouched by the myriad dangers of the Pennsylvania frontier. Usually the practice soothed the guilt that coiled inside him like a rattler ready to strike. Tonight, he wondered if any of them would live to see another nightfall.

In the loft above, four-year-old Isaac snored softly. Henry, age seven, turned on his cornshuck mattress with a faint rustling sound like a mouse skittering across a barn floor. Sebastian could picture his son: eyes closed, sturdy body curled into a ball. Jane was quiet, unmoving as usual. But at age 13, even a dreamer like Jane was old enough to pick up the tension in the air. He doubted she'd missed the significance of his talk with Papunhank earlier.

Sebastian looked toward the fireplace where the Indian slept on a bearskin. The fire crackled with an occasional loud pop. The glow from the flames flickered across the turtle clan tattoo on Papunhank's chest and highlighted the glistening bear oil on his shaved scalp. Last night while staring into the flames as they smoked tobacco Papunhank had muttered about a troubling dream, one in which a cabin erupted in flames and people fled through the woods, pursued by wolves with painted faces. Sebastian suspected the tale was a way to send him a warning. With Papunhank's tribe, the Lenni Lenape, under the thumb of the Iroquois, he had veiled his message, refusing to say more. Sebastian exhaled heavily. It was difficult enough for a man to fight the dangers he could see without trying to decipher riddles. In the loft, he heard Jane sigh and stir restlessly.

Turning on her side, Jane fought to subdue the fright rising in her. It was like trying to hold down morning fog. She'd pretended not to listen to Papunhank while she cleaned up the supper dishes, afraid Papa would send her from the room. Even though she was thirteen, he still treated her like a child. Often, he complained she was woolgathering, and she knew she should pay more attention, but sometimes she got lost in imagining the future, when she'd be grown and with a house of her own. One in town with smooth walls and glass windows with pretty drapes. No more oiled windows, log walls, rough floors. It would be heavenly. Then she'd come to with a start to realize her mother stood waiting, hands on hips, for her to complete a chore, or that her father had called her name again and again.

Still, she'd heard enough last night to make her afraid. The wolves in Papunhank's dream must be Indians, but was it this cabin that burned? For a moment, as she stared down at the fireplace, she imagined what it would be like to have flames licking at the walls, smoke filling the room. Her body stiffened. It's not real, she reminded herself. Mama always said don't borrow trouble. Deliberately, she thought of pleasant things: deer lifting their head from the brook to study her with soft brown eyes, geese winging overhead with noisy honks, apple blossoms drifting around her in spring. As usual, it helped. But in the back of her mind, the dream lingered.

Sebastian turned on his side and looked at his wife, Lydia, lying next to him. Her blue eyes, even by the dim light, mirrored his concern. He reached for her hand and squeezed it under the bed furs. After a long, painful second of delay, she returned the pressure and he felt the calluses from the spinning wheel, the roughness from a dozen daily chores. He marveled again at how God had made women so frail but so strong at the same time. He'd tried once to talk to his brother about it but John had stared at him, then turned away as if embarrassed.

"What do you think Papunhank was trying to tell us?" Lydia whispered, a tremor in her voice.

"Use German," he whispered back. "Jane may be awake still."

The language, absorbed in childhood, was becoming their private province. In their new life, English was supplanting it for daily use. Now the children spoke German imperfectly and knowledge of the mother tongue was fading like linen bleached in the sun.

"What do you think Papunhank meant?" Lydia repeated in German, her lips close to his ear so that her breath was almost a caress. He felt a shiver of desire run through him, quickly squelched as useless.

"Indian trouble's coming, I vow," he replied. "I wish Papunhank knew more English so I could be sure what's going to happen and how soon."

"But we've always been friendly with the Indians. And we always do our Christian duty and give a warm welcome. As the Good Book says, be kind to strangers because you might entertain angels unawares." She paused. "Wouldn't that be something?" she said, "an angel in our kitchen?"

"It would." He smiled in the darkness. Lydia's mother, Jannetje, had drilled a sense of duty into Lydia since childhood, and though Jannetje had died five years ago, her admonitions lived on inside Lydia, a presence so constant as to be invisible to her.

"The Lenni Lenape are friendly, yes," Sebastian said. "But the Senecas, I don't know. Since they decided to side with the British, things have changed."

"If we hadn't...," she said, then stopped, struggling not to finish the familiar sentence. He appreciated the effort even while the unspoken words grated on him. He knew how the sentence went. "If we hadn't moved here. If we'd stayed with your parents on the Hudson."

But he'd wanted more. If they had remained in New York state until his father died, the family farm would have been subdivided among him, John, and their brother Wilhelm. It was better to have land of his own, no matter how hard the taming of it. To be the first at something.

"This all may come to naught," he said. "Remember a month ago when we heard rumors of Indian attacks and I rode to Forty Fort to arrange for protection from the soldiers? Nothing happened. Mayhap it's another false alarm."

"Mayhap it is, God willing," she said, "but we have to warn John and Margaretha."

Outside, wolves howled in the May evening and in the distance, a panther screamed like a woman in pain. "Indians don't attack at night," he said. "First thing in the morning I'll find out more. Get some sleep."

Her bare feet brushed against his ankle as she turned on her side away from him, adjusting the coverings. "Your feet are cold," he said. "Let me warm them."

She stiffened, a reaction he had grown to know all too well over the past year, then relaxed. He reached down and rubbed her feet gently, feeling the hardness of the soles from going barefoot.

"That's better," she said. "Thank you." She withdrew them and turned on her side again. In a few minutes her breathing became soft and regular.

Sebastian lay awake thinking, his muscles stiff as an Indian drum. The soldiers hadn't been happy last time to discover that they'd ridden hard for a false alarm. What if they refused to come? And how would his brother

John react? Big John everyone called him for his large frame and 6'4" height. The brothers had done everything together, despite their differing personalities. They'd even married twins, Lydia and Margaretha. Sebastian still remembered his excitement three years ago when he'd heard about virgin land in northeastern Pennsylvania, land waiting for the plow, waiting for him.

"It's our chance to carve out places for ourselves, something to hand down to our sons," he'd told John. Yet John had been strangely reluctant.

"It's a verdammt wilderness," John had said. Sebastian, who usually deferred to his brother, had pushed hard, and eventually he'd persuaded John that opportunity lay along the rich bottom lands of Wysox on the Susquehanna River.

Now help was more than sixty miles downriver near Wilkes-Barre along a trail too rugged and dangerous to travel in darkness. God, he wished he could do something now, instead of lying here helpless. Sebastian smacked his fist into his palm in frustration. Lydia, awake after all, touched him lightly on the shoulder. He pressed his hand against hers, then stretched out flat on his back and decided to pray. He had never understood prayer, how it worked, whether it worked. He couldn't confess a thing like that to anyone though, especially not to Lydia with her deep faith. But if prayer did work, he didn't want to take a chance on not using it. Lord, save us from peril, he prayed silently. Help me to protect my family from harm. And, he thought, with a familiar pang, let me do a better job than I did with my son Gideon.

Chapter Two

Morning dawned cool and gray. The Susquehanna was a slow-flowing swath of dull silver as the sun struggled to break through the low-lying clouds. The light trickling through the greased paper windows did little to alleviate the gloom. Buzzing insects wandered in through the half-open door to land on the food. Not even the strong smell of bear oil emanating from Papunhank, who sat beside Sebastian at the table, deterred them. All through breakfast the Indian had been quiet. Enough silence, Sebastian thought. I must have answers.

"Jane, take the children outside," he commanded. With a worried glance backward, Jane shepherded her brothers out.

"What were you trying to tell us last night?" Sebastian asked Papunhank. "Are we in danger? If so, how soon?"

Papunhank took a final bite of venison and stood up. "I tell dream. You listen. I go now. Wanishi, nitschu. My thanks, friend."

"Wait," Sebastian said, stepping in front of him. "It's my family's safety we're talking about for God's sake."

Papunhank stared at him, arms folded. "I say all I can."

The two stood with gazes locked. I can't force him to talk, Sebastian thought. He's risked a lot as it is. "Go in peace then," he said, stepping aside. Papunhank hurried toward the door. The feathers on his scalp lock waved faintly in the breeze as he jogged across the clearing.

When Papunhank faded into the trees, Sebastian turned to Lydia. "I'm going to see John," he said. "Stay close to the cabin."

He took his long rifle from its peg on the wall, tucked a knife in his belt and strode the half mile north through the woods to John's house. The heavy branches of pines veiled the rough path in dimness. He stopped for a second to look up at the patterns the sunlight made filtering through the fresh spring leaves of a maple tree. Look at all the shades of green, he thought. It's a wonderment how pretty the world can be. He shook his head, impatient at himself. He was as bad as Jane. He broke into a jog, reaching the cabin just as John finished turning his cows out to forage in the woods. Their bells clanked as they ambled across the clearing. The chickens, fresh from the safety of their overnight roosts in the trees, scratched and pecked in the yard, their clucking a counterpoint to the bells of the cattle.

Sebastian stopped for a second, listening to the familiar sounds. God, how he loved the land. Resolutely, he headed toward John.

"Indian trouble is on the way," Sebastian called out.

John stiffened. "Ach. What makes you think so?"

"Papunhank. He spent the night with us. All he'd do is hint. But something bad is coming soon."

"I knew it. That trapper who came through last week said the British were paying the Indians for scalps of patriots. Eight dollars a head." John ran his fingers through his long blond hair as if reassuring himself it was still there. "I vow someone has told the British about your trips to Forty Fort and they have marked us as supporters of the fight for independence."

Why did John so often find fault? I'll not rise to the bait this time, Sebastian thought. "My contacts with the fort may prove our salvation now," he said.

"Not likely. It will be more than a day before a military escort can get here. A lot can happen in that time. We should have chosen someplace closer to civilization."

A sharp reply rose to Sebastian's lips and died aborning. Now was not the time to rehash discussions worn dull with repetition. "Should have is no use. Here we are," he said.

"Yes, here we are. Well, come in and we'll talk."

Inside the cabin, Margaretha rose from her spinning wheel to greet them, her pregnancy clearly visible under her loose gown. Looking at her pinched face and swollen belly, Sebastian suddenly wondered if it had been Margaretha who hadn't wanted to come to Wysox, and John had been thinking only of his wife when he objected. Before they moved here, she'd lost two children in childbirth. It had taken a long time to recover her strength. But if Margaretha's fears had influenced him, John would never admit it. Still, Sebastian was glad he hadn't argued with his brother.

"Sebastian, welcome," Margaretha said in her soft voice, so different from Lydia's matter-of-fact tones.

"Lydia sends greetings," he said. "How are you this day?"

She rubbed her back, then sat back down heavily. "As well as can be expected," she said, picking up her flax, and soon the noise of the spinning wheel filled the room.

"You're the logical one to go to the fort. When can you leave?" John asked.

As usual, John, the older brother, was supremely confident he knew who should do what.

"I'm the strongest. I should stay to protect the women," John said. He looked at Sebastian's thin, sinewy frame, then punched him on the arm, rocking him. "Anyway, you're lighter. You'd tire a horse less than I would."

John was right. But it rankled to admit it. John had done the bulk of the heavy work when they were hewing logs for the cabins and barns. But, Sebastian thought, I can work until I drop, even if I'm not as strong as you. And I'm a better rider.

"Then it's settled," John said. "When you get back with the soldiers, we can decide whether to take the women and children to safety."

"It's settled," Sebastian echoed. "I'll count on you to watch over Lydia and the children until I get back."

"Of course. I'll talk to Lydia after I finish my chores."

Sebastian nodded, hating to leave his family when harm threatened, no matter how logical it might seem. Well, all he could do was ride for help like the devil was chasing him. Considering the tales of Indian atrocities, maybe the devil was.

Chapter Three

Lydia stuffed johnnycake and dried meat into Sebastian's pack with abrupt motions. She'd known he would be the one to go. John knew just how to play him to get him to do what he wanted. But no, that was a selfish thought. John needed to be with Margaretha. The pregnancy was eight months along, so perhaps all would go well this time. Margaretha had never kept a baby this long. Her sister's ankles were swollen lately, and that was a bad sign. Maybe later in the day, she could take Margaretha some nettle leaf tea to help with the swelling.

Sometimes I wish we were back on the Hudson, Lydia thought, then felt guilty. It said in the Bible, "Whither thou goest, I will go." And Sebastian wouldn't have been happy elsewhere. He loved working the fields. Sometimes she thought he cared for the land as much as he cared for her. And for all he chided Jane for daydreaming, sometimes he'd stand with a hoe in his hand staring at a red-winged blackbird on a branch like he was in some other world.

She tucked a stray wisp of auburn hair under her linen cap and straightened. Her duty as a wife and mother was plain. Sebastian needed her support, and the children would be worried and afraid. Not Isaac, of course. He was too young. She smiled, thinking of her chubby son, her little sunshine. Was it wrong to love one child more than another? Or did a mother just love each one differently?

She pushed down the ache for Gideon, buried under the elm tree on the knoll for a year now. "The Lord giveth and the Lord taketh away," she murmured. Surely God must have reasons humans couldn't comprehend. But the loss still hurt bone-deep. Sometimes, she'd be doing the simplest chore, churning butter or weeding the vegetable patch, and grief would spring at her like a cougar, raking her with its claws. Other times, a quiet contentment stole over her at the sight of a row of glistening preserves, a patchwork quilt fresh from her hands, dried herbs from the garden — all fruits of her labor. Maybe that's how Sebastian felt about the land. It was a new thought, and one to cherish. She hated the distance between them since Gideon died, but she couldn't seem to help it.

No use to think of that now. She returned to the problem at hand. The children would have to be kept busy while Sebastian was away, so there'd be no time for fear. They would make soap today. Last spring's supply was almost gone. And they could sing while they worked. That would distract the children.

She looked around. Jane was sweeping the floor with the hickory broom while Isaac watched a bug trundle across the hearth. Henry was outside, probably doing a chore his father had set him.

What advice did the Good Book offer, she wondered. Lydia lifted the huge family Bible down from the mantel. She unhooked the brass clasp and opened the oak cover. As always, she paused to look at the title page and its inscription "In the slow storm of ages." It was a reminder of the eternal Father. Closing her eyes, she uttered a brief prayer for guidance and opened the book at random, stabbing with her finger. She opened her eyes and glanced down to see what wisdom God had to offer her. Psalms 119: 17: "Deal bountifully with Your servant, that I may live and keep Your word." She nodded in satisfaction. A good sign.

She looked up to see Sebastian silhouetted in the doorway. He had not yet tied his blond hair back behind his neck with a rawhide string. In its loose state, outlined by the pale sunlight, it shone like a halo, blond like Gideon's.

"What was it this time?" he asked. He didn't share her practice of seeking random divine guidance, but neither did he mock her. He stepped toward her and looked over her shoulder where her finger hovered.

"May it be so," he said as he put his arm around her waist. She swayed against him like a sheaf of rye before the wind. "I'm ready to go," he said. "I'm leaving my gun with you."

"But you may need it."

"I'll be fine. You remember how to shoot it?"

She nodded. "Let's practice anyway," he said. Her fingers trembled as he guided her through the loading sequence, and gunpowder spilled on the floor.

"I'm sorry," she said. "Let me try again." This time, she willed herself to stillness with a swift prayer and they repeated the sequence without mishap.

"Good enough," he said. "John will be over as soon as he finishes his chores. I've let the cattle out so they can forage. The crops can wait a day. I'll be back as fast as I can."

Lydia nodded, then busied herself with refastening the clasp on the Bible lest she weaken and send her husband off with tears.

When they trooped outside to say farewell, Sebastian took a long look around, seeing the homestead as if for the first time. The springhouse that kept their milk and butter cold was almost invisible from here. He'd had to build it farther than he liked from the house but at least the creek didn't dry up in the heat of summer. The sturdy, two-story barn, built with the help of neighbors across the river, was his special pride. It comforted him to know his livestock were properly housed. Only a poor farmer wouldn't see to his animals.

He shifted his gaze to the fields. The rye, sowed last fall, was well up, aided by the warmer climate near the river and the mild spring. Weeds were creeping in around the edges of the rye. Lydia would see to them with her usual thoroughness. Sebastian thought of the turnip seeds they'd planted earlier in the week. John would have called the notion fanciful, and likely he'd be right, but Sebastian sometimes imagined seeds stirring under the ground, climbing toward the light, eager to become food for his family. He felt a surge of anger to think the war for independence from England, a war he supported but had hoped to stay apart from, might bring harm to him and his. I shouldn't be surprised, he thought. My grandparents fled Germany to escape famine and war. War follows men everywhere.

He became aware Jane was studying him. She was always the watcher, the dreamer. He smiled at her reassuringly. Leaning down, he hugged her.

"Help your mother while I'm gone, Little Bit," he said. Then he pulled Henry close and lifted Isaac high in the air. Isaac laughed and reached for his father's face until Sebastian, eyes glistening but face calm, gave him to Jane to hold and turned to his wife. For one long moment, Lydia clung to Sebastian, then she forced a smile and handed him his pack.

"God be with you," she said, stepping back.

"And with you, dear wife," he said.

Jane hugged her father hard, burying her face on his chest, smelling the leathery tang of his deerskin pants and overjacket, the sweat from his homespun shirt, the hint of fireplace smoke that clung to all their clothes. Then she pulled back while he said goodbye to her brothers and mother. Little Bit, he'd called her. The nickname had fit when she was younger. She knew she was short, skinny, small-boned. But lately her body had started to fill out. One of these days, she would outgrow her nickname.

She watched him take a last look around, wondering what he saw. It seemed as if people could look at the very same thing and see something different. She followed the sweep of his gaze. The massive barn, the pigs rooting in the woods, the shoots of corn pricking through the earth. In the vegetable garden, carrots and peas were smudges of green. Her father's expression was unreadable, then he noticed her watching and smiled as if to say, don't worry.

As her father rode off, Jane turned to look at her mother. Her mother's mouth hoisted into a smile as she waved goodbye, then drooped downward, and Lydia murmured to herself, no doubt in prayer. How many times Jane had seen those lips move in silent prayer for her daughter's failings. Jane was tempted to edge away. She longed for time to sit and look at clouds and trees until she felt calm again. In a minute, her mother would have a list of chores for her. She sighed and stepped forward, facing the inevitable.

"Henry, weed the vegetable garden," Lydia ordered, "then bring in some firewood." He trotted off obediently. "That's a good boy," she called after him.

Lydia looked at the overcast sky calculatingly, then turned to Jane. "I think the rain will hold off. We're not going to hide inside the house like a bunch of frightened cows. We'll make soap this morning. Bring the big kettles, then fetch some water from the creek. I'll get the fire going. When Henry gets back from his chores, he can watch Isaac while we work."

Reassured by the normalcy of her mother's actions, Jane sauntered to the nearby creek that emptied into the Susquehanna, dipped a wooden bucket deep into the cool water and carried it back, trying not to spill any. As she passed the laurel thicket near the creek, she looked longingly at it. Gradually, on each visit to the creek, she had worked away at the thick, almost impenetrable branches until she had carved a private place inside where she could sit undetected, surrounded by green, and listen to the gurgle of the creek, the rustle of laurel leaves, the calls of birds as silence descended. There was no place to be alone in the cabin.

Sometimes, as she sat quietly, she fingered the fossils she'd found in the creek, gray shells imbedded in gray rock. Papa said the land must have been under the sea long ago. Mama said maybe it was from the Great Flood in the Bible. Jane tried to imagine what it would be like to have water covering everything and fish swimming where she stood now. She paused to imagine yet again what it would be like to live in a city in a fancy house with a feather mattress and to wear a silk dress, one your fingers wouldn't catch on because the cloth and the fingers would both be smooth. She looked ruefully at her hands. Buckskin gloves helped protect them for the worst work, but they were rough and reddened. When she complained once, her mother smiled and said, "If rough hands are the worst you ever have to worry about, how blessed you will be."

Back at the house, Jane helped drag out the boxes of lye and fat and combine them in the kettle. Soon she was stirring the mixture over the fire, trying not to gag from the acrid vapors. Sweat poured down her face and she wiped her forehead on her sleeve.

"Ah. It's starting to thicken. I'll take a turn," her mother said. "You can fetch more water. And cool your face in the creek. You've done well."

Jane raced toward the creek, long red hair flying free, bucket bumping against her side. If she hurried she might have time to duck into the thicket before her mother wondered at her tardiness.

As she passed her hiding place, she slowed, drawn toward it like a bee to clover. In the distance, she heard scuffing noises and stopped to listen. Bears sometimes came to the creek, and while they usually didn't bother anyone, it wasn't wise to get in their way. Or maybe the deer and fawn she'd seen recently were coming to take a last drink before retiring for the day and she could spy on them. Deer had to be killed, of course. How else would the family get food and clothing? But they were so graceful she wished it wasn't so.

She edged off the path, set down the bucket and crouched motionless as the sounds came closer, became more identifiable as marching feet. She thought of her father's conversation with Papunhank the night before. Alarmed, she crept into the thicket, dragging the bucket with her, and peered out. She counted ten braves and three squaws walking along the path. The men carried tomahawks, bows and guns and their faces were painted red and black. War paint. The women wore their hair in braids with red paint at the part. In the back of the pack, between two warriors, limped Uncle John, his arms tied, his face bloodied. She stifled a gasp. At the end of the line, hurried along by one of the women, Aunt Margaretha stumbled forward, breathing heavily.

The Indians padded along in moccasins. But their effort to approach silently was spoiled by the way their captives crackled twigs underfoot. Uncle John seemed to be deliberately noisy. The warrior holding John smacked him on the cheek. The blow rocked him, but John continued to scuff along. The Indian struck him again, and John lurched forward, then walked more silently. Farther back, two Indians led horses, their hands over the muzzles to keep them quiet.

Jane's thoughts darted here and there like waterbugs on a pond. What should she do? Should she yell and warn the family? But where could they flee? No neighbors were close enough to help. Feeling like a coward, she crouched silently until the procession passed, then crept after them. When they turned toward the cabin, she veered off toward the springhouse, ducked inside and peered through a chink in the logs.

Chapter Four

Sebastian rode south downriver through the woods at a steady pace. He yearned to gallop, but that would only exhaust Pferd and risk a broken leg if the horse fell. As Lydia was fond of saying, "Eile mit Weile," hurry with leisure. He would have to, like it or not. Miles of rough terrain lay ahead.

At least Pferd was young and well fed and would stand up under some pushing. Pferd was a whimsical name for a horse. When Jane was nine, she had looked at the newborn colt and asked her father the German word for horse. The name stuck and now he had a horse named Pferd, Horse. John had teased him, saying next the family's two cows would become Kuh Ein and Kuh Zwei, cows one and two, and what would happen when the sow farrowed and Jane wanted to name the piglets? Pferd was a silly name, but what did it matter? Jane loved the horse so much, too much. He had warned her it wasn't wise to treat livestock as pets. It hurt when they died or had to be killed for food. Animals should be well cared for, of course. To do otherwise was shameful. But they were one more tool to provide for his family.

His thoughts drifted to what was happening at the farm. Best not to think of that. But that particular furrow was hard not to plow. Were Indians even now creeping up on the house? Or was this another false alarm?

He thought of the way Lydia had swayed against him before he left. Whenever she yielded like that for a moment, he felt a stirring of hope. Since the death of Gideon, she had taken more and more solace in religion. She came late to bed, kept busy, pleaded fatigue, found ways to avoid lovemaking without outright refusal. She was too obedient a wife for that. But when she lay stiffly beneath him as he thrust at her unwilling body, he felt desire draining away and frustration filled him. Yet surely that involuntary sway against him meant something. He had to believe that desire and love still lay buried like seeds beneath the ground, ready to grow in their season.

At a shallow place, he forded the river, putting his shoes in his saddlebag to keep them above the water. The Susquehanna was no longer swollen with spring melt, but the water was cold and the current swift. He shivered as his leggings became drenched. Once on the other side, he wiped his wet feet dry on grass, donned his shoes and guided Pferd along the Indian path that ran near the Susquehanna between the high hills. Following the path was risky, but quicker than going through the tangled woods. Now he paused to rest his horse near the rock known as Standing Stone. On the opposite bank he could see the huge gray stone and hear the rustle of water swirling around the base. It loomed twenty five feet high and some thirteen feet wide, impaled in the river bed where it had fallen from the cliff above long ago.

The sun peeked out, warming his hands and face. A fish broached the surface, leaving ripples that faded quickly in the current. On the opposite shore, oaks and black walnut trees cast wavering reflections in the water. The swarms of mosquitoes that had feasted on his hands had dissipated. Under other circumstances he would have enjoyed the scenery.

He looked at the stone as memory battered him. This was the spot where five-year-old Gideon drowned last June. The scene brought it all back, clear as a mountain lake. Gideon had waded into the river while Sebastian explored the stone monolith, his attention off his son for a few critical minutes. He had been sure Gideon was happily playing with the shiny pebbles on the shore. When Sebastian heard his son's frantic splashing, he'd plunged into the river at a full run, but already the current had carried Gideon to deeper water. The images of that day still haunted Sebastian: Flailing in the muddy water for a hand, a foot, anything. Lungs burning and eyes watering as he searched through the brown murk. Dragging the limp body to shore and pushing on the tiny chest to force water out. Then came the long canoe ride home with Gideon's body sprawled in the bottom. His son's blond hair dried on the way and shone silkily in the sun. His eyes were closed as if he were only asleep. Worst of all had been facing Lydia with Gideon's body in his arms. Three days later, Lydia had miscarried of a daughter. Ever since, Gideon's death lay unspoken between them, a silence that grew louder with each passing month, bitter as wormwood as it said in the Bible. Almost every day, Lydia visited the spot on the knoll where Gideon lay buried beneath a rough shale headstone with his name and a cross scratched into it.

Pferd stirred restlessly, recalling him to the present. On the opposite bank, a heron, startled by the horse's movement, took flight, racing low over the Susquehanna with its wings spread wide.

God help him, he still thought the river was beautiful. It wasn't the river that killed Gideon. He was the guilty one. Sebastian shook his head vigorously as if he could jolt the memories away. The past couldn't be changed. All a man could do was try to guard his family better in the future. Sebastian urged the horse forward at a trot, farther down the valley toward Forty Fort and help.

Chapter Five

The stream running through the springhouse gurgled softly as it flowed over the red clay crocks of milk and butter. Usually Jane loved the cool dimness and the earthy smell. Today, hiding in terror, she noticed nothing except the scene unfolding in front of her. Uncle John swayed on his feet and Aunt Margaretha sat slumped on the ground.

Her mother stood in the yard, one arm around Isaac and the other around Henry. Her posture was straight and her face ashen but calm. Jane strained to listen.

"What can I do for you?" Lydia asked, her quavering voice unnaturally loud as her eyes darted toward the creek. She's trying to warn me, Jane thought.

"Where is Sebastian?" a tall Indian with a breastplate of reeds demanded, stepping forward and shouting inches from her face.

"He's not here," Lydia said. "Why do you want him? He has never done you any harm."

"He is not our friend or friend to the British. He is a friend to soldiers at the fort. Always, he talks to them."

"We are friends to all," Lydia said. "What is your name?"

After a long second, the man replied. "Tokayundisey."

"Would you like some food, Tokayundisey?" she asked, stumbling over the name. "Take whatever you want and go in peace. We have tobacco and some beer, too."

Tokayundisey laughed, but there seemed an undercurrent of respect. Papa always said you shouldn't show fear to Indians, Jane thought.

"No food," Tokayundisey growled. "We want Bastian. We will find him."

He motioned to two of the men and they entered the house, only to emerge a few minutes later grim-faced.

"Not here," one of the men said. Lydia was silent.

"He thinks he can visit the fort and be friendly with soldiers and nothing will happen. He is wrong. And if we find him, we will scalp him," Tokayundisey yelled.

Jane drew in a sharp breath. Her thoughts were muddled, as if her brain wasn't working right. She watched through a crack in the springhouse door as the Indians pulled the meager furniture from the cabin and piled it in the yard. With a big push, they overturned the kettle of soap and began throwing the furniture on the blaze.

Big John, who seemed dazed, stood motionless as the soap mixture oozed toward him and lapped at his shoes. Margaretha lay curled into a ball on the ground beyond him holding her swollen abdomen and weeping.

A warrior carried out the big family Bible and tossed it on the fire.

"No," Lydia screamed. She let go of the children, reached into the flames, ignoring the heat, and snatched the book out, beating at the smoldering leather binding. "Not this," she said, staring at him. "You will not burn God's word."

Tokayundisey stared back, looking as if he might rip it from her hands and return it to the flames. "Then you must carry it."

"Fine. I will."

He pointed at his men. "You and you, round up livestock. You and you, wrap belongings in blankets to carry with us. I will burn the house myself."

He touched a torch to the interior and roof in several places. Flames leapt forth, bright against the sullen sky. Lydia stood white-faced, while Henry buried his face in her skirt. She patted his head reassuringly, continuing to stare at the flames as her lips moved silently.

Tokayundisey turned and spotted the springhouse almost hidden behind the trees. "Ah," he said, and headed toward it.

The action broke Jane's paralysis. She looked around frantically, but there was no place to hide inside and the Indian might spot her if she went out the front door. She dove for the narrow opening under the logs through which the creek ran. The rocks bit into her stomach. Small as she was, it still seemed for a moment as if she would become stuck. Mud and green slime coated her hands and face as she scrabbled in the wet muck. Frantic, she wriggled through, scraping her head on the top of the logs. The area behind the springhouse was wooded. Hoping the building would hide her flight, she pelted for the nearest thick bush, dove behind it and sat motionless. The pounding of her heart seemed so loud surely the Indians must hear it. She breathed shallowly, trying to make no sound. Don't let him see me, God, she prayed. Don't let him see me and I'll never skip my prayers again. And save my family. Please, please, please, save my family.

The smell of the burning house drifted to her on the breeze that rustled the bush where she crouched. Footsteps drew near. This was how the rabbit must feel when the hawk soared overhead. She prayed harder. If God would only spare her and her family, she would never talk back to her mother again. She would do her chores cheerfully. No more dallying or dreaming. Ever.

Suddenly, she heard shouts in the distance. Uncle John was yelling incomprehensible words. The footsteps coming her way stopped, then faded as if the person were running back toward the house.

For a long time she sat on the ground, straining to hear, not moving as bugs crawled over her legs and arms. A wasp landed on her mud-caked face, and she blew softly, trying to dislodge it. There were no more sounds from the house. Her breathing quickened as she imagined what might be happening. Finally, shivering with fear, she parted the branches and peered through. No one was in sight. It was impossible to see the house clearly, but smoke rose beyond the trees. A second plume of smoke marked where the Indians must have burned the barn.

She stood, her muscles painful after so long in one position, and tiptoed toward the springhouse. A ruffed grouse flushed from the nearby brush, its wings thrumming as it took flight. Startled, Jane let out an involuntary scream and froze. No, she must be strong. Mama said that since God was always present, there was no need for fear. She thought of her mother's favorite hymn, "A Mighty Fortress is Our God," and tried to feel brave. Either the Indians were gone or they weren't. If they were gone, she was safe. If not, at least she would share the fate of her family. Standing straight, she walked around the springhouse and toward the house, but she could not stop the trembling in her legs.

The yard was deserted. Pieces of furniture smoldered beside the overturned soap kettle. In the distance, smoke rose from Uncle John's farm. A trail of footprints and hoofmarks from livestock led off through the woods.

Jane stared at the scene with mingled horror and relief. Glowing timbers from the house threw out heat while tiny flames feasted here and there. The stone chimney rose bleakly above the ruins. Crouching behind the springhouse, she had imagined worse — the scalped, tomahawked bodies of her mother and brothers sprawled on the ground, their blood coating the dirt. Her breathing was rapid and she felt dizzy. She sat down abruptly and put her head between her legs. In a few seconds, her mind cleared and her eyes fell on the trail leading into the woods. She stood and walked toward the hoofprints. She clung to the fact that her father would be back with help tomorrow. Maybe he and the soldiers could follow the trail and get everyone back safely.

She wanted nothing so much as to stay where she was. But that was a coward's way. Once, when a bear threatened Henry, Jane had seen her mother face down the animal, running full tilt at it, screaming and waving.

Papa praised her, but he said she was lucky it turned out that way. Then Mama said nothing was ever going to hurt her children while she had breath in her body. Better something happen to her than to Henry. Papa looked away and didn't say anything more after that. Jane suspected he was thinking of her dead brother, Gideon, but no one was supposed to talk about that.

I have to be brave like Mama, Jane thought. Maybe she could help by seeing which way the group was headed. Stifling sobs, she followed the trail back toward Uncle John's house. The scene that greeted her was the same. Burning buildings. Fields green with new growth. And no people. She was alone.

A pile of brown fur lay at the edge of the clearing. Jane moved closer, then jumped back. It was Uncle John's dog, Gertie, with an arrow through her body. That was why there'd been no barking to raise an alarm. Their own dog, Jager, had been killed by a bear a month ago. Uncle John had promised to breed Gertie to a distant neighbor's dog and give her one of the puppies. Now this. It was too much. Despite herself, tears ran down her cheeks and sobs shook her.

Her thoughts fixed on the idea of burying Gertie, making one thing right amidst all that was wrong. In the rubble near the barn she retrieved an axe, its wooden haft charred and still hot to the touch, but the blade usable. Near the edge of the cornfield, where Gertie loved to chase squirrels, Jane hacked at the dirt while tears streamed down her sooty face. Already flies were buzzing over the dog. After an hour, thirsty and tired with blisters rising on her palms, she acknowledged it wasn't going to work. Finally, she settled for cutting a few branches from a nearby pine tree and piling them over Gertie's body where it lay. She bowed her head. "God bless Gertie. She was a good dog," she prayed. "Please, please, keep Mama and the boys safe. And bring Papa back soon with help."

She took a last look around, then picked up the trail of hoofprints and crushed branches. After an hour of following the trail, she decided the party was headed north up the river. A rustling in the brush startled her. She jumped and picked up a fallen branch, holding it half raised. A raccoon scuttled away and she laughed wildly with relief. The sun's rays, penetrating dimly, slanted low across the trees. Intent on tracking the captives, she hadn't realized how late it was. There was nothing she could do here, and soon wolves would be out. Papa said they rarely attacked humans, but they were scary all the same. Panthers and bears prowled the woods, too.

Clutching the branch like a talisman, she hurried home and looked around more carefully, the first shock turned to a sense of unreality as if someone else were inside her peering out. The crops and the herb garden were undamaged. Off to one side lay pieces of her mother's prized linen chest. She knelt and ran her hands over the scrap of wood with the red and gray tulips her father had painted on it so her mother would have something "for pretty," as he said. The hollowed-out stump they used to grind corn sat undamaged with the heavy pestle beside it. A handful of unground corn rested in the bottom of the mortar. Her stomach knotted with hunger, but when she tried to chew the corn, it was gritty and made her nauseous. As she surveyed the smoking ruins, a light rain began to fall, the drops hissing as they hit the hot embers. The rain mingled with the dirt coating her cheeks. She shivered as she walked back toward her family's undamaged springhouse. After a bit, she opened a crock and drank deeply of the cool milk inside, wrapped her shawl around her, then settled back against the rough wall to wait for morning and her father's return.

Chapter Six

Lydia walked along the forest trail, clutching the Bible to her chest and grasping Henry's hand. His face was smeared with soot where she had wiped away his tears with hands stained from retrieving the Good Book. *God is with us, even though I can't see how right now,* she thought. *I've got to be strong for my family.* She didn't feel strong. Her legs quivered so that it was hard to walk, and shock and fear lurked behind her set expression, ready to pounce if she loosened her control. She let out a tiny, involuntary sigh, and Henry looked up at her. She tightened her grip on his hand and tried to smile. "Everything will be all right, son," she said. *And if not,* she thought, *there's no point in frightening him any more than he is.*

The group was spread out single file or in twos. At the head of the procession, an Indian drove the cows. They had left the wildest part of the forest and joined with the Indian path near Wysox. The narrow path was worn deep from hundreds of Indian feet through the years.

Lydia glanced back. One of the squaws, surprisingly, had volunteered to carry Isaac when he got tired. But then, the Indians were said to love children and to spoil their own. Isaac looked scared and she mustered another reassuring smile.

John's head had stopped bleeding, and he urged Margaretha forward. Her breath came in gasps, but she had ceased moaning and stumbled doggedly forward. At the end of the procession, an Indian rode John's horse, holding a white pillowcase filled with their pewter dishes and linens. Her mother had sewn and embroidered that pillowcase for her as a gift in their new home. She saw Tokayundisey's eyes on her and blinked back tears. She would not let him see her cry. Her lips compressed in anger and she stared at him until he looked away. A tiny sense of victory flared in her.

Thanks be that Jane was free. But would she be safe when night fell and panthers came out? Would she be able to find food with everything burned? What would Sebastian do when he returned tomorrow with the soldiers? Too many questions. *Be strong,* she reminded herself. *Your sons need you.*

It looked as if they were headed north to Tioga Point, where the Susquehanna and Chemung rivers merged. Perhaps twenty miles. She hoped Margaretha could make it. John had said the Indians had no mercy for captives who fell behind. Burning the homestead and rounding up the cattle had taken time. She estimated they had left about noon. Now with the livestock to slow them, they might spend the night on the trail, giving her sister some needed rest. Henry tripped over a root and she pulled on his arm.

"You must keep up, my son," she whispered.

"I'm tired," he complained.

"I know. How about if I tell you a story? Here's one. Once upon a time there was a fish who could talk."

Henry trudged along beside her, listening. It began to rain lightly, soaking their clothing and making them shiver. After an hour or so it stopped.

"I'm cold," Henry said.

"Walking will warm us up," she said. "How about another story?"

"Yes, a story, please."

Lydia shifted the heavy Bible slightly, ignoring the shivers that shook her body. "Let's see," she said. "Once there was a miller who had three sons..."

By sundown, her voice was hoarse and her feet and back ached. Despite the stories, she had had to carry Henry several times. She wasn't sure how much longer they could go on. As long as they had to, she supposed. She blessed the lessons she'd learned from her mother now. When Lydia had been a child, she been the only girl in a family of six boys. She was twelve when her mother got sick, and she'd had to do both their work. At times, she'd resented it. But it had taught her that you did what you had to without whining when times got tough. Sometimes she worried that her upbringing had made her tough, too, that Sebastian would have preferred a softer woman. She pushed the errant thought away. The thing to do now was to concentrate on putting one foot in front of another, just as she'd done as a girl.

When the sun sank behind the trees, Tokayundisey finally called a halt. The Indians passed around strips of dried venison and corn cakes. Lydia yearned to sink to the ground and rest, but uneasiness filled her when she saw the way the squaw kept Isaac by her side, patting his shoulder and talking to him in broken English. Lydia walked over to her.

"What is your name?" she asked.

"Rebecca." A white name. A Biblical name. More and more Indians were adopting them as they came in contact with Christian missionaries.

"Thank you for watching my son."

Lydia scooped up Isaac and carried him to where John, Margaretha and Henry sat. Rebecca shrugged and Henry began to chew his venison.

"Wait, son," Lydia admonished. "We must pray." Obediently they bowed their heads and closed their eyes. "God guard us and bring us safely home," Lydia said. Surely a brief, heartfelt prayer was as good as the longer one they usually said. The corn cakes, laced with berries and nuts, tasted surprisingly good and she ate eagerly.

Looking around, Henry spotted a tree with carved, painted figures. "What are those?" he asked John.

"It's how the Indians mark their exploits," he said. "How many captives or settlers scalped, how many warriors they lost, that kind of thing."

"What does it say?" Henry asked.

"I can't read Indian markings," John said. He touched his head and winced. At least it had stopped bleeding.

Henry stared at the carved figures on the tree in fascination. "That one looks like someone holding a club," he said.

Tokayundisey took a knife from his belt and walked toward the tree. John and Lydia tensed. "It's a war club," Tokayundisey said. He carved three large stick figures and two smaller ones into the bark. Three adult captives and two children then. He pointed at the tree, then at each captive, gave a slow smile and returned to his place.

Abruptly, Margaretha, who sat with her back against a nearby oak, moaned and doubled over.

"The pains are getting worse," she gasped. "The baby is coming soon."

Not here, not now, Lydia thought. "Are you sure?"

Margaretha nodded. "I've been feeling them for a while."

John started to get to his feet. Tokayundisey motioned to an Indian. "Tie him," he said.

"I won't try to escape. My wife is going to have her baby," John protested. Tokayundisey looked at him. "Tie him."

As the Indian approached with strips of rawhide, Lydia could see John tense, ready to fight. "Please. We need you," Lydia said.

Trembling with rage or frustration, John stood still and let his hands be tied behind his back. "Sit," the Indian commanded and John slid down against a tree and let the cords be wrapped around it.

"Now, a cowbell for the boy," Tokayundisey said, and another Indian fastened a bell securely around Henry's neck. Henry flushed and reached to remove it.

"Would you rather be tied tonight?" Tokayundisey asked. "Now, if you should try to flee, we'll hear you."

"Accept it, son," Lydia said. "It's not the worst thing that could happen."

Margaretha groaned again. "I can't give birth in front of these men," she whispered. "It isn't seemly."

Indeed it was not, but nothing was the way it should be, Lydia thought. The most important thing right now was to help her sister. But how far did she dare to try Tokayundisey? Margaretha whimpered as a labor pain tore through her, and Lydia strengthened her resolve. She stood and approached Tokayundisey.

"My sister is about to give birth. She needs privacy, a place alone."

He continued stuffing tobacco in his pipe without looking up. "So you can escape? No."

"How can we escape? And do you think I would leave my children?"

He locked eyes with her. "I give you my word as a Christian," she said.

He snorted. "I know about Christians who give their word to Indians," he said.

"My word is good," she said. "I have never broken it."

The other Senecas watched as Lydia stared at him, her chin up. She refused to look away first despite her inner trembling. Finally, he nodded.

"Behind there," he said, motioning to some bushes. The other Indians murmured, but he quelled them with a look. He stared at Lydia again. "If you flee, he dies," he said, pointing to John.

"I won't flee." Lydia looked at Henry and Isaac. "Stay here, children" she ordered. "I need to help Aunt Margaretha."

Rebecca moved forward and took Isaac while Henry stayed beside John, looking as if he wanted to cry but was trying to be brave.

Lydia led her sister behind the bushes where Margaretha sank down on the ground with a sigh. Daylight was gone, and the woods were lit only by moonlight filtering through the trees and the flickering glow of the campfire. Lydia looked around uncertainly. Wolves usually wouldn't bother adults, but would they attack a baby? Maybe this semi-seclusion was a bad idea. But she couldn't have asked Margaretha to bare her nether parts to a bunch of men. Margaretha moaned as fresh pains struck her. Lydia longed for some papoose root to ease her or a knife to slip under her to cut the pains.

"Pant," she said. "It will help."

A breeze soughed through the trees and the crackle of flames from the fire reached them faintly. Margaretha panted more rapidly, then was reduced to moans. As the night wore on, the pains came closer together.

"I can see the baby's head," Lydia said. "Push. Push." Exhausted, Margaretha made one last scream-filled effort and the slippery, blood-streaked baby emerged into Lydia's waiting hands.

"It's a boy," Lydia said. She cleared the infant's throat, slapped him on the back and he let out a wail. His tiny face turned red and his fists pummeled the air. "God be praised, it's a healthy baby boy," she said.

Margaretha smiled. "A healthy baby boy," she repeated. The two sisters stared at each other, locked in momentary joy.

"I have to cut the cord," Lydia said. She hurried back to the fire where Tokayundisey sat smoking his pipe and gazing into the flames. He lifted his head and looked at her inquiringly.

"I need a knife to cut the birth cord," she said.

Tokayundisey hesitated and his face clouded.

"It's a boy," she announced loudly. "And the mother is fine." John's weary face lit with pleasure.

Shrugging, Tokayundisey sat down his pipe and handed her his knife. "If you do not behave, he dies," he said, pointing to John again. "If she can not keep up in the morning, she dies."

"I understood the first time," Lydia snapped, nerves frayed. "She dies. He dies. Everyone dies."

Tokayundisey's eyes narrowed and he gave her a look she couldn't interpret.

Ignoring him, Lydia rushed back, severed the cord and kneaded Margaretha's stomach to stop the bleeding. With the knife and her hands, she dug a depression in the punk under a pine tree and buried the afterbirth.

"What is your son's name?" she asked.

"Elisha Gideon," Margaretha said. "His name is Elisha Gideon Strope." She smiled weakly at Lydia.

Lydia felt a sharp blend of pain and pleasure. A new Gideon. No one could replace her dead son, but it was a loving gesture.

"A good name," she said. "Here is your son, Elisha Gideon." She faltered on the second name. It had been so long since she'd said it aloud. She put the squirming infant to Margaretha's breast. Margaretha held him close, then checked his fingers and toes, caressed the wet, dark hair on his head.

"He's beautiful," she said.

"He's shivering," Lydia said practically. "Wait." She tore off part of her underslip to wrap him in. "Now sleep. You'll need all your strength tomorrow."

The morning dawned mild and sunny. Despite Lydia's fears, no one moved to harm the newborn. Margaretha, moving stiffly and looking pale, nursed the baby, turning away from the group, then held it up so John could see his son. When his hands were freed, he stretched and winced, then awkwardly held Elisha.

Lydia looked with apprehension at Margaretha. Her sister seemed too tired to walk the remaining distance carrying the baby. Something had to be done. Lydia faced Tokayundisey. "My sister needs to ride today," she said, hating the quiver in her voice. "Please let her have the horse. That way we won't slow you down."

"No," he said.

"But she is tired and ..."

"No. Enough," he barked, turning away.

For a few seconds, Lydia's shoulders slumped. She was so tired, the farm lay in ruins, God knew what was happening with Jane and now somehow she would have to see that Margaretha kept up, manage the newborn, keep Henry on track, carry the Bible. She considered leaving the Bible behind. But it was her only physical tie with home, filled with the record of family births, weddings and deaths stretching back to when the first Stropes left Germany in 1709. Besides, if ever there was a time when she needed the solace of God's word this was it. With a silent prayer for strength, she straightened her shoulders and lifted the Bible. "The Almighty suits the back to the burden," she murmured. Hacking a farm out of the wilderness had seemed impossible at first. She remembered the many nights she'd gone to bed exhausted in mind and body. But they'd done it. Somehow, they'd get through this, too.

Before they started off, Rebecca took Isaac to one side and replaced his shoes with a tiny pair of moccasins decorated with white beads and orange porcupine quills. Reaching in a deerskin pouch, she pulled out dye and painted Isaac's face red.

Alarm raced through Lydia. "What are you doing?" she demanded. She stalked over and pulled off one of the moccasins. "His own shoes are fine," she said.

Silently, the woman took the moccasin from Lydia and replaced it. Lydia removed it. Rebecca replaced it. She glared at Lydia when she reached for the moccasin again.

"We go now," Tokayundisey said suddenly. He shot Lydia a glance that silenced any further objections.

Lydia stared at the moccasins on her son's feet, troubled. She had heard of Indians adopting white children to replace family members killed by settlers. Pray God that wasn't what this behavior meant. She'd lost Gideon; she couldn't stand to lose Isaac too. She felt a flash of resentment toward Sebastian. If he hadn't brought them to this wilderness. If he'd moved them to safety sooner instead of this arrangement where he had to ride miles and miles for help. She knew it wasn't fair or Christian, but there it was, a hard spot in her heart like a rock in the middle of a river.

They headed out again, with Henry holding Lydia's hand and Rebecca carrying Isaac, who kept looking down at his new moccasins in delight.

Briefly, Lydia looked back at his leather shoes sitting by a tree. Shoes can be replaced, she thought.

She glanced up to see Tokayundisey watching her. During the journey, she felt his eyes on her from time to time. When their gazes met, he smiled at her, a long smile that reminded her of the way Sebastian used to look when he was thinking of bed play. Nervously, she dropped her eyes.

Shortly after sunrise, they crossed a creek. Tokayundisey called a halt and sent a warrior running back to pull the baby from Margaretha's hands. She screamed as the Indian carried the newborn to the chilly water and dunked him. Lydia rushed forward while two Indians restrained John. Another one grabbed for her and held her arms tightly. Oh God, they're drowning him just the way my Gideon was drowned, she thought. "No," she yelled. "No. Stop."

But in a minute, the baby emerged from the creek, cleaner and squalling indignantly.

"Cold will make him strong," Tokayundisey said, as the warrior returned the wet baby to Margaretha. "Now, we march."

They were reeling with fatigue by the time they approached Tioga Point. Sighting the buildings, Tokayundisey gave five sharp whoops. One for each prisoner, Lydia wondered. Blades of corn showed in the fields, and she thought of Sebastian returning to their ruined farm. She grimaced as she saw scalps on poles at the entrance to the palisade surrounding the encampment. Inside, Indians moved here and there, along with British soldiers in Tory green. Barking dogs ran loose among the dozens of wooden houses and the familiar smell of wood smoke hung over all.

A tall, well-built woman in her fifties strode toward them as they entered the grounds, walking proudly erect without the forward stoop and turned-out toes that often marked Indian woman who had spent their life carrying burdens with a strap around their forehead. Her lighter complexion showed the French side of her mixed parentage. She wore a knee-length blue top decorated with brooches of silver, pantalets of blue cloth, and stockings. Her long black hair flowed behind her and a necklace of white beads ending in a stone cross adorned her neck. It's Queen Esther, Lydia thought. Thank God.

Chapter Seven

Halfway between waking and sleeping, Jane imagined that Henry was tickling her hand to pester her, as he liked to do. She brushed impatiently at the spot, then jerked away. It was a spider crawling across her skin. She catapulted into wakefulness, momentarily disoriented. Around her, a dim, rosy light filled the springhouse. The previous day's events came rushing back. The raid, the destruction, her family captured. Tears sprang to her eyes and she lay on her back sobbing. Finally, she wiped her eyes and sat up with a groan, her body sore and chilled from sleeping on the cold, stone floor. Brushing off her clothing and running her fingers through her tangled hair, Jane stumbled to the door and peered out.

Dawn painted the eastern sky with pink, promising a fair day. The barn still smoldered, and the smell of charred wood hung heavy in the air. She knew it would be so, yet somehow she had hoped it was all a dream. Rather, it was a nightmare. After a moment, seeing no movement and hearing only early-morning birdsong, she stepped outside and looked around. Her mouth was dry with thirst and her hands grimy and sore. She picked her way toward the creek. Gradually, the stiffness left her. Tendrils of mist hovered over the creek as the sun's rays warmed the surface. A deer, head bowed to drink, looked up with wide eyes, then bounded away through the woods, white tail flashing. For once, she felt no surge of pleasure at the sight. Who cared about a stupid animal when her family was torn from her? Bracing herself, she knelt at the stream and splashed water on her hands and face. The cold made her gasp, but it helped clear the fuzziness from her brain. It felt good to wash away at least part of the previous day.

She sat on the creek bank and stared at the moving water. She had never been truly alone before. It felt so much lonelier than choosing to be by herself when her family was nearby. Her stomach reminded her that she hadn't eaten since yesterday. Usually, she would be busy milking the cows by now, then breaking her fast with cold meat, corn bread dripping with maple syrup and still-warm milk. No use thinking about that. She stood up and trudged back to the springhouse. She sniffed at the jug of milk from yesterday. It smelled fine and when she took a taste, it was cool. Probably it would be all right, and she was so hungry. Taking the jug in both hands, she lifted it to her mouth and drank deeply.

She tensed when she heard scuffling noises in the distance. Peering out the door, she saw the family's boar trot into out of the clearing and stand still, moving its pink head back and forth inquiringly. She had always been wary of the mean-dispositioned boar, but now gladness filled her. Papa would be pleased to see that at least one animal had survived the raid. But it hadn't been fed yesterday or today. How long would it stay around without food? Looking at the boar, an idea struck her. If she could capture it for her father, something would have survived that meant a fresh start. She clung to the idea and began to plan how she could trap it. The boar, left loose to forage for nuts in the woods, was half wild. To keep it from wandering away permanently, Jane regularly put out slop for it and the boar associated her with food. Nevertheless, she knew how hard it was to catch a pig.

She looked around for a way to confine it, but there was only the springhouse. It would have to do. Edging over to the mortar, she scooped up the grains of corn in the bottom. The pig watched her with beady, black eyes.

"Sooie, sooie," she crooned, as if she were doing her normal morning chores. It felt weird, as if at any moment Mama would call to her from the open door of the kitchen. Jane glanced at the smoldering ruins of the house, then quickly away.

"Sooie," she crooned again and scattered a few grains of corn on the ground. The boar trotted closer. Its sides were coated with dried mud and a rank smell rose from it. The boar edged forward and gobbled up the corn. Gradually, she laid a trail toward the springhouse. Now if the pig would just enter so she could trap it, how proud Papa would be of her. Moving slowly, she picked up a charred log from the yard. The pig grunted and shook its snout, tusks gleaming in the sun.

"Sooie, sooie," she called, aware more than hunger was tightening her stomach. Papa had told her what to listen for when a pig was getting ready to charge, a deep, chuckling uh, uh, uh sound like a series of sharp grunts. "They're fast," he'd said. "If you hear that sound, get out of the way. There won't be any other warning. And sometimes not even that."

They were close to the springhouse now and the corn was almost gone. She put the last handful just inside the open door, grateful the sill was almost even with the ground. The pig studied the situation, then stepped partway inside the structure, intent on eating. Swinging the log, Jane booted him on the rear, then slammed the door shut. She leaned against it triumphant. One good thing had happened. It didn't wipe away all that was lost, but her accomplishment steadied her. Inside, the pig bumped against the walls, then settled down. Jane's hands were coated with soot again and she walked toward the creek to wash them off, wondering what she should do next.

On the way back from Forty Fort with the soldiers, Sebastian swayed in the saddle and jerked upright. Exhausted from the ride for help and a sleepless night, he rode homeward in a fog.

"Stay lively, man," Lt. Lazarus Stewart, the notorious Indian fighter, called out. Sebastian waved a hand in acknowledgment. Lazarus, a short, stocky man with a bushy beard, rode behind him, along with eight other soldiers on horseback spread out single file along the trail. They had gotten a late start, what with explaining his mission, mustering the men, changing to a fresh horse. Despite his frantic pleas, the fort had refused to send the soldiers out before sunrise, when there would be less risk. Now the sun was well up the sky. The party had passed Standing Stone not long ago and Wysox creek lay just ahead. Apprehension at what he'd find warred with Sebastian's fatigue.

"It's just around the next bend," he called to Lazarus. The smell of smoke drifted on the air. Let it be from the fireplace, he thought, even while he knew the smell was too strong for that. He urged his gelding to a trot. Emerging from the woods to the clearing around the farm, he saw the burned buildings. He vaulted from his horse and ran across the yard. "Lydia," he shouted. "Lydia, Jane, Henry, Isaac."

His voice seemed to echo off the surrounding hills, mocking him with the lack of an answer. He spun in a circle, searching for any sign of life.

"Lydia," he shouted. Still nothing.

Lazarus surveyed the scene from his horse, peering into the woods. "It doesn't look as if anyone is here," he said. "We're too late."

Sebastian turned toward Lazarus. "We can't be," Sebastian said. "We can't be."

The soldiers, rifles at the ready, spread out in a semicircle and kept watch while Sebastian strode around the yard, poking here and there under debris, dreading what he might find. Here the spokes of Lydia's spinning wheel, there a shattered leg from the table. But, God be thanked, no bodies, no blood.

He stood for long moments stunned. His knees felt weak and he fought to keep from falling. His wife and children gone. Everything he'd worked for destroyed, not that burned buildings meant anything if his family was dead.

Lazarus stood to one side watching with a stricken expression, seeming to share his anguish.

Noticing the intact springhouse, Sebastian raced toward it. A low noise, like someone bumping against the wall, came from inside. He motioned to Lazarus, who pointed his rifle at the door. Sebastian knelt to one side. If someone with a weapon lurked inside, he would expect Sebastian to be at eye level.

"Whoever is in there, come out now," Sebastian called. No answer. Cautiously, he pushed the door open. The boar exploded from the springhouse, raking Sebastian's face with a tusk, and raced across the clearing. Lazarus fired, but missed while Sebastian fell to the ground clutching his bleeding face.

"Are you all right, man?" Lazarus asked, striding over. "Let me see." He pulled Sebastian's fingers away. "It missed the eye, but I'd wash that off right away. Pigs are filthy beasts. Here." He pulled a cloth from the front of his shirt and handed it to Sebastian, who dabbed at the deep slash.

"I'll clean this later," Sebastian said. "I need to know the worst. Let's push on to my brother's farm. It's only a half mile."

Just then, Jane came flying up the path. "Papa, Papa," she cried and flung her arms around his waist, sobbing. He staggered and dropped the handkerchief, where it lay forgotten on the ground as he crushed her to him. "You're safe," he said. "Thank God. You're safe." Joy exploded inside him. For long seconds he hugged her, feeling her solid warmth. She was alive.

"Oh, Papa, they..." The blood from his cheek fell on her arm and she stopped in midsentence.

"You're hurt," she said, drawing back. "I heard a gunshot. Are you all right?"

"I'm fine. But the strangest thing happened. The boar was shut up in the springhouse. When I opened the door, it charged out and gored me."

Her face changed as she saw the gash on his cheek. "Oh no," she said, putting her hand to her mouth.

"What is it?"

"It's my fault. I put the... Nothing."

"Your mother and brothers," he said. "Where are they?"

"The Indians took everyone," she said, bursting into tears again.

"Was anyone hurt?" he demanded.

"I don't know," she said. The story came out in a rush, between gulps and sobs. "The Indians came and I hid in the springhouse, and before that they hit Uncle John and he was bleeding, and Aunt Margaretha was on the ground and they burned the house and Mama snatched the Bible from the fire and..."

"Whoa, whoa," he said. "Take a deep breath. And slow down."

Obediently, she inhaled, brushing at the tears on her cheeks. "I was hiding and I didn't see what happened when the Indians took them away." Another sob escaped her. "But the last time I saw them, Mama and the boys were all right."

He closed his eyes in gratitude. "That's something, then."

"How long ago were the Indians here?" Lazarus broke in.

"They came yesterday morning not long after Papa left," Jane said. "There were ten men and three women."

Sebastian turned to Lazarus. "We need to find out which way they're headed."

"I trailed them through the woods for a ways," Jane said. "They were headed north up the river."

"You did? My brave, smart girl," Sebastian said, and was rewarded with a fleeting smile.

"Can we go after them?" she asked. "Can we?"

Lazarus broke in, his expression grim. "It's no use. They have too big a head start. And even if we caught up, they might…"

"Enough," Sebastian said quickly. He suspected that Lazarus had been about to point out that the Indians might kill the captives. Jane didn't need to hear that. He didn't need to think that.

Lazarus paused, then went on. "Even if we caught up, we might not be able to free them. No, they're probably bound for Tioga Point and there are hundreds of Indians and British there. Too many for us to fight. Or they might even take them on to Fort Niagara,"

"God, I hope not," Sebastian said. Their Indian friend Queen Esther might be at Tioga Point, and it was a lot closer and less heavily fortified than Fort Niagara.

"We could try," he said.

Lazarus shook his head. "You know better."

Sebastian blew out a long breath and nodded. "You're right, damn it." He touched his wounded cheek absentmindedly, then winced at the pain. Jane winced too in sympathy.

"Let's see what's happened at John's farm, although I expect it will be the same," he said.

"It is," Jane said. "I've been there, and everything is burned, just like here. And they killed Gertie."

"I'm sorry," he said, hating the feeling of powerlessness. "I know it doesn't help now, but when this is all over, I'll get you a dog of your own. I promise."

"Thank you, Papa," she whispered. "Can we bury Gertie before we leave? I tried, but I couldn't do it."

His throat closed up as he looked at her. "Yes, daughter," he said, patting her shoulder. "We'll take care of that."

Lazarus looked at the angle of the sun. "We'd best head back soon," he said.

Jane made a tiny noise of protest.

"After we bury Gertie," Sebastian said.

"But the dog's been dead a day already," Lazarus said.

"Nevertheless," Sebastian said, "we're not leaving until we bury Gertie."

Lazarus looked at Jane's stricken face, then shrugged. "All right. If we must."

When they arrived at John's farm, Lazarus motioned to two soldiers to dig a grave for the dog and pile stones on it. He fidgeted the whole time and looked around the clearing constantly as if expecting, or perhaps hoping, Indians would spring forth. "There's nothing more we can do here," he said, as soon as the last stone was in place. "We'd best head back directly."

Sebastian stared in the direction the Indians had gone. The desire to go after them tugged at him like a current in a river. Finally, he nodded. "You're right. Let's go."

He hoisted Jane in front of him on the horse, and they headed south toward Forty Fort. As they rode away, Sebastian looked back one last time at the ruined homestead. He'd planned to add a room to the house next month. Lydia had been asking for it, and it would have given them more privacy. Maybe then things would have been different between them. Sweet Jesus. His family had to be all right. They had to.

As they camped that night, Sebastian stared into the campfire, thinking again about flames devouring his home, about his missing family. Off to one side, Jane lay curled under a blanket Lazarus had placed over her. Her breathing was soft and even, although she jerked in her sleep now and then as if reliving the terrors of the previous day. Sebastian felt in a dream state himself, exhausted but unable to sleep.

"I know it's a shock," Lazarus said. "I remember when the Indians burned my affianced's house, butchered the whole family, beheaded her. I swore then I wouldn't rest until we'd driven them out of the whole area. Every time I see another burned farm it comes back to me. God damn them." He'd been picking his teeth with a twig. Now he hurled it into the fire.

Jane stirred restlessly and Sebastian motioned with his head toward where she lay. "My daughter," he said warningly.

"Let her learn young what they're really like," Lazarus said.

"But," Sebastian protested, "I've lived in peace with the Lenni Lenape. One of them warned us of the raid."

"You're not an Indian lover, are you?" Lazarus asked.

Sebastian thought of Lydia and his sons. What was happening to them?

And what of Margaretha? Had she lost another baby? John, that stubborn hothead, wouldn't submit peacefully to captivity. What might the Indians do to him? He looked into the fire and saw again the burned farms, the backbreaking work of three years destroyed, his family torn from him.

"No. I'm not an Indian lover," he said.

"Good. I hate Indians," Lazarus said.

"I reckon I hate the Indians who captured my family," Sebastian said. "I hate what they did, what they're doing. But I can't say I hate all Indians. It's not that simple."

"Yes, it is," Lazarus said. He lowered his voice.

"At least the Iroquois don't..." he paused. "Well, you know, trifle with the women."

Sebastian stared at him. "For the love of God, stop talking about it."

"Sorry. I thought knowing that would comfort you."

"It doesn't," Sebastian said. But then, he thought, I know better than to count on other people for comfort or protection. I learned that lesson a long time ago. The gash on Sebastian's cheek had stopped bleeding, but it gaped slightly open and the pain from the wound, combined with his inner pain, made him feel like weeping like a woman. He felt Lazarus' eyes on him and stared silently into the fire, face set, betraying nothing.

"What do you plan to do about your daughter?" Lazarus asked.

Sebastian roused himself. At least he could take care of Jane. "Take her to my parents' farm on the Hudson River, as soon as it's safe."

Lazarus had treated Jane with kindness, showing a side at odds with his ruthless reputation as an Indian fighter. "My wife, Martha, is expecting a child in six weeks or so," he said, "our seventh. Maybe she can look after your daughter until then, or there's a new widow, Faith Hollenbeck. She's German, like you. Her husband was killed by Indians. Taking care of Jane for a bit might take her mind off her loss."

"Thank you. That's mighty kind of you," Sebastian said.

"After you take Jane up to New York state, you ought to come back and join us at the fort. The army needs all the soldiers it can get."

"I might well do that," he said. "I support the cause of independence from the British. But I'm a farmer, not a soldier."

"Every man's a soldier these days. Or a coward."

Sebastian stiffened. "I'm no coward."

Chapter Eight

Relief flooded Lydia when Queen Esther walked toward them as they entered Tioga Point. Many a time before the war broke out, the half-French, half-Indian woman had visited the Strope home in friendship. Maybe the raid was a dreadful mistake, and Queen Esther would order them set free, even return their livestock. The British had dubbed her queen because she was a tribal leader and the widow of a chief. Lydia hoped she had as much influence as she claimed.

Other Indians streamed out now, the bells on the moccasins of the women jingling and the silver trinkets sewn on their clothes twinkling in the sun.

"Welcome, Lydia, and welcome to your sons," Queen Esther said with no hint of surprise at seeing them. Lydia felt a little hope die.

The baby made a soft mewing sound. "Ah, a newborn," Queen Esther said and reached toward him. Unwillingness in every line of her body, Margaretha drew back. "I won't hurt him," Queen Esther said. Reluctantly, Margaretha released Elisha to her.

"The last time I saw you, you were pregnant," Queen Esther said.

"My baby was born on the way," Margaretha said. "Tokayundisey camped for the night."

Queen Esther looked at Tokayundisey with raised eyebrows. "Did he?" She held up the baby and moved the swaddling cloth aside. "A fine son. Good." She handed Elisha back, then seemed to notice Big John's wounds for the first time.

"What happened?"

"He resisted," Tokayundisey said.

She nodded. "I'm sorry to hear that." She turned to Lydia. "I'll take you and your family to your quarters now. You will be well treated if you cooperate and don't try to escape. If you don't behave, I can't help you."

"But I thought we were friends," Lydia said. "We need your help."

Queen Esther threw up both hands as if in apology. "The Americans drive us away from our homes. Our land is taken from us. The British have promised to help us regain them. I did not wish war, but here it is, and these are my people. I will do what I can for you, but I must stand with them."

Lydia opened her mouth to reply, then stopped. Even through the haze of her weariness and shock, she realized nothing would be served by arguing. The important thing was to keep Queen Esther happy so her family would be treated well.

"Tonight, Big John runs the gauntlet," Tokayundisey announced.

Margaretha gasped. "No," she said. Lydia put a hand on her shoulder in support. She felt sick at the thought of her brother in-law running half naked through rows of Indians wielding sticks and clubs. He was strong, but even the strongest man sometimes suffered fatal injuries before reaching the end of the gauntlet. Lydia looked appealingly at Queen Esther, who looked away.

As the Indians led them to a log cabin, Rebecca swerved to one side, taking Isaac with her.

"Wait," Lydia called. "He needs to stay with us."

"He is mine now," Rebecca said.

Lydia dropped the Bible, hurried toward Rebecca and clutched Isaac, who stifled a cry.

"No," Lydia said, glaring at Rebecca. "He's mine. Leave him alone."

Queen Esther, who had been leading the way, looked back. "Lydia, calm yourself. This is my niece, Rebecca. She means no harm to Isaac. Her own son, just ten years old, was killed by the American soldiers. You are a mother. You know what sorrow that is. It is only fair that she get a son in return as is our custom."

"It's not fair at all," Lydia said, clasping Isaac closer. "Isaac is my son. Mine."

"I know it is hard. But nothing bad will happen to him," Queen Esther said. "He will be adopted into the tribe and treated as one of us."

She motioned to several Indians. One pried Isaac from Lydia's arms and the other two held her as she lunged toward Isaac. Lydia kicked one of the Indians holding her, but failed to free herself. Isaac began to cry. Margaretha, eyes wide and frightened, hugged Elisha closer as if afraid he would be next. When John moved to intervene, an Indian raised a rifle and pointed it at him, finger on the trigger. John froze where he was.

A tall, blond white man passing by paused and looked as if he wanted to interfere, but Queen Esther stared at him.

"This is not your affair, Zach," she said. The man glanced at Lydia, hesitated, then moved on.

"I'm sorry," Queen Esther said to Lydia. "I truly am. But there is nothing

I can do. I promised her a child from the next raid. I did not think that it might be yours. I can not go back on my word. Unless..."

She turned to Rebecca. "Will you accept another child in this one's place? On our next raid?"

Rebecca shook her head and hugged the squalling Isaac.

"Then it is settled," Queen Esther said. "Take the others to their quarters. The women and children over there, John with the male prisoners."

"No, no," Lydia screamed. She bit the hand of one of the Indians. He yelped as she twisted frantically, dragging them a few paces through the dirt toward Isaac before one Indian slapped her hard on the face, making her ears ring.

Queen Esther shook her head. "Please," she said. "You aren't helping yourself." She picked up the Bible and handed it to Lydia. "Find comfort in Scripture. In time, you will get used to it. We all have lost loved ones and gone on."

"You never get used to losing a child," Lydia said. "Never.

"Don't be afraid, Isaac. I'll come for you," she called over her shoulder as they led her and Henry away.

Their cabin was small with a fireplace at one end and rude beds piled with furs and quilts along the walls, a wooden table and two benches. A subdued light shone through the greased paper at the windows, while the pitch torches set into chinks in the walls filled the room with smoke that stung the eyes.

Lydia looked around vaguely, dazed. Elisha began to cry and Margaretha seated herself on the bench, turned her back to undo her dress and suckled him. Henry ran over and dove under one of the beds, which was elevated above the floor on wooden legs. "A cave," he said. "I'm a bear, and this is my cave. Look, Mama. I'm hiding in my cave. I'll be safe here."

"Be still," Margaretha said. "Don't bother your mother. She has enough on her mind."

Lydia blinked as if awakening from a nightmare. "Let him be. We'd all like to hide somewhere safe," she said and walked over to put the Bible on the table, then plopped down on the other bench. She sat staring into space for long moments. First Gideon drowned, and now the farm burned, Isaac taken from her. Where would it end? She sighed heavily and brushed away tears. Somehow she had to go on. She looked around the cabin, trying to focus on what they would need to survive here. A knock on the door made her jump and she stood eagerly. Perhaps Queen Esther had relented and was bringing Isaac back. The young man who had looked sympathetically at them earlier stood in the doorway. His tall, skinny frame and the way his blond hair was outlined by the sunlight reminded her momentarily of Sebastian and she stifled a renewed stab of pain.

"Do you know where my son is?" Lydia asked. "Is he all right?"

"He's in the biggest log cabin, the one we call Queen Esther's castle."

"Can I see him? Can you take me to him?"

The man shifted from foot to foot.

"Please, oh, please. I won't make trouble. Just let me see him," she begged.

He backed away. "I'm truly sorry. I don't rightly think I can. It would only cause problems for both of us. But I got one piece of good news. I come to tell you that Queen Esther done some talking and John won't have to run the gauntlet after all."

"Thank God," Margaretha said.

"Thank you," Lydia said. "That's some comfort at least. What is your name?"

"Zach. Zach Wilson. I'm a trader here. I bring in flour and other goods to sell."

Henry peered out at the trader, who had a rifle slung over his shoulder. Zach winked at him and Henry retreated. "Is there anything I can get for you folks?" Zach asked.

"Diapers, and clothes for the baby," Margaretha said.

"And food," Lydia added. "We've haven't eaten since early this morning."

The thought of food was unappealing, but Henry and Margaretha needed to eat. And she had to force down food too. It was vital to keep up her strength, even though escape seemed unlikely at this point. Palisades surrounded the settlement, and the narrow doors at each end were guarded. Still if Daniel could escape the lion's den, the Hebrew children escape the fiery furnace and Jonah be cast from the belly of the whale, perhaps with God's help, they, too, could come out of this safely. The biggest problem would probably be freeing Isaac so he could go with them.

She thanked Zach profusely when he arrived with the food and a few diapers for the baby and gave him a weak smile.

"My pleasure," he said, smiling and giving a half bow as he left. Later, he brought her pen and ink so she could record Elisha's birth in the family Bible. The entry comforted her. It made her feel that someday they'd all be together again and life would return to normal.

The day passed in relative freedom as they wandered around, exploring. Constantly, she looked for signs of Isaac, feeling his absence as if part of her had been torn away, but she saw nothing. The land where the rivers met was flat, and neat fields of corn and other crops stretched all around. The captives were watched constantly but not interfered with as long as they didn't stray. But Lydia didn't fool herself that they would be allowed to leave. Carefully, she began noting what routine she could. Watchfulness, knowledge, patience would all be required if they were to escape. She vowed to be calm. Anger and wailing clearly would get her nowhere. Inside, she might burn with the agony of her losses. But Henry and Isaac needed her.

Toward evening, Queen Esther stopped by. "How are you?" she asked. "I'm told the trader brought you food."

"Yes. Thank you. Now I want to see Isaac," Lydia said.

"That's not possible. The adoption ceremony will be tonight. Then he is Indian."

"What do you mean?" Her voice rose despite her resolve to act calm.

"We will wash him clean of his white blood with water and robe him in new garments. Then, we will mourn my niece's lost son and welcome Isaac as her new son. Truly, no harm will come to him. We love our children."

"He already has a mother. This is wrong. Surely you can see that,"

Queen Esther looked at her, shaking her head. "My own grandmother was taken captive as a teenager and adopted into the tribe," she said. "She thought it was a tragedy and talked of killing herself. But in time, she found it a good life. And so have I. Now I have a position of trust and honor. Isaac will have a good life too." She left without another word.

"This is wrong," Lydia whispered again as she watched Queen Esther walk away.

Lydia had thought she would be unable to sleep, but the physical and emotional rigors of the past two days had left her exhausted. She awoke to a dream of her dead son, Gideon, calling to her through a veil of water, and realized her eyes were wet with tears. For a few moments, she lay still, orienting herself. Around her, the others still slept. Henry's soft snore wrenched her back to the night before their capture when Sebastian lay beside her. How she would welcome that now. She looked over to where Margaretha slept with Elisha curled against her. At least Lydia knew Sebastian was alive and Margaretha knew naught of what was happening to John.

"This is the day the Lord hath made," Lydia murmured, as she did every morning. I can't rejoice and be glad in it like the rest of the verse says, she thought, but God is still with us. "Help me to get Isaac back again safe, and to be a good mother and sister," she prayed.

Strengthened, she tiptoed to the door and looked out. Dawn was breaking, but inside the cabin it was still too dark to read. With a prayer for guidance, she took the Bible outside, opened it and pointed. Her finger fell on Numbers 35: 3. "They shall have the cities to dwell in; and their common-land shall be for their cattle, for their herds and for all their animals." Did that mean the Indians or the settlers? This was going to be one of those times when the way ahead was unclear. Well, she'd just use the wits God gave her. Behind her she heard the sleepy voice of Henry calling "Mama?" and turned to go in again.

Later in the morning, she approached Queen Esther's dwelling. Women looked up curiously from stretching skins on wooden frames or paused in stirring kettles as she passed. Margaretha had asked her to find out when she could see John, and Lydia intended to demand again that Isaac be returned. Or at least that she be allowed to see him.

Queen Esther's home was a long, low building made of planks and hewn logs. Over the porch was a sculpture of a wolf, the symbol of her clan. Esther stood outside talking to a young, well-muscled Indian with a scalp lock adorned with feathers. He wore a red cloak, and a necklace of bear claws encircled his neck.

"Ah, Lydia, meet my son, Gencho," Queen Esther said, pride in her voice. She hugged him as he left, then turned to Lydia. "How do you fare?" she asked.

"How should I fare?" Lydia responded. "You know I lost my Gideon a year ago. How can you take a son away from me now?"

"I am truly sorry for your loss," Queen Esther said. "What is done cannot be undone."

"When you supped at our house last autumn, you said you hated war and wanted the Indians and settlers to live in peace," Lydia said. "Was that all a pretense?"

"We do not always get what we want. You know that well."

Lydia looked at the cross around the Seneca's neck. "You call yourself a Christian. Is this a way for one Christian to behave toward another?"

A pained looked passed over Queen Esther's face. "Do not judge until you have tried to walk in two worlds," she said.

"Thank you for sparing John the gauntlet," Lydia said. "My sister would like to talk to him, and I want to see Isaac."

"It is best if you forget Isaac, difficult as that may be. Let him be a sweet memory. As for Margaretha, if she wants to see John, she had best be quick about it. The British have decided to transfer him and some other male prisoners to Fort Niagara. They leave within the hour. I have told Tokayundisey to go with them."

Lydia started to protest.

"I am doing a good deed for you," Queen Esther said.

Lydia thought uneasily of the way Tokayundisey had looked at her on the trail. "I'll tell Margaretha about John," she said.

"Good. I will send someone to show her the way."

Lydia's thoughts were busy on the way back to their cabin. They had to escape. Her mother had taught her about herbs. If the Indians let her forage in the woods for medicinals and cooking herbs, escape might be possible. But not, she vowed, without the others. As she walked, her eyes scanned passersby, hoping for a sight of Rebecca and Isaac. She paused at the entrance to the cabin, girding herself to tell Margaretha she would be parted from John. Momentarily, she thought of the grief and uncertainty Sebastian and Jane must be feeling now. Then she took a deep breath and went inside.

As Jane entered Forty Fort with her father, she examined her temporary home through a blur of fatigue and shock. At least it looked sturdy, a place where they would be safe. Wooden logs, pointed at the top, formed walls the height of two men. In each of the four corners, blockhouses protruded. As she rode through the massive gate, a confusing mix of sight and sound greeted her. Dogs barked and soldiers drilled in a giant field, while against the walls children played outside huts and women talked or sewed.

"Let me get my wife for you," Lazarus told Sebastian.

"Then can we go see Pferd?" Jane asked. The horse seemed a familiar anchor in a sea of change.

"When we've properly greeted Mrs. Stewart, Liebchen," her father said. "Pferd will manage for a while longer without us."

"She really loves that horse, doesn't she?" Lazarus said.

"Yes. And he loves her, as much as a horse can love anyone. I swear she knows as much as a grown man about horses. She has a way with them."

Jane felt a momentary glow at the unexpected praise.

In a few minutes, a plump, smiling woman in her late thirties came toward them, moving slowly. She was heavy with child. Behind her came a slender, plain-faced woman of perhaps twenty two. Strands of curly brown hair hung from under her cap.

"This is my wife, Martha," the lieutenant said, introducing the older woman. "And this is Faith Hollenbeck, the widow I told you about."

Jane studied them. One of these women would be her companion until Papa took her to the farm on the Hudson. She remembered what Lt. Stewart had said about his wife when he thought Jane was sleeping. Six children already, and another on the way. All would require tending, no doubt. The decision of which woman to choose was easy. Jane nodded politely to Mrs. Stewart and smiled warmly at Faith, who partly hid her mouth with her hand as she smiled back.

"It looks as if the young people have taken a fancy to each other already," Mrs. Stewart said. Jane edged closer to Faith and looked appealingly at her father.

"So it would seem," Sebastian said.

"That's good," Lazarus said, "because we're crowded here. More and more families are coming in. You'll have to bunk with five other men over there."

He gestured abruptly toward one of the cabins. At the sudden movement, Faith winced and stepped back. Jane stared at her, and Faith reddened.

"Jane can stay with Mrs. Hollenbeck and some other single women," Lazarus went on.

"Can we go to the stables now?" Jane asked.

Faith looked at her curiously. "The stables?"

"Our horse, Pferd, is there. I want to see him."

"Your horse is named Pferd?" Faith laughed, covering her mouth again.

"It's not funny," Jane said. She wondered if she'd made the wrong choice of companion.

Instantly Faith sobered. "I'm sorry. I didn't mean to poke fun. I just never heard of a horse named Horse before."

"We have to go that way anyway," Lazarus said. "Then I'll get your father settled."

At the stable, Pferd whickered and nudged Jane with his nose. He's glad to see me, she thought. She longed to talk to him as usual about what had been happening, even though he wouldn't understand. But others were watching so she settled for petting him. His skin felt comfortingly warm and velvety.

"The Indians took our horse," Faith said suddenly. "We had a dog, but they killed him." Her voice was sad.

Jane's irritation at Faith vanished. "The same thing happened to my uncle's dog," she said.

In a friendly mood, the two walked across the big open yard. On the way, they passed a woman making soap in a big kettle. For a few seconds, the events of the previous morning flooded back, and Jane's step faltered.

"What's wrong?" Faith asked.

"Just remembering," Jane said. "You know, when the Indians came."

"I try not to remember things like that," Faith replied. "It's not easy, but I try." She put her hand to her face again.

"Did the Indians hit you?" Jane asked.

"No." Faith looked startled. "Why?"

"I just thought perhaps your mouth got hurt."

Faith faced her square on. "I know why you said that." She opened her mouth in a parody of a smile, revealing a gap in her front teeth and a broken tooth beside the gap. "Yes, my smile is ugly," she said. "You didn't have to tell me."

"No," Jane protested. "You have a nice smile." Although truth to tell, the gap did mar Faith's looks.

"So you say."

"No. It's true. I'm sorry if I was rude." Mother would be horrified at my behavior, Jane thought. She wished fervently her mother was there beside her to be horrified.

"It's not important," Faith said. "Anyway, it wasn't the Indians. Come on. I want to show you where we get water. The springhouse is outside the fort, and there's a hidden tunnel so we can draw water without being attacked."

Jane followed her, still wondering what happened to Faith's mouth.

A week later, Jane stood watching three girls play hopscotch on a grid drawn on the ground with a sharp stick. Last week at this time, she thought, I was at home with my parents. It seemed like months ago. The first days at the fort had been a blur. She did what she was told, helped cook, wash clothes, mend, answered when people talked to her. Yet all the time, it was as if she were watching someone else do these things. Papa came by to talk to her every day, and she tried to smile and act natural so he wouldn't worry. But inside she felt like one of those cornhusk dolls, dry and brittle, ready to break. Even talking to Pferd didn't help, because what was there to say after the first recital of the facts?

It hadn't all been horrible. Early on, Faith pulled out a checkered board and some round playing pieces and introduced her to the game of draughts. Jane liked figuring out which piece to jump over and how to capture Faith's pieces. Sometimes her father joined them. Then Faith seemed to lose every time, laugh and ask him for tips on strategy.

The day before, on Sunday, soldiers had piled two drums on top of each other for a pulpit and a minister preached a long, boring sermon about being soldiers of God, after which everyone sang "Awake my soul, stretch every nerve" so slowly and gloomily that Jane felt as if her every nerve was indeed being stretched.

The evenings, when darkness fell, were the most difficult. There was nothing to do but lie in bed, worrying about her mother and brothers.

Now as Jane watched the children play hopscotch, she began to notice more of her surroundings. One of the girls reached down to grab the pebble being used for a tile, overbalanced and fell to the ground, giggling. Jane smiled involuntarily.

Faith walked up and put her hand on Jane's shoulder. Jane was growing fond of Faith, who was young enough to be a companion but old enough to be motherly.

"You've watched the game long enough. Give it a try," Faith said.

Jane nodded and walked forward.

"Can I play, too?" she asked.

"Sure," a girl about her age said.

When Jane hopped to square ten and back to the start without falling, she beamed and looked at Faith. Her father was standing beside Faith and they were smiling at each other.

Chapter Nine

June, 1778

Sebastian knelt in a row of soldiers in the middle of the Forty Fort parade ground as they drilled for battle. The afternoon sun beat down relentlessly, making him sweat beneath his fringed linen shirt and buckskin trousers.

The row behind him stepped forward while his row began reloading. A third row stood ready to replace the second row in a seemingly endless drill. The drilling was boring, but at least it kept him busy. A man needed work to do.

Continuing Indian raids the past month had made it too dangerous to take Jane all the way to his parents on the Hudson River, and he was no closer to finding out how his wife and children fared. Instead, he had become a part of the volunteer group of farmers being whipped into shape by Lazarus Stewart. Lazarus had pressed him to join the army officially, but Sebastian thought of his obligation to Jane and refused. As word of atrocities drifted in, he began to wonder if Lazarus was right about Indians. Still, he reminded himself of Queen Esther and the Indian who had warned him of the raid. Not all Indians were alike, no matter what Lazarus said.

After an hour, Lazarus dismissed the men, and Sebastian headed toward the cabin where Jane was staying.

"Your daughter isn't here," Faith said as he walked up. "I'm not sure where she's gone. I heard that Mrs. Stewart's dog had puppies, and she may be there."

"Ah, that would attract her." He scratched at the scar where he'd gotten the new smallpox injection all the soldiers were getting, then wiped his neck with his handkerchief.

"You look like you could use a dipper of water."

He smiled. "That would be most welcome."

He had come to know the widow better in the past four weeks. She had a gentle, friendly way he found admirable in a woman.

"It is powerful hot today," Faith said. "I thought I might cool off by wading at the edge of the river, if I could find someone to stand watch. It's shallow at this time of year."

Sebastian considered. Wintermoot, a stockade a few miles upriver, had reported all quiet the last day or two. No telling how long it would last, but it was tempting to enjoy it while they could.

"I could stand guard for you," he said, "if we're not gone too long."

"Thank you," she said. "That is most kind." She smiled, covering her mouth.

Jane had told him about the conversation she and Faith had had, and he suspected Faith's husband had struck her, damaging her teeth. He was grateful that explanation had not occurred to Jane. She had never seen a man hit a woman and pray God she never would. Nausea filled him at the thought of blows falling on a defenseless woman or child. The strong should protect the weak. Yes, it was a man's duty to rule his household, but with kindness. He didn't hold with everything in the Bible, but he liked that verse in Proverbs about the worthy woman and how her husband called her blessed for her hard work. A longing for Lydia filled him so strong he thought it couldn't be borne. But it must be borne.

Where was she now? Lazarus had said the Iroquois didn't molest their female captives. But what about the British? And if he got his family back, how willing would Lydia be to start over at Wysox, especially if John and Margaretha abandoned their homestead? Yet he couldn't bear to give up his dream of a farm of his own. He was building for his family's future. Many questions, no answers. An excursion to the river was just what he needed.

Faith and Sebastian walked in silence toward the Susquehanna. "You seem very serious today," she said. "Lt. Stewart is working you too hard."

"No. It's not that," he said. "I was thinking about my family."

"Ah, I know you worry about them and miss them." Her voice was gentle.

"I do. I know you must miss your late husband even more."

"Of course," she said.

At the river, he watched with pleasure as Faith took off her shoes and waded barefoot in the shallows, holding up the hem of her dress and displaying her trim ankles. She saw his gaze, hesitated, then smiled. "Come on in," she urged. "It's refreshing. It will do you good."

The water shimmered in the sunlight. He looked around, seeing no sign of danger, laid his rifle on the bank, pulled off his shoes and stockings and stepped into the cool water.

"It feels good," he said. She laughed and splashed playfully at him. He dodged and flicked water back, almost slipping on the algae-covered rocks on the bottom. They splashed back and forth at each other, wetting their clothes. Her skirt clung to her, outlining her thighs. The river, which had been a place of bad memories since Gideon's death, became briefly a place of sunshine and laughter with a young, pleasant woman.

Faith waded toward him smiling, then put her hand to her mouth. Gently he reached to pull her arm down. "You don't need to do that," he said. "You have a nice smile."

At his touch, she stiffened, then relaxed.

"Not all men hurt women," he said.

Tears filled her eyes. "I know you never would," she said. She started to step up on to the bank, but appeared to lose her balance. Her cap fell off as he grabbed for her. They fell backward to the ground together. He looked at her, seeing her wide eyes, her hair flowing loose, her barely parted lips.

She started to cover her mouth again and he stopped her, putting one arm around her.

"I know I'm ugly," she said.

"No, you're not," he said. "You're pretty."

"Truly?" she said. "Thank you." She reached up and kissed him lightly on the lips.

Startled, he froze. Then, almost without thinking, he kissed her back, feeling her lips soften under his. His arms tightened around her, and he kissed her again. Her breasts pressed against his chest, seeming to burn into him, and she slid one hip over his. His body responded instantly, but instead of pulling away at the feel of his maleness, she pressed closer. Half-formed thoughts raced through his passion-fogged mind. It had been so long since he'd held a willing woman in his arms. God knows, Lydia loved him, but since Gideon died, she hadn't been willing. A man yearned to be wanted by his woman. What would be the harm? No one would know. He loosened his hold, sliding one hand toward her breast. It felt wonderfully soft and exciting. She gasped and he hesitated, wondering if he had misread the signs. When she left his hand there, he was tempted to go farther. No, he thought. No. I must not. I made a vow to Lydia and God, and I will not break it just because I am tired and lonely. Lydia likely is tired and lonely, too. With a groan, he wrenched himself away from Faith and sat up.

"This is wrong," he said.

She gave a quick half nod, then looked away. "I know. But…" Her voice dropped to a whisper. "But I feel so alone. And scared. And I like you."

She lay back, her body spread out before him like a banquet for a hungry man. He stared at her for several long seconds. Then he jumped to his feet. "We need to get back," he said, turning away. "All right," she said. "If that's what you want."

He reached out to help her to her feet, still feeling desire racing through him at her touch. He released her hand as if it might burn him, retrieved her cap and handed it to her, watching her tuck her glistening long hair back in place.

They brushed at their clothing, straightening and cleaning it as best they could.

As they started back, Sebastian saw someone running far ahead of them. My god, he thought. I hope no one saw us.

They walked the rest of the way without speaking, avoiding each other's eyes. Just before they reached the fort, Faith turned to him. "I have something to say. I am ashamed."

"No. I am the one who should be ashamed," he said.

"Let me finish. I shouldn't have done that. I let my loneliness speak instead of what I know is right. But I thank you for telling me I am pretty. Your wife is lucky. Almost, you make me believe there are still good men." Then she hurried on ahead.

Still unsettled, he went straight to his cabin and lay on the bed, trying to make sense of the afternoon. He relived the moments when she lay against him, the feel of her lips on his, her body pressed against his. Yet he loved his wife. Just that morning he had awakened thinking about Lydia, about how she used to laugh when he kissed the back of her neck as she bent her head over some task. About the tiny, crescent-shaped scar on her thigh where she'd fallen on a stick as a child. God knew what she was suffering now. What kind of man was he?

About 4 o'clock, Lazarus poked his head in the door.

"We've gotten word that the British and Indians are building boats and making canoes at Tioga Point," he announced. "They must be planning something big."

"Is the fort in danger?" Sebastian asked, sitting up.

Lazarus' eyes glistened. "Let them come," he said. "We can whip them. Maybe I'll get to kill a few murdering copperheads."

A wave of revulsion swept Sebastian. He longed to be back on the farm in a world where people didn't scalp others or kidnap innocents or burn homes that men had poured their sweat into. "What do we need to do to prepare?" he asked.

"We'll convene the men at dawn and talk about strategies," Lazarus said.

As soon as Lazarus left, Sebastian thought of Faith. He needed to talk to her, to let her know they could still be friends. She needed a kind man as a friend. He would be a model of proper behavior from now on. Determined to set the right tone, he went to Faith's cabin. She stood in the yard surrounded by other women and he had to content himself with a request to watch over Jane if things went wrong.

"You can both flee to Fort Penn at Stroudsburg if things go badly. Leave word with a pastor there so if I have to flee, too, I'll have news of you. If you deem it safe and can find someone to escort you, take Jane on to my parents' farm on the Hudson."

He paused as she nodded, then gave her instructions on how to get to the farm.

She smiled tremulously at him. "You may count on my caring for Jane as if she were my own daughter," she said.

He found his daughter at Mrs. Stewart's house, looking at five puppies tumbling around beside their mother in a big wooden crate. As he entered, Jane reached in and picked up a brown puppy with a white spot on the tip of its tail. It wriggled in her grasp.

"This is my favorite," she said. "She's smart and she's always exploring. And she looks a little like Gertie."

Sebastian knelt. "She does, doesn't she?"

"Mrs. Stewart says they'll be ready to leave their mother any time now," Jane said, darting a glance at him.

It was obvious Jane hoped for a puppy, and he was determined to fulfill his promise. But now was not the time. Fighting might begin soon. Plus there was the long trip to his parents' home still to come. He scratched the puppy's neck, and Jane held it up, its legs kicking wildly, and cooed to it. Her face was alight with happiness.

He smiled at her. A puppy was still wildly impractical, but who knew what the future held? She had little enough to make her happy here.

"All right. Ask Mrs. Stewart if you can have one of the puppies," he said.

She looked up at him, still clutching the puppy. "Oh, Papa, do you mean it?"

"I do. But you'll have to be the one to take care of it."

"I will," she said. "I will. I already have a name picked out. Gertie."

"A good name," he said. "Now, there's something I need to talk to you about."

She looked at him gravely and cuddled the puppy. "All right, Papa."

"It may be that the fort will be attacked. If it is, I'll have to help fight. I want you to stay with Faith Hollenbeck so I won't have to worry about you. Will you do that?"

Her eyes were wide with alarm. "But you'll be safe, won't you?"

"Of course. But things can get confusing, and I'll feel better if we have a plan. I just talked with Mrs. Hollenbeck, and she has agreed to look after you."

She frowned. "What about Mrs. Stewart? Can't she do it?"

"She'll have her hands full, and Mrs. Hollenbeck has no other responsibilities. It's better this way."

He paused. He knew he was scaring her, but facts were facts. People got killed or separated during battles.

"If worse comes to worst and the fort falls, you two should make your way east to Stroudsburg. Now listen: From there, go over the Water Gap into New York state and on up to your grandparents at Round Top on the Hudson," he said. "I've told Mrs. Hollenbeck how to get there."

He put his hand on her shoulder, reminded of how young and small she was. "All right, Little Bit?"

Jane nodded without speaking and put the puppy back in the box.

Lydia walked across the enclosure at Tioga Point carrying a woven basket. The meadows were bursting with strawberries; they would make a good addition to supper. Earlier in the week, the Indians had held a ceremony to celebrate the ripening of the strawberries. Drums had beat loudly and there had been high-pitched ululating, singing and carrying on. The Indians had worn flowers in their hair and waved wands and turtleshell rattles while they danced. Queen Esther said it was to thank the spirits for their bounty. And she had shared with Lydia how to make a strawberry drink that Henry enjoyed. It would be good for supper tonight. She had yet to figure out a way that everyone could escape. Instead, one day seemed to slide into another with nothing happening.

Now as Lydia ambled along in the sunshine, the breeze tugging at her skirts, she was lulled into some faint semblance of peace. The trader, Zach Wilson, walked beside her. He had been a godsend during the past month, keeping them company, helping with the heavy chores, building a bench outside the cabin for them to sit on. And he had brought her news of Isaac from time to time. She had spotted her son in the distance, but never been close enough to talk to him. If not for Isaac's absence, the captivity would have been endurable. The war couldn't last forever. Then they could start life over. She hoped desperately that Sebastian would forsake the Susquehanna farm and return to the Hudson.

"How long have you been a trader?" she asked. Zach had spoken little of his background.

"Oh, maybe five years. I'm a restless sort and trading suits me. I get to go here and there, see things, meet people."

"Have you no home then, no one special in your life?"

"Not yet. Waiting for the right one, I suppose." He looked sideways at her.

"And your family?" she asked. It was pleasant to walk and talk in the sun, even far from home.

"I haven't got much to speak of. My pa died when I was little. Bled to death when he cut his foot with an axe chopping wood." His tone was matter of fact. "My ma's still alive over Stroudsburg way near the Delaware River. That's where I hang my hat when I'm not out trading."

"Oh, yes. I've heard of the town. What of your brothers and sisters?"

"I have a brother who's reading for the law in Philadelphia. And a sister who married an innkeeper there. I had another sister, but she died in a fall from a wagon last year. I guess our family is under a curse."

"I'm sorry for your loss," she said. "I had a son who drowned. And a brother who died of smallpox. So I know how painful it can be. But faith can be a comfort."

He said nothing. She'd never heard him speak of God and suspected religion played little part in his life. How did people manage without the comfort of knowing God was with them no matter what?

"Do you see your family in Philadelphia much?" she asked as they approached the gate nearest the river.

He shrugged. "No. They don't have a lot of truck with me. I'm the black sheep of the family. Or maybe the prodigal son." His voice had an edge to it.

"Even the prodigal son was welcomed home," Lydia said.

Abruptly, Zach reached out and grabbed her arm. She'd been startled the first time he took her arm when they walked. But he'd made no improper moves and she concluded it was just his way. "Look there," he said. "Off to the right beside that cabin in the shadows. Isn't that Isaac under that pine tree?"

Lydia's step faltered and her heart raced. It was Isaac, naked like the young Indian boys his age, a custom that bothered her. He was tanned but bits of sunburned skin peeled from his back and arms. She looked around, keeping herself from running toward him by main force. She mustn't do anything to alert the Indians or they would swoop down and take him away.

With trembling legs she edged closer, then sidled to one side. "Isaac," she said softly. He looked up from drawing in the dust with a stick. "Mama" he cried and flung himself into her arms. Her basket fell to the ground and she hugged him close, feeling his sturdy body while tears streamed down both their faces.

"Mama, I want to go with you," Isaac wailed. "I want to see Henry."

"I know, Isaac. I hope we'll be together again soon."

"That woman said she is my new mama and my name is Joshua now," he said.

"I'm your mother. And your name is Isaac, Isaac Strope. Never forget that," she said, her voice fierce. She'd heard of captives who became so indoctrinated they stayed with the Indians rather than return to their white families. That mustn't happen to Isaac.

"Say it," she said. "My name is Isaac Strope."

"My name is Isaac Strope," Isaac repeated.

"And my mother is Lydia Strope and my father is Sebastian Strope," Lydia said. "Say it every night so you don't forget it."

"You're holding me too tight, Mama," he said. "You're hurting me."

"What's happening here?" a voice interrupted.

Rebecca stood behind them, hands on her hips. She gestured to Isaac.

"Go inside, Joshua," she said, looking at him kindly.

Isaac looked from one woman to the other uncertainly.

"I want to stay with Mama," he said.

"It might be best if he does what Rebecca says," Zach said.

Lydia sighed and nodded. She couldn't win this engagement. At least she had seen and held him. He looked healthy, and maybe if she yielded without a struggle, she'd be allowed to see him again.

"Go inside, son," she said. "Remember what I told you."

As soon as Isaac closed the door, Rebecca faced Lydia. "You are confusing Joshua," she said. "I will make sure you don't see him again."

"No, please," Lydia said. "Let me look at him from a distance now and then. I promise I won't talk to him. Just don't send him away."

"That rests with you. We will see how well you keep your promise," Rebecca said. "Now leave."

Zach picked up the basket. "You're trembling," he said, taking Lydia's arm. "You can't go back to your cabin all upset like that. Come on."

He led her outside to the strawberry-filled meadow that had been their original destination.

"I don't care about picking berries now," she said.

"All right," he said. "Just sit down for a spell and get more settled."

She sank down into the grass and clover. "It's too much," she said, tears in her eyes again. "It's too much."

"I know," he said. He stroked her hair softly and she leaned against him, seeking comfort. He bent toward her and kissed her gently. Appalled, she pushed firmly on his chest.

"Stop," she said. "What are you doing?"

He reddened. "I'm sorry. It's just you're so..." His expression darkened and he jerked her to her feet. "Let's go back," he said.

"Mayhap you meant no harm," she said, pulling away. "But I am married. I would not be a cause of temptation to you. I think we should not be alone together any more." She picked up the basket and hurried back to the cabin without looking back.

As the days in June dwindled, Zach stayed away, although she often saw him staring at her, turning up too often for it to be coincidence. Perhaps she had been too harsh. But it was best not to provide an opportunity for sin. Still, she missed talking with him.

Occasionally, she saw Isaac at a distance. True to her word she made no effort to approach although the longing seemed unendurable at times. So Moses must have felt, barred from the Promised Land.

It was on the Sabbath, a time to sing hymns, pray and read the Bible with Margaretha and Henry, that things changed. The Scripture was from Genesis about how Joseph interpreted the pharaoh's dreams and thereby gained favor. They finished the final prayer by giving thanks for God's mercies during a difficult time and Margaretha sat suckling Elisha while Henry spun a wooden top Zach had whittled for him.

In an effort to keep Queen Esther friendly, Lydia had started talking with her regularly. Her feelings toward the woman troubled her. She was angry that Queen Esther had been involved in taking Isaac away. Yet she could see that the woman's power had limits, and she knew she should turn the other cheek. But I don't want to, she thought. She recalled how Jesus had forgiven those who crucified him and suspected it was easier to forgive people who hurt you than people who hurt your children. When Lydia arrived at the castle, Queen Esther was sitting on her porch rubbing sunflower oil on her long hair and working it in with a bone comb.

"You should try this oil," Queen Esther said, proffering the half-full bowl. "It will make your hair shine."

"No, thank you," Lydia said. She thought of the morning's Bible reading and the store that Indians set by dreams, believing them full of meaning. In some ways that was like the Israelites in the Bible. It was a new and intriguing thought.

"I have a question for you," she said as she sat down.

Queen Esther looked at her. "Ask on."

"This morning, I was reading in the Bible about dreams. And I remembered that dreams are important to Indians. Would you tell me what dreams mean to your tribe?"

"Dreams." Queen Esther hesitated. "Dreams are sacred to us. If someone dreams that someone gave them an object, a knife, perhaps, or a pipe, that person must give it to them in waking life. If they don't, bad luck may follow. And if a person is sick, it is especially important to help them fulfill their dreams."

Lydia felt a surge of anger. "I am sick. Sick at heart over the loss of my son, and I have dreamed over and over that Rebecca gave Isaac back to me," she burst out. "Why don't you fulfill my dream if dreams are so important?"

Queen Esther stopped combing her hair and stared at Lydia, her expression troubled. "Yours are not an Indian's dreams," she said at last. "I cannot let them bind us."

She stood up and came over to Lydia. "Listen to me. You know that Rebecca's son was killed by American soldiers. What you do not know is that it was before her very eyes. They caught the two of them near their camp and said they were spying. They held her while they stuck a knife in him over and over and she listened to him try to be silent like a brave warrior. But he was only ten, and he could not help himself. Soon he began to scream. Then they abused her in the way of evil men with women. She has regained a son in Joshua, and she has no love for Americans. She is owed something for her loss, and she will never, never let him go."

Lydia stepped back, struck by a fuller realization of the pain Rebecca had endured.

"What they did isn't right," she said. "I am sorry it happened. But it doesn't make it right to take my son either. I am like Rebecca. I will never, never give up on getting my son back."

Queen Esther sighed. "I see you cannot let this matter go. I hate to see you in pain, but I cannot have you causing trouble and confusing Joshua. I will do what must be done."

Chapter Ten

Lydia sat on the bench in front of her cabin hulling strawberries and worrying about what Queen Esther had said that morning. A shadow fell across her lap. She looked up to see Zach standing there, his blond hair outlined by the sun. She was struck again by his resemblance to Sebastian and felt a warming toward him.

"I know you were upset with me," he said, "but I deserve another chance. Haven't I been a friend to you and your family?"

Fairness compelled her to nod. "You have."

He smiled. "Good. I have some news for you about Isaac."

"Isaac? Is he all right?"

He squatted down in front of her. "Yes. But I found out that Rebecca and Isaac are leaving the settlement tomorrow afternoon."

She put her hand to her mouth. "Oh no. Where are they taking him?"

"I'm not sure. Maybe Fort Niagara. But there are Indian encampments all over the western part of New York state. It could be any of them. Or even up in Canada. But I've thought on it and I have a plan to rescue him."

"What? What plan?"

"I'm leaving tomorrow to pick up some trade goods and bring them back. I could smuggle Isaac out with me."

"Smuggle him?" Her voice rose. "How?"

"Not so loud," he said. "Just trust me. The less you know the better. But basically, I know a white couple who favor the American cause. They could be trusted to keep him safe and take him down the river."

"Down the river to where?"

"To Forty Fort. I found out that's where your husband and daughter are." He smiled broadly.

"Are they all right?" Her voice rose again with her excitement.

"Fit as can be. I could take Isaac there and they'd all be safe together."

Joy flared in Lydia like summer lightning. Jane was safe and with her father. If Isaac could join them, how wonderful that would be. "You could do that? It sounds dangerous. What if you are caught?"

"I won't be. They trust me. They won't imagine I'd come back here with supplies if I'd freed Isaac."

"But if you *were* caught? And what about my son?" It was hard to talk over the tightness in her throat as she veered wildly between hope and fear.

"Isaac wouldn't be harmed. I know Indians. The worst they'd do is take him away, which they were going to do anyway, so you have nothing to lose. I'm the one taking a risk. For you." He paused, glanced around, then reached out and took both her hands in his. "But I deserve something in return."

"What? Anything."

"I want you to lie with me tonight. It will give me courage." He tightened his grip.

She jerked her hands loose. "I can't do that. Get away from me."

"Hold on. Don't decide so fast. See, it's like a trade. I give you something you want; you give me something I want. That's the way the world works. Trading is what I do. Of course, it's your choice. Isaac can vanish into the wilderness. Or I can deliver him to his father." He looked at her appealingly. "Am I that terrible? I've wanted you since I saw you looking so upset the day you arrived. I could tell you needed a man to take care of you. I'm doing this to make you happy. I'm only asking for one favor in return."

"Leave," she said. "Please." Her pulse hammered in her throat so hard she felt he could see it.

"All right. But think about it. I'll wait for you an hour after sunset behind the cabin if you change your mind. Otherwise, Isaac will be gone and it will be too late."

After he left, she continued hulling berries without seeing them. What he asked was sinful, heinous. She could never consent. And yet, to lose Isaac forever, to have him brought up by Indians, never to see or touch him again. That was horrible and wrong, too. The act with Zach need not take long. It would be over and Isaac would be safe. But what if she yielded and Zach didn't keep his word? Or if he wanted to lie with her again and again? How could she endure that? No, yielding to him was unthinkable, a betrayal of her sacred marriage vows. But it was the best chance she had of saving Isaac. She was his mother. Only she could do this for him. True, she would come to her husband with a stain of sin on her. But, unlike Sebastian, she would at least have saved their son. No, Gideon's drowning was different, an act of omission on Sebastian's part, not commission. Her thoughts grew as tangled as a skein of badly spun flax. Her head ached and her body felt stiff with tension. I have to pray, she thought. But could God ever bless something like this?

She stood and took the berries inside. Margaretha sat at the table sewing while the baby slept on a blanket on the floor. Henry was outside somewhere playing. He'd been spending more time than she liked with the Indian boys his age, but it wasn't fair to keep him inside all the time.

"What's wrong?" Margaretha asked as Lydia entered. "You look as if you've seen Old Nick himself."

"It's…too much sun," Lydia said. "I feel faint."

"Ach. Rest yourself. Did I hear you talking to someone?"

"Zach stopped by for a few minutes."

"Have you two become friends again? That would be good. He was a big help. I never did understand what happened."

"He told me they're moving Isaac to another village tomorrow," Lydia said. "What am I going to do?"

"Oh no." Margaretha dropped her sewing and jumped up to hug her sister. "I'm so sorry. Perhaps when this war is over…" She let the thought trail off.

"Perhaps," Lydia said dully. Her eyes fell on the Bible. "I sorely need guidance," she said. "And I need to pray."

"Of course," Margaretha said. "I'll pray with you."

"Thank you, but I need to be alone for a bit," Lydia said. She often talked things over with her sister. But not this. No one must ever know about this.

"Are you sure?" Margaretha asked, eyebrows raised.

Lydia nodded. "Please, sister."

"As you wish." Margaretha picked up her sewing and walked outside, back straight.

Lydia stood with her hand on the Bible for a few seconds, then with a fervent prayer for guidance, she stabbed with her finger. Joshua 19:49: "When they had made an end of dividing the land for inheritance by their coasts, the children of Israel gave an inheritance to Joshua, the son of Nun, among them." The hairs on her arms stood up when she saw the verse dealt with Joshua, the name the Indians had given Isaac. Joshua, the son of Nun, could mean that if Isaac stayed with Rebecca he would become "the son of none." And how could he inherit his father's land if he were with the Indians? The verse might indicate she should lie with Zach. Her stomach roiled at the thought.

Maybe there was some other way. With something this important, she should consult the New Testament, too. Despairingly, she opened the Bible again. Her shaking finger fell on Matthew 9:6: "But that ye may know that the Son of man hath power on earth to forgive sins, (then sayeth he to the sick of the palsy,) Arise, take up thy bed and go unto thine house."

So Jesus could forgive her, even if she sinned. It said in Isaiah that though one's sins were as scarlet, God could make them white as snow.

Shame swept over her. She feared that instead of truly seeking divine guidance she was finding reasons to believe whatever would save her son. Lydia shut the Bible with a bang, making Elisha stir on the floor beside her. She looked at his chubby face, so sweet in sleep, and thought of the day Gideon was brought home in the canoe dead and the day the newborn Isaac was thrust squalling into her arms. If I am finding excuses for this act, so be it, she thought. I will save Isaac no matter how hateful the means.

Jane stood outside the gate to Forty Fort clutching the yellow and white daisies she had picked. They would look pretty in Mrs. Stewart's clay vase. Off to one side, her father and Lazarus Stewart were practicing throwing a tomahawk. They stood ten feet away from an oak tree, hurling overhand. The tomahawk flashed in the sun as it made two turns before landing with a thunk in the bark. Several rifle-toting men standing around cheered when her father hit close to the center of a circle painted on the tree.

He turned, saw her watching and waved. With a half smile, she waved back. It was hard to know how to respond to him these days. Sebastian turned back as the men roared at Lazarus' accurate throw. The boar's tusk had left a scar down one side of Sebastian's face. Every time she looked at it, Jane felt guilty. He would carry it forever. But he's the one who should feel guilty, she thought. Her face screwed up into a scowl under her sunbonnet. It was so confusing to love someone and be angry at them at the same time. She'd seen him and that Hollenbeck woman rolling in the grass by the river like animals. She knew what stallions did with mares and bulls with cows and had seen her brothers' private parts when she tended them. Although no one had told her, she knew what must happen between a man and a woman.

It was all Mrs. Hollenbeck's fault. She made Papa behave that way. Since that afternoon, Jane had avoided Faith as much as possible. Faith had never asked why. And Papa acted as if everything was fine. Maybe he didn't know that she knew. Or maybe no one wanted to talk about it, as if it was easier that way. Easier for them maybe. I wish Mama were here, she thought. Then this wouldn't have happened.

Papa still talked to Faith, although to be honest Jane couldn't see anything improper in their behavior. Who knows what they do when no one is watching, she thought, with a fresh stab of anger toward Faith.

It was better to think about something else. She headed for Mrs. Stewart's cabin and the litter of puppies. She found her mixing up a batch of johnny cake. Her belly was huge now. The baby would arrive soon.

"Come to see the puppies?" Mrs. Stewart said, smiling broadly. Jane smiled in return. Mrs. Stewart always seemed happy even though children ran everywhere, shouting and knocking things over. Today, everyone was outside except a toddler sucking on his fingers and four-year-old Elizabeth who played with a corn husk doll in a corner.

"Those puppies are really getting around," Mrs. Stewart said. "Soon I'll have to find homes for them."

She scratched at several mosquito bites on her hand "Those pesky gollynippers are vicious at night now. It's because we're so close to the river. They don't seem to bother Mr. Stewart, but they really love me."

"It's the same with me and Mama," Jane said. "They bother me more than they do her. Papa says it's because I'm so sweet."

Mrs. Stewart laughed heartily. "I'll have to remember that. It's because I'm so sweet." She poured the johnnycake batter into a long-handled frying pan and thrust it over the fireplace, then wiped sweat from her forehead. "Keeping the door open lets the gollynippers in," she said, "but it's so hot in here with a fire going, I can't stand it. But you didn't come to listen to me talk. Go play with the puppies."

Jane picked up the puppy she had named Gertie. Its smooth tongue felt warm as it licked her cheek. She played with the other puppies for a few minutes, then picked up Gertie again. When Mrs. Stewart came over to her, Jane was petting Gertie while the puppy tugged at her shoe with its tiny teeth. The woman couldn't stop talking for long, Jane had found. One of the worst things about being at Forty Fort was how hard it was to find a place to be alone. Often, Jane longed for her hollowed-out bush by the river at home. Just when a person started to settle down and think about things, along came someone to interrupt. It was nice to make new friends. It was also nice to sit and look at trees and clouds all by yourself.

At least Mrs. Stewart was cheerful. Life with Faith was tense all the time now.

"What kind of puppies are these?" Jane asked.

"Part terrier, part who knows what." Mrs. Stewart nudged the puppy worrying at Jane's shoe. "Nipping and yipping, nipping and yipping, that's about all they do," she said. She rubbed the small of her back as if it hurt. "So, have you settled on a puppy to call your own?"

"This one," Jane said. "She looks like my Uncle John's dog, the one the Indians killed."

"A good choice. She seems friendly and lively."

"I've named her Gertie, just like the other dog," Jane said. "Do you think the Indians will attack Forty Fort? People say a big army is gathering at Tioga Point."

"I don't know whether they'll attack or not. But this is a strong fort and we have several hundred men here so I'm sure we'll be safe."

"But what would you do if the fort fell?" Jane persisted.

"Why, I'd take the children and go downriver to Bloomsburg. I have a friend I can stay with until the baby is born. Then I'll go on to my sister, Mrs. McClure, in Lancaster," Mrs. Stewart said. "We'd figure out something from there. Your father told me Mrs. Hollenbeck would look after you. But don't worry. These walls are solid and we have our own water supply. Everything will be fine."

Maybe so, Jane thought. But if anything happened, she wasn't going anywhere with Faith Hollenbeck. She'd stick with Mrs. Stewart or leave alone if she had to, no matter what Papa said.

Darkness covered Queen Esther's camp when Lydia slipped out to meet Zach behind the cabin. Fireflies blinked on and off in the fields. He greeted her softly. "Thanks for coming," he said, as if this were some social engagement.

"Did I have a choice," she said.

"Sure you did. But now we've got a deal and I don't take kindly to people who welsh on deals."

"A deal," she whispered. "Is that what you call this?"

"It could be more if you'd let it. I could protect you. Maybe get special treatment for you and your children. And I'd treat you right."

"Never. I'm doing this for Isaac."

He shook his head and stared into her eyes. "Ah, Lydia," he said. "You're pretty in the moonlight."

He bent to kiss her and she twisted her lips away. Zach pinned her against the back of the cabin wall.

"Don't be that way," he said. "I'm not gonna hurt you. You'll see." He fumbled at her breasts while she stood rigid, then he hoisted her skirts. He stopped at the sight of the white of her thighs. On her right thigh, the crescent scar from an earlier accident shone palely by moonlight and he ran his finger over it, making her shiver with revulsion.

She closed her eyes to block out the sight of his face so close to hers. Anger surged through her, at him, at herself, at a world that brought people to such straits.

Abruptly, Zach entered her. Lydia bit her lip to keep from crying out at the pain. Isaac, she thought over and over. "Isaac. Isaac." The logs scraped her back as Zach thrust back and forth. His breath reeked of tobacco, and she turned her head away. In a few minutes his body stiffened, he gave a soft groan and it was over. She pulled her skirts down and turned away, leaning her cheek against the logs. Isaac, she thought again. Pray God, her son would be safe now.

"Don't fret yourself. I'll be sure Isaac gets to his father," he said as he refastened his trousers. He turned her face toward him and brushed her cheek with his fingers. "Now that wasn't so bad, was it? I should be back in a week or two with no one the wiser."

No, she thought. Don't ever come back. He slipped away and Lydia stood for a few minutes as tears slipped down her cheeks. She could feel the wet stickiness of his spilled seed on her thigh. She pushed down the nausea that rose in her throat, bent over, plucked some grass and rubbed vigorously until her skin was raw. Swiping at her mouth where he had kissed her, she took a deep breath, straightened her garments and went back inside. God forgive me, she thought.

Henry stirred sleepily as she lay down beside him. "Mama?" he said.

"Go to sleep, son," she said. "Everything's going to be all right."

Once in the night, she awoke and cried out in terror, dreaming that Zach's disembodied face hung over her, smiling. The next morning, Lydia busied herself with sorting out clothes for a washing. It was too hard to stay inside and do nothing. It seemed as if she could still feel Zach's hands on her, his male part inside her. She shook herself like a dog trying to rid its coat of water, but it was no use. The images remained. Deliberately, she tried to focus on the practical. When Isaac's absence was discovered, it might be best if she was in plain sight, clearly busy at something. She borrowed lye soap from another captive and went to the river to pound their clothes on the rocks there.

At the bank, she looked at herself in the river, wondering if what had happened showed on her face. It seemed as if it must. But it was hard to tell. Her reflection was blurred and wavering in the flowing water. Just like me, she thought. Who am I now? A wife foresworn. But Isaac's loving mother, at least. After she rinsed the clothes and set them to dry in the sun, she leaned back on the bank, tireder than her exertions warranted. She closed her eyes and, exhausted, fell asleep.

The sun was directly overhead when she awoke. She listened carefully, but heard no signs of undue commotion. Gathering the dry clothes, she headed back to the enclosure, passing other women on the way.

As she reached her cabin door, Rebecca confronted her, blocking the entrance. "Where is Joshua?" she demanded. "I can't find him anywhere."

"I don't know," Lydia said. "I haven't seen him today. I've been down at the river all morning washing clothes." She felt a surge of relief. Zach had kept his word and Isaac was on his way to freedom and his father. It was worth it, even if she'd never feel the same again.

"That may be, but you still might know where he is."

"I don't," Lydia said. "Nothing better have happened to him. Now please let me pass."

Rebecca stared at her, then stepped aside. "I'll be back," she said, and hurried off in the direction of Queen Esther's castle.

Lydia sank down on the bed, thankful Margaretha had taken Henry with her to pick berries. Tension filled her body. She wondered how long Zach needed to get Isaac to safety. She breathed a brief prayer for his safety.

The cabin door was flung open without a preliminary knock. Queen Esther stood in the doorway with Rebecca and a warrior with a gun.

"Where is Joshua?" Queen Esther demanded. "Tell us now and no harm will come to you."

"I told Rebecca already that I haven't seen him. If no one knows where he is, we should be searching the fields, not wasting time talking. He could be lost. We have to find him." It was easy to sound frantic. She felt frantic with worry.

"Come outside," Queen Esther said. "I would see you in the sunlight."

Lydia walked outside, head held high.

"I checked. No one left the fort this morning except the trader Zach," Queen Esther said, studying Lydia's face. "No one saw him leave, but Joshua is gone. I would not have believed it of Zach, but then..." She hesitated and Lydia schooled her face to impassiveness. Apparently Queen Esther saw something though because she nodded slowly. "Ah," she said. "I wish this were not so. Go back inside your cabin and stay there until I come again."

She turned to the warrior. "Take three warriors and track the trader. Be quick about it. If he doesn't have the boy, let him go. Meanwhile, Lydia is right. Joshua could have wandered off. We need to search the fields and around the river."

The hours passed tensely. At midafternoon, Margaretha returned.

"What's happening?" she asked, taking off her bonnet. "People are out in lines in the fields calling for Joshua. Sometimes they call for Isaac. Is he lost?"

I mustn't tell Margaretha the truth Lydia thought, although she longed to do so. What she doesn't know, she can't tell.

"It seems he is," Lydia said. "Queen Esther told me to stay here while they search. I pray he is safe. Have you heard anything?"

"Just that people are looking for him."

Lydia let out her breath. Maybe it would turn out all right. Zach had a head start.

"You seem calm about this," Margaretha said.

"I am anything but calm," Lydia said. "But it's out of my hands. All I can do is wait and pray."

"That is all any of us can do anymore," Margaretha said, coming over to lay a hand on her sister's shoulder. "Shall we pray together?"

"I would like that very much."

The sun was setting when Queen Esther came to the cabin again. Lydia looked up with frightened eyes as she entered.

"Joshua is restored to us," Queen Esther said. "We found him and the trader together. The trader claimed he found him wandering in the woods and was returning him to us. But on the way back, Zach broke free and fled, so I doubt that. I cannot prove you had anything to do with this, so in fairness and for the sake of our past friendship, I will not pursue it. In the morning, Joshua and his new mother will leave Tioga Point for Fort Niagara as planned. That had better be the end of it."

Lydia, who had risen from the bench at Queen Esther's knock, felt her knees give way and sat down abruptly. Isaac would be torn from her. Her honor was gone for nothing. Thank God Zach had fled. The Indians might have tortured him to find out the truth. And while she despised him, at least, that wouldn't be on her conscience, too.

Queen Esther looked at her for a moment. "Any debt of friendship we had is discharged," she announced, then stalked from the cabin.

The next few days passed in a daze of automatic rising, eating, sleeping, making conversation behind a blanket of deadness. Daily, Lydia opened her Bible. Over and over she read the same two passages. The first, from the sixth chapter of Luke, urged Christians to love their enemies, to judge not, to forgive. The second passage in John 8 comforted her. Jesus had refused to condemn the woman taken in adultery, telling her to go and sin no more. She tried not to think about the day she would face Sebastian, knowing the choice she had made. Could he possibly understand? Perhaps if the plan had succeeded. As it was…

Finally the last week of June as Lydia sat outside the cabin, Margaretha walked past her with Elisha balanced on her hip and a spray of fresh roses in one hand. The aroma penetrated Lydia's fog, sweeping her back to the profusion of wild roses that even now would be perfuming the air near their house in Wysox. If they were home, Sebastian would be working in the fields. She and Jane would be tending the vegetable and herb gardens. Stumbling to her feet, she walked behind the cabin and stared at the spot where Zach had violated her. Guilt, shame, anger, despair threatened to overwhelm her. She could feel her heartbeat racing and she swayed. She felt like a leaf floating on a pond, needing only a touch to break the surface tension and send it spiraling to the muddy depths. She leaned against the side of the cabin to steady herself. But the feel of logs on her spine brought everything back. The horrid kiss, the groping at her breast, the violation, the pain. Ever since she had felt tainted. Her throat closed up and tears pricked her eyes, but she blinked them away. Tears changed nothing. I would do it over if I knew it would save Isaac, she thought fiercely. It didn't save him, and I have to go on anyway. She straightened, drew a hand across her burning eyes and took a deep breath. Things were what they were, and she would make the best of them.

She emerged to see Henry walking behind a soldier toward the gate. I've been neglecting him, she thought. I've lost two sons. But I still have a son and daughter and a husband. And my son needs me. She walked rapidly after Henry. When she caught up with him, she put her arm around his shoulder, rejoicing in the feel of his sturdy body.

"Hello, son," she said, making her voice calm and light. "How are you doing?"

He looked up at her and smiled. "Look, Mama," he said. "They're building all these boats and canoes."

The river bank was alive with activity. Everywhere Indians and British soldiers were hollowing out logs, stretching bark over frames, hammering at planks. She counted almost two hundred canoes and thirty or forty larger boats. They must have been building for days while she walked around in a fog. Approaching one of the soldiers, she asked, "What's going on?"

He hesitated. "I guess it won't do no harm to tell you. We're going downriver with the Royal Greens."

An officer saw him talking to her and motioned sharply for him to return to work.

That afternoon, the Indians sacrificed a white dog to the Great Spirit. Henry watched with fascination as they marked it with red paint. When a chief strangled it, the Indians let out a yell and Henry, wincing, stepped back into the shadows. In the evening, bonfires flared. Around them, warriors with painted faces danced and chanted. Alcohol ran freely. As the clamor rose, Lydia pulled Henry inside the cabin. "What's going on, Mama? Why are they dancing and singing? And why did they kill that dog?" he asked.

"Their ways are not our ways. Don't concern yourself. It has nothing to do with us."

In truth, she found it confusing that Queen Esther could proclaim herself a Christian yet participate in these pagan ceremonies.

Henry looked puzzled, then turned to playing with the tiny carved horse that Queen Esther had given him. The wooden horse, who he'd named Thunder, pranced across the bed under Henry's guidance while Lydia fretted about what the ceremonies might mean.

In the morning, more than a thousand Indians and soldiers left, heading down the river in a flotilla, Queen Esther among them.

"Where are you going?" Lydia asked as Queen Esther prepared to step into a canoe.

"To watch my son, Gencho, in battle against the American soldiers," she said. "I know he will make me proud with his courage."

"In battle where?"

"To Forty Fort, of course."

Chapter Eleven

July, 1778

Sebastian shook Lazarus Stewart's hand vigorously. "Congratulations," he said. "I understand your wife has presented you with another fine daughter."

Lazarus smiled. "Indeed. And a little early. Jane is already over there looking at the baby."

"And playing with the puppies, I warrant," Sebastian said with a laugh.

The two stood in front of Lazarus' cabin looking out over the Forty Fort parade ground where soldiers stood around in small knots. Off to one side Col. Zeb Butler and Col. Denison talked in low tones. Denison held a letter in one hand and glanced at it frequently, as if the words would change.

"I wish the baby had arrived at different time," Lazarus said. "I love a good battle against the Indians. But my wife, she's weak right now. And the expedition from Tioga Point already captured Wintermoot and Jenkins forts just up the way, so we may be in for some hard fighting. Still, there's some good news."

Sebastian looked at him. There seemed nothing good about the situation. Women and children terrorized. Farmers penned inside a fort when they should be tending their crops. The enemy on their doorstep.

"What would that be?" he asked.

"It's that Indian half breed, Queen Esther. Didn't you say you knew her?"

"Yes. Why?"

"She's traveling with the Indians. I heard her son, Gencho, was killed by an American scouting party near Forty Fort yesterday. They shot him dead and mutilated his body. The word is his mother is wild with grief."

Sebastian's stomach tightened. He'd taken comfort in the fact his family might be at Tioga Point with Queen Esther, a friend. But if she were marching with the British instead of just lending support, she must have had a change of heart. He'd met Gencho once. A nice-looking young man. He knew the pain of losing a son. Yet the Indians were scalping settlers and burning farms all along the frontier.

"Why so somber?" Lazarus asked. "This is good news. One less copperhead."

Lazarus would never understand this mix of emotions, Sebastian thought. It was all so simple to him. Drive out the Indians. Rail against the Quakers with their lily-livered talk of peace. If you are not with us, you are against us. Lazarus plowed the same furrow over and over, sowing the same bitter seeds.

Instead of responding, Sebastian pointed toward Denison and Butler. "What about that?" he asked. The day before three of the enemy had arrived with a letter demanding the surrender of Forty Fort.

Lazarus waved a hand dismissively. "Butler told them we won't surrender. Maybe we'll show some backbone and fight instead of cowering here. Teach them a lesson they won't soon forget." He paused. "You're with me, aren't you?"

"I don't see we have much choice."

Lazarus clapped him on the back. "Good man."

Out on the parade ground, a soldier pointed their way and a tall, thin man clad in a white linen shirt and brown breeches walked toward them. The breeze ruffled his flowing blond hair. He reached up to push it back, never taking his eyes off them.

"Are you Sebastian Strope?" the man asked.

"I am."

The stranger reached out and shook his hand. "Pleased to meet you. I'm Zach Wilson, lately come from Tioga Point."

Excitement raced through Sebastian. Here, at last, might be news.

"Have you any word of my wife, Lydia, and my two sons?" he demanded. "They might be at Tioga Point. She's a tiny woman with blue eyes and reddish brown hair. My son Isaac is four and Henry is eight."

Lazarus broke in before Zach could answer. "Hold your horses." He turned to address Zach. "What were you doing at Tioga Point? That's Indian country."

"Hey, I'm just a trader," Zach said, stepping back a pace. "I got plumb tired of trading with Indians and British against my countrymen and decided to pull out. I've got kin at Fort Penn in Stroudsburg. I thought it safest to stop at Forty Fort first and get the lay of the land. I have to allow as how I didn't expect to be in the middle of this mess. But at least I'm among friends now, instead of those benighted savages."

Lazarus continued to regard him with suspicion. "If that's true, we're glad to have you. But if not..."

A ruffle of drumbeat interrupted him.

"That's the signal to assemble and discuss how to proceed. We have to go," Lazarus said. "I'm going to push to attack." He grabbed Sebastian's arm." I need you to back me up."

"What about my family? Do you know anything about them?" Sebastian asked Zach, standing where he was.

"Later," Zach said. "We can get to that later."

Sebastian shook free of Lazarus' hold. "No, not later. Mr. Wilson, tell me if you have news of my wife and children *now*."

"Don't worry," Zach mumbled, and strode away.

"There, you see. It must be good news," Lazarus said. "Now come on. There'll be time to learn more after the meeting."

Sebastian ignored him and headed after Zach, who waded into the crowd of soldiers and disappeared.

The leaders had been arguing for twenty minutes in the hot July sun with no resolution. Sebastian looked over to where Jane stood in the shade of a hut a few feet from Faith. They must be terrified by all this. He tried to smile reassuringly, then turned to listen to the argument again. He'd lost track of the trader. Perhaps after this battle, he'd get news at last.

"We're not provisioned for a siege," Lazarus said. "If we stay bottled up in here, they can burn our farms with impunity. There aren't that many more than we are, from what the scouts tell us. I say send them running. Or are you a bunch of cowards?"

Denison interrupted. "We don't have reliable information on their numbers. What if they have a lot more men than we know about? We've sent for reinforcements. It's smarter to hunker down until more troops arrive in a few days."

"And what if it's a few weeks before they get here?" Lazarus said, turning to address the men. "The Indians will burn your homes to the ground, steal your livestock. Then where will we be?"

A low murmur of agreement rose from the men. It might be smarter to stay inside, Sebastian thought, but he could understand the urge to protect your home and loved ones. Indecision left him. He couldn't miraculously restore his own farm, but he could fight to save some other family from what he'd gone through.

"Let's go," he called out.

Someone yelled from the back of the group. "I say we wait for reinforcements. Why get ourselves killed?"

Lazarus spun around with a scowl, then turned toward Butler and Denison. "If our leaders won't fight, I say they're cowards," he shouted. Silence settled over the field.

Butler's face turned red. "Do not mistake prudence for cowardice," he ground out. He took a deep breath. "We'll see how the majority feels. I call for a show of hands of those who want to attack." A forest of hands shot up.

" So be it," he said. "It's a mistake, but if that's your wish, Denison and I will lead you."

Lazarus led a rousing cheer and Sebastian joined in.

"We'll leave the women and children and the elderly in the fort under Lt. Jenkins," Denison said. He paused. "Quartermaster, a round of rum for each man before we go." Another cheer rose.

"We'll count off by odds and evens," Butler said as the pails went around. "Odds will fire first, then kneel to reload, go five paces and be ready to fire when the evens are through. Stand firm, men. If you withstand the first shock of battle, the Indians will lose heart and leave."

A scout slipped forward and whispered in Denison's ear. "A small force of the enemy is on the way," Denison announced. "Prepare to do battle."

Sebastian hurried to get his rifle and say his farewells. Jane's face was white.

"Papa, be careful," she whispered.

"I will, Little Bit," he said. He felt her trembling as he hugged her. "Don't worry. Your father won't take any unnecessary chances." He looked at the midafternoon sun. "We'll be back in time to eat supper together."

When he turned to Faith, she smiled unconvincingly. "Be safe," she said. He felt a sudden urge to hug her, too, but didn't dare.

Jane's face clouded when Faith spoke. Sebastian suspected she knew what had gone on between them, but how could a father bring something like that up with his daughter? Instead, he'd ignored the growing tension, hoping Jane would see from his current behavior that there was nothing to worry about. When he returned, he'd make things right.

With a wave, he went off to get in formation. The huge gate was thrown open, the drums sounded the command to march and the pipers struck up a lively tune. The women and children broke into applause and cheers. Excitement and hope filled Sebastian as he marched out into the sunny afternoon.

At a stone bridge about a mile from the fort, the company stopped and Col. Butler again urged a return to the fort to wait for reinforcements. "Farms can be rebuilt. Dead men can't walk again," he said.

"I say we go on," Lazarus shouted. Sebastian joined in the cheer that rose from the ranks.

Butler shook his head and gave the order to advance. Bands of Indians raced across the fields ahead of them, firing as they fled. The men surged forward in pursuit, crossing a field bordered by stone fences. A rush of excitement poured through Sebastian, making his hands shake, and he found it hard to kneel, reload and advance in an orderly manner.

"They're running like rabbits," Butler shouted. "Press on and we'll win the day."

As they approached the end of the field, hundreds of Indians poured out from hiding. The noise and smoke of gunfire filled the air.

It's a trap, Sebastian thought. My god, they outnumber us three to one.

"Fall back," an officer shouted. Soldiers raced across the field fleeing from the advancing Indians. Streams of blood mixed with the waters of the Susquehanna as some men plunged in, only to be shot in midstream

Sebastian ran wildly, angling off toward the trees and away from Forty Fort. Off to one side he spied a huge gorse bush. He dove behind it and peered out to see Indians racing across the field toward his position. He reached for his priming horn to reload his rifle, then paused. He might hit one, maybe two, of the enemy. But then what? There were too many to fool himself that he might turn the tide of the battle. No, eventually, they'd find him, and he'd die, either quickly or more slowly and terribly. What would happen to Jane then? How would Lydia and the boys manage without him? His life wasn't his to throw away.

Reluctantly, he replace his priming horn and scrambled inside the bush, wincing as the sharp spines pricked and tore at his hands and face. The straps on his ammunition pouch and his wooden canteen caught on the branches. He jerked them free, praying that in the confusion no one would hear the noise. Heart pounding, he listened to the screams of his comrades, curling his fingers into fists so hard his fingernails cut into his palms.

Hours later, as darkness fell, the glow of a bonfire penetrated the bush. Cautiously, Sebastian peered out. Crowds of Indians stood around a flat, wide rock. Their belt pouches bulged with scalps, the leather stained dark with blood. In front of the Indians, captives were arrayed. He counted. Sixteen soldiers. On top of the rock. a tall woman waved a war club. Circles of white paint rimmed her eyes, giving her a ghostly appearance, and sworls of black and white paint marked her skin. My God, Sebastian thought, it's Queen Esther. She motioned and the Indians led a captive forward, forcing the back of his head against the rock so he stared upward into Queen Esther's face.

"Gencho," she screamed, burying her war club in the man's skull. Blood trickled down the rock and spattered on her bare legs. A towheaded boy, barely old enough to fight, wrenched free and ran straight toward Sebastian's hiding place. A few yards short, he tripped and fell. The Indian chasing him grabbed him and began beating him. The Indian faced toward Queen Esther, but the screaming boy faced Sebastian, seeming to stare straight at him. Torn between the urge to help and the knowledge it was useless to try, Sebastian sat frozen, every muscle so tight he ached. This must have been what Jane felt like when she watched Lydia and the boys being captured. He had thought he understood what she went through, now he realized he hadn't understood at all. Seething with helplessness, he closed his eyes to block out the scene, but he couldn't escape the sounds of wood rhythmically hitting flesh or the dull sound of a tomahawk smashing the boy's skull. Sebastian shifted his gaze to the rock where Queen Esther was dispatching the remaining captives with a scream of "Gencho" at each blow. He willed himself not to vomit. Finally, Queen Esther jumped from the rock, almost slipping on the blood, and the Indians raced away toward Forty Fort.

The glow of the bonfire died and the sound of crickets and the hoot of owls replaced the crackle of flames. The smell of smoke hung heavy on the air.

Sebastian crouched in the gorse bush, stunned. If this was what Queen Esther had become, he feared for his family. That Zach Wilson fellow had told him not to worry about them, but that was impossible. If Zach had survived, Sebastian would find him and demand details. Uncertainty left too much room to conjure scenes of horror. But right now, he feared for Jane. If he returned to the fort, he would be killed. Yet Jane was there. He refused to think she might have been harmed. Faith must be reliving her husband's death, too. There had been no more incidents between them like that time at the river, but still their paths seemed to cross constantly, and he looked forward to it more and more.

Rage filled him as he stared at the blood-covered rock. Lazarus was right. You couldn't trust an Indian. Look at Queen Esther, who he had thought was a friend. He'd find a way to get back at the savages.

Wincing as he removed thorns, he worked his way out of the gorse bush, crawled on his stomach to the river and swam to the far side to collapse exhausted under a patch of willows. The British are sure to let the women and children go, he thought. Tomorrow, I'll push on to Stroudsburg. That's where Jane and Faith expect to find me.

Jane had reached a stage of numbness beyond terror. All afternoon, she had stayed busy inside the fort, helping prepare food, watching Mrs.

Stewart's children, mending clothing. Mrs. Stewart had let her take the puppy Gertie and that was some comfort. But it was impossible to shut out the sounds of gunfire in the distance.

Denison and Butler limped in with a few men, confirming a terrible loss. Denison ordered the casks of whiskey destroyed, lest they fall into the hands of the Indians. Several families fled through the springhouse tunnel at dusk, taking their chances. Jane wondered if the blond stranger she had seen talking with her father was one of them. He had stayed behind when the others left the fort, enduring scowls and whispers of "coward" from the women. Earlier, the stranger had asked Faith where she and Jane would go if the fort fell.

"What did you tell him?" Jane asked.

"Why, to Stroudsburg, of course."

The night was filled with screams. She listened in vain to see if she could pick out her father's voice.

With sunrise, fearful families huddled inside the cabins waiting. Jane sat on a bed with Faith. During the night, Faith had sat frozen, biting her bottom lip until it bled, while Jane hugged herself tightly as if she could keep the fear inside if she tried hard enough. She looked around at the other white-faced women and girls. Some were weeping. Others stared straight ahead or talked in low tones. Jane thought of how she had hidden in the springhouse and watched like a frightened rabbit while her family was taken captive. She couldn't stand to hide again. Scared, but determined, she went to the door and lifted the latchstring.

"What are you doing?" Faith asked.

"I want to see for myself what's going on."

Behind her, several of the women stood up, smoothed their dresses or tucked their hair under their caps and joined her outside.

The gates were open. As drums beat, a column of British soldiers marched through the north gate, flags flying,.

The fort had surrendered.

Jane sucked in her breath. Let Papa be safe, she prayed.

Her gaze swung to the south gate where a group of whooping, laughing Indians jogged in, led by a woman. As they drew closer, Jane realized with a shock that it was Queen Esther, dressed in her usual red and blue broadcloth, now marred by dark stains. She looked haggard and traces of white paint rimmed her eyes, but her walk was proud. It was confusing. Queen Esther was their friend, yet here she was with the enemy.

More people came out of huts to watch, huddling near the doorways.

Queen Esther turned to Col. Denison. "Well, she said loudly, "once you made me promise to bring more Indians here." She waved her hand. "See. I bring all these."

Butler flushed. "Women should be seen, not heard," he said.

Esther laughed. "Hear this. I was never so tired in my life as from killing all those damned soldiers."

Jane stepped backward in horror and the movement caught Queen Esther's attention. They stared at each other, until Queen Esther turned away.

"You women, stop standing around. Fix food for us," she snapped. "And no tricks. We won't eat a bite until you taste it first."

While the women prepared food, Denison ordered the firearms piled in the center of the yard. Jane watched nervously as the British leader gave them to the Indians.

A soldier dragged out a table, and Butler signed papers of capitulation, giving up the fort. A murmur of apprehension swept through the crowd.

What will happen to us now? Jane wondered.

A few feet away Mrs. Stewart, who had just learned her husband had fallen in battle, cried while she jiggled her newborn against her shoulder. Her children stood around her in varying degrees of shock and grief.

What about Papa? Had he been killed too? Jane had tried to find out earlier, but she was just one of a large group of frantic women and children who had besieged the returning men with questions. Finally one of the officers, blood on his clothes and one arm hanging useless from a wound, had bellowed, "I don't know. I don't know. Anyone who's not here is either fled or dead."

Maybe Queen Esther knew something about Papa. Jane's legs felt wobbly and her breath came in shallow gasps as she walked toward her.

Some Senecas were eating, but Queen Esther and the other Indian women were rifling through the clothing of the settlers. Already, she had donned two chintz dresses, one atop the other. Two bonnets were stacked on her head. She smiled with pleasure as she picked up a scarlet riding cloak and flung it around her shoulders. Her companions laughed.

"Excuse me," Jane said.

Queen Esther spun around and the women fell silent, staring at Jane.

"What?" she demanded.

"It's Jane Strope," she said. "Remember you ate at our house lots of times. Do you know what happened to my papa, Sebastian Strope?"

"No. Leave me be." Her voice was harsh. Seeing Jane's stricken face she spoke more softly. "The scale is balanced now. I can't help you."

"But..."

"I can't help you," Queen Esther repeated. "Go." She turned away decisively.

Jane stood a moment, shoulders slumped, then started back to the cabin.

Faith hurried toward her. "What did she say?" Faith asked.

"She said the scale was balanced."

"What does that mean?"

"I don't know. But I don't think it's good."

Around them, Indians were drawing out pots of war paint. Jane watched with mounting fear. Was this a prelude to some Indian ceremony that would end in death?

Queen Esther clapped her hands and spoke loudly in the sudden silence.

"We have agreed that women and children are free to go," she announced. "Your faces will be marked with paint to show you are not to be harmed."

"Come on," Faith said. "Let's get marked before they change their minds."

She took Jane's hand and they stood in one of the lines of settlers that quickly formed. When her turn came, Jane stared into the eyes of the young Indian marking her. His arms were covered with what she feared was dried blood. Perhaps even her father's. Her mind veered away from the thought like a frightened deer, and she scowled at the Indian. Roughly, he swabbed her face with a twig brush and pushed her aside to daub Faith's face.

Together, she and Faith headed for their cabin and began gathering what belongings the Indians hadn't plundered.

"We'll head east, toward Stroudsburg, " Faith announced.

"I'm not going with you," Jane said, determined to have control over at least one thing in her life. "Mrs. Stewart will take care of me."

"What? Your father told you to go with me."

"I've changed my mind. Tell him I'm going downriver with Mrs. Stewart to Bloomsburg. He can look for me there."

Jane turned and raised her voice. "Is anyone here going to Stroudsburg?" Two women nodded.

"Tell my father to look for me in Bloomsburg with Mrs. Stewart. She'll be staying with a friend there to rest for a while," Jane said. There, she had just tripled the chances her father would find her. And if he was coming to get her, he wouldn't be with Faith.

"Is it because of the puppy?" Faith asked. "You know we can't take a puppy through that swamp and over those mountains. How would it survive?"

"It's not the puppy," Jane said, her voice cold.

Faith's face reddened. "Oh," she said.

"Yes, oh," Jane said and darted off before Faith could reply.

Papa might be mad at first, Jane thought. But he could find her at Bloomsburg. This way she wouldn't have to go with Faith, and she could take Gertie with her. The puppy was old enough to leave her mother now.

She thought of Pferd. What would happen to him?

She found Mrs. Stewart and her brood loading themselves with food, water and clothing. Everyone carried something.

"I want to go with you," Jane announced.

"I thought you were to go with Mrs. Hollenbeck," Mrs. Stewart said, startled.

"The plans have been changed," Jane said.

Mrs. Stewart's face was pale and she swayed on her feet. She shouldn't be doing all this so soon after having the baby, Jane thought. "I can help look after the children," Jane said. "And I'd like to take Gertie with us."

Mrs. Stewart continued to gather possessions. "All right, child," she said. "But you have to take care of her. We'll turn the other pups loose to forage."

"What will they eat?"

"They're almost four months old. They can find worms, grubs, squirrels, baby rabbits, something. Maybe they'll go with the Indians."

"What about Pferd?"

Mrs. Stewart turned to her, clutching a coil of rope. "I'm sorry," she said, "but the Indians will take all the horses. They'll never let us leave with Pferd. They take good care of their animals."

Not as good as Papa or I would, Jane thought, but she knew she had to accept it.

Mrs. Stewart thrust the rope at Jane. "Now, come along. We need to find some boards and lash them between two canoes to make a raft. And we need to be quick about it. I don't have any faith in how long the British major will be able to restrain the Indians from killing us all."

Soon they joined the rafts, canoes and boats filled with families and their belongings. As soon as they pushed off, the baby began to cry. Mrs. Stewart nursed him discreetly while their lashed canoes glided along on the slow-moving river, rocking with the current or being bumped by another raft in the flotilla of refugees.

Mrs. Stewart's three-year-old son whimpered and she reached over to pat him.

"I know," she said. "But before you know it we'll be at Bloomsburg and we can all rest and catch our breath. We surely need that."

Gertie wriggled in Jane's arms and tried to bite at the twine around her neck. Jane looked out over the sea of crafts, absorbing the impact of what had happened. On some rafts, people sat in silence. On others, women called to each other, exchanging news. Occasional laughter or sobs rose above the hubbub. The tinny sound of a fife drifted over the water.

Things will get better, Jane thought. Papa is alive and will find me. The war will end soon and they'll set Mama and the boys free. We just have to soldier through this bad time. She hugged the puppy closer, feeling vaguely comforted when it licked her hand.

The water grew choppier as they approached the rock-strewn Nanticoke rapids, ten miles below the fort. In places the paddles scraped the bottom and Jane could see stones beneath them as they drifted by. Finally, they hung up on a large rock, and joined other craft piled up along the fall line. Only the lightest canoes sailed on, pitching and turning in the rough water.

Men lined the shore, drawn from somewhere nearby by the opportunity for profit. "We'll carry any boat around for a price," one called.

Mrs. Stewart lifted a hand in acknowledgment as six men headed their way.

"Everyone out," Mrs. Stewart ordered. "Off with your shoes first." Jane waded to shore, shoes in one hand, Gertie cradled against her chest. The river soaked her skirt and the stones were slippery underfoot but the cool water felt good. Somewhere she had lost her cap. The wind whipped her long red hair against her face. On shore, she watched while men heaved at the various boats. The puppy whined and wriggled in her arms. Nearby, in a clearing, dozens of yellow butterflies fluttered above clover blossoms and daisies.

"There you go," she said, placing Gertie on the ground in the midst of the blossoms. The puppy explored busily, sniffing at everything, while Jane followed, glad to be moving instead of sitting jammed up among children and possessions. She glanced toward the river. Their craft was third in line, time enough to slip behind the big oak at the edge of the field and relieve herself. She put on her shoes, conscious of how prickly the forest floor could be, and stepped behind the tree. A startled squirrel bounded away through the woods and Gertie jerked the twine from Jane's hand and raced after it.

"Gertie, come back," Jane called. She pelted into the woods in pursuit, tripped on a root, picked herself up and spotted the puppy ahead. "Come back," she called again. Gertie stopped and looked at her. When Jane got close enough to grab her, Gertie dodged, ran deeper into the woods as Jane chased after her, then stopped again, tongue out, forepaws extended and hindquarters up in the air.

"No, Gertie. This is no time to play," Jane said. She held out her hand, moving slowly, then dove for the puppy. Another miss. Giving excited yips, Gertie moved off. This time, Jane sat on the ground and waited. Gertie cocked her head, then trotted toward her. Jane resisted the temptation to move. Gertie stopped a hand's breadth away and Jane scooped her up.

"Bad puppy," she admonished, half crying. "Bad puppy." The puppy, uncowed, licked her cheek.

Jane looked around. Which way had she come? She listened for the sound of the children and men shouting, but heard only the wind soughing through the pines and the gurgling of a creek somewhere ahead. Nothing looked familiar. She headed back the way she thought she had come. Her breathing quickened and her heart beat faster as she realized she was lost. She stopped short and tried to take stock. It was foolish to keep wandering aimlessly. Her father had told her that creeks flowed to larger bodies of water. If she followed the creek, she was bound to arrive back at the Susquehanna, maybe even near the spot where she'd entered the woods. Surely they'd search for her, and she might hear them calling her name. She hurried toward the sound of water.

Chapter Twelve

The creek was farther away than she expected, cascading over rocks in a small waterfall. At a shallow spot, she and the puppy drank thirstily, then she began making her way downstream. Willows and tangled vines lined the banks, slowing her progress. Soon, her hands were crisscrossed with red, stinging scratches from branches. The sun, glimpsed through the trees, sank ever lower in the sky. From time to time, she called out, then listened, but the only sounds were the creek and the wind. Finally the creek widened. With relief, she burst out of the woods onto the shores of the Susquehanna. The river had never looked more beautiful to her. The puppy, unconcerned, dug in the dirt. Boats crowded the water, moving freely. She was probably below Nanticoke Rapids then. By the length of her shadow on the ground, it was midafternoon. Mrs. Stewart might have given up and gone on. So it was best to hail a passing boat and continue to Bloomsburg. Once there, she would find Mrs. Stewart somehow.

Jane lifted one hand and waved. People in boats waved back but kept going, apparently thinking she was greeting them.

"Help," she called. "I need help."

Several more boats swept by unheeding. Finally, a big man alone in a canoe looked her way and put one hand to his ear inquiringly.

"Help," she shouted. "I'm lost. I need to get to Bloomsburg."

He nodded and paddled toward her. She picked up Gertie and ran to meet him as he pulled the canoe up on the bank. He was a burly study in brown from his long hair and unkempt beard on down to his brown leather shoes. "What's a little girl like you doing out here all alone?" he asked. The puppy yipped, startled by his booming voice.

"I came down from Forty Fort," she said, "but I got separated from Mrs. Stewart and her family. Now I need to get to Bloomsburg to meet up with them."

He looked at her. "You look familiar," he said. "What's your name?"

"Jane Strope."

He gave a half bow, just as if she were a grown-up lady. "Pleased to make your acquaintance. I'm Hiram Landon. Come on, I'm heading that way. I'll give you a ride."

The canoe was packed with bundles.

"How long ago did you get separated?" Hiram asked as they pushed off.

"A few hours, I guess."

"And you came down from Forty Fort?"

She nodded.

"It was terrible there from what I hear."

Again she nodded, unwilling to talk about her ordeal. Better to concentrate on the river, the passing scenery, this kind man.

He looked at her sympathetically. "Are you hungry?"

"I could eat a bear," she said. He laughed and pointed to one of the bundles. "There's some corn cakes and meat in there, but no bear," he said. "Help yourself."

"Were you at Forty Fort?" Jane asked, tearing into the food and taking a long swallow from the canteen he handed her.

"No," he said, "I was farther downriver." He paused. "What about your family? Are they all right?"

"I don't know," she said. She didn't want to talk about it. It was too fresh. "Gertie is hungry, too," she said.

"There's a pan in that pack," he said. "If you moisten the cornbread, she'll probably eat it. And she might make some headway on the jerky."

He paddled vigorously downstream while Jane fed Gertie, then held the wriggling puppy over the side to urinate. The canoe rocked with Gertie's motions. Hiram laughed. "Feisty little thing," he said.

At times, the river became so shallow the canoe scraped on the rocks and Hiram pushed them free with his paddle.

Skillfully, he navigated into deeper water. She studied his strong hands, his broad back.

"What kind of work do you do, Mr. Landon?" she asked.

"Oh, I'm good with my hands. I build things for rich people." He chuckled. "I do just about anything a person might want done. Wherever there's opportunity, I grab it. You can be sure of that."

Every now and then he studied her face as if puzzled. Suddenly he snapped his fingers. "I've got it," he said. "You favor Betsy Jamieson right smart. The same red hair, same blue eyes."

"Who is she?" Jane asked.

"Betsy died somewhere near Harris Ferry nigh on a month ago. How old are you?"

"Thirteen."

"Hmm. You look younger."

"How old was Betsy?" Jane asked.

"Twelve, but small like you. Not a perfect resemblance, but still close," he said, and paddled silently for the next hour, outdistancing the heavier craft on the river. Jane stared dreamily at the passing trees, grateful for the respite. Forty Fort seemed far away.

"Does anyone know where you are?" Hiram asked suddenly.

"Not really," she said.

He paddled in silence and Jane fell into a kind of daze, stroking the puppy rhythmically.

Once, they stopped to stretch and relieve themselves. Jane slipped behind a tree, feeling awkward and embarrassed. But when she emerged she saw Hiram staring pointedly away at the river. How lucky I was to meet up with such a nice man, she thought. Maybe more luck would come her way. She'd connect with Mrs. Stewart soon and Papa would find her. She passed the time with thoughts of their happy reunion until she fell asleep slumped forward over her seat in the canoe.

They reached Bloomsburg at dusk. The low hills sloping down to the shore and the islands dotting the river were barely visible; the light of the full moon lay in ripples of silver across the water. All along the bank, boats were drawn up in a crowded jumble.

"We can't put in here. Too crowded," Hiram said suddenly, startling Jane awake. "I'll try farther down."

Sleepily she rubbed her eyes. The puppy, curled in the bottom of the canoe, slept on.

Hiram paddled steadily on, apparently alerted to whitewater by the light of the moon.

"Shouldn't we beach the canoe?" Jane said. "It's a long way back to Bloomsburg."

"Everything will be all right," Hiram said, and kept paddling.

Alarm swelled in Jane. Where was this stranger taking them? Maybe he wasn't so kind after all. She considered jumping out and swimming to shore. But they were in midchannel in the dark. The current was swift and the river broad here. Plus there was the puppy.

"Stop now," Jane said, trying to sound firm. "I can go back upriver by myself."

"I'm sorry. I can't do that," he said, his voice gentle. "I have a better plan."

Jane sat silently as Hiram landed his canoe at Harris Ferry, miles farther south from Bloomsburg. They had stopped to rest earlier, but he had watched her constantly and she had seen no way to escape. Papa will never find me now, she thought. Why didn't I stay with Faith like he asked? I've really gotten myself in a stew this time.

"My father said I should go to my grandparents' farm on the Hudson," she said, refusing to get out of the canoe. "You could take me there. They'd pay you for your trouble."

"That sounds good," he said. "But first, we're going to my house. My wife will feed you and the dog. Her name is Gertie, right?" We'll clean you up and you can get some rest. Then I'll explain."

Maybe it will be all right, Jane thought. If not, maybe someone here can help me.

Above them on a rise, barely visible in the moonlight sat an imposing two-story home of limestone surrounded by a stockade, the gate open.

"That's John Harris' house," Hiram explained. "He's a big man hereabouts. He trades with the Indians for furs and owns the ferry. Now and then I do chores for him."

She followed Hiram through the settlement, gazing around with curiosity despite her concern. There must be almost two hundred houses here, she thought.

She looked down at her bedraggled skirts and muddy shoes. A chance to wash up and hot food would be welcome, and Gertie needed to be fed. Mr. Landon wouldn't take her to his wife if he planned to hurt her. Maybe he really did have a better plan.

Chapter Thirteen

Hiram didn't introduce Jane to his wife except to say he had plans for her. Hiram and Jane sat in the kitchen at a carved walnut table that he proudly explained he had made.

Silently, his wife set loosestrife tea, fresh berries and cornbread smeared with honey in front of them. When they finished eating, she knelt to give the puppy the scraps, petting his head. Gertie devoured the food and nosed around under the table for more. The woman looked questioningly at Hiram. When he nodded, she put down more scraps.

"I'll take the dog outside to relieve herself," the woman said in a low voice.

"Thank you," Jane said and was rewarded with a faint smile.

After his wife left the room, Hiram turned to her. "Feeling better?"

"Yes, I guess so."

"Good. Now here's my plan. That girl I told you about, Betsy Jamieson, her mother is really rich. And touched, if you know what I mean." He pointed to his forehead. "Nothing but bad luck for her. She lost a child two years ago to a bee sting. Darndest thing. The boy's throat swolled all up and bam, he was dead. Then her husband up and died of typhoid and left her everything. Within days, Betsy, their other child, disappeared. Her horse came back without her. They searched, but they never found her. That was a month ago. That really sent her around the bend, poor thing. Anyway, now Mrs. Jamieson's all alone in that big house and purely touched in the head. When I was over there last week doing carpentry work, she vowed her daughter was still alive out there and would come back. She's offering a reward for information. So I'll take you to her house and say you're Betsy and I found you wandering lost near the river."

He paused as his wife brought Gertie back inside.

"See, if Mrs. Jamieson doesn't believe me, I'll say I made a mistake," he said. "No harm done. But she's so full of grief and half crazy, she'll believe me. Either way, I'll finagle the reward out of her. You'll stay with her for a day or two. Then I'll come get you and share some of the money with you. She can't prove I lied. An honest mistake. I'll take you to your grandparents and get money for my trouble there, too. Everyone will be happy." He sat back with a satisfied grin. "I told you it was a better plan."

His wife shot him a surreptitious look so full of venom Jane was surprised he didn't wince.

Jane stared at him. She thought of the pain she and her parents had felt after Gideon drowned. Now this man wanted to take advantage of someone who had lost not one, but two children.

"That's horrible. It's a stupid plan," she burst out. "It won't work and I won't do it. Take me to Round Top now and you'll get plenty of money." Jane wasn't sure her grandparents had plenty of money, but surely they'd find enough somehow.

Hiram scowled. "It will work."

Behind him, his wife rolled her eyes.

"People believe what they want to believe," Hiram said. "Especially if they're crazy to begin with. And don't say you won't do it." He walked over to where Gertie lay sprawled asleep, stomach distended with food and paws twitching as if she were chasing something, and pointed at the puppy. "You wouldn't want anything to happen to your dog, would you? We'll just keep her here where she can be well cared for, until we finish up with what we need to do."

Something inside Jane shifted. This was an evil man. She had to protect Gertie and get them both away from him somehow. A proverb her mother quoted came to mind, one she had hated because it smacked of giving in: In der Not frisst der Teufel Fliegen. When in need, the devil eats flies. If she had to eat flies for a day or two, she would. Once she met the widow, she could explain everything.

She gave a jerky nod.

"To success," he said, lifting his mug. She sat down her tea, folded her hand in her lap and glared at him. She might have to eat flies, but she didn't have to pretend to like it.

Acting on Hiram's instructions, Jane stayed behind him as he walked up to Mrs. Jamieson's front door. Hiram's wife had altered her hairstyle to resemble Betsy's and given her a clean, though faded, dress that she pinned up to keep it from dragging the ground. "Good luck, child," she had whispered.

"I'll tell her your own clothes were ruined," Hiram said.

Along the way they passed dozens of houses, some with lights shining through the windows.

Jane thought about shouting for help, but doubted anyone would hear her, and Hiram had a firm grip on her arm.

"Come along," he said.

Mrs. Jamieson's two-story house with its pillared front porch was made of the same native limestone as John Harris' mansion. Hiram climbed the steps and knocked. "Remember, let me do the talking," he said.

In a moment, a petite woman with auburn hair and eyes rimmed with red entered the hallway. Her silk dress was wrinkled and she clutched a wadded handkerchief.

"Why, Mr. Landon," Mrs. Jamieson said. "What brings you here at this time of night?"

"A miracle. A sure-enough miracle the Lord has performed."

"I could use a miracle," Mrs. Jamieson said, her voice high and quavering.

"Well, I have one for you. I was coming down the river when this girl stepped out of the woods, lost as could be. She called to me and when I pulled my canoe to shore, I couldn't believe my eyes." He paused. "Who should it be but Betsy." He dragged Jane forward with a flourish. "And I've brought her back to you."

Mrs. Jamieson staggered back against the wall, staring at Jane's face. "Betsy?" she said.

Jane stood mute. This was horrible. Hiram nudged her. "Betsy, is that any way to greet your mother."

"I..." Despite her resolve to cooperate, Jane couldn't force words past the tightening in her throat.

"What? How...?" Mrs. Jamieson seemed equally speechless. She swayed, white-faced and would have fallen if Hiram had not grabbed her arm. "Come in," she whispered.

She led them to the drawing room and collapsed on a settee, waving them to chairs. She sat motionless for long moments staring at Jane.

"It's a lot to absorb, I know," Hiram said. "God must have been looking out for both of you, when he led me to her."

Mrs. Jamieson ignored him, concentrating on Jane by the dim light of two oil lamps. "Is it really you?" she asked. She passed her hand over her eyes. "Has God answered my prayers?"

Hiram cut in quickly. "Maybe Betsy would like to rest in her room while you and I talk. I understand there's a reward."

"What?" She looked at Jane again and seemed to come to a decision.

"Oh yes, of course. But I don't have the funds with me. You'll need to come back in the morning."

He frowned. "But…" He looked at Jane and jerked his head slightly.

Jane was torn. Would he do something to Gertie if he didn't get his money? She couldn't contradict him now. She had to let him believe she was going along with the scheme.

She gave a big yawn that was only half feigned.

"Betsy is exhausted," Hiram said.

The woman looked at her with concern. "You do look worn out. Would you like to lay down?"

Hiram stared at Jane and she nodded.

"All right. Follow me."

Mrs. Jamieson led her up the stairs to a bedroom with lace curtains and a deep green quilt. "Just rest," she said. "I can tell you've been through a lot."

She leaned over and stroked Jane's hair.

As soon as Mrs. Jamieson left, Jane crept to the door and listened. Voices drifted up from downstairs, but the words were unintelligible. In a few minutes, Hiram left, and Mrs. Jamieson came back upstairs. She stood in the doorway a few seconds, her hands trembling.

"Child," she began.

"I'm not Betsy," Jane burst out. "I just look like her. I'm Jane Strope and Mr. Landon forced me to come here because he has my puppy and he'll kill it if I don't do what he wants. You have to help me."

Mrs. Jamieson stared at her, forehead wrinkled. "You're not making any sense."

"I'm not your daughter," Jane repeated.

"For a few minutes there, I imagined…" Mrs. Jamieson looked like she was ready to cry.

"I'm sorry, but I'm not," Jane said.

Mrs. Jamieson ran her hands down her face and slumped against the door frame, then straightened.

"You're exhausted. A good night's sleep will make everything clearer to both of us."

That night, lying on the soft feather bed, so different from the rustling, uncomfortable corn shucks at home, Jane looked around the room at the fine furniture and flowered rug. She thought of the times she'd sat hidden in the thicket at home and dreamed of a room like this. Now that she was here, it was a nightmare. Too much had happened too fast. She curled into a ball and sobbed herself to sleep.

She awakened at dawn and lay in bed staring at the ceiling, wondering how Gertie was and what the day would bring. A knock on the bedroom door interrupted her musings.

"Good morning, child," Mrs. Jamieson said. "My servant, Susanna, is fixing us buckwheat cakes with maple syrup as a special treat."

"You know I'm not Betsy, don't you?" Jane demanded.

Rather than answering, Mrs. Jamieson stared at her ragged clothes.

"You can't go around looking like that." She opened the chifferobe where a row of pretty dresses hung and pulled out a brown and white print dress with a white collar. She ran her fingers over it and pressed her face against the garment, inhaling. Then she gave a big sigh and pulled it out.

"You can wear this," she said. She picked up a bottle from the dresser. "And here's some lavender water to sprinkle on it. When you're ready, come to breakfast. Then we can talk."

She whirled and hurried down the stairs before Jane could speak.

Jane looked at the dress, unwilling to wear the dead girl's clothing. She still wasn't sure what Mrs. Jamieson thought. Wearing the dress would make her look even more like Betsy. But then she looked at the ragged, too large dress Hiram had provided and donned Betsy's dress. She looked at herself in the mirror. The dress fit almost perfectly. She smoothed the fabric, her rough fingers catching on the fine material, then picked up a comb and ran it through her hair.

Afterward, she glanced around the room. On the wall hung a needlework sampler Betsy must have made. It read: "When I was Young and in my Prime, You see how well I spent my Time And by my Sampler you may see What care my Parents took of me."

When Jane came down the stairs, Mrs. Jamieson rose from the sofa. She put her hand to her heart and staggered backward a step.

"Betsy," she said, then more softly and with a break in her voice. "Betsy."

The curtains were open. "Come here," she said, "where the light is good. Let me look at you."

Jane stood in the sunlight trembling.

Mrs. Jamieson shook her head. "The resemblance is amazing. God, how I wish all this were real. I laid awake all last night thinking, hoping, and finally knowing that my daughter is gone. I've been living in a dream. But oh, it's so hard to leave it." A sob escaped her.

Jane put her hand out and touched Mrs. Jamieson's shoulder.

"I'm sorry," she said.

Mrs. Jamieson's hand closed over hers, then Mrs. Jamieson swept her into a long hug and sobbed in earnest.

Jane stood frozen, feeling her own losses rise in her. She pulled back a little.

Quickly, Mrs. Jamieson released her.

"Well," she said. "Let's eat and you can tell me your story."

When Jane finished, Mrs. Jamieson sat back in her chair. "You have had a time of it."

"What about my puppy? Can you help me? And I have to find Mrs. Stewart."

"It will be my pleasure," she said, standing up. "First we'll retrieve your dog."

At last, Jane thought. Things are going well.

"As to Mrs. Stewart, why don't you stay here a few days and rest up? We can find a way to get you two together later."

Jane looked at her.

"I..."

"Please. It's so nice to have a daughter...now you're not my daughter – but it's just...so nice."

"I really have to find Mrs. Stewart so Papa can find me."

Mrs. Jamieson nodded. "All right. If you must. Then, let's get it over with."

She reached for her bonnet, donned it, and, holding Jane's hand, they walked out of the house and up the street.

As they approached Hiram Landon's cottage, Jane's apprehension mounted. Was Gertie all right? How would he react?

His wife answered the door.

"My husband's not here," she said. "He's gone to Philadelphia for a few weeks, right sudden like." She gave a lopsided grin. "I suppose you've come for the dog."

"Yes," Mrs. Jamieson and Jane said at the same time.

Mrs. Landon led them out back where Gertie was tied to a post.

In a paroxysm of delight, Jane flung herself down beside the puppy, then held Gertie up and checked her all over. "She looks wonderful," Jane said. "Thank you, thank you."

Mrs. Jamieson knelt beside her and petted the puppy. Even Mrs. Landon smiled.

Jane cradled Gertie in her arms as they left.

"You're never getting away again," she said.

"Now we'll inquire about Mrs. Stewart," Mrs. Jamieson said, "unless you've changed your mind..."

Jane shook her head.

"Ah well."

When they neared the river, they found the bank still crowded with canoes and boats. People milled about. After a dozen queries and several dead ends, they couldn't find anyone who knew for sure if she was at Bloomsburg. Peering around, Jane spotted a familiar face from Forty Fort and relief flooded her. "Maybe Mrs. Whittaker knows something," she said, heading toward a stout, middle-aged woman and waving to attract her attention.

"Why, Jane, I'm glad to see you," Mrs. Whittaker said when they reached her. "Mrs. Stewart was so worried when you disappeared. She decided to bypass Bloomsburg. Her friend was ready to flee herself. And it wasn't safe anyway with the baby and all. Everything's total chaos. Anyway, Mrs. Whittaker pushed on to her sister in Lancaster early this morning. She said if anyone saw you, they should send you there."

"Lancaster? But Mrs. Hollenbeck will tell my father to meet me in Bloomsburg." Jane frowned. "And Mrs. Stewart didn't stop there after all, so he may not know where I am. Will anyone there know she went on to Lancaster."

She felt like crying with frustration. "Maybe I should to Lancaster and wait for him. Or should I go to Bloomsburg?"

"Do you know anyone in Bloomsburg?"

"No."

"And I doubt anyone is eager to go back upriver to Bloomsburg right now. I'm sorry, Jane." Mrs. Whittaker paused and put her finger to her lips in thought. "I know. Why don't you come with us? We're leaving for Philadelphia in the morning by way of Lancaster. The road from there to Philadelphia is dreadful, but at least it's a road. We can drop you off in Lancaster. We'll leave word here as best we can as to what's happened."

Mrs. Jamieson put her arm around her. "Are you sure you'll be all right?"

"We'll take good care of her," Mrs. Whittaker said.

Mrs. Jamieson nodded and swept Jane into a fierce embrace.

"Maybe you could write me and let me know you're safe," she said.

"I will." Jane hesitated, then reached up and kissed her on the cheek.

Mrs. Jamieson smiled, turned and walked away without looking back.

After Mrs. Jamieson left, Mrs. Whittaker took in Jane's fancy print dress and slippers, coupled with the puppy who tugged at the rope. "It looks as if you have an interesting story to tell."

Chapter Fourteen

Sebastian staggered in to Stroudsburg exhausted. He'd lost weight from his already slender frame and knew he looked skeletal. But not as bad as some of the poor devils he'd encountered. Many of the fleeing settlers had perished en route in the swamp and over the Pennsylvania mountains. Sebastian shifted his rifle and scratched at the blackfly bites on his arms. Thank God he was here at last and could find out about Faith and Jane. Most of those who died on the way were old or weak, but Jane and Faith were young and strong. They should be fine.

Stroudsburg residents had set up a huge kettle of stew on a fire inside the fort. Gulping down a bowlful, he went in search of the pastor. He found the Rev. Hollister Strait sitting at a table while a line of people waited to talk to him. As each one approached, Strait questioned them, wrote on parchment and clasped hands in prayer. After twenty minutes, it was Sebastian's turn. The minister turned weary eyes toward him. "How can I help you?" he asked.

"I'm seeking word of Faith Hollenbeck and Jane Strope, a woman of about twenty two with a missing front tooth, and a small girl of thirteen with straight, red hair. They fled from Forty Fort."

"I'm sorry. I don't remember them. But I've seen so many souls it's hard to recall names or faces," Strait said. He paused. "Can you read?"

Sebastian nodded. Strait handed him another parchment filled with writing.

"I've noted what names I could here. And I'm still taking names. Take a look while I help the next person."

Sebastian studied the list, spotting Faith's name halfway down, but no mention of Jane. Fear filled him. What did it mean? Maybe Faith had assumed there was no need to give Jane's name since she was a child.

He turned to the minister. "Where are the refugees staying?" he asked.

Strait finished his pen stroke before replying. "Anywhere someone will take them in. A few have already gone on to relatives in Connecticut or on the Hudson."

"Thank you," Sebastian said and walked over to squat down in the shade and think. The settlement was small. It wouldn't take long to check every house. If they had moved on, he could head for his parents' home and meet them there. Wearily, he rose to his feet, made the rounds of the fort and began knocking on doors.

At the fifth house, an elderly woman with gray hair answered. When he gave Faith's name, she invited him in and led the way to the kitchen. "There's someone here to see you, Faith," she said. Faith jumped up from a bench.

"Sebastian," she exclaimed. "You're alive. Thank God. I was so worried." She ran across the room and hugged him, tears streaming down her face. Sebastian hugged her back, while the owner of the house looked on with a smile. The depth of his pleasure at seeing Faith startled him.

He stepped back and looked around. "Where's Jane?"

"She went with Mrs. Stewart to Bloomsburg," Faith said.

"Bloomsburg?" All this way and Jane wasn't here. He felt weary to the bone. "Why Bloomsburg? She was supposed to go with you."

"Because of...the puppy, I suppose. She knew it would be too hard to bring it here."

"The puppy?" He became aware of the woman listening to their conversation. "Let's take a walk," he said.

They stepped outside and strolled toward the fort.

"We can go get her," Faith said.

"We? I can't take you with me all that way."

"Why not?"

"It's dangerous," he said. And, he thought, it's best if we don't spend a lot of time together.

"Where can I go?" she asked. "I don't know anyone. My husband is dead. Everything I have has been taken from me." She reached out and clasped his hand. It was true, she was alone in the world. He left her hand in his as he tried to think what to do next.

Across the street, he saw a tall, blond man watching them.

"Isn't that the fellow from the fort?" he asked Faith, "the one who knew something about my family."

"It might be."

"Hello," Sebastian called. What was the fellow's name? Zach something.

The man started toward them. "Hello. I'm Zach Wilson," he said. "We met at Forty Fort just before the gates of hell opened up."

"You have the right of that," Sebastian said. "I see you escaped unscathed."

"God be praised. I'm safe at home at last." Zach's gaze raked Faith. "And I see your *friend* is safe, too."

Sebastian flushed and dropped Faith's hand. "When last we met, you said you had news of my family," he said. "What can you tell me?"

Zach hesitated. He looked from Faith to Sebastian and back again. "I'm sorry to have to tell you this, but your wife, Lydia, and son Henry are dead, and the Indians adopted Isaac."

"What? Are you sure?"

"I saw your wife and son with my own eyes," Zach said.

"But back at Forty Fort you told me not to worry. Why did you say that if they were dead?"

Zach dropped his eyes. "I guess I didn't have the heart to tell you then. I'm right sorry."

Sebastian felt pain split him open like an axe through kindling. He let out a groan and bent over, putting his hands on his knees to keep from falling. Faith put her hand on his shoulder.

After a moment, he raised his head and forced himself erect.

"What about…" Words stuck in Sebastian's throat. He stopped and tried again. "What about Margaretha, my sister-in-law?"

An uncertain look crossed Zach's face. "She's. uh…she's alive."

"And her baby?"

"Born a few weeks after they were captured and doing fine."

"My brother John?"

"He's a prisoner at Fort Niagara."

"When did my wife and son die?"

"The same day they got to Tioga Point."

So soon. "How did it happen?" Sebastian choked on the words.

"I don't want to talk about it," Zach said.

"I understand, but I'd like to know."

"It's best you leave it be, man. You don't want to know."

Then it must have been horrible. Sebastian wiped his hand across his eyes as if he could rid himself of the visions of scalping and torture that leaped to mind.

"Thank you for telling me," he rasped.

Zach shifted from foot to foot uncomfortably. "You're welcome," he muttered. "I must be going." He turned and hurried away. Sebastian called after him, but Zach disappeared into the woods.

"I have to go to Bloomsburg to get Jane," Sebastian said dully. "She's all I have left."

"You need to rest first," Faith said. "Another night won't make a difference. You're exhausted. And you've had shock after shock. We all have."

"You're right," he said. Numbly, he escorted Faith back to the house where she was staying and found a place to bed down inside Fort Penn. He lay unsleeping most of the night, staring into the outer darkness that mirrored the darkness within. Over and over he imagined scenes of horror. The more he tried to wipe them out, the more they returned, until he felt like an ox chained to a pole, endlessly turning a millstone

Maybe, he thought, he could remember their pleasant times together and that would wipe out the darker thoughts. He recalled the many evenings they'd sat by candlelight in silence. He might be mending a harness while she shucked peas in a wooden bowl. He would look over at her intent face, then back to his work and a sense of peace would sweep over him. It was womanish almost the way he felt at times like that, but there it was. Or sometimes he'd ponder which crops to plant and she would offer her advice. He'd compliment her on her cherry pie and she would say, "Oh, it's not that good." He'd insist and she'd turn away, still protesting, but with a smile on her lips. He loved the practical side of her, but he loved the less-rarely-seen soft side even more.

But these visions of their times together tortured him just as much as the scenes of horror he'd imagined. Finally, he got up and went outside. He stumbled over a root in the dark, stood up and struck the tree over and over with both fists until his hands were bloody, then staggered back to bed.

The next morning, exhausted and empty, he sought out the pastor and told him what had happened.

"So many losses," Strait said. "It's hard to understand, I know. Let me pray with you." Obediently, Sebastian bowed his head.

"Lord, your ways are beyond human understanding. Be with this poor man and succor him in his time of grief. Reunite him with his daughter and keep him safe until that blessed day when he will rejoin his family in paradise. And help us to accept your will."

I don't see how this is God's will, Sebastian thought. And it was cold comfort to think some distant day they might be together in heaven. A coal of fresh anger sparked to life and he welcomed it. Anything to replace the hollowness that filled him. The British and Indians did this, he thought. Damn them to hell. They've taken everything from me. As soon as Jane is safe, I'm striking back.

"Thank you for your prayers, Pastor Strait," he said. "What I really need is something more earthly. I need to borrow a horse to ride to Bloomsburg and get Jane."

"That could be difficult. Everyone needs horses right now." He looked at Sebastian's bloodshot eyes and drawn face, the scrapes on his hands. "I'll see what I can do."

Bloomsburg, a small settlement to begin with, was almost deserted when Sebastian reached it. Houses sat empty; weeds encroached on flower and herb gardens in the noon heat. A few men worked in the fields while dogs lay panting under the shade of trees, barely lifting their heads to notice when Sebastian rode by.

Most of the settlers had fled south or east in terror when news of the Forty Fort massacre reached them.

Sebastian had pushed himself and his borrowed horse hard, focusing on finding Jane. Now, he tied the sorrel mare to a hickory tree and walked over to a young man chopping a log. The man pushed his straw hat back on his head and wiped sweat from his face with a bandana.

"What can I do for you?" he asked.

"I'm looking for word of Mrs. Lazarus Stewart and a girl of thirteen with her. Mrs. Stewart has seven children, including a newborn, and the girl, my daughter, has red hair and is small for her age. Jane Strope is her name."

"Ah. You're the father. Come over in the shade," the man said.

"So you do know her?" Sebastian asked, pulse racing, as they walked toward a large oak.

"Not exactly. I know of her. I heard that she got separated from her party at Nanticoke Rapids. She went into the woods after a dog, and no one has seen her since. I'm sorry."

"Oh." Sebastian had passed into a place beyond shock.

"What about Mrs. Stewart? Do you know where she is?"

"Sorry. I don't."

"But she was going to stop here, so she must know someone in Bloomsburg."

"That may be, but as you can see, most folks have fled. We're all that's left."

"I'll ask around anyway," Sebastian said. He went from house to deserted house, hoping to find someone who knew where Mrs. Stewart had gone, then returned to the man he'd first met.

"No luck?" the man said.

Sebastian shook his head.

"Your daughter could have met up with someone else from Forty Fort and be just fine," the man said. "If I hear anything, is there someplace I can send word?"

"What?" Sebastian said. The world had taken on an unreal quality and he was having trouble focusing. "Oh, send word to Johann Strope, my father, at Round Top on Shingle Kill in New York state. His farm is on the Hudson."

"I'll do that," the man said. "You don't look so good. Why don't you sit down and rest? My wife, Judith, might know more and she would be happy to fix you a bite of food."

But Judith didn't know more. Sebastian poked at the venison on his plate, no longer hungry. Judith gently touched his shoulder as she put biscuits in front of him. The gentle woman's touch threatened to break through his numbness.

I have to be strong, Sebastian thought. My daughter is alive somewhere. She has to be. The next morning, armed with fresh provisions but still dazed from lack of sleep, he continued down river, asking for word of Jane. But in the confusion and with the way folks had scattered, no one remembered seeing her.

A week later he sat in despair by a campfire, staring into the flames. This way isn't working, he thought. I could search forever and never find her. I need to be where she can find me. He thought of his parents' farmhouse at Round Top, the cattle grazing in the fields, the barn loaded with sweet-smelling hay, his mother's kitchen table piled high with green and gold bounty from the garden. A longing for a place of respite, however temporary, swept over him. The farmhouse was where Jane would send word, so he needed to be there. He would turn his steps toward the place where he was born.

The next morning, he headed back to Stroudsburg to return the horse.

When he arrived, he sought out Faith at the house where she was staying. She was picking flowers from a bush in front of the cottage. When she saw him, she dropped the flowers, rushed to him and flung her arms around his neck.

"You came back," she said.

For a moment, he returned her embrace, realizing how glad he was to see her. But now, with a clearer head, he also realized he needed to be careful that in his grief and loneliness he didn't give her a false impression of his feelings. No one could ever replace Lydia. Gently, he removed her arms and stepped back.

"Of course I returned," he said. "I said I would. But I've had hard news. My wife and son are dead." He said the sentence flatly, as if he could deny the emotions it raised in him. "And I didn't find Jane."

"Oh. I'm so sorry for your loss. How terrible." Her voice was rich with sympathy. She put her hand lightly over his. For a moment they stood in mutual silence. Then he stirred.

"I don't understand something," he said. "Why did Jane go with Mrs. Stewart instead of you?" he asked. "I thought it was all arranged."

"Well, there was the puppy. But really I think she saw us together that day and didn't want to go anywhere with me." She looked at his stricken face. "It's not your fault. She was headstrong and foolish."

"Don't speak ill of my daughter," he said. "Ever."

She covered her mouth with her hand in a gesture he thought she'd abandoned. Instantly, he was ashamed. He had made a woman fear him, but Lord knew with all that had happened it was all he could do to contain his emotions and act like a man.

"Don't be afraid," he said. "I would never hurt you." He took a deep breath, struggling for control. "I have to believe that Jane is alive and will send word to her grandparents. I'm going to my parents' farm."

"Please take me with you," Faith begged. "I don't have anywhere else to go. The woman here is wondering how long I plan to stay. I can sew and do needlework and I could make my living in a village near your parents' farm."

"The nearest village isn't very big or close to our farm," he said.

"I can find some way to earn a living. I'm sure of it. I need a safe place to start over."

"We all do," he said.

Sunlight fell full on her face, highlighting the lines of worry and the dark circles under her eyes. Compassion swelled in him. Her plight was real and she had been a friend to him and to Jane. At the same time, some part of him doubted the wisdom of this plan. He pushed his misgivings aside.

"We'll start for Round Top tomorrow," he said.

Faith smiled and kissed him on the cheek.

Chapter Fifteen

Lydia stepped into the canoe at Bainbridge, New York, fifty miles upriver from Tioga Point. It rocked in the shallow water under her weight. An Indian handed in Henry and she gripped her son firmly. Margaretha and Elisha settled into another canoe beside them, each manned by an Indian.

She wondered what had happened at Forty Fort while she and the other captives had been harvesting flax. As they paddled back, Lydia tried to stop worrying. Nothing she did could change the outcome. She had prayed fervently, but the mysteries of prayer were hard to understand, why God answered some pleas and not others. That morning when she and Margaretha did their devotions, Lydia had recited the verses about God clothing the lilies of the field and about taking no thought for the morrow. It had calmed her for a while. But lilies weren't people. At times it seemed to her that the waters of her faith were being roiled, that some change was stirring deep inside that she couldn't yet discern.

When the group stopped for the night, the Indians wove bushes to make tents, while Henry helped catch eels and trout for supper and the women picked berries.

"I miss salt," Margaretha said, popping a berry into her mouth. "I don't understand why they rarely give us any."

"I don't either," Lydia snapped. It was hard to concentrate on trivial things like salt with her new worry. Her monthly courses were late. It had happened before, after Gideon died and at other times of stress. Please let that be the reason, she prayed. If she were with child, soon Margaretha would notice. She could never pass the baby off as Sebastian's. The timing was wrong. She would be shamed in front of friends and family. There were certain herbs that might solve the problem. But that was a sin. Sebastian was a good man, but would he understand this? She felt a surge of longing to see him, to hear his voice. At the same time, the idea of lying with any man now, even her husband, made her freeze inside. Her thoughts went round and round, going nowhere. What was it Sebastian said when she worried about things that hadn't happened? "You're grinding the corn before it's been planted."

Pray God he was right. She settled back to enjoy the day as best she could.

The canoes arrived back at Tioga Point at nightfall. The next morning, Lydia stepped outside the cabin to see a group of Indians sitting around bending twigs into circles and carefully attaching objects to them. One of them scraped away blood; another daubed red paint on a center part. Scalps, she realized. The battle must have been a disaster for the Americans. She hurried to Queen Esther's castle. An Indian waved a blond scalp as she went past. "Your husband," he said. She stopped, snatched it from him and examined it. The length and color were wrong. Thank God. She flung it to the ground and hurried on, his laughter drifting after her.

She waited for long minutes in the sun until Esther finally stepped out on her porch.

"What do you want?" Queen Esther demanded.

"News of the battle and my husband," Lydia said. "Please. I beg you."

"News of the battle I will tell you. I went to see my son fight. And he fought bravely until an American scout shot him. Even then, wounded, he raised his rifle, fired and wounded the man before he died. That is how the battle went."

"I am so sorry," Lydia said. "I know the pain of losing a child. I grieve for you. But I beg you, tell me about Sebastian."

"Do you indeed grieve with me?" Queen Esther's expression softened. "I believe you do. So I will tell you what I know. Of your husband, I have no news. I did not see him among the dead, but there were so many who fell. Still, there is hope. Your daughter was there and is safe as far as I know. She fled with the women and children I know not where." Her expression darkened again. "And the soldiers paid and paid for killing my son. Now leave me to my grief."

She turned and went inside. Lydia stared after her, then walked back toward the cabin. Around her, Indians were painting the hoops and undersides of scalps black, red, green, blue, yellow, white. What did it mean? Finally, she asked an elderly Indian who had been friendly to her before the battle.

"The colors are to mark what kind of person was killed so the British know how much to pay us for each scalp," he said. He picked up a green hoop and pointed to the painted skin. "This for a farmer killed in the fields. This black mark shows he was killed by a bullet. This mark…"

An Indian sitting nearby laughed. "And a red hoop — that's for a man who isn't a soldier or a farmer in the field. Maybe like your husband." Earlier, the Indians had noted how she examined blond scalps closely and concluded her man had yellow hair. Now the Indian shook a blond trophy at her and watched her expression. She backed away, then with deliberate slowness despite her shaking legs, she walked to the cabin. I won't give them the satisfaction of looking, she thought. I could never be sure anyway. And Queen Esther gave me hope. Yet from time to time her eyes strayed to the hoops.

In front of the cabin, Henry was drawing pictures in the dirt with a stick. He looked up at her approach, his eyes red and swollen. "You've been crying. What's wrong?" she asked.

"One of the Indians said Papa is dead," Henry said in a shaky voice. "But another said they didn't know that for sure and to leave me alone. Is Papa dead?"

She hugged him and ruffled his hair, blond like Sebastian's. The temptation to lie was strong. But she tried never to lie. Except to myself, she thought.

"I don't know, son," Lydia said. "Queen Esther didn't think so. We'll keep on believing he's alive. Soon this war will be over. We'll go free and return home to the farm where your father and Jane will be with us. Queen Esther says your sister is alive, and was fine when she saw her." She stifled a sigh. "We have to be like the lilies of the field now. They don't worry. Neither should we. God will take care of us."

"But what about Isaac? Will he be with us, too?"

"We can only hope and pray," Lydia said. "Now go play outside. I need to talk to Aunt Margaretha."

Once Henry was gone, she opened the door to the cabin. Margaretha looked up when she entered. Elisha lay on the bed, trying to roll over, while Margaretha cooed encouragingly at him. "What is it?" Margaretha said, seeing Lydia's white face.

"Terrible news," Lydia said. "Forty Fort was a disaster."

When Lydia finished her recital, Margaretha stared down at Elisha, then hugged him.

Lydia walked to the Bible and opened it to seek guidance, then shut it with a bang that made Margaretha's head snap up. No more seeking God's will in random Bible verses, Lydia thought. Look where it led me. I committed adultery and lost Isaac anyway. Instead, she turned to Margaretha.

"I'd like us to pray," she said.

Together they knelt on the rough wooden floor. "Keep our loved ones safe," Lydia prayed, "and help us to be strong in our faith even when darkness and despair surrounds us."

Margaretha looked at her. "You doubt God's hand in this? His ways are beyond human understanding."

"I surely don't understand," Lydia said, "but I can't afford to doubt."

"Good. Doubt is of the devil," Margaretha said.

Is it, Lydia thought. Or is it human to doubt?

Jane looked around curiously as she and Mrs. Whittaker entered Lancaster, Pennsylvania. Jane's spirits had grown lighter on the journey, and her optimism had returned. From Lancaster, she could surely get word to her father, and in the meantime she would be safe and have experiences she would never have had on the farm. Not that what happened was good. But dwelling on it wouldn't change it.

They rode past the Center Square with its brick courthouse and leaded windows. A stock and pillory sat near it. Jane glanced at the man with his head sticking through the hole. What did he do? she wondered.

Dozens of shops lined the edges of the square. It was early evening, and laughter and music drifted from the Golden Swan tavern. Carriages clattered through the street. A red and blue Conestoga wagon rumbled by. She stared at the four matched bay horses pulling it, the bells on their harnesses jingling and their colorful ribbons fluttering in the breeze. She wondered briefly how Pferd was doing, then was drawn by the sound of a knife sharpener calling out his services on the other side of the street.

Mrs. Whittaker laughed. "If you keep swiveling your head to look at things, it will fall off," she said. "But it is a big town, isn't it? Why, more than three thousand people live here."

"It's the biggest town I've ever seen," Jane said.

They stopped in front of a tavern with a painting of grapes hanging from a signpost. "We'll stay here tonight," Mrs. Whittaker said. "We can look for Mrs. Stewart tomorrow."

The next morning, a series of inquiries led them to the home of Mrs. Stewart's sister.

When they arrived, Mrs. Stewart crushed Jane against her ample bosom. "Jane, oh Jane," You're safe. Thank God," she exclaimed. Gertie, her paw pinched by Mrs. Stewart's foot, let out a yelp. "Oh, and the little dog is with you, too. How wonderful. What happened? Tell me all about it. But wait. I bet you're hungry. Let me fix some loosestrife tea — liberty tea they call it now — and get something for us to eat. Both of you, come along. I'm not letting you out of my sight." She swept Jane and Mrs. Whittaker into the kitchen with her, chattering while she heated water, poured tea, set out small cakes.

"Do you know anything about my father?" Jane asked, darting into a gap in Mrs. Stewart's monologue.

"Oh, my dear, I'm sorry. I don't. So many people are unaccounted for, or gone forever." Her cheer faltered. "But we mustn't give up hope. Every day brings fresh news."

Mrs. Whittaker spoke up. "Jane was hoping she could stay here with you until she finds out more about her father," she said. Just then, two screaming boys tore through the kitchen, one chasing the other.

"Of course. One more won't make a difference. I doubt we would even notice," Mrs. Stewart said.

"I can help with the children," Jane volunteered.

"Then it's settled," Mrs. Whittaker said. After a cup of tea and exchange of news, she stood up. "I'll be on my way. I hope things turn out well for you, Jane."

"Thank you. I'm sure they will."

Sebastian and Faith huddled under the overhang of a huge rock and watched the rain pouring down in sheets in front of them. The sun was low in the sky; already darkness invaded the forest.

"We'd best spend the night here," he said. "We'll not find anyplace drier. Tomorrow should see us at Shingle Kill, the creek where my parents' farm lies."

Faith shivered and wrapped her wool scarf around her. Sebastian looked at her. "I could build a small fire," he said. "If I can find any dry wood."

"You don't need to go out in that," she said, gesturing to the rain, then patting the dry ground by her side. "Come rest yourself." Obediently, he went to sit with her. They stared out at the rain together. Suddenly, Faith spoke. "Tell me about your family," she said. "I'll be meeting them soon."

Sebastian cleared his throat. "Well, there's my brother John. He's a captive now, of course."

"What kind of man is he?" she asked. He hesitated, unused to sharing his thoughts.

"He likes to be in charge," he said at last.

"Ah," she said, as if he'd imparted more information than he'd planned.

"And there's my brother Wilhelm. His wife died a year ago and he's not yet remarried."

"And what's he like?"

"Hmm. A little quick to rile, I guess. A good farmer. A hard worker. I don't know. I've never thought much about it."

"Who else?"

"My sister, Anna. She's married with three children and she and her husband, Jacob, live with my parents. She's friendly, a good wife, a good mother."

"What are your parents like?" Faith asked.

"People say I'm a lot like my father, Johann. At least, everyone says we look alike. He's known as a generous neighbor, always willing to help. Now my mother, Maria, if she went to visit Hell, she'd have the devil begging her to leave." He laughed fondly. "Only she'd chase him out instead and put his imps to work scrubbing the place clean, then fix a feast for everyone."

"She sounds…formidable. What about you, Sebastian? What do you want to do when the war is over?"

"Farm in peace," he said as a wave of longing swept over him. He couldn't bear to mention Lydia or his children. The hollow place inside him was too big, too full of jagged shards of pain.

"I've told you about my family," he said. "It's only fair you tell me about yours."

Her face clouded. "Oh, all right. Let's see. My mother was an orphan. She fell in love with my father." She paused. "Do you want to hear this? It's not that interesting."

"Yes. I do," he said. "Go on."

"They were both young and in love. My mother was beautiful. That's what I remember most about her. And kind."

Sebastian listened to her low, gentle voice while they sat in the darkness in a silence broken by the dripping of the rain and the sound of the wind in the trees. He looked at her, then away, feeling an odd closeness, despite his pain. This was different than any conversation he'd had with a woman. Not like Lydia, he thought with a touch of disloyalty. He'd loved her, but they'd known each other since they were children. Everyone assumed they would marry, and there was little he didn't know about her past. Faith was an unknown, interesting quantity.

"What about your father?" he asked.

"Not much to tell. Unfortunately, he had a weakness for whiskey. When he had a snootful, he'd take his belt to my mother or my younger brother, Josh, or me." Her voice was brittle. "No need for details there. Anyway, Josh ran away when he was fourteen. I haven't heard from him since. Then my mother died of consumption and I met my husband. He was a hard worker and good looking. I thought I'd made a good choice. Let's just say

I was wrong." She drew the scarf closer around her and lay down. "I'm tired," she said. "I think I'll try to get some sleep."

He lay down beside her, conscious of her nearness. Her eyes closed and he looked at her, then stared up at the overhang, thinking about what she'd said. She'd had little enough happiness in life. Maybe things would turn around for her now.

The next morning, no more was said about the revelations of the night. As they neared Round Top, the dome-shaped hill that overshadowed the farm, Sebastian's uneasiness about bringing Faith along returned. He had been scrupulous about avoiding physical contact, a task made easier by the hardships of the journey and his numbed state. But, looking at Round Top in the distance, he realized only the extraordinary circumstances of the massacre and subsequent flight could ever explain why he had spent days in the wilderness alone with a young widow.

Faith seemed nervous, too. "What will your family say?" she asked.

"I suspect they'll be so filled with grief, but glad to see I'm alive, that nothing else will matter."

"I hope they like me," Faith said, touching his arm with a hand that trembled. This was another way she differed from Lydia. Faith wanted, even needed, a man to lean on. Her attitude made him want to protect her. Lydia had been strong and had seemed to need no one except God. Surely she was with Him now.

"Let's push on," he said.

As they approached, his gaze swept over the massive wooden barn, the two-story stone farmhouse with its steep tile roof and bright red door, the benches under the tree by the front steps, the fields ripe with crops, the chickens scratching in the yard. A red-winged blackbird, startled by their approach, skimmed low over the corn. In the distance his father, Johann, and his brother Jacob worked side by side. Someday I'll have a farm of my own again, Sebastian thought. Someday. I won't let this be the end of all my dreams.

When they crossed the yard, a huge, furry dog rushed toward them, barking furiously.

"Bear," Sebastian called. "Bear." The dog's barks turned to woofs of welcome and it danced in front of Sebastian wagging its tail, then circled Faith, sniffing at her bedraggled skirt and tattered leather shoes.

"The dog's name is Bear?" Faith asked.

Sebastian smiled as he scratched behind Bear's ears. "Well, Jane named him."

"Ah. Like Pferd the horse."

Sebastian's mother, Maria, drawn by the sound of barking, stood in the doorway shading her eyes. Her red hair had escaped her cap. Sebastian noticed with a shock that since his last visit three years ago, gray had crept in and her sturdy frame had thickened.

Suddenly, his mother let out a scream and ran across the yard to envelop him in a hug. Her arms felt comforting, even at his age, and tears pricked his eyes.

"Son," she said, "what a wonderful surprise." She stepped back. "Let me look at you. You're so thin." She dropped her arms and looked inquiringly at Faith.

"This is Faith Hollenbeck," Sebastian said. "We've come over together from Forty Fort after the Indian massacre there."

"Welcome," Maria said. "Come in, both of you. Where are Lydia and the children?"

Her smile faded as she took in his expression. "What is it? What's wrong?"

"I have a lot to tell, Mama, but let's wait until everyone is here. Once is enough."

Maria called to the men in the field while Anna came running toward Sebastian with her children in her wake and swept him up in another hug.

In minutes, they were seated around the wooden table. He looked around, avoiding people's eyes. The pewter plates that once stood in rows in the side cupboard were gone, probably melted down for bullets for the war effort, and a new rag rug covered the pine floor. But his father's gun still hung on brackets over the mantle, above the Bible, hymnbook and the well-worn "Habermann's Prayerbook." If only he could turn back time to before he had taken his family to the Susquehanna. It might have been better after all to stay here and farm with his father. At least everyone would be alive. He braced himself for what must come next.

"Now, son, tell us what happened," Maria said.

He started the recital calmly enough, including the death of Faith's husband and the massacre, but when he reached the part where Zach told him of Lydia's death, his throat closed and his mouth tugged downward. He sat unspeaking, trying to control himself.

"Oh my God," Maria said in the silence. "I knew something terrible had happened. Last Monday, a bird flew in the house. And two nights ago I dreamed I lost a tooth. Two sure signs of death. But this, who could imagine this?"

Swallowing hard, Sebastian finished his story, ending with his hope that Jane was somewhere in Pennsylvania, safe with Mrs. Stewart.

"I searched and searched," he said, "but folks are scattered to the four winds. No one seems to know where anyone is."

"I'm sure she's alive. She's a plucky little thing," Maria said, then rocked back and forth, hugging herself.

Johann stared into space, his face working like his son's as he struggled to master his emotions. Wilhelm and Anna's husband, Jacob, looked at the floor, while Faith sat unmoving, an outsider during this outpouring of grief.

"Well," Maria said at last, "all we can do now is pray." She looked around the room blankly, then seemed to gather herself. She stood up, putting one hand on the table as if for support.

"Are you hungry?" she asked. "Let me fix you something to eat."

Sebastian started to say he had no appetite, but his mother was already moving toward the dishes. "That sounds fine, Mama," he said. Prayer, food and house cleaning were her way of dealing with things.

"I can help you," Faith said, jumping up.

"Come on, son, and let the women work," his father said. The two walked outside and sat on a bench looking out over the fields. The shrill noise of crickets rose on the summer air.

"The crops look good," Sebastian said.

"They do, don't they?"

After a bit, his father patted him awkwardly on the shoulder. They sat in a silence broken only by the wind in the trees and the distant lowing of cattle until Maria called them to the table.

Before they ate, Johann said a prayer for healing and strength. When they opened their eyes, Maria, as usual, added "Nimm, was du magst, iss, was du nimmst." Take all you want; eat all you take. It was all so familiar, yet everything was different.

The abundant board, laden with fresh bread, apple butter, pork, slaw, cheese, carrots, pie, failed to spark Sebastian's appetite, but he drank heavily of the beer. His mother raised her eyebrows as he filled mug after mug, but said nothing. Only Faith looked frightened as first mellowness, then depression settled over Sebastian.

The meal over, Maria busied herself cleaning up and finding a place for Faith to sleep.

Sebastian mumbled an early good night and climbed the stairs to his old bedroom. A familiar red-checked coverlet lay on the bed, and in the corner sat the huge schank with its carved doors that served as a wardrobe for clothes. At least here things are the same, he thought, before sleep claimed him.

A dull scratching noise outside his bedroom awoke him. Sunlight streamed through the window. It must be seven in the morning, later than he'd slept in years. His head ached from last night's overindulgence in beer, but the deep fatigue that dogged him since leaving Forty Fort had started to abate. He struggled to identify the sound. His mother must be sweeping the pine floor with the fine white sand she used as an abrasive. In the distance, he could hear a clanking as someone worked the hand pump that drew water to the house. Half awake, he reached across the bed to touch Lydia, and his hand brushed the rough sheet. Memory swept over him, destroying the moment of peace.

"Good morning," his mother greeted him when he entered the kitchen. "I hope you slept well."

"Well enough."

"Good. I've set out food for you. After you eat, we need to talk."

"All right." His stomach tightened. His mother, like John, had definite ideas about the course other people should follow.

"Where is everyone?" he asked.

"Anna is mending shirts. The children are playing or doing chores outside. Jacob and Wilhelm are in the fields with your father."

"What about Faith?"

"She got up early and asked if there was something she could do to help." Her voice held a note of approval. "I sent her to pick marigolds so we can dye wool later."

While she talked, his mother was busy boiling toadflax in milk to poison flies. He'd never been sure it worked, but she was convinced.

The food, as usual, was plentiful. She smiled approvingly when he reached for seconds. As he washed down the last bite, she whisked his plate away, then returned to sit down facing him.

"Now," she said, "I know you're tired, but I wanted to talk about Faith. When she and I spoke this morning, she was very vague on where she would go or what she would do next. She seemed to think she would stay here until you decided otherwise. Does she have any plans of her own? Of course she is welcome here for a while. But she needs to look to the future."

"Mama, we just got here."

"I know, son. But we need to help her start a new life as soon as she is able. Work is the best cure for many problems."

"She hopes to get work sewing and teaching needlework."

"Really? She didn't mention that." Maria was silent as she poured the fly poison into a dish.

"If that's what she wants, I'll ask around. But I suspect she'll have to go to a city to find that kind of work."

Sebastian stood up, scraping his chair against the wood floor. "I'm going to help Papa." He turned at the door. "I don't see why we need to rush her."

Chapter Sixteen

Jane watched anxiously as Mrs. Stewart folded the letter for the post rider and sealed it with hot wax.

"How long do you think it will take the letter to reach my grandparents?" she asked.

"It's hard to say. The rider will have to find them, since it's not in a town. It could be two weeks, depending on the weather and the fighting. You mustn't get your hopes up that a message will get through the first time. Since the war broke out, service is spotty. If we don't hear anything in a month, we'll try again."

"I hope it makes it the first time," Jane said.

Since they'd arrived in Lancaster three days ago, life had been a mixture of good and bad. Mrs. Stewart's sister, Mrs. McClure, had three sons and no daughter, so she delighted in fussing with Jane's hair and clothes and supplying her with feminine trinkets. Being cosseted was pleasant and soothing. But Jane was expected to watch out for ten children, ranging from the newborn up to age 12. The middle ones acted as if Gertie was a new toy, and Jane constantly had to rescue the dog. Eight-year-old Silas, Mrs. McClure's youngest son, had turned sullen and begun pulling Gertie's ears or tail. When Gertie yelped with pain, he insisted he was only playing. The last time, Jane threatened to pull Silas' ears until he yelped. He complained to his mother, who reminded Silas to be kind to animals, then apologized to Jane for her son's behavior. Since then, Silas had been more circumspect, but Jane didn't trust him.

Now it might be a month or more before her father came for her. If he was alive. Quickly she shooed the idea away. I should be grateful for all they are doing for me, she thought. And I am. I just wish I could find something to do besides tend children and rescue Gertie.

"I'm going over to Center Square for a while," she told Mrs. Stewart.

"Oh, could you take some of the children with you? It will do them good to get out. And could you pick up some items at the market? I'll make a list."

"Of course."

Mrs. Stewart bustled in shortly and handed her a short list. "Here's what we need, and here's some money to pay for it. Now let's see. Who should accompany you?"

Jane sighed heavily, and Mrs. Stewart looked at her. "Ah, I see. All right. Why don't you run on by yourself, take a little time alone? But I'll need you to watch the children this evening."

"Thank you, thank you," Jane said, feeling guilty and elated at the same time.

Bypassing the markets and ignoring the fascination of the shops and the fur traders and soldiers on the streets, Jane headed straight for the stables she had spotted earlier.

The pungent smell of fresh hay, sawdust and manure greeted her as she entered the dim enclosure.

The hostler, a small, wizened man with frizzy gray hair and a leathery, wrinkled face, looked up from oiling a harness. "Good morning, young miss. Can I help you?"

"Good morning. My name is Jane Strope," she said.

"Ephraim Shoemaker," he said with an acknowledging nod.

"I wondered if I could just look at the horses, Mr. Shoemaker"

He raised an eyebrow. "Just look? Hmm. I suppose there's no harm in that. But mind you don't get too close."

"I won't," Jane said, already moving across the yellow paving bricks toward the stalls. He set down the harness and hurried to catch up.

She greeted the horses, asking Ephraim the names of each one, and told him about Pferd while he looked on, seeming torn between bemusement and amusement.

Finally, he said, "That's enough, young miss. I've work to do."

"Can I come back again?" she asked.

"I don't care if your folks don't mind."

"They won't care," she said as they emerged blinking into the sunlight.

A Conestoga wagon rolled to a stop in front of them, the chains of the traces clanking as the tension was released. The tallest man Jane had ever seen, with a bulk to match, climbed down from the left rear horse. His nose was bulbous and his skin ruddy. A leather patch covered his left eye and an odor of whiskey wafted from him like morning mist from a river. Spotting Jane, he gave a little bow, almost losing his balance.

"Good morning, miss," he boomed in a slight brogue. "One Eye O'Rourke at your service."

Eyes wide, Jane whispered a greeting in return.

"Ephraim," he said, "I'm plumb out of stogies. Lost my last one somewhere last night, and I'm plumb out of money until payday, too. You've got to help me out. A man can't face these roads without his cigars."

Ephraim laughed. "Come inside, you old dog," he said. "I'll fix you up. But this is the last time until you settle up."

One Eye winked at Jane. She doubted it was really the last time.

While the men transacted their business, Jane walked around O'Rourke's huge horses. They stood placidly, not even seeming to breathe heavily. She walked to the back of the wagon and stared inside. It was packed with trade goods. She stepped back as One Eye emerged and climbed into the saddle. Jiggling the rein and calling to the team, he drove off with a wave. A puff of cigar smoke drifted back on the still air.

"Who was that?" Jane asked.

"Old One Eye? He's been driving wagons ever since I can remember. Even half lit, he's one hell of... beg pardon, miss. He's one fine driver. Never has a cross word for anyone, never has any money either."

"How did he lose his eye?"

"Ah now, that's a good question. He has a dozen versions of how it happened. He lost it in a sword fight while rescuing a woman who turned out to be royalty. He lost it when a jealous husband... well, never mind about that story. Anyway, nobody really knows."

"Does he have any family?"

"Another good question that nobody knows the answer to. Now I'd best be getting back to work. You run along."

"Thank you for letting me visit," she said, staring after the wagon.

August, 1778

Lydia watched in amazement as hundreds of Indians swept back and forth across the open field at Tioga Point playing lacrosse. Beside her, Henry bounced with excitement and Margaretha held Elisha, who, in the miraculous way of youngsters, slept through the uproar.

The field was awash in sweating, leaping, diving, falling players, all striving to use their rackets to hurl the deerskin ball through the opposing party's goal. Spectators cheered, roared at good moves, laughed when one player fell, turned a somersault and knocked down another player. Lydia gave an involuntary smile at the two men's expressions. These are the same people who take scalps and torture enemies, she thought. Yet they love to play and they're as kind to their children as we are. Just yesterday, another Indian had tormented her by claiming Sebastian had been killed at Forty

Fort. Outwardly, she no longer listened. The day before, another Indian had given Henry an intricately carved toy horse.

Yesterday, the green corn ceremony had begun to celebrate harvest time for the corn, and the same Indians now dashing across the field had danced and sung late in the night. If I were at home, she thought, I would be picking the corn from our fields. Instead, the deer are probably feasting on the ears. Will this war never end?

Queen Esther strolled up and stopped beside her. "Do you know this game?" she asked.

Lydia shook her head and patted the ground in hopes Queen Esther would join them. She had been cool since the battle at Forty Fort and Lydia was reluctant to lose any more of her good will. Queen Esther hesitated, then squatted beside her.

"I'm amazed they have the energy after the festival last night," Lydia said.

"There are more ceremonies and feasting tonight," Queen Esther said. "The corn is our life."

"I wish there were a ceremony to get over loss," Lydia blurted.

Queen Esther looked at her. "There is. It comes down to us from the time of Hiawatha."

The customs of the Indians had begun to both fascinate and repel Lydia. Unless a miracle happened, this might be the only life Isaac knew. These customs might be the only way of knowing what was happening with her son. The forces arrayed against him remembering even his name were strong. The knowledge was wrenching, but there it was.

"Can you tell me about the ritual?" Lydia asked.

"I suppose so. We wipe away the mourner's tears so she can see clearly, touch her ears so she can hear freely and her throat so she can speak and breathe freely. I found comfort in it after my son was murdered by the soldiers."

The last words seemed to shift Queen Esther's mood. She got to her feet and stalked off.

That night Lydia lay in bed waiting until everyone was asleep. Her courses still had not started, and she felt certain she was pregnant. Her thoughts turned to the various herbs that might solve her problem. She'd need to act soon. It would spare her shame, and the baby the stigma of bastardy. She was the only one who knew about the pregnancy. Except God, she thought. I can't do it. Not only would I add to my sin, but I would lose any remaining chance of seeing Gideon in Heaven. And that would be unbearable.

Thoughts of Gideon led to the memory of her earlier conversation with Queen Esther. Since they had talked, she had pondered whether it would be wrong for a Christian to use a heathen ceremony. But God hears all our prayers, she decided.

Tentatively, she touched her eyes. "God, please wipe away my tears so I can see clearly," she prayed. She touched her ears. "God, please unstop my ears so I can hear freely." She laid her hand on her throat. "God, please help me to be able to speak and breath freely."

The constriction in her chest since Isaac had been taken seemed to ease a little.

"Thank you, God," she whispered. "Amen."

Chapter Seventeen

September 1778

Jane shifted on the wooden bench she shared with two other girls and stared out the schoolhouse window. The boys' school had ended; now it was the girls' turn for a few hours of instruction. It was almost four o'clock and the September sun sent long shadows across the streets of Lancaster. Only a few more minutes, Jane thought, and the dismissal bell would ring. Then she could slip away to the stable on her way home. True, she'd have to take two of the Stewart children with her, but she'd bribed and threatened them into silence about her visits. By now, she had asked enough questions of the usually patient Ephraim that she knew a lot more about the care and training of horses. Not that he ever let her practice any of it, but you could learn quite a bit by watching.

Maybe One Eye O'Rourke would stop by, as he'd taken to doing, and tell her a few funny stories about life on the wagon roads. His tab for cigars must be huge by now, since he never seemed to pay. But he did bring Ephraim presents now and then. Once he'd brought dress goods for Ephraim's wife; another time, he'd given Ephraim a huge cone of hard sugar wrapped in blue paper, then produced one for Jane. She was tempted to accept and take the cone home to Mrs. Stewart for her kindness, but then she'd have to explain where she got it, and she doubted Mrs. Stewart would want her talking with a wagon driver who smelled of whiskey and used rough language when he thought she couldn't hear. She wasn't sure what some of the words meant, but her vocabulary was expanding.

Instead, she asked O'Rourke to shave off some pieces from the cone. She and the children savored a few bites, then she fed the rest to the horses while he shook his head and laughed.

It was all so fascinating, she thought, so different from the farm. Even school in a real schoolhouse was interesting. At home, she would be through with schooling except for helping teach the boys. If only there were some word from Papa, she could be content. Clearly, the first message never reached him. And waiting was becoming increasingly difficult. The teasing from that brat Silas was making Gertie more nervous.

The voice of the schoolmaster interrupted her musings.

"Mistress Strope, we're ready to end with prayer. Perhaps you'd care to close your eyes with the rest of us?"

Flushing, she bowed her head. Finally, the bell rang and the children burst out the door.

At the stables, O'Rourke's wagon stood in front. He was inside talking with Ephraim when she walked up. "Ah, Miss Jane," he said, greeting her with his usual bow. "Wait right there." He went out to the wagon and returned with a shiny ribbon. "Red for a redhead," he said.

She hesitated. Was this proper? But it was pretty.

"Thank you," she said, stuffing it in her pocket to admire privately later. He looked at the two Stewart girls accompanying her. "And for you, young ladies..." With a flourish, he whipped out some candy and handed it to them.

On the way home, Jane reminded the children, "This is our secret." They nodded solemnly, mouths full of candy.

The Stewart children were playing "Blindman's Buff" in the sitting room. Their shrieks echoed through the house. Mrs. Stewart stuck her head out of the kitchen. "Having fun?" she asked. "I'll have a treat for you later."

"Jane, your turn," Silas called. She fastened the blindfold and waited.

"How many horses has your father got?" the children chanted.

"Three," Jane replied.

"What colors are they?"

"Black, white and gray."

"Turn about and turn about and catch whom you can."

Silas whirled her around three times, sending her staggering. "Tell me if I'm near anything I might trip over," she said.

The children giggled and scattered as she reached toward them. Flailing, she grabbed at a sleeve, overbalanced and fell heavily on someone. The children gasped. She tore off the blindfold. Silas lay silent on the floor beneath her, eyes closed.

"He hit his head on the table," one of the girls said.

"Run and get his mother," Jane ordered.

Mrs. Stewart, alerted by the silence, peered in, then hurried over to where Silas lay motionless. Jane, kneeling beside him, looked at her, full of fright.

Silas' eyelids fluttered and he moaned.

Thank God, Jane thought. Mrs. McClure came running in, her face white. "Are you all right? What happened?" she asked as Silas struggled to a sitting position.

"We were playing a game and Jane pushed me," Silas said.

"No," Jane cried. "It was an accident. I had the blindfold on and I couldn't see and I fell on him. I didn't mean to do it."

Mrs. McClure looked around at the other children. "It was an accident," one said, and the others agreed.

"Well, accidents happen," Mrs. McClure said. "Thank goodness it wasn't worse. Come on, son. You've got a cut on the back of your head. Let's get it taken care of."

After supper, Mrs. Stewart called Jane aside. "I've been told that you have been stopping by the stable with some of the children and are associating with a wagon driver, the one they call One Eye O'Rourke. That has to stop."

Jane stared at her.

"Do you hear me?" Mrs. Stewart asked. "I know you love horses, but it isn't seemly, Jane. I don't want to hear of this happening again."

"All right," Jane said. "But I don't see how it hurts anything."

"I wish your mother were here to explain it better. Trust me; O'Rourke is not a fit companion for a young girl entering womanhood."

Jane blushed. It was true her figure was beginning to develop, but O'Rourke had never behaved improperly.

"He's just a friend," Jane said. "More like a father."

"I doubt your father would appreciate the comparison," Mrs. Stewart said. "Now, we'll say no more about it. Why don't you go check on Silas, then come in the kitchen and get some pie?"

"Yes, ma'am," Jane said. It isn't fair, she thought. I'm not doing anything wrong.

The next afternoon, Jane looked longingly at the stable, but headed straight home. Mrs. Stewart greeted her at the door. "There's been an accident," she said. "Your little dog's leg is broken. I have her in a box in the kitchen."

"What happened?" Jane asked, hurrying toward the kitchen.

"I don't know. One of the children heard her yelping, and came for me. When I went out, there she was. I put a splint on it, and she's resting now."

Gertie looked up at Jane and wagged her tail. Her right hind leg was wrapped in a bandage.

"Will the leg be all right?" Jane asked.

"I would think so. She's young. It should heal in a month or so."

Satisfied Gertie was all right, Jane sought out Silas. "You did this," she said. "I know you did."

"I did not," he said. "Your stupid dog must've fallen or something."

She glared at him. "I can't prove it," she said. "But you better watch out."

"Ooh, I'm scared," he said, but he backed away.

That's it, Jane thought later, cradling Gertie. There's been no word from Papa. Now Gertie has been hurt. I'm not waiting any longer for other people to do things. Somehow I'm going to Grandpa's house by myself.

Chapter Eighteen

Sebastian looked at Faith as she crossed the field toward his parents' farmhouse. Her arms were full of goldenrod, gathered to make dye, and her face was flushed from her time in the sun. The wind blew her dress against her body, outlining her figure. Feelings dormant since he'd learned of Lydia's death surfaced. Most widows and widowers remarried quickly, he knew. One person couldn't manage a farm alone. But he still ached daily for Lydia. It was too soon for such thoughts, but he continued to stare at Faith.

He heard a sound behind him and turned. His mother was watching him watch Faith.

"It's been two months now, son," she said, "and Faith is no closer to making a place for herself. I'll grant you she's a hard worker, and she's taken over the sewing and mending." She paused. "Truth to tell, she does as good a job as I do. But she's in no hurry to find a situation elsewhere. Anyone can see she has her eye on you."

"Mama," Sebastian said, flushing. Sometimes her plain talk and honesty was embarrassing.

"It's true. It's too soon to think seriously about anyone. But it's not good for her to go on here in limbo. Just yesterday your brother Wilhelm..."

She broke off as Faith moved within hearing distance.

"I'll think about it," Sebastian muttered.

As Faith moved up on the porch, she greeted them with a smile. "So serious on such a beautiful day?" she asked.

Maria smiled back. "It is a beautiful day. Let's set those flowers to boiling."

That evening at supper, Sebastian, freshly aware, saw the way Faith looked at him, how she noticed if his plate needed filling. And he saw the looks Wilhelm gave her. He felt a sense of possessiveness, yet he wasn't ready to declare anything. His mother was right. Things needed to change.

In the morning, his sister Anna's husband, Jacob, offered a temporary solution.

"When I was over at Wynkoop's Mill, " he said, "I heard Col. Thomas Hartley is assembling an expedition to head north to Tioga Point and destroy the Indian village there, Queen Esther's flats I think they call it. He's looking for volunteers."

All eyes turned toward Sebastian.

"You knew Queen Esther, didn't you?" Wilhelm asked.

"I thought I did," Sebastian said. "That was before the massacre at Forty Fort." The comfort of his family and the slow, steady rhythm of farm life had banked the fires of revenge. Now they blazed forth.

"I'm volunteering," he said. The words surprised him. It was as if someone else had uttered them. But they felt right. He could get away, sort things out, maybe get news of Lydia and his sons or John. And he could strike back at those who killed his family instead of hiding here like a fox in its den. "I'm volunteering," he repeated.

"Oh, son," his mother said. "We don't want to lose you too."

"Do what you must," Johann said.

"Aye," Wilhelm echoed.

Faith's face turned white. She poked at the food on her plate, but said nothing.

Two weeks later when he finally left, her goodbye embrace was passionate. He wished he could give her what she wanted. But it was too soon. Maybe when he returned things would be clearer.

A rock dug into Sebastian's back, and he shifted on the damp ground. His leather trousers were stiff from the last five days spent crossing and recrossing the swollen Lycoming river with the army, and his skin was scratched and bruised from crawling along precipices, slogging through Pennsylvania swamps. Even shifting his bone-tired body was an effort. But soon it would all prove worthwhile. They were within two days march of Tioga Point.

He shivered in the chill of the late September evening. If only they could build a fire. But that might alert the Indians. Beside him, Darius Jones, a fellow volunteer who had also lost a wife in the war, sat up with an oath. "I vow these rocks are multiplying," he growled. He pulled a jagged lump from under his blanket and tossed it into the woods. "I'll be glad when we meet up with some of them copperheads. I can hardly wait to kill a few."

Sebastian thought of Lydia and his family as he had last seen them in

May, smiling, hugging him, waving goodbye as he rode off for help. "I feel the same," he said. "I can hardly wait."

The next morning, he got his chance. Their advance scouting party of nineteen men surprised an equal number of Indians. Darius and Sebastian fired simultaneously and the leader crumpled to the ground. Darius ran forward, yelling and waving his rifle in the air. Sebastian and the other men followed, screaming and whooping as the Indians fled. Adrenaline raced through Sebastian's veins like fire through a field. The leader, who looked to be in his twenties, lay bleeding from a chest wound. Blood welled from it in a steady rhythm.

"Are there more of you?" Darius demanded. "Where are they? How many?"

The Indian stared up without speaking, then his eyes glazed and his hand fell limply to his side.

"Damn," Darius said. "Dead." He reached back and pulled his tomahawk from its belt loop. "Might as well give him what he gave my wife," he said. He sliced around the edge of the chief's scalp, grabbed the hair in his teeth, put both feet on the chest and jerked the scalp free.

Some men whooped with delight; others watched silently. As Sebastian stared sickened at Darius holding the bloody trophy aloft, his thoughts flashed back to the night he had hidden in the gorse bush and watched Queen Esther scalp soldier after soldier. He forced himself not to turn away.

Darius capered around, as if dancing with the scalp. Could you learn to love killing? Sebastian wondered.

After an uneasy night, he sought out Col. Hartley. "We're only a few miles from my farm — or what's left of it," Sebastian said. "There's plenty of space to camp there for the night, and good water from the creek. Maybe even some corn left to eat."

Hartley nodded and called to the men to move out. As they entered the clearing around Sebastian's farm, crows cawed and took flight. The blackened timbers of his house rose like brooding sentinels. Wild cucumber weeds, almost six feet tall, covered much of one field. Hoof marks showed that deer had nibbled on the ripening corn. Unless the war ended in the next few years, nature would reclaim the clearing. It was all so wrong.

The springhouse still stood. He walked toward it while the men milled around setting up camp. Small animals had made nests in it. He fingered the long white scar on his cheek where the boar had gored him. Where are you now, Jane? he wondered. I would come for you if I could.

He stood inside the springhouse, listening to the water gurgle, then sat on the stone floor and waited for the waves of memory to stop pounding him. Through the partly open door, he heard Col. Hartley calling the men to order. Reluctantly, he went out to join them.

Sebastian knew little about Hartley. He looked to be in his thirties and Darius had said he was a Pennsylvania lawyer until he joined the military and rose to commandant of the Northern Frontiers. The whole journey he had looked unhappy to be here. But then, perhaps he hadn't lost loved ones like the rest of them.

Now the men stood in front of Hartley, some leaning on their guns. Hartley climbed on a stump. His face was grim. "Fate ordained," he said, "that we are here making war on the savages instead of fighting the British, who accept, at least in principle, the laws of warfare. Nevertheless..." He jabbed a finger in the air for emphasis.

"Nevertheless, we will follow the rules of civilized beings. There will be no more scalpings."

A low rumble rose from the men.

"Dismissed," Hartley said.

"He can say what he wants, but if I get me a redskin, I'm going to do what I damn well please," Darius said.

He sounds like Lazarus Stewart, Sebastian thought. Lazarus, who now lay dead at the hands of Indians.

"If we all agree, he can't do anything about it. Are you with me?" Darius demanded.

"I don't think so," Sebastian said.

Lydia watched curiously as a party of exhausted Indians trotted toward Queen Esther's house at Tioga Point. In minutes, the word spread. An expedition of hundreds of American soldiers headed north was almost upon them. Queen Esther conferred with the tribal leaders and the British, then came out on the porch. "We'll move out to Chemung immediately," she said. Almost a thousand British troops were encamped at Chemung, about fifteen miles away.

Soon, the village resembled a beehive after a bear attack with people running here and there gathering things. Lydia and Margaretha quickly packed a few possessions and what food was at hand. I wonder if Sebastian is with them, Lydia thought. Or perhaps he lay in a grave at Forty Fort. And what of Jane? The uncertainty ate at her.

When the order to move out came, she grabbed Henry with one hand and cradled the Bible with the other as the two sisters and their children joined those hurrying into the woods. Queen Esther rode at the front, and mounted warriors with guns lingered near the rear.

"They're not paying attention to us," Margaretha said.

Lydia looked around. It was true. "Maybe we can escape in the confusion," she said. "They couldn't come after us right away, so we might make it."

"You have the best chance," Margaretha said. "It will be harder with a baby who can't even walk yet."

"We should both try."

"I'm willing, but I would only slow us down. Jane needs you. I'll be fine. Besides, I heard a rumor we might go on to Fort Niagara, and my John is there. Maybe he and I could be together."

"I think he'd rather you be free," Lydia said. "But it's your decision. I'm going to try."

They drifted farther back and toward the edges of the strung-out group.

"This looks good," Lydia whispered. Holding Henry's hand, she edged behind a tall bush and crouched low, heart pounding. Putting her finger to her lips, she signaled a wide-eyed Henry to silence. Five minutes went by. She heard the steady beat of feet and hooves outside as the queue passed. They crouched motionless, afraid the branches might sway and give them away. Her knees ached from the prolonged position. More minutes passed. I'm going to make it, she thought, hope rising. I'll wait until everyone has left, then head back to Tioga Point and meet the soldiers.

But a few minutes later, she heard someone coming closer. She hugged Henry and froze, feeling like a rabbit targeted by a hawk.

Let whoever it is go by, she prayed. Please God, let him go by.

Henry shifted, making a tiny noise. The Indian poked their bush hard with his rifle, hitting Henry's foot. Startled, Henry jerked back.

The searcher pulled the branches apart and stared at them.

"Out," he ordered.

"Please let us go," she said as they crawled from the bush. "No one needs to know."

"Get back in line."

She stood unsteadily and stumbled over a root. The Bible fell from her hands. She grabbed for it, but he pulled her away.

"Leave it," he said. When she hesitated, he jabbed her twice in the abdomen with his rifle butt. She winced with the force of the blows.

"Leave the book," he repeated. Tears in her eyes, she rejoined the others. Once she looked back at the big Bible lying on the edge of the trail. My last link with home, she thought. Now it's gone. But no one could erase Scripture from her mind. "Thy word have I hid in my heart," she murmured. Everything has a purpose, she thought, although doubts assailed her more and more. It has to.

They forged steadily ahead. Soon, she felt nauseous, and cramps laced through her stomach.

"Are you all right, Mama?" Henry asked as Lydia gasped and grabbed her abdomen.

"I'm fine," she said. "Just a little upset stomach."

By the time they reached Chemung and she rejoined Margaretha, sweat beaded her forehead and she walked bent over from the pains piercing her. In the hut provided for them, she lay on her side, knees drawn up, trying not to cry out. Warm blood trickled between her legs.

"Send Henry outside," she gasped.

Margaretha sat beside her as Lydia expelled the bloody fetus. Lydia averted her eyes from the sight. She didn't want to think about the child that would never be, Zach's child who would have been a huge problem if it had lived. But still an innocent soul.

Afterward, Lydia lay spent, crying with such a mixture of relief and regret that she could hardly think. She saw Margaretha staring white faced at the fetus. This must bring back memories for her of the two children she lost, children she desperately wanted.

"Oh, sister, what have you done?" Margaretha said. "What have you done?"

Chapter Nineteen

Sebastian and the rest of the army trudged into Queen Esther's encampment at Tioga Point at dusk. Buoyed by the hope of freeing loved ones, they had marched double time to get here. At Sheshequin, just downstream, the troops had recaptured more than 50 cattle and freed fifteen prisoners. Perhaps, Sebastian thought, they could rescue Margaretha, too.

An empty town greeted them. Possessions were strewn here and there and two dozen canoes lay on the bank of the river. The only sign of life was a lame dog who barked nonstop as they marched into town.

Exhausted, the men dropped to the ground and slept. At dawn, Sebastian visited cabin after cabin seeking some sign of Margaretha or Isaac. Nothing. Men fanned out to pick through the plunder and follow the trail toward Chemung. Sebastian picked up a wooden comb decorated with silver and stuffed it in his shirt. Faith might like it.

"Hey," one of the men called. "Look at this. Someone lost a Bible." He picked it up and opened it. "It's in German," he said, and tossed it down.

Another soldier picked up the book. "Don't treat a Bible that way," he said. He looked at the ornate Fraktur type curiously. "Hey, Sebastian, " he called, "I bet you can read this stuff. You want it?"

Sebastian walked over and opened the thick volume. On the inside cover, he saw his name, written in Lydia's careful hand. With a shaking hand, he closed the book. Jane had said Lydia took the Bible with her when the Indians captured them. Margaretha must have kept it. Perhaps she dropped it as the Indians and captives fled. Sebastian ran his fingers over the cover, picturing Lydia holding it, reading from it as she'd done so many times. His grasp tightened and he stood clutching the Bible until he heard Darius yelp with excitement in the distance.

"I got me one," Darius said. He pushed an elderly Indian forward.

Hartley emerged from Queen Esther's castle. "Bring him here," he ordered. "We need to find out what he knows."

Darius stared at the colonel. "Aw, leave him to me. I can make him talk," he said.

Hartley stared back. "I believe my methods will be more efficacious," he said. Darius looked confused, then shoved the man toward him. Sebastian let out a breath he hadn't known he was holding.

In twenty minutes, Hartley emerged. "The British have eight hundred troops at Chemung," he announced. "They're bound to find out there are only two hundred of us. And we have only one day's supply of cooked rations. It galls me, but we have to retreat."

The men looked at each other. "Eight hundred men," the soldier beside Sebastian murmured. "We'll be lucky to get home alive."

"But first," Hartley said, "we'll fire the town. Give them something to remember us by. They won't use this for a staging area again."

A cheer rose. One of the scouts fashioned a torch and set it ablaze. Sebastian thought about the Indians burning his home and barn. He grabbed a torch and joined the men as they ran from house to house, hut to hut, until the sky was dark with smoke. When the last building had been fired, he stood, panting, watching flames lick the roofs and clouds of smoke fill the air. Flushed with adrenaline, for a moment he understood the lure of the power to destroy.

As the flames died, Sebastian picked up the Bible. It was bulky, too big to carry and still keep his rifle ready, but he couldn't bear to leave it behind. Finally, he took his extra homespun shirt, contrived a crude sling and slung the Bible on his back.

"You look like a hunchback," one of the men joked. Another snorted with laughter.

"Shut your yaps," Darius said. "It belonged to his dead wife."

Days later, safely back at Fort Muncy, Sebastian gratefully dropped on the floor of a cabin with other men and curled up to sleep. But sleep fled at his approach as he replayed the events of the past few days. This was the third time, he mused, that he had been spared. First, his family had been taken while he was gone. Would that it had been him instead. Then at Forty Fort, while hundreds died, he had escaped. Now, confronted by a superior enemy force, he again had emerged unscathed. Why him? Better men than he had fallen.

He turned on his side to see Darius lying there, eyes open.

"You can't sleep either?" Sebastian asked.

"Too tired I guess," Darius said. "Ain't that a bitch."

"Have you ever wondered why some men die in battle and others right beside them live?"

"Can't say as I have."

"Do you suppose it's luck or something else?" Sebastian persisted.

"You think too much," Darius said and rolled over. Soon he was snoring with a peculiar whistling sound.

Sebastian lay awake, staring into the darkness. Lydia would have said God had a plan for him. With a twinge of childhood fear that he might be risking hellfire, he wondered if God really had a plan for anyone. If so, God was keeping mighty quiet in his case.

He thought about the Bible. Could Lydia have dropped it and she and Henry still be alive? No, wanting something to be true didn't make it so.

For a week after Jane decided to leave Lancaster, she checked the stable each day on the way home from school, ignoring Mrs. Stewart's warning. Finally, she spotted O'Rourke's wagon outside. If he followed his routine, he would leave early in the morning for Philadelphia. Before dawn, she slipped into Mrs. McClure's kitchen and packed a bundle of food. Last of all, she left a short note on the wooden table. "Gone to my grandparents. I have a ride. Don't worry. Thank you for everything. Jane."

If I get caught, they'll never let me out of their sight again, she thought. So I better not get caught.

Holding Gertie, she slunk to the stable through darkened back streets. She looked doubtfully at the high, sloping rear gate of the wagon. It hadn't seemed this high before. And the wagon was packed full of goods. But it was the only place to hide. She reached up and placed Gertie inside, hoping the puppy wouldn't bark and alert anyone. All week she had worked on getting Gertie to bark less. The effort had been a total failure.

After several tries, she climbed on to the feed trough fastened to the back of the wagon and used the chains that held it in place to pull herself up over the tailgate and into the wagon. With effort, she pushed aside enough boxes to crawl partly under a tarpaulin with Gertie. A dizzying array of scents — tobacco, ginger, cinnamon, iron, leather — assaulted her senses.

She hoped One Eye would leave soon. I only have to stay hidden a day, she thought. He won't send me back then. And in a few days I'll be in Philadelphia. Even though Hiram Landon turned out to be an awful man, everybody isn't like that. Someone is bound to be willing to take me to the Hudson if Grandpapa pays them for their trouble. But I'm still scared.

They rumbled off a few minutes after she was settled. The team forged steadily on for several hours. The noise of the wheels and steady clopping of the horses hid the sound when Gertie began to whine to be let down.

Jane tried holding Gertie over the edge of the wagon, hoping the dog would relieve herself, but Gertie kicked and started to bark. Jane pulled her back in alarm. "Hush," she said. "Just a few more miles. You don't want to be sent back to where Silas is do you?" Gertie continued to whine, and Jane fed her scraps of ham until the dog settled down.

When the sun was high overhead, One Eye pulled the wagon to a stop. This should be far enough from Lancaster, Jane thought. The heat under the tarpaulin made her head hurt and Gertie was panting.

She climbed down from the wagon and reached for Gertie. Another wagon passed them, and the driver looked at them curiously.

This is it, she thought. Clutching Gertie, she walked to the front of the wagon.

One Eye jumped back when he saw her with such a shocked expression it would have been comical if she hadn't been so tense.

"Holy Mary, Mother of God," he exclaimed. "What the blazes are you doing here?"

"I'm going to my grandparents," she said. "If you can give me a ride to Philadelphia, I can find someone to take me to them. They'll pay the person back. Maybe you could even do it."

He seemed stunned. "It's a ride to Philadelphia you want, is it? You don't know what you're getting into. The road is no place for a young girl."

Wagons rumbled in both directions in a steady stream.

"I'll find someone to escort you back," he said. "You can't come with me." He studied the drivers on the wagons heading toward Lancaster as if assessing which one would be best.

She had pictured the reunion at her grandparents' farm so many times it seemed as if it had almost happened. Grandma staring out above the double door, then running toward her. Grandpa in the field turning at Grandma's shout of welcome. Bear woofing in welcome. And most of all her surprised father sweeping her up in a big hug and calling her his brave, wonderful girl. Giving up the dream seemed impossible.

"I won't go back," she said. "You can't make me."

His six-foot, six-inch frame towered over her. He looked down in amusement.

"Ah now, I think I could hoist you aboard a wagon without any trouble," he said.

"But you can't make me stay there," she said. "Papa never got my message and Silas broke Gertie's leg and I'm not waiting any more. I'll just stow away again." She paused as an idea struck her. "And you can't be sure it will be someone as nice as you."

He shook his head. "And here I thought you was a sweet little slip of a girl. Let me think."

In the shade of a tree, while dust from passing wagons settled over their food and covered their clothes, they swatted at flies and devoured salt beef, washed down with rum for One Eye and water for Jane. She studied his face and tried to discern what he was thinking.

"Hmm," he said at last, "maybe when you get a sip or two of what the road is really like, you'll know when you were well off. You can go on with me for a bit. I'm betting you'll see things differently before we get to the big city. I'll send you back then."

"Oh, thank you," she said. "Thank you."

"We'll see if you thank me later," he said. "Do you understand what I'm saying? I'm not coddling you."

"I've seen my home burned and my mother and brothers taken captive and I was at Forty Fort during the massacre. I can handle it."

"We'll see how you're feelin' in a few days."

When they started again, Jane alternately trudged along or sat in the wagoner's saddle, carrying Gertie, who seemed to get heavier every mile. The dust made her cough and irritated her eyes. She looked at the cloudless sky. If only it would rain. But then this would be a sea of mud and that might be worse.

Farmers driving cattle and pigs to market joined the procession and the wagon jolted along over heavy ruts and deep holes, crossing occasional streams. She held her shoes in one hand, fording with her bare feet, but her skirts became drenched and clung to her until the warmth of the sun dried them.

One Eye said little, although he glanced at her often.

By midafternoon, her feet and back ached, her skin was turning pink from the sun and she felt lightheaded.

When she swayed and almost fell, he yelled "Whoa" to his team. One Eye waved his straw hat in front of his face like a fan, then turned and plopped it on her head. The inside was sweaty and the hat slid down on her forehead, but the shade felt good. "Here," he said, thrusting a canteen at her. "Drink some water."

She wanted to ask how much farther before they stopped for the night, but knew he would take it as a sign of weakening. Instead she asked, "How did you get started driving a wagon?"

"It was a long time ago," he said. "I wasn't much older than you when I left home and took to the road."

"Do you like it?"

"Mostly I do. I like being outdoors. I never could stand being cooped up inside. It's best in the spring when the trees start greening up or in fall when the leaves change to pretty colors."

"But don't you miss your family?"

"I get along just fine on my own," he said, and snapped his seven-foot blacksnake whip over the back of the team. They traveled in silence for a while, broken only by the jingling of the bells in the arch over each horse.

She looked at the big horses lumbering steadily along. Their coats gleamed in the sun.

"What do the horses do at night?"

"Stay out under the sky," he said.

"What do you feed them?"

"You saw the feed trough on the rear of the wagon. I bring it up front, fill it with grain and they line up three to a side. Whisht, don't worry about the horses. They get treated better than I do."

She looked over at the side of the wagon. "What's that?" she asked, pointing to a long iron lever.

"The brake, for going down hills."

"How do you make the horses go with just one rein?"

"Jerk line, not rein," he corrected her. "Training."

A pot hung from a hook near the rear of the wagon. "What's that for?"

"Tar pot, to grease the axles. Sure, and you're a curious little thing, aren't you. I'll tell you what. Instead of so many questions, let's sing. What songs do you know?"

"I know 'A Mighty Fortress Is Our God' and 'All Hail the Power of Jesus' Name'."

"Not hymns. I don't sing hymns any more. Do you know anything else?"

"I learned a few songs in Lancaster," she said. "How about 'Froggy Went A Courtin'?"

"Perfect. We need something lively to perk us up."

His rumbling bass joined with her light soprano, rising over the rumble of the wagon.

"Wasn't that grand," he said when they finished. "Do you know 'Chester?' That's a fine marching song."

"I'm not sure of the words."

"I'll start. And you join in. Ready?"

Where she couldn't remember the lyrics, she hummed along. After that, they moved on to "Yankee Doodle." For a while she forgot how tired and thirsty she was and how uncertain her future.

As evening approached, her feet began to burn and the urge to relive herself became unbearable.

"One Eye," she said, feeling pink rise to her cheeks. "Can we stop? I ... I need to go aside for a moment."

He looked at her. "Aye, lass." She darted behind some bushes as the team halted. This was so embarrassing. She lifted her skirts and wiped herself with leaves.

When she stepped back out on the main road, One Eye stared at her.

"You don't look so good. Are you ready to be sent back."

"No. I'm fine," she said, leaning against the wagon wheel for support.

"Oh, Holy Joseph and all the saints," he muttered. Then he lifted her up on the lazy board on the side of the wagon.

"Could I ride in back of the wagon out of the sun?" she asked.

"Good Lord, no. If the cargo shifted going down a hill, you could be crushed. You must have the luck of the Irish not to have had something bad happen earlier."

"Oh," she said. "I didn't think of that."

He grunted. "Didn't think at all."

He let her ride until they reached the Blasted Elm wagon stop, giving her sips of water from time to time. Outside, a giant tree partly split by lightning explained the tavern's name.

"Come along," he said. "I have to unhitch and feed the team and figure out what to do with you."

The inside of the inn was full of wagoners, talking and laughing. She sidled along with her back to the wall. The smell of liquor hung so strongly in the air it seemed almost visible.

"Have you got money to pay for your food and lodging?" he asked.

"No," she said.

"You see why this fine plan of yours won't work? How could you get all the way to the Hudson alone and you with not a coin to your name?"

"I told you. My grandpa would pay them when I got there."

He waved his hand around. "You see these men? They're rough and loud and, while most of them are decent lads, there are a few here and elsewhere who would take advantage of you in ways you can't imagine."

She said nothing.

He gave a big sigh. "All right. I'll pay for your meal."

Hungry from her exertions, Jane wolfed down the salt pork, boiled turnips and sour bread. One Eye washed his meal down with amazing amounts of rum.

The server, a heavyset woman with a thick German accent who reminded Jane of her grandmother, looked from her to One Eye with raised eyebrows, but refilled the community platters without comment.

After supper, the men broke out decks of cards and began to play and drink.

"So, O'Rourke," one of them said, "tell us again how you lost that eye."

"Sure, 'tis a terrible tale. I was servin' on a sailing ship. How I got there is a tale in itself. Anyway, in the middle of winter it was, and a gale howlin' down on us, and the masts so thick with ice we thought they'd snap off..."

The woman came over to Jane where she sat beside One Eye holding Gertie.

"Are you all right?" the woman asked.

Maybe the woman would have something to help her feet.

"Could I talk to you?" Jane asked, her voice low. "Alone."

The woman scowled at One Eye. He broke off his story and scowled back. "She's come to no harm," he said. "You know me better than that."

"I'm Frau Reinhardt," the woman told Jane,. "Come with me. Bring the dog if you want."

When Jane explained, the woman nodded. "I've some salve that may help your feet. And tell One-Eye I said you need to ride. I can't imagine what he was thinking letting you walk."

"He was trying to show me that I didn't belong on the road."

"He's right about that. How old are you?"

"I'll be fourteen in December."

"You look younger. How is it you come to be with One Eye anyway? You're way too young for his tastes, if you'll pardon my bluntness."

"He's helping me get somewhere," she said.

Frau Reinhardt persisted until the whole story came out. "One Eye is right," she said. "You're too young to travel alone. Now, what are we going to do with you tonight? You certainly can't sleep with the wagoners on the floor of the common room. I guess I can put you up in my bedroom. You'll be safe there. Once these fellows get a little more drink in them, they can get rowdy."

Relief flooded Jane. She was determined to get to the Hudson, but it felt good to have a woman to turn to.

"Thank you," she said. "I'll go tell him."

Frau Reinhardt hesitated. "All right, go ahead." She flung open the door and a raucous combination of singing, fiddle music, shouting and cursing filled Jane's ears. A few men turned and watched her as she walked across the room. It's just men having fun, she thought, but she felt nervous. One Eye, still talking, sat at the card table in a cloud of cigar smoke.

"Just then a giant wave broke over the stern and washed the captain and the steersman overboard, and..."

He broke off and stared at her blearily.

"I'm sleeping in Frau Reinhardt's room tonight," she said.

"Good. Very good. I'll see you tomorrow then."

A blast on a cow's horn at six in the morning proclaimed time for breakfast. Jane swam up through layers of sleep, aching all over. Frau Reinhardt had slipped out and Jane lay alone in the bed. Only one or two more days, she thought, then I'll be in Philadelphia. I know I can find someone there to help me, no matter what One Eye and Frau Reinhardt say. She pushed down the bubble of uncertainty that rose in her.

At breakfast, One Eye devoured the eggs and buckwheat pancakes, but ignored the pitcher of beer being passed around, contenting himself with the roasted rye beverage that passed for coffee since the British blockade. He was freshly shaved and wore a clean, if wrinkled, linen shirt.

"One Eye musta got hisself a gal," one of the men joked.

"Twins," he shot back. "Both eternally grateful and willing to show it."

"Why's that?"

"Musta been the way I saved them from that grizzly bear," he said.

"Tell us about it," another wagoner said. And O'Rourke was off on a rambling tale involving not only a grizzly but a pack of wolves, ending with, "and that's why they're so wild about me. And now I'd best be off. Can't keep them waiting."

Laughter followed Jane and One Eye out the door.

At midmorning, eyes bloodshot and complaining of a headache but as sober as Jane had yet seen him, One Eye pulled off the main road and wound his way down a side trail and across a stream, bringing the team to rest in the midst of a secluded maple grove.

"Where are we going?" Jane asked.

"You'll see," he said. "I never bring people here, but I don't have much choice this time. Just don't be gabbing about it."

He pulled a sack from the rear of the wagon. "Come on. We walk from here." A quarter mile farther on they came to a small, shabby log cabin in a clearing. Outside the door, which hung loose on its frame, flowers struggled to bloom amid weeds. An unsmiling gray-haired woman and a girl of about four appeared at the door. The girl raced toward One Eye and flung herself into his arms.

"Daddy," she squealed. He swung her in a circle until they both collapsed in a tangle of laughter.

"Meet my daughter, Kathleen," he said, getting to his feet.

Jane stared at the girl's black hair, dark eyes and bronze skin. Her mother must be Indian. One Eye watched her closely as if gauging her reaction.

Jane bubbled with questions she knew she couldn't ask. She smiled at the girl. "Hello," she said. "I'm Jane Strope."

One Eye turned to the elderly woman who watched from the doorway, leaning on a cane. "And this is Mrs. Hewett. She looks after Kathleen for me."

"Hello," Jane said. Mrs. Hewett looked at her quizzically. ""Good morning," she said. She studied the sky. "It's clouding over. My joints tell me it's going to rain soon. Let's get inside."

The interior of the cabin was clean but sparse. "Did you bring me something?" Kathleen demanded.

"Now would I come without a present?" He opened the sack and pulled out bright ribbons and a rag doll with black yarn hair. While Kathleen played happily with it, he talked to Mrs. Hewett.

"How has she been?" he asked.

"All right. But she's getting to where she needs other children to play with."

He sighed. "I know. But what can I do? Maybe her mother's people would raise her, even though Red Deer died — God rest her soul — but I don't want that. I'd lose her. And the way people feel toward Indians because of the war, this isn't a good time for white families to be accepting a half-Iroquois child."

"You'll have to think of something soon." Mrs. Hewett held up her hands to show fingers deformed by rheumatism. "It's getting to be too much for me, and I may have to go stay with my daughter."

"I know. I'll study on it," he said. He pulled a small leather pouch from inside his shirt and handed it to her. "This should be enough until I come back this way again," he said.

For the next hour he watched Kathleen play. At the patter of rain on the roof, he stood up. "We have to be going," he said. "This rain will turn the roads to mud."

Kathleen ran to him and threw her arms around his legs. "Don't go, Daddy," she said. "Please don't go."

"I have to, poppet." He pulled her arms loose, lifted her above his head and pretended to drop her. She laughed as he caught her at the last second.

"I'll be back soon," One Eye promised. "And I'll bring you something pretty."

A pang of longing for her father swept over Jane and she turned away.

The patter of rain changed to a downpour as she and One Eye trudged to where the team waited.

Already the ground under the trees was soaked. In the distance, lightning split the sky and a long peal of thunder rolled.

"Maybe we should wait for this to pass over," Jane said.

"We're wet clear through already," One Eye said, raising his voice to be heard above the steady downpour. "A little more won't hurt us. And I'm not wanting to wait out a thunderstorm under big trees."

He urged the team forward and slowly they moved on to the side trail.

Lightning sounded closer, making Jane jump.

"If you can hear it, you're still safe," he said. "I kind of like it. All rumbly and loud and bright. Standing on the shore of the ocean at night, it's a sight to behold. Why, I remember one time…Well, I'll tell that tale later."

One Eye frowned as he studied the creek. The water had risen dramatically. "Should be all right," he said. "This wagon is heavy enough." He lifted her up on the lazy board and she clutched Gertie with one hand, holding on to the seat with the other.

"We'll be fine," he said. "Luck of the Irish."

He climbed into the saddle and cracked his whip. The horses sloshed forward, pricking their ears back at a roll of thunder. Water rushed past the wheels, making the wagon sway, but it remained upright. A large branch, swept downstream, hurtled toward them. It struck One Eye's horse, making it shy. He lurched in the saddle and fell, still holding the jerk line. The force of the water pushed him under the wagon where the massive left rear wheel struck him, knocking him under.

Jane screamed and jumped from the lazy board into the water. Gertie barked frantically and leapt in after her.

"One Eye," Jane yelled. She grabbed for his shirt, then lost her footing and the two of them were swept downstream until a log fallen partway across the stream halted their progress. Sobbing, Jane straddled it as water roared by. With an effort, she held One Eye's head above the stream and screamed for help. The creek was stained pink with bleeding from his leg. Thunder cracked overhead, and she realized there was no one around to hear.

Chapter Twenty

The first hints of autumn color mottled the trees as Lydia trudged with an assortment of Indians and captives into the ruins at Tioga Point. On the way back, she had searched for the Bible, but it was gone.

They were going to rebuild the town, Queen Esther insisted. Crude huts at first, but they would be shelter from the winter, and in the spring they could begin again. Lydia eyed the blackened corn fields and wondered what they would eat.

Margaretha walked beside her with Henry a little ahead.

"Are you feeling better?" Margaretha asked.

"Yes." In truth she felt weak and sore from the miscarriage, but there was nothing to do but bear it.

"I'm glad to hear that." They walked on. Suddenly Margaretha burst out, "How could you let this happen?"

"Do we have to talk about this now?" Lydia asked.

"If we don't talk now, I don't know when we'll have privacy. We'll have to build lean-tos tonight or sleep on the ground. People will be even closer and there'll be no noise to cover our conversation. So tell me, what have you done?"

"What I had to do," Lydia said, staring straight ahead.

"What does that mean? What you had to do?"

"It was Zach," Lydia whispered.

Margaretha's hand rose to her cheek. "Oh, no. How horrible. He forced you."

Lydia started to agree. It would be so easy. She would still be tainted, but there would be pity along with the shame. I made this mess, she thought, and I won't run away from it.

"Not exactly," she said, her voice low.

"I didn't hear you. What did you say?"

"Not exactly. He said if I let him...you know...that he would take Isaac to safety."

"And you agreed?"

"Yes. I did. I know the Bible says it's wrong. But I'd do it over if I thought his plan would succeed and Isaac would be safe and we could be together when this is over."

Margaretha stared at her. "I understand loving your son. But you knowingly slept with another man. That's a sin." She walked without speaking for several minutes. "Are you going to tell Sebastian?"

Was she? If she did, it would lie between them always. There were enough walls already. Better to keep her shame a secret. "No," Lydia said. "No good could come of that."

"And you don't repent of your sin." Margaretha sighed. "There's no more to say then, is there? I will pray for your soul." Her voice was sad.

Lydia felt as if she'd been slapped. "Sebastian said once that he'd never seen you and me quarrel," she said. "I told him, 'Why should we? We think alike.' Sister, we've done everything together all our life. We even married brothers. Don't turn away from me now. Can't you understand why I might do this?"

Margaretha gave a pained sigh. "I can understand the temptation. I love my son, too. But sin is sin. Now that we're among savages, we especially must hold fast to what is right. Otherwise, we're no better than they are."

Lydia looked at her sister's set face. Anger rose in her. "Judge not that ye be not judged," she said.

"Thou shalt not commit adultery," Margaretha shot back.

The quote so nearly echoed Lydia's own ambivalence that she fell silent.

Margaretha stared at her for a long moment.

"I'm sorry. I'm going on ahead," she said, striding forward. "I need to think."

Lydia stared at her sister's stiff, retreating back, feeling more alone than ever.

The next morning, Queen Esther announced that because of the potential shortage of food, some captives and Indians would move to Fort Niagara.

"I'm going to ask to go," Margaretha told Lydia. "John is supposed to be there. And I want to be with him."

"As you wish."

Jane's legs felt numb from the cold water of the creek, and her arms ached from holding One Eye. The water level had dropped somewhat, and the rain had stopped. Upstream, the wagon team had halted on the far bank. Gertie was nowhere to be seen. One Eye moaned and opened his eyes.

"Holy Jesus. What happened?" he mumbled.

"A big branch hit one of the horses and you fell into the water," she said. "I can touch bottom, and I think if I brace against the tree trunk, I can make it to shore. It's not far. But can you walk?"

"Only one way to find out." He struggled to get his feet under him, yelping with pain as the wounded leg took part of his weight. With one arm around her shoulder, he limped to shore and collapsed. When he tried again to stand, he sank to his knees. "I don't think I can walk after all," he said.

"I'll fetch Mrs. Hewett," Jane said. "I'll be right back." His face was white, his skin cold and clammy and his breath came in gasps.

"Wait," he whispered, grasping her sleeve. "If I don't make it, see that my daughter is taken care of."

"You'll be fine." Her voice quavered with uncertainty and shock.

"No, listen. Under the left rear wheel of the wagon, there's a box. I fixed a spot for it so you can't see it if you don't know where to look. A little indentation. There's money in the box. See Kathleen gets settled and take some for yourself for your trouble. Mrs. Hewett will help you."

"I need to get help."

"Promise me." His breath came in gasps, but he kept his grip on her arm.

"I promise," she said, anything to get him to let go so she could run for Mrs. Hewett.

Satisfied, he slumped backward on the ground and his eyes closed.

When Mrs. Hewett arrived, leaning heavily on her cane, he was still unconscious. Mrs. Hewett pulled a knife from one of the pocket sacks inside her gown and slashed at one leg of the buckskin trousers to reveal a mangled bloody mess. Jane winced and turned her head away.

Mrs. Hewett pressed her lips tightly together.

"It's not good, is it?" Jane asked.

"No. I'm afraid not." She wrapped a clean rag around the wound and together, they tried to drag his limp body to the cabin.

After about fifty torturous yards, marked by a smeared path through weeds and mud, Mrs. Hewett stopped. Jane leaned on her knees, breathless.

"He's too heavy. We're doing more harm than good," Mrs. Hewett said. "Run back to the main road and find some men there to help us."

Jane hurried upstream to where the horses stood on the far side. Debris floated downstream, but the level was definitely lower. She stood on the bank looking at the muddy water. If she stayed here, One Eye might die. If she tried to cross, she might be swept away. Quickly, before she could lose her nerve, she murmured a prayer and plunged in, fighting the current, to emerge safely on the other side. As she passed the wagon, she hesitated. It would take time to find the money, but once people arrived, there would be no way to retrieve it undetected. One Eye might be fine. But what if he wasn't? She lay on the ground and shimmied under the rear wheel, praying the horses wouldn't spook. In the dimness, she spied an indentation in the underside of the wagon. Much tugging freed a small metal box. Clutching it, she worked her way out. A small, bedraggled brown form limped toward her as she emerged.

"Gertie," Jane screamed. "You're alive." She dropped the box, knelt and hugged Gertie, who licked her face.

"Stay here," Jane ordered. Not that Gertie would obey. She worried the dog might be injured, but there was no time to check. One-Eye needed her more. Off to one side, the flash flood had piled brush against a tree. Hastily she tucked the box out of sight amid the debris and ran toward the main road.

It had been three days since One Eye's injury. Wagoners had rallied to help, unhitched his team, divided his load among them and constructed a crude corral for the horses before going on their way. The grain they donated was ample, and Jane enjoyed feeding the horses, finding peace as she listened to them munching in the quiet of the morning. Gertie, except for some scrapes, seemed fine.

But One Eye, who'd insisted on remaining at the cabin with his daughter, proved slow to recover. In the morning, he burned with fever and the leg felt hot and swollen. Streaks of red ran up his thigh. He smiled weakly when she brought him breakfast.

"We need a doctor," Jane declared.

"I know. But I don't have money for a doctor," Mrs. Hewett said. Beside them, Kathleen played with her doll, seemingly ignoring their talk.

Jane recalled the pouch One Eye had handed to Mrs. Hewett.

"What about what he gave you to take care of his daughter?"

"I need that for supplies to last us until he's up on his feet again."

Jane hesitated, thinking of the hidden money box. "I can pay," she said.

Mrs. Hewett looked at her. "You? You can pay?"

"Yes. One Eye gave me money for Kathleen."

"All right. Something has to be done. I don't know what we'd do if he died." I don't either, Jane thought.

It took until nightfall to find and fetch a doctor, and Jane reeled with fatigue. Dr. Franklin's face was grave as he examined the swollen, streaked leg. He sniffed at the wound, then stood up and sighed. "Things don't look good," he announced. "Putrefaction has set in. We'll have to amputate immediately."

One Eye, who had been drifting in and out of consciousness, roused himself.

"Jesus, no. I'd rather die."

"That's what will happen if we don't amputate," the doctor said.

"I don't care," One Eye said weakly.

"Is that your little girl I saw playing out front when I drove up?"

"Yes."

"Well, if that leg doesn't come off, she won't have a daddy. Is that what you want?"

One Eye closed his eyes for a moment. "Do what you have to," he said.

Dr. Franklin pulled a vial from his bag. "Laudanum, for the pain." He turned to Mrs. Hewett. "Do you have some whiskey to mix it in?"

She nodded.

"At least there are some benefits to this," One Eye said.

Dr. Franklin looked at Jane dubiously. "You're a little thing, but you'll have to do. I need you and Mrs. Hewett to stand on each side and hold the leg steady."

"All right," Jane said. Mrs. Hewett nodded and limped forward.

When One Eye was drunk, Dr. Franklin pulled a saw from his bag and wrapped a tourniquet around the leg above the wound and a leather strap below it. Jane looked away as he began sawing, but nothing could block out the rasping sound of the saw going through the bone. One Eye moaned, then fainted. Jane swayed on her feet.

"Here now. None of that," the doctor said. "Think of something pleasant."

Jane pictured a colt standing on wobbly legs beside its mother and felt a little better.

"We're almost through," Dr. Franklin said.

Jane dared a look. Deftly, the doctor tied off an artery and wrapped pledgets of lint over the bone end. She looked away again.

"It's all over now. Just don't let the bandage get wet," Dr. Franklin said. He felt One Eye's forehead. "I don't like this fever. I think it best to bleed him. It will counter the excessive irritability. But no more than a quart." He looked at Mrs. Hewett. "Can you help? I'll need a basin."

"Yes," she said, as white-faced as Jane.

"Good. After I bleed him, he should sleep. I'll be back to check on him tomorrow."

While he let the blood, Jane walked outside and retrieved One Eye's box from its hiding place. Under the money she found a silver crucifix and a tiny white seashell that reminded her of the ones trapped in the gray rocks in her secret shelter at home. Where had the shell come from? she wondered. Why had he saved it?

As Jane paid the doctor, she asked, "What are his chances?"

"It's in God's hands now."

In the morning, One Eye's fever was worse, despite being bled. He called Jane to his bedside. "The team," he whispered. "Are they all right?" His voice was so low Jane had to bend close to hear him.

"They're fine."

"I don't think I'm going to make it," he said. "I'm sorry to put this on you."

He waved a hand weakly when Jane opened her mouth to protest. "No, you have to know this. The other drivers will sell the wagon and horses for you. I figure they'll bring $1,000. That's for Kathleen. And for you for your trouble."

He stopped talking and rested for a few minutes. A thousand dollars, Kathleen thought. She couldn't imagine that much money.

One Eye roused himself. "Fetch me a priest," he said. "I've a few things to confess."

When Jane trudged back to the main road, she was told the nearest priest was miles away. A wagoner offered to go for one, but by early afternoon, One Eye was dead, still unshriven. Jane, entering the bedroom to bring him water, tried to rouse him, then backed away from his still form and called for Mrs. Hewett.

Mrs. Hewett checked his pulse, leaned close to listen for a heartbeat, sighed and pulled the tattered sheet over his face. "What a shame," she said. "He was a good man in his way. God rest his soul."

Jane stared at the shrouded form on the bed, eyes filling with tears. He had seemed larger than life. How could he be dead? And what would happen to them now? She murmured a silent prayer that he was in Heaven where there was no sickness or pain, then followed Mrs. Hewett outside. Kathleen sat on the grass cradling a doll. "Can I see Daddy now?" she asked.

"Not now, child," Mrs. Hewett said.

Jane wandered toward the horses and stared at them blankly. She looked up at the clouds scudding across the sky and wished she could see farther, all the way to Heaven. It had to be invisible. She hoped there was an ocean so One Eye could stand on the shore and watch lightning strikes over the waves.

Mrs. Hewett came up behind her. "Do you have anywhere to go?" Mrs. Hewett asked.

"My grandparents' house," Jane said. "But I promised One Eye I'd see Kathleen was safe. I don't know what to do." Why me? she thought. He made me promise. I don't have to do it. I am tired of taking care of people. I want someone to take care of me.

Mrs. Hewett's gaze softened. "Ah well, time enough to figure this out when we've done what has to be done," she said. "I'm sorry, but you'll have to walk out for help again. My hips won't let me. I'll prepare the body while you're gone."

"Does he have any relatives we should tell?" Jane asked.

"None that I ever heard him mention."

Jane's promise weighed heavier on her by the moment. "Can't Kathleen stay here with you?"

Mrs. Hewett shook her head. "Not much longer. These old bones have been telling me for a while that it's time to go live with my daughter in Philadelphia, but One Eye kept persuading me to put it off. I can hardly bend over enough to weed the vegetable patch. And this house needs repairs I can't make."

"If it's money," Jane said, "I can help with that."

"Money would help, but for how long? And winter's coming on. It's past time for a change. My daughter and I don't get along that well, but she won't refuse to take me in."

"But…"

"We'll sort it out," Mrs. Hewett said.

October 1778

Sebastian stood with his father and brothers and looked at the heaps of hay, laid in neat stacks in the fields of his father's farm. The sugar maples blazed with color on the hills around them. He loved autumn. Looking at the trees made a man feel peaceful inside, not like the time he'd spent with Hartley's army. "Trees are as good as church," he'd told Lydia once. But this fall, his pleasure was muted. Finding the Bible had brought his loss home again in a concrete way. He'd tucked it away in a storage chest. Every time he'd looked at the cover on the long way back to the Hudson, an image of Lydia leafing through its pages flashed through his mind. It was better to put it out of sight where it wouldn't be a daily reminder of loss. Someday it would belong to Jane. There had been no word from her, but he refused to give up hope. Surely God would not be so cruel as to take Jane, too.

Beside him, his father spoke. "Let's put on the covers." Jacob and Wilhelm moved forward. Together, the men wrestled the roofs over the hay to protect it from rain. Sebastian's hand slipped and the cover slid toward Wilhelm, jolting him.

"Watch what you're doing," Wilhelm snarled.

"Sorry," Sebastian said.

Wilhelm helped hoist the cover in place without speaking. Johann looked from one to the other, then shook his head. In silence, they tromped to the next mound to put on another cover.

Later, Sebastian waited to find Wilhelm alone. He was mending a fence when Sebastian found him. "Let me help you," Sebastian said. Wilhelm nodded. "Hand me that sledgehammer and hold the post."

Sebastian had wondered how to bring up the incident, but Wilhelm spoke first. "I'm sorry I was irritable before," he said. He raised the hammer over his head with both hands and slammed it down on top of the fence post. Sebastian's hands stung from the force of the blow transmitted through the wood.

"Put it out of your mind," Sebastian said. "We all get out of sorts at times. How are you getting along since Zipporah died?"

"Well enough," Wilhelm said. "I get up, I work, I go to bed. I get up. I work. I go to bed. I'm tired of being alone."

"I know. We've both lost a lot," Sebastian said.

Wilhelm wiped sweat from his forehead. "How did you come to meet Faith?" he asked.

"She was at Forty Fort and had no relatives, nowhere to go, so she ended up here somehow."

"She said she has no children," Wilhelm said.

"Right."

"Hmmm."

Sebastian pondered what that drawn-out sound meant. Zipporah had been barren and Wilhelm wanted a family. The idea he fancied Faith was disturbing.

"Let me take a swing," Sebastian said.

"I got to know her better while you were gone," Wilhelm said as he handed over the sledgehammer. "She's a fine-looking woman. And sweet, too. She'll make some man a fine wife."

He looked sideways at Sebastian assessingly.

"Yes, she will," Sebastian said. He brought the sledgehammer down with all his strength, driving the post deeper into the ground.

"My turn," Wilhelm said and moved to the next post.

Chapter Twenty One

Perched on a Conestoga wagon, Jane entered Philadelphia. Lancaster had seemed big, but this city was huge. She stared at the broad, flagstone-paved streets and the horses and wagons filling the road. Dogs ran free, barking at passersby. Gertie wriggled excitedly and barked back. Trash was piled in gutters, and a stench filled the air.

"It stinks," Jane exclaimed.

Mrs. Hewett, behind her on a second wagon, laughed. "Be glad you're visiting in the fall instead of the summer," she shouted over the noise of traffic. "It's really rank then." She called to the driver. "Turn here, please. Our street is just ahead."

They entered a quieter area of fine brick homes and pulled up in front of the house of Mrs. Hewett's daughter. A wagoner lifted Mrs. Hewett and Kathleen O'Rourke down from the lazy board. Mrs. Hewett stifled a groan. The trip had been torture for her, but she hadn't complained. "The Lord suits the back to the burden," she said.

Tears sprang to Jane's eyes. "My mama always said the same thing."

"She was right," Mrs. Hewett said. "Or at least we might as well act that way. Moaning and groaning never changed anything that I could see."

The second wagoner reached for Jane, who clutched Gertie, and set her down in front of the two-story home.

"Quite a procession," Mrs. Hewett said. "Dorcas won't like this."

Jane looked at the teams. They did seem out of place.

"They're all friends of One Eye and I think it's nice they gave us a ride for free," she said.

"I do too," Mrs. Hewett said. She brushed at her clothes and puffs of dust flew off them. "I'm just saying, Dorcas won't like it."

Jane wasn't sure she would like Dorcas either. During the trip, Mrs. Hewett had confided that her three sons all lived in New York, now in British hands, and couldn't take her in. But Dorcas had married a rich lawyer, Benjamin Sutton, and had plenty of room. Yet Mrs. Hewett seemed uncertain of their reception.

Mrs. Sutton better be nice to us, Jane thought. I'm tired and hungry and I don't see how I can take care of Kathleen by myself.

The front door opened and a slender middle-age woman in a low-necked silk gown stood there. Her face with its large, dark eyes, generous mouth and high cheekbones was attractive, but a scowl spoiled the effect.

"What's all this?" she demanded. "Get those wagons out of here. You'll crack the brick pavement." She wrinkled her nose. Jane had to admit the horses did smell strong. In fact, they all were in need of a bath.

"Dorcas," Mrs. Hewett said, limping forward.

"Mother?" Dorcas' voice rose. "Mother, is that you?"

Dorcas' gaze swept to Kathleen, Jane and Gertie. "What in the world?" she said. She shook her head as if absorbing the scene.

"My goodness. Well, come on in," she said. "No need to stand out in the street for people to gawk."

"This is Kathleen, Jane and her dog, Gertie. They're with me," Mrs. Hewett said. Jane smiled and bobbed her head. Kathleen stared at Dorcas with wide eyes.

"I see," Dorcas said.

Jane turned to the wagoners. "Thank you for everything. We'll be fine now."

The lead wagoner looked at Dorcas, then at them. "If you're sure. Send word to the Green Tree Inn if you need anything."

Jane waved as they drove off. She wished One Eye could have known how much the other wagoners missed his stories and how willing they had been to help her and Kathleen get to their destination safely.

Dorcas looked doubtfully at Gertie, who was covered with dust. "The dog will have to stay out back," she said. "I don't want dirt tracked in." Seeing Jane's stricken look, her tone moderated. "I'll get a servant to tend to your pet. He will be well cared for."

"Gertie's a girl dog," Jane said. Then, remembering her manners, she added, "Thank you for your hospitality."

She had thought Mrs. Jamieson's home was fancy, but the interior of this house made it pale by comparison. Dorcas saw her looking at the furniture with its polished wood and curved lines. "Philadelphia Chippendale," she said with the first smile she'd shown.

After they washed up and were seated in the parlor sipping herbal tea and munching on biscuits, Dorcas turned to her mother. "What a surprise," she said. "I'm glad to see you and get caught up. It's been too long, but I wish I'd known you were coming. How long can you stay?"

Mrs. Hewett's smile did little to hide her apprehension. "Actually, there have been some changes in my life." She went on to recount One Eye's death and the decline in her health. "So," she concluded, "I have nowhere to go but to my daughter."

"Oh, Mother." Silence fell. Jane wanted to shake Dorcas. What she wouldn't give to have her own mother show up unexpectedly. She'd fall on her neck and hug her and never let her go.

"We'll have to make the best of it then. You're welcome here, of course."

Of course, Jane thought. She stared at Dorcas' slender hands wrapped around the flowered teacup. They were so smooth, the nails so neatly trimmed. It made her want to hide her own rough hands with their ragged nails, made worse by the struggle to pull One Eye from the river.

"What about your companions?" Dorcas asked, gesturing toward Jane and Kathleen. "I assume you have some plans for them."

"Jane and Gertie need to get to her grandparents in New York state and Kathleen needs a home. That's as far as I've gotten in planning," Dorcas said.

Dorcas looked at Kathleen and shook her head. "She's a pretty child and sweet, I'm sure, but she's clearly part Indian. Benjamin won't want her here a second longer than necessary. And she's too young to be a servant. This could be difficult."

As the weeks went by, it proved difficult indeed. Daily, Jane fought a growing sense of depression and a hunger to move on to her grandparents' house. And almost daily, Dorcas or her husband hinted at their desire to have Jane, Kathleen and Gertie move on. I'm as eager to leave as they are to see me go, Jane thought. It's no fun being where you're not wanted. But I promised One Eye and I'm not leaving until Kathleen has a new home.

So far, the quest had been fruitless. Many of Mrs. Hewett's friends had died or moved and her health made it difficult for her to get out and about to help search. She'd heard of a school for Indians in New Hampshire where girls learned housekeeping, but no one was sure where it was or even if it was still in existence.

If Jane could just get Kathleen settled, she could be on her way. She had the means now. The wagoners had sold One Eye's wagon for $900, but the driver who showed up on their doorstep handed her only $100. "One Eye owed all of us considerable money," he said, not meeting her eyes. "I know he'd want to repay his debts. This is all that's left. I'm sorry." He'd thrust it at her and hurried off. Still $100 was more than she'd had in her entire life. With what was in the box, there should be enough for both her and Kathleen.

The last rays of the setting sun cloaked the streets of Philadelphia in a dim light as Jane hurried home from the market, her basket clutched in her hand. She'd dallied too long and was going to be late getting back. But it was getting harder and harder to stay in that house with the disapproval that seemed to seep from the very walls. Besides, doing chores was one way she could help earn her keep until she found a home for Kathleen.

Vandals had broken several street lamps and she almost passed by a small building without noticing it. Friends Bettering and Alms House the sign said. She stared at it. Friends sounded like a good thing, and Alms meant help for the needy. Maybe someone here would know a safe place for Kathleen. She pushed open the heavy door and was greeted by a young man in a plain black coat and knee breeches with a white cravat.

"Art thou in need of help?" he asked.

She hesitated. What an unusual way of talking.

"The sign said something about alms. Do you help Indian children."

"Ah, our dusky brethren. But allow me to introduce myself. I am Ishmael Rotch. And thou art?"

"Jane Strope. What is this place, please?"

"The Society of Friends runs it. The Bettering House is a workhouse that helps the able-bodied poor find work. The almshouse wing cares for those unfortunates who have no one and who can not work. There is also an infirmary."

"What about children? Do you take children?"

"More the aged and infirm. I take it thou hast need?"

"Not me. I'm trying to find a place for a half Indian, half white girl."

"How old is she?"

"Four."

"Too young, I fear. But tell me about it and we will see what might be done."

The story of One Eye and Kathleen rolled off her tongue easily now. She'd told it so many times trying to find help.

"The poor child," Rotch said. He looked at her. "And hard on you, too, I'll warrant."

A lump formed in her throat. "I guess," she said. "Do you know anyone who could give Kathleen a good home?"

"Let me study on it," he said. "How can I get in touch?"

"I'm staying with Dorcas and Benjamin Sutton," she said.

"I know the house. Today is Monday. I'll call on thee at 10 on Thursday if that's convenient."

Anything that might solve her problem would be convenient.

"That would be perfect," she said.

Over the next few days, she alternated between hope and doubt. Promptly at 10 on Thursday, she heard the rap of the brass knocker and rushed to open the door.

Rotch stood there with a smile. That must be a good sign.

"Come in," she said, and led him to the parlor, glad that Dorcas was out visiting.

"I know of a couple who might take her as an indentured servant," he said. "She's too young now, but when she got older, she could work off the debt for her care. Many people do it. I told them you had a little money to contribute, so the debt shouldn't be that much. However, they are not Friends."

"So you don't know them? How can you be sure they are nice people?"

He looked puzzled, then his face cleared. "Oh, I see. I meant they are not members of the Society of Friends. I don't know them well, but they are respectable members of the community. They promise to treat her kindly and to teach her to read and write."

An indentured servant. One Eye must have hoped for more for his daughter.

"May I see the child?" Rotch asked.

Jane called to Kathleen, who came running into the room, then stopped short at sight of a stranger. She sidled over to Jane and stood by her knee, looking at Rotch with wide, dark eyes.

"A lovely child," he said. "They would want to meet her, of course. What say you?"

"All right," Jane said. It was the best, indeed the only, offer they had after weeks of trying.

Dorcas insisted on being present for the interview with the couple. The man, with his stomach bulging over his gray trousers, and the equally plump woman in her red cloak sat side by side, perched on a settee like a catbird and a cardinal on a branch. Jane disliked them as soon as the woman began talking. It wasn't the woman's fault she was richly dressed, but she acted as if Jane wasn't there, addressing her remarks to Dorcas and calling Jane "the child." They sipped tea and chatted while Kathleen stood by Jane's knee staring solemnly at them.

"Come here, child," the man said, motioning to Kathleen. When she clung to Jane, he frowned. "Has the child no manners? Ah well, that can be set right." He walked over, knelt down and pried Kathleen's fingers loose. She started to cry.

"Now, now, none of that," he said. "You must learn to obey your elders."

Jane looked down at the sobbing child. The man's fingers were crushing Kathleen's hand.

"I've changed my mind," Jane said. "This isn't the right situation for her."

Dorcas sat bolt upright. "What are you talking about? Here is a chance for the child to have a good, Christian home."

The man still gripped Kathleen's hand. She whimpered and tried to pull free. With a frown, he released her and went back to the settee.

"Well," he said, "I should hope we are good Christians. This child," he waved one hand toward Jane, "doesn't understand what is best for Kathleen. Not everyone would take a half breed in."

Jane sighed, tempted to let someone else take over responsibility for Kathleen. Then she thought of One-Eye lying wounded on the bank of the creek. I made a promise, she thought, and I have to keep it. But oh I wish it was easier.

"I'm sorry. But One Eye said I was to look out for his daughter and I say she isn't going with them," Jane said.

"I know you care about her," Dorcas said. "But really, you're too young to judge what's best."

"No," Jane repeated. Mama and Papa would never treat a child that way. They could be strict, but they never deliberately hurt her or her brothers.

The woman and Dorcas exchanged glances. "We'll see," Dorcas said. As Dorcas ushered the couple out, she spoke softly to the woman, who inclined her head and smiled.

They're going to do this no matter what I say, Jane thought. She looked at the red marks on Kathleen's hand from the man's grip, marks that were only now starting to fade. If he acted that way in public, how might he act when no one was around?

Maybe I'm being foolish, but I won't do it, she thought. But how could she keep the couple from taking Kathleen? They'd just have to leave before that happened. She repressed a sigh. Another journey. Well, she'd done it before. She could do it again.

In a few minutes, she put on her bonnet and slipped out to see if she could find the Green Tree Inn and a wagoner who would help a child of One Eye's.

Chapter Twenty Two

November 1778

Lydia shivered and stuck her hands inside the sleeves of her ragged coat as she and the other captives crossed the drawbridge and walked under the stone arch into Fort Niagara. A cold winter wind blew off Lake Ontario. So much water, stretching into the distance, more than she'd ever seen. Henry covered his reddened nose with his hand and stared in fascination at the gray waves washing up on the narrow shore. Their color matched the gray stone of the imposing buildings inside the fort and the mood of the hungry, footsore prisoners, forced here by the lack of food and adequate shelter at Tioga Point. Off to one side a group of soldiers in tan breeches and green jackets drilled smartly to the shouted commands of an officer.

Were Margaretha and John still here? Lydia wondered. How would Margaretha receive her? She had missed her sister more than she would have thought possible. For years, the two saw each other daily. And daily in the past month, Lydia had noticed the absence, like a child touching the spot where a tooth had been pulled. Her anger at Margaretha's rejection had faded, although the hurt remained. She longed to repair the breach. If she had to listen to preaching and be prayed over, so be it.

A group of women and children watched in silence as the captives filed inside. Suddenly, Lydia spotted Margaretha, holding Elisha. Gladness rose in her. Margaretha waved and she waved back. "Aunt Margaretha," Henry said. He tried to jerk free of Lydia's hold on his hand.

"Welcome. I'll see you later," Margaretha called to them.

Lydia had barely put down their belongings on a bed in their new quarters when Margaretha burst in. "I missed you," Margaretha said, setting Elisha down and sweeping Lydia up in an embrace.

"And I missed you. So much." Margaretha's arms around her felt so good, so natural. It had been lonely on her own, not knowing what had happened to anyone she held dear.

"How have things gone since we saw each other last?" Lydia asked. "How is John?"

"Not good. He tried to escape and they caught him. He has scars all over his body from where they beat him. I thought they might let us be together, but we're being kept apart. I only get to talk to him now and then. But at least I can see him."

"That's something," Lydia said. A longing to see Sebastian swept over her.

"Have you heard anything about Isaac?" she asked.

"I've spotted Rebecca, that Indian woman who took him, from a distance once or twice, but Isaac wasn't with her. I asked someone and they said she lives in a village near here."

Lydia's stomach felt hollow. Her son was nearby. She had to find a way to see him.

"Perhaps one of us will see Rebecca and can ask how he is faring," Lydia said.

"Perhaps," Margaretha said. "What about you? How has it been with you and Henry?"

"We didn't have enough food, and the march was long and tiring. We went partway by boat but we're well enough, considering. The squaws mostly ignore us or stare at us and laugh behind their hands."

Unspoken was the way the two had parted. Lydia hoped they could leave it that way.

"I've prayed for you nightly," Margaretha said.

"And I for you."

"Have you had time to reflect on what we spoke of last?" Margaretha asked.

"I've given it much thought," Lydia said. Too much. Too many sleepless nights and the ache of being at odds with someone she loved.

"And?" Margaretha prompted.

"Can't we put that behind us? We're together now. Let it go."

"I wish I could. I have struggled with this. I hate being at odds, then I think about how you haven't repented, and it hurts my heart. Can't you say you're sorry for your sin, even if you did it for Isaac? God is gracious and ready to forgive. Remember the Prodigal Son? His father welcomed him back with a feast." Tears rose in Margaretha's eyes. "Your immortal soul is in danger and I would be a poor sister if I didn't try to help you become right with the Almighty."

Lydia remembered her decision to let Margaretha view her however she liked as long as they were together. It was harder in reality than in imagination. Once again she'd been branded a sinner. Maybe God, a father, would understand and forgive without repentance. But He let His son die. How could He do that? Shaken, she thrust the thought away. She felt like someone standing in a swift current, unsure whether she would be swept away and where the current might take her if she yielded for even a second.

"I wish I could make you understand," Margaretha said. "All that we had has been taken away from us. We have to hold onto God's laws. We have to. I have to. It's my anchor in the storm."

Lydia sorted through and rejected various responses. She understood the feeling, and yet things seemed more complicated. "Well," she said at last, "I appreciate your concern and your prayers, sister."

Off in the distance toward the south Lydia heard a dull roar. "What's that?" she asked, eager to change the subject.

"The Falls," Margaretha said. "It's said to be a great cataract that drops more than a hundred feet. And they say the mist from the water rises up above the trees. On overcast days like this and when the wind is right, you can hear it."

"Do you think we could go see it?" Henry asked.

Margaretha smiled at him. "Oh, it's miles away. Come, there are dozens of children here. Let me introduce you to a boy your age."

A week later, when Lydia had begun to adapt to their new life, she and Margaretha spotted John working with other prisoners hauling stone to repair a wall. His appearance shook her. He had lost weight from his huge frame and his resemblance to Sebastian was heightened. She thought of the burly man who had fought off a cougar in his youth. Scars marred John's once-handsome face. She shuddered to think what the rest of his body must look like. John's eyes widened as they passed by.

Margaretha held Elisha high so he could see his son. He put down the rock he was carrying and started toward them.

"Back to work," a British soldier said. John glared at him and kept walking. His stubbornness had not changed. Lydia and Margaretha shook their heads simultaneously.

The soldier lengthened his stride. "I said, back to work," he shouted.

"Please, John," Margaretha called.

John paused just as the soldier raised the butt of his rifle to strike him. Reluctantly, he turned back toward the work crew. He stared at the soldier, then waved at his family before picking up his load again.

Later that day, Lydia saw Rebecca in the midst of a group of Indian women. She hurried over to her.

"Excuse me," she said, stepping in front of her. "Remember me? I'm Lydia Strope, Isaac's mother."

Rebecca stopped short and frowned. "I know who you are."

"Could you tell me how Isaac fares? Please. It would sooth my heart."

"Joshua is well."

"Could I see him? Talk to him for just a few minutes. I wouldn't make any trouble. I promise."

"No. He has a new life. Now get out of my way."

The other women stood watching with blank faces. Rebecca flushed, then took a step forward. Reluctantly, Lydia stood aside. At least she knew Isaac was well. Now, she needed to find out where he was being kept.

But how? She hated what captivity was doing to her, always passively following other people's orders, no longer in control of her actions. Her mother would have reminded her that mein gedanken sind frei, my thoughts are free. True enough. But she longed to be free in action, too.

She walked a little ways away to where she could see the lake and stared out at the gray water ruffled by the wind. And the spirit of God moved upon the face of the waters, she thought. And God said let there be light. And there was light. It didn't seem that way right now. If God was all powerful, how could He let all this happen? Faith had sustained her since childhood. But I'm a grown woman now, she thought, fighting down fear of divine retribution. I'm not a child to blindly follow everything my mother taught me. I will choose this time. And I choose to believe that God didn't cause this, that He is with me and hurts for my loss just as much as I do. And I will never give up on finding Isaac.

A feeling of lightness filled her. She spread her arms wide, as if she could fly away if she tried, and lifted her face to the breeze, not caring that the cold raised goosebumps on her skin.

In the morning, still with the faint sense a burden had been lifted, she lay in bed and thought of what steps to take to see her son. First, she needed to find out where he was. For that, she needed an ally. What came after that, she didn't know. But it was a place to start.

Over breakfast, she discarded the idea of an Indian ally. A few were friendly; a few were hostile, but most ignored the captives. She would start with the chaplain for the British troops. He wouldn't be Lutheran, but that didn't matter.

When she asked to speak to the chaplain, the officer in charge stared at her.

"Chaplain? We don't have a chaplain," he said. "He stayed back in London where it's safe."

"So you have no pastor among you?"

"That's right. The men who are so inclined can hold prayer services on Sunday."

Lydia stood for a minute thinking. "Then do you have an interpreter, someone who speaks Seneca? I'd like to learn the language."

The officer stood. "Madam, I don't wish to be rude. But I have no interest in arranging language lessons. I suggest you return to your cabin and devote yourself to sewing and cooking."

He motioned to a stocky soldier in a red uniform with yellow facings. "Private Wheeler, take her back."

"Come along, ma'am," Wheeler said. When she hesitated, he said, "Please, ma'am. Don't make trouble for yourself."

She turned to face Wheeler. His hair was tied up with a ribbon that matched his uniform. He was young enough to be plagued with acne and his harelip made him look as if he was snarling, but his brown eyes were kind. If one door closes, open another, she thought. She smiled at him. "I have no desire to make trouble, Private Wheeler," she said. "By all means, let's go back."

"So," Lydia said as they walked toward her hut, "I'm Lydia Strope. You may know my brother-in-law, John."

"Indeed, I do, Mrs. Strope. Indeed I do." His tone sounded as if it was cause for regret. John, that proud, stubborn man, would be known anywhere he went and especially in a situation like this.

"Where are you from, Private?" Lydia asked, slowing her steps to give them more time to talk.

"Oh, a little village you never heard of. In northern England."

Gradually, Lydia drew out that his first name was Trevor and that he had worked on his father's farm before the war and longed to return to that life. By the time they reached her hut, they were deep in talk of crops and livestock.

"Do you know anything about the Indians hereabouts?" Lydia asked as they stood outside in the sun.

"A little, Not much. I go out on patrol sometimes."

An officer passed and stared pointedly at Trevor, who flushed. "I must be getting back to my post, ma'am," he said. "I enjoyed talking with you. Good luck."

"I enjoyed it, too," Lydia said. "I often walk near the building they call the French Castle at dusk. Perhaps we'll find a chance to talk again some evening."

He tipped his hat. "I'd like that," he said. "You remind me of my older sister, Maria. She has the same kind of smile."

"Your sister is named Maria? That's my mother-in-law's name." She gifted him with another smile, trying hard to make it sisterly. She didn't want another incident like the one with Zach. She'd have preferred the help of a woman, but, as the saying went, better a sparrow in the hand, than a pigeon on the roof.

And this sparrow might lead her to a pigeon.

"I'll hope to see you some evening soon," she said.

The aroma of baking bread suffused the kitchen of the Strope farm at Round Top. Sebastian, chilled from working outdoors, sniffed appreciatively as he and the other men entered.

"You're just in time," Faith said. She cut slices of warm bread and put it on platters in front of them.

Sebastian watched as Faith took small bites, then flicked out her tongue to catch a stray crumb on her lips. She smiled at him, and he smiled back.

"That was mighty tasty," Wilhelm said as they downed the last crumbs.

Faith smiled at him, too. "Thank you, kind sir," she said with a mock curtsey.

Johann frowned. "Sebastian, let's butcher the hog today. It's cold enough that the meat won't spoil. And the moon is waxing, so that's a good sign. Can you and Wilhelm see to it? I'll send Jacob up in a bit."

Sebastian touched the white scar on his cheek where the boar's tusks had grazed him what seemed a lifetime ago. "Of course, Papa."

"I'll get the pot and start the fire," Faith said. While she dragged the huge iron pot closer to the hog pen and set water to boiling, Sebastian and Wilhelm penned the boar.

"We can take it from here, Faith," Wilhelm said. She smiled at each of them individually. Both men's eyes followed her as she walked away, swinging her hips.

"I want to talk to you," Wilhelm said.

Sebastian had been expecting this. "All right," he said. "Let me take care of this first."

He raised his rifle and shot the hog between the eyes. Sebastian's body shook with the gun's recoil and the sound echoed back from the mountain overshadowing the farm. The hog fell to its knees, then toppled over, kicking.

Wilhelm took out a knife and slit the jugular vein. Blood poured from the wound. Sebastian held the head and directed the flow of the blood into the bowl set there to receive it. It would help make good bloodworst sausage.

"It's about Faith I want to talk," Wilhelm said, staring at the blood in the bowl. "What are your intentions? She's been here a while. It's been even longer since my wife died, and I'm tired of being alone. I want to know where you stand."

The hog lay still. Wilhelm slit the animal down the middle.

"I don't know where I stand," Sebastian said. "I wish I did."

"You better figure it out, because it isn't fair to her. And if you're not interested," Wilhelm paused and stood up, holding the bloody knife, "I am. So get it settled in your mind."

Together they began removing the entrails, which steamed in the cold. A foul odor filled the air. As they lowered the hog into the hot water to scald the hairs, Sebastian thought about what Wilhelm had said.

"You're right," he said. "I'll decide something soon."

Wilhelm grunted. "Good, because I'm not hanging back any longer. She won't look at me seriously as long as there's a chance with you." He threw the knife down and the blade stuck in the dirt, quivering.

That night Sebastian lay awake for hours. He had known Faith for six months, and Lydia had been dead that same amount of time. Wilhelm was right that something had to change. In the morning, Sebastian decided, I'll tell Wilhelm that I'm going to court her and see if she'll have me.

But in the morning, he thought of Lydia. Soon, he thought. I'll tell Wilhelm soon.

Chapter Twenty Three

Jane's heart beat faster as she and Kathleen trudged down the path leading to her grandparents' farm at Round Top. It was hard to believe they were almost there. She was so very tired. Tired of being brave, tired of taking care of Kathleen, tired of cajoling people to help. Just plain tired.

Gertie trotted along beside them, stopping to sniff every few seconds. Jane's feet were cold and her nose numb. Mrs. Hewett had given her most of One Eye's money and Jane had slipped out of the house with Kathleen before the couple returned to claim her. After that, aided by One-Eye's friends, it had been a long and arduous journey by wagon, horseback, on foot, through good weather and bad. Much of the money was gone, spent for food or to pay for shelter. And Jane had learned a lot about how kind or callous people could be to a half-Indian little girl like Kathleen. But no matter. The end was in sight. Safety and security lay in the farmhouse below with the curls of smoke from the two chimneys.

Weeds and snow would cover One Eye's grave now, she thought. The wooden cross lashed above it probably had fallen, but the rock with his name, Brendan "One Eye" O'Rourke, carved on it would mark the spot. Maybe someday she could take Kathleen there and show her where her father was buried. She wished she'd found out how he'd lost his eye so she could share that story, but no one seemed to know. One Eye might have wanted it that way.

Squinting, she saw figures working in the barnyard. She stopped short, filled with fear now that the end of her journey was so close. Was Papa alive? Would there be more heartbreak and loss?

Kathleen looked up at her. "I'm hungry," she said. Her practical words were like a pebble thrown in a pond, breaking the tension on the surface.

"All right. Come on," Jane said. "My grandmama will have some good food for us."

As she got closer, she studied the men at work. Was that…could it be her father?

Sebastian looked up and stared in her direction, shading his eyes. The two stood frozen, then Jane broke into an awkward run, still carrying Kathleen. This was too slow.

"Follow me," Jane said, putting Kathleen down, and raced toward her father at the same time that he dropped his shovel and ran toward her. The minute he reached her, she burst into tears. He swept her up in his arms, murmuring her name over and over and burying his face in her hair. His tears leaked down and mingled with hers.

He pulled back. "Oh God, Jane. It's you. It's really you."

"Papa," Jane said. Her throat closed up and she shook her head.

"It's all right," he said. "Don't try to talk. Just let me look at you."

They stared at each other. He looks older, she thought. And tired. But wonderful.

"I thought I'd never get here," she said, the words coming out jerkily. "It was awful."

"I know," he said. "I know. But we're together now." He gave her another long hug.

Gertie jumped and yapped, ignored, while Kathleen, her short, thin legs tired from running down the lane, stood and stared, chest heaving.

"I'm hungry," Kathleen announced. Sebastian stared at her.

Jane wiped her eyes and laughed shakily. "Papa, this is Kathleen O'Rourke," she said. "I have a lot to tell."

She gripped his hand tightly as they walked toward the farmhouse.

"Look who's come home," he called as they neared the kitchen door. Her grandmother peered out, then rushed toward her, apron flapping, exclaiming with joy.

Later, seated at the kitchen table, Jane wolfed down stew while Kathleen stared wide-eyed at everyone.

"What about Mama," Jane asked, setting her spoon down. "Is she OK?"

Her grandmother walked over and stood behind her, one hand on her shoulder. Her father, seated beside her, took her hand.

"What?" Jane demanded, dread rising in her.

"Oh, Jane, I'm so sorry to have to tell you this, but your mother and Henry are dead," he said.

"No. They can't be."

"It's true," he said, voice catching.

"They can't be dead," she repeated. Black spots filled her vision and she felt on the verge of sliding away. Mama and Henry dead. This wasn't happening. Papa had to be mistaken. She swayed in her chair and he reached over and put his arm around her. All through the journey, thoughts of her mother and their eventual reunion had sustained her. His words shattered something inside her. It had been such a long ordeal and she'd tried hard to be brave, and now this. Jane began to sob, long, keening sobs wrenched from deep inside. She stood up, pushing her chair back, as if somehow she could flee from the news.

Sebastian caught her in his arms while she cried and cried and cried.

December, 1778

Sebastian breathed in the sharp, clean scent of the Christmas tree in the main room of the farmhouse. The stars and angels Jane and the children had made from colored paper lay waiting. Tomorrow was Christmas Eve, when the family would decorate the tree, and Grischkindel, the Christ Child, would bring gifts. The best gift of all had already arrived with Jane's return.

He wasn't sure what to do with this half-Indian child, Kathleen. Every time he looked at her he remembered the smoke rising from the timbers of the farmhouse at Wysox and the massacre at Forty Fort. But when she smiled shyly at him with those dark eyes and her hair gleaming in the sun like a raven's wing or came running to him crying with a skinned knee like his own children had done, he saw a sweet little girl. They'd have to find someplace safe for her to go.

This Christmas, Sebastian had agreed to play the role of Der Belsnickel and bring nuts and candies to the children. It threw him back to childhood when he had been on the receiving end, shivering when Der Belsnickel rattled a stick on the windows to get attention, hoping he would receive sweets and not be threatened with the whip. It was a good decision to keep the traditions this year. His sister's children deserved it. And so did Jane. She'd grown up a lot in the past months, but he could see the child in her. Still, it was hard to be joyful on this first Christmas without his wife and sons.

Faith came up beside him. "The decorations are lovely, aren't they," she said.

He nodded without speaking. She hesitated and laid her hand on his arm.

The hesitation was his fault for not declaring himself, he thought. Wilhelm entered the room, his face darkening as he saw them standing close together. He glared at Sebastian, turned and left.

"I need to leave," Faith said. "This can't go on. I'll find a place for myself somewhere." She swayed against him. Her breasts seemed to burn into him. God knows it wasn't lack of desire that made him hesitate to propose. "That is, if you want me to leave," she said, looking up at him.

Would she appreciate his honesty? Perhaps not, but he owed it to her.

"I don't know. When I'm with you, I want us to make a life together. But at night, when I lie in bed, I think of Lydia, especially at this time of year, and…" He trailed off, wishing he were better with words. It was so much easier to deal with animals and farm chores than women.

She pulled away, and her lips firmed into a straight line. For a moment, she raised her hand as if to cover her mouth in the way she used to, then let her hand drop. "I think I should leave," she said. "I can't wait forever. There are other…Well, I'm not waiting forever."

"I don't expect you to. But don't leave until after the holidays, at least," he said. "We'll all help you get situated."

Later, he sought out Wilhelm. Brother shouldn't be angry with brother.

"Faith plans to leave sometime after the new year," he said.

"No wonder," Wilhelm said. "You've dithered long enough. I give you fair warning. I plan to court her. And I think I'll be well-received." He smiled without warmth.

Sebastian felt a pang of pain, wishing he were certain enough to propose to Faith right now. But that wouldn't be fair to either of them. He returned Wilhelm's frosty smile and they parted without further words.

His mother, when he told her of Faith's decision, threw her hands in the air.

"Praise God," she said. "Two stallions and one mare is nothing but trouble."

Sebastian lowered his eyes, wishing his mother didn't speak so plainly at times.

"Of course we'll help her make her way," Maria, always practical, went on. "I can provide some household goods and the pastor may know of a place she can stay until she finds something permanent. She does beautiful needlework."

She busied herself scraping cracklings from a pan. "Son, if you're getting serious about her, there's something you need to think about. She was married before but she never had any children. You've lost two sons. I wonder if she's able to breed. A man needs sons to help him farm the land."

It was a legitimate consideration, but he was embarrassed to discuss it with his mother.

"I'm not ready to think about that yet," he said.

She looked at his somber face. "This isn't all your fault, son."

"What do you mean?"

"A woman like Faith, she needs a man. If she can't have the one she wants, she'll find another."

He flushed with anger. "Faith's not like that," he said.

His mother looked at him, then shrugged. "Bring me some milk from the springhouse," she said. "I think I'll make some noodles. A warm dish will taste good on a cold night like this."

Sebastian lit a lantern and donned his winter coat, glad to escape the kitchen. A visit to the springhouse meant going outside. The sound of water greeted him as he entered. Someday, he'd divert the creek at his farm in Wysox and build the springhouse closer to the main house. It would be more convenient, warmer in winter. Someday lots of things would happen.

The pews of the Lutheran Church near Round Top were packed with settlers who'd driven their sleighs for miles through deep snow for the Christmas Eve service. Neighbors smiled and nodded by the glow of the candles filling the sanctuary. Jane tried to recapture the feeling this holy night had always given her. But how could she be joyful when Ma and Henry were dead? Since she'd found out, the lifeless feeling she'd had after the farm burned, as if she were a corncob doll, had returned. She walked and talked and did all the things she was supposed to. But she wasn't really there. Grandmama said their loved ones were looking down from Heaven and wouldn't want them to be sad. But how did you stop hurting?

Kathleen stirred restlessly beside her and pulled on Jane's sleeve. "I want to stay up and hear the animals talk tonight," Kathleen whispered.

"We'll see," Jane whispered back. The story of the animals speaking on Christmas Eve was the same one Mama had told Jane when she was a girl. Jane had enjoyed passing it on, feeling a momentary connection with her mother.

Grandmama put her finger to her lips in a signal to be quiet. She had accepted Kathleen's presence calmly, even though everyone was crowded together. "We'll work something out," Grandmama had said when she heard about how One Eye had befriended Jane. "Of course we must help someone who helped you." Papa often looked at Kathleen with a strange expression, but he hadn't objected to her presence.

Deliberately, Jane turned her thoughts to more pleasant channels. In two days, on Dec. 26, she would be 14 years old. Grandmama said anyone born on Christmas Day could understand what cows said. When Jane was little, she'd crept outside to listen one night, hoping a Dec. 26 birthday was close enough for the magic to work. But the mooing sounded like the same old noise.

Thoughts of her mother intruded even as the pastor, standing in the elevated pulpit, announced the next hymn, "Himmel hoch da komm ich her," From Heaven above to Earth I come. It was one of her favorites.

Around her people stood. Her father nudged her, and she rose to her feet.

The verses rolled on, and she sang through a tight throat, "Glad tidings of great joy I bring, Whereof I now will say and sing."

Faith stood on the other side of Sebastian singing in a halting voice. From time to time, she looked first at him, then at Wilhelm and smiled equally. Jane was glad Faith was going to stay with Widow Bowman. While Faith was at Round Top, everyone was cross and tense. Things would be more peaceful when she was gone. At least she hoped so. Right now it seemed as if she'd never be peaceful again.

Chapter Twenty Four

February 1779

S ebastian pulled his horse to a stop and dismounted in front of Widow Bowman's house. It had been a long ride from his parents' farm at Round Top to the town and he was tired and cold. Snow had begun to fall in big, wet flakes and showed no signs of stopping. A gust of wind struck him, scattering the snowflakes before it like sheep before wolves. He brushed flakes from his jacket and smoothed his ruffled hair. Yesterday, he'd awakened sure of what he wanted to do at last. The fading bruise on his cheek from a shoving match with Wilhelm had helped him decide. When he and Wilhelm were as ready to fight as two rutting elks in springtime, it was time to do something.

Jane might not like his plan, but she was only a child, a wonderfully brave child, but still a child. Once he explained, she would come to understand that he was lonely, that a farmer needed a helpmate, that he cared for Faith. And Jane would have a stepmother she might grow to love, someone to guide her through becoming a young woman in a way he couldn't. His hard-won decision was the right thing for everyone. Today, he would ask Faith to marry him. He still didn't know whether she could have children, but he wanted her to be his wife anyway.

When he entered the house, Faith was perched on a stool in the front room that served as a small millinery shop for Widow Bowman. He watched as she pushed a needle through blue fabric, her brow furrowing in concentration. There was something intimate and endearing about watching someone you loved when they weren't aware of your gaze.

He cleared his throat.

She looked his way, then jumped down and came over.

"Sebastian, what a surprise." The warmth in her voice and her smile eased the tension of his mission and the discomfort he felt at being surrounded by female fripperies.

Now that he was here, the words he'd rehearsed stuck in his throat. He stood there, turning his hat over and over in his hands. Snow melted on his great coat, and still he said nothing.

"Is something wrong?" Faith asked.

"No. I....something is right, I hope." The words rushed back to him. "Will you do me the honor of becoming my wife?"

She stared at him. "Oh Sebastian. Are you sure? Don't say it if you're not sure."

"I'm sure," he said.

She smiled and he reached out and hugged her just as Widow Bowman pushed aside the curtain that led to the back room. Her wooden cane made a thumping sound as she pushed into the room.

"What did I just hear?" she asked in a voice raspy with age.

Sebastian turned red.

"Sebastian asked me to marry him."

"And your answer?"

Faith turned to Sebastian. "Yes," she said, voice firm and eyes shining. "My answer is yes."

Sebastian tiptoed down the hall to Faith's room, wincing as a board squeaked under his foot. Widow Bowman had agreed that in light of the snowstorm, Sebastian could spend the night asleep on furs in the front room. After she retired, he and Faith had spent a few precious minutes hugging and kissing. Desire flared in him, and he felt certain from Faith's rapid breathing and the way she clung to him, that Faith felt it too. Reluctantly, not wanting to pressure her, he'd forced himself to pull away. But as she retired for the evening, she whispered an invitation in his ear. For a moment, he worried that she was doing what she'd done with her late husband: giving the man what he wanted regardless of her own desires. Or perhaps she was uncertain of his resolve and wanted to bind him to her. He looked at her questioningly as she walked away. She smiled over her shoulder, nodded, then entered her bedroom, leaving the door slightly ajar.

Now, he paused, listened for any sounds he'd awakened the widow asleep farther back in the house. All was quiet. When he tiptoed into Faith's room, she lay under the quilt clad in a white nightgown. Shivering in the chilly room, he shucked off his pants and joined her, unable to stop himself from trembling with eagerness as well as cold. Any doubts he'd entertained about whether they should wait until the wedding disappeared when his hand touched hers. After all, they were both adults and widowed. And now they were engaged.

"It's cold under here," he said.

"It will soon be warm enough," she whispered. Her breath so close to his ear sent a shiver through him. He'd planned to woo her gently, take his time. But the minute he pressed his body against hers through the nightclothes, he felt a fresh surge of desire. He put his arms around her and drew her to him in a long kiss, then loosened the drawstring on her nightgown and cupped her breast in his hand. A sigh escaped him. It had been too long.

He hesitated a moment.

"It's all right," she said, feeling his arousal.

Then without another word, he kissed her again and again. Her lips parted in response and in a few minutes, he raised her nightgown above her hips and entered her, barely able to withdraw before spilling his seed, lest there be a child before wedlock. When it was over, he kissed her and dropped beside her, satiated, but worried about her reaction.

"I know I was too quick," he said.

"It was fine," she said.

"But it's better if we take more time."

"I give you pleasure," she said. "What more could I ask for?"

He laughed, almost a growl. "Wait a little bit and I'll show you," he said.

"Do you feel like talking?" she asked.

Truthfully, all he wanted was to lie there spent and bask in the relaxation that permeated every pore.

"If you wish," he said.

"I was wondering where we would live. We have to plan for the future."

The future. The word had meaning now. It shone before him like a pale sun peeking out after unending rain.

"For now, I thought I'd build a small cabin in the lower field here," he said. "When the war ends, we can go back to my farm at Wysox and start over."

"That sounds good. How does Jane feel about that?"

"I haven't told her yet. But I'm sure she'll be fine once she's used to the idea."

"I hope so. I don't think she likes me very much."

"She'll learn to, once she gets to know you. She's been through a lot."

"We all have," Faith said.

Sebastian lay quietly for a moment, then he spoke in the darkness. "Someday we'll have sons of our own." For a second he thought of Lydia and the sons he would never see again. Pain filled him, but he pushed it away. Staying single wouldn't bring them back. Better to think of what lay ahead, than dwell on the unhappy past.

"I hope we have sons together, too," Faith said. "Tall, slender ones like you."

She snuggled against him and desire filled him. It was like being eighteen again, the way he responded so quickly.

"Let's try that again, more slowly," he said, cupping her breast in his hand.

This time, when they finished, she spoke haltingly. "That was.... never.... my goodness."

He laughed, pleased. Later, as he fell asleep, he thought of Jane. If only she would be as happy about this as he was.

As Jane and her father walked through the woods near the farm, she reveled in the way the snow coated the branches of the fir tree.

"Fresh snow is so pretty," she said.

"Yes, it is." Snow crunched underfoot. He brushed against a tree, and a clump fell to the ground beside them. "Jane, there's something I need to tell you," he said.

She braced herself for more bad news.

"Faith and I plan to marry at the end of March. You'll have a new mother. And after the war is over, we can leave Round Top and go back to Wysox."

"I don't need a new mother," Jane said, kicking at clumps of snow. "I don't want a new mother."

"I know she'll never replace your mother, but you're getting older. In a few more years, you'll be starting your own home."

It felt funny to hear him talk that way, although she had noticed young Luther Vanderhook in church recently. Luther, two years her senior, had winked at her several times, and once he called her "Red" as they left the service.

"That's a few years from now. I can cook and clean for you until then."

She knew she was being unreasonable, but it felt wrong. Faith was only seven years older than she was. And Papa was almost forty. Ancient. Of course, lots of widowers married younger women. But still.

"Don't make this difficult," he said. "Don't you want me to be happy?"

She kicked at the snow again, harder. The thought of Faith back at the farm, tending her mother's flowers, cooking at her mother's hearth, filled her with a confusing mix of anger and sadness.

"Yes," she said. "I want you to be happy."

"Then you'll give Faith a chance."

"I'll try, Papa. I wish..."

He waited for her to finish.

"Nothing," she said. "I need some time to get used to the idea. I only found out a few months ago that Mama and the boys were gone. I still miss her so much."

"I know," he said, laying his hand on her shoulder. "I miss her, too. But she would want us to go on. Everything will be all right. You'll see."

March, 1779

Lydia smiled as Henry picked maple sugar candy from the snow and crunched it, smacking his lips at the taste. The sweet smell of boiling sap filled the air. After a long, hard winter inside Fort Niagara, it was wonderful to be allowed outside to help with maple sugaring. Trevor Wheeler, the young private she'd gotten to know as a friend in the past few months, was among those guarding the small group of women and children.

She walked over to him, bringing a cookie. He closed his eyes for a second as he bit into it.

"Thanks. That tastes good," he said.

"Are you sure the Indian women and children will be coming?" she asked.

"That's what I was told. I hope your little boy is among them. But, please, don't do anything to get yourself or me in trouble."

"I won't," she said. Just to see Isaac would have to be enough.

When she spotted the first Indian women coming through the woods, she was carrying buckets of sap from a trough by a tree to the boiling kettles. And there was Isaac, dressed in Indian clothing and slightly taller now, but his light hair made him instantly recognizable. Her step faltered, then she recovered and sat the buckets down near the fire. She'd argued and pleaded before and it had changed nothing. This time, she would watch and wait. This was only Step One in her plan. Trevor had led her to a bigger fish, one of the Army surgeons, Roswell Kingsley. She'd spent weeks cultivating Kingsley and impressing him with her knowledge of herbal medicine. In winter, nothing had been possible. But with luck, he'd let her go out to gather herbs in the spring and summer. Then opportunity might present itself to find out more about the layout of the Indian village and where Isaac was being kept. What would happen after that, she didn't know. But the knowledge might somehow be useful later.

For now, she feasted on the sight of Isaac, trudging along with other Indian children. Rebecca went immediately to the troughs of sap beneath the trees. Lydia edged closer to Isaac. His gaze passed over her. Then, uncertainly it shifted back. His brow wrinkled and his lips formed the word Mama. Her resolve to just watch evaporated. She jerked her head sideways and motioned him to move over under the trees. With a quick glance at Rebecca, who was talking with another woman, she went over to stand beside him, afraid to kneel lest she call too much attention to them.

"Isaac, it's Mama," she said. "How are you, son?"

"Mama? Is it really you?"

"Yes, son. It's Mama."

He spoke to her in a mixture of English and Seneca, and she put her hand to her mouth. Was he losing his English? She tried again. "Are you well?"

"Yes," he said in English.

She looked toward Rebecca again.

"Do they treat you kindly?"

"Yes. I like my new mama. But I miss you."

"I'm your mother. I will try to come for you when the weather is warmer," Lydia said. "Then we can go home again to Papa and Henry and Jane."

He took a step toward her. Quickly, she bent and hugged him. Letting go was torture. "Remember, your name is Isaac Strope," she said. Rebecca looked their way and Lydia turned and hurried away, leaving Isaac staring after her.

He's going to forget who he is, she thought. God help me to get my son back — and soon.

Chapter Twenty Five

Sebastian stroked the covers of the Strope family Bible. In a few weeks, he and Faith would marry. But now, as dawn flooded his bedroom with a pink glow, he sat quietly remembering Lydia. He could picture her clearly, stabbing with her finger to locate a Bible passage for guidance, then declaiming what the verse meant. I'll never forget you, he thought. But I have to go on.

He leafed through the Bible, lingering over the pages her hands had touched, then stopped at the section that recorded family history. Elisha Gideon Strope, the most recent entry read: Born May 20, 1778.

Margaretha's son. The child would be almost a year old by now. The handwriting looked like Lydia's. He stared at the date again.

"My God," he whispered. Zach said the baby was born several weeks after they were taken prisoner. But the date in the Bible was the night they were captured. Lydia would never put something in the Bible that wasn't true. Had Zach lied?

If he lied about that, could he have lied about Lydia's death? At Forty Fort, he'd said not to worry. Later at Stroudsburg he said she was dead. Slowly, Sebastian reconstructed the scene in his mind. At the time he'd been too dazed to notice much. Now he recalled the way Zach had hesitated and looked at Faith, then hemmed and hawed about exactly how Lydia died.

What would be his motive? An ugly suspicion rose in Sebastian. Lydia was an attractive woman and a captive. If Zach had harmed her, he'd kill him with his bare hands.

The important thing was she and Henry might be alive. And Isaac might not be adopted by Indians. His family might be restored to him. A joy sharper than any knife ever honed pierced him. Traume sind Schaume, he reminded himself quickly. Dreams are foam. And foam evaporates.

Abruptly, he thought of Faith, whom he loved, too. What a tangle. They couldn't marry until he found out whether Lydia was dead. And then there was Jane. He had to sort this out before he even hinted at the possibility her mother was alive.

He sat a little longer with the Bible on his lap, absorbing the new situation and planning. He'd have to tell Faith and swear her to secrecy. God knew how she would react. Then he'd go to Zach's home in Stroudsburg and see if he could find him and get the truth out of him, one way or another. Steeling himself, he went to saddle his horse for the long ride to town to talk with Faith.

He found her sweeping the stoop of the shop. When she saw him, her face lit up. He tried and failed to produce an answering smile. She looked at him questioningly.

"Let's walk around back where we can talk," he said. She smiled again, and followed him.

And so he spilled out the story. When he finished, Faith was silent, staring at the ground.

"Life never goes the way we wish, does it," she said, raising her eyes to look at him. "I should have known this was too good to be true."

"We don't know anything for sure yet," he said. "I'm sorry."

"May God forgive me, but I hardly know what to wish for," she said.

He could think of no good answer. As he looked at her, he realized although he loved her, his heart still yearned for Lydia.

"I know it's a tangle," he said. "I'll be back with news as soon as I can."

She reached up and kissed him on the cheek. "God speed," she said in a strangled voice. "Do what you must. And so will I."

She turned away abruptly, leaving him staring after her.

Jane watched Uncle Wilhelm escort Faith into the kitchen of the farmhouse. Lately, life at Round Top had been like staring at the ripples in a muddy pond. You knew something made the ripples. But nothing showed beneath the surface, leaving you to guess. Papa had gone to Stroudsburg, saying he had to look up a man on business. It must be incredibly important business as tense and evasive as he'd been.

Now here was Faith visiting. Jane supposed that part was all right, since she and Papa were going to be married, but even there something strange was going on. Faith didn't act very happy. Maybe she didn't want to marry Papa. Well, Jane would just have to watch. You could learn a lot by studying people's expressions and listening to the way they said things. Like now. Uncle Wilhelm held Faith's elbow as if she didn't know her way or might fall. Faith looked down at his hand, then up at him and smiled. Something is going on, Jane thought, and I don't like it.

Stroudsburg was a sleepier village now that the flood of refugees had mostly moved on. It should be easier to find Zach, if he were still here, Sebastian thought. Zach had said this was his home, but he seemed like someone who went where the river took him.

Sebastian found the pastor, Samuel Strait, at home. "Can I help you?" Strait asked.

"I'm Sebastian Strope."

The pastor continued to look at him politely. "I'm sorry. Have we met?"

"I was one of those who fled here from Forty Fort. You loaned me a horse to go in search of my daughter, Jane, and I brought it back again."

The pastor's face cleared. "Ah yes. There were so many who needed help it is hard to keep them all straight. Did you find her?"

"Not immediately. But she's home at last."

"God be praised. Now I remember. You had just found out your wife and son had been killed by Indians. A terrible blow. How are you faring?"

"That's what I want to talk to you about," Sebastian said.

"Come in and be welcome."

The interior of the home was clean, but cluttered. More books than Sebastian had ever seen lay piled on the floor and on a desk by a window.

"Excuse the way things look," Strait said. "My wife is off visiting her sister, and I fear I'm not as neat as she is."

Sebastian laughed. "What man is as neat as a woman would want him to be?"

Strait removed books from a chair, motioned him to a seat and sat down across from him. "Now, what brings you to Stroudsburg?"

"I'm in search of a man named Zach Wilson. Do you know where I might find him?" Sebastian's voice was harsh and Strait looked at him.

"The trader. Why do you ask?"

"Because I think he might have lied to me about my wife being dead." The flat statement hung in the air.

Strait sat back in his chair. "My Lord. Why do you think that?"

Sebastian found himself telling the bare bones of the entry in the Bible. His relationship with Faith was his own business.

"And what will you do if you find he has lied?"

Beat the bastard half to death, Sebastian thought. Would the reverend understand an impulse like that? He skirted the truth. "I can't rightly say."

"Vengeance is mine. I will repay, sayeth the Lord," Strait said. "It isn't for us to do."

"So we just turn the other cheek? That's a good way to get slapped."

"I know it's difficult. But it is what our Lord commands."

That's what Lydia would say, Sebastian thought. Or, if she was still alive, maybe captivity had changed her, made her as angry as he was right now.

But there was no use arguing with the pastor. "Do you know where I might find Zach?" he asked.

Strait looked at him a second, then sighed. "He travels a lot, but I believe he just got back. His is the third house on the left on the second street over after you leave here."

As Strait said goodbye, he put a hand on Sebastian's shoulder. "Remember what I said about vengeance."

"Thanks for your help, Pastor. Be well," Sebastian said.

Zach answered the door, looking as if he'd just awakened, even though it was nine in the morning. He yawned and ran his fingers through his tousled hair, then stepped back as he realized who was at his doorstep.

"Sebastian Strope. What do you want?" he said.

"To talk."

"I'm half asleep. Come back later. We can talk then." He started to close the door.

Sebastian pushed his way in. "I would appreciate it if you made time now," he said.

Zach scowled, then shrugged. "If it's that urgent. Give me a minute to get myself together."

While Sebastian waited, he looked around. Trade goods, ranging from bundles of fur to jugs of whiskey, lined the walls and filled half the floor. An odor of rum wafted from an open bottle on a table. Streaks of mud covered the wooden floor. No woman here, then.

When Zach returned, his demeanor had changed. "Sorry if I was a mite churlish. I'm always grouchy in the morning. Let's start over." He stuck out his hand with a smile, and Sebastian took it. He could be wrong about Zach.

"Now, what can I do for you?" He waved a hand at the clutter. "I'd ask you to sit down, but as you can see, there ain't much room."

The two stood facing each other. "When you and I talked, you said Margaretha's baby was born several weeks after they arrived at Forty Fort," Sebastian said. "But the entry in our family Bible says the baby was born the night they were captured. I wondered if you could explain that."

"I guess my memory was faulty."

"The entry was in Lydia's handwriting. She wouldn't have had pen and ink on the trail. And it would have taken a few days to find writing material, I would think. But you said she was killed the day she arrived at Forty Fort."

"What difference does the day make? She's dead. Look, I'm sorry for your loss, but I can't help you."

Maybe I'm going about this the wrong way, Sebastian thought. When you want to catch game, you don't charge straight at it. You sidle up gradual like.

"How have you been since Forty Fort?" Sebastian asked. "I hope things have gone well with you."

"Tolerable. Thanks for asking."

"I imagine your relatives were happy to see you safe and sound. I know mine were." I wish Lydia were here, Sebastian thought. She's better at this.

"My relatives and me, well, never mind. I'm glad for you if your affairs are looking up."

"Thank you. About my wife and son, I can see how a man could make a mistake in a confusing situation like new captives coming in. If you have even a glimmer of hope for me, I'd surely like to know."

He stood with his hands at his side, looking earnestly at Zach.

"Look, I allowed as how I was sorry," Zach said. "but I can't help you. And I don't appreciate you keeping on like this. Now, if you don't mind…" He gestured toward the door. Sebastian half turned, but hesitated. Impatiently, Zach pushed his shoulder.

Sebastian took a deep breath, fighting for control. "There's no need for that," he said, planting his feet firmly. "But I have to know for sure."

"Get out," Zach said, and pushed him again.

At Zach's touch, Sebastian's frustration spilled over. He swung around, knocking the trader backward. Zach lurched, caught his balance and swung at him. Sebastian ducked. He fell to his knees with Zach landing on top of him. They tussled on the floor, rolling back and forth, hitting packages and bottles. Sebastian felt a bottle break under him. He twisted to avoid being cut by a shard of glass. Zach took advantage of the moment to grab the stem of the bottle and slash at him with the jagged edge.

Sebastian yelped as the bottle cut the back of his hand. He grabbed for it and wrested it from Zach. Panting, Sebastian threw himself over Zach. He held the bottle inches from Zach's face with one hand and throttled his neck with the other.

"Now," Sebastian grated. "Tell me the truth."

"I done told you the truth already."

Sebastian tightened his grip and pushed the bottle closer.

"The truth, or you'll be minus an eye."

"All right, you bastard. I lied. Your wife is alive."

Sebastian eased his pressure on Zach's throat. Did he dare believe him?

"My son too?"

"Yes, damn you."

Zach glared at him. "You know what else? She gave herself to me. How do you like that?"

The temptation to maim Zach filled Sebastian and he pressed the bottle closer while Zach closed his eyes with a look of horror. At the last second, Sebastian pulled the bottle away. He couldn't do it.

"You're lying. Lydia would never do that."

"Am I? How'd she get that little crescent scar on her thigh? And she loved it, too, having a real man."

Sebastian raked Zach's ear with the bottle, opening a deep jagged cut. Zach twisted under him and pulled free, knocking Sebastian aside as he surged to his feet.

"Get out of my house before I kill you," Zach snarled, clutching his ear.

Trembling with adrenaline, Sebastian backed away and walked out into the street while Zach slammed the door.

Sebastian stood dazed in the sunlight, blood dripping from the cut on his hand. I've got to do something, but what, he thought. I don't know where Lydia is. I can't prove he's done anything illegal. I attacked him first. The authorities won't help me.

At last, he mounted his horse and rode to the stable, where he watered his horse, downed a sketchy meal, and decided to get some rest, clear his head before he made his next move. But visions of Zach assaulting his wife filled his mind. No matter what the fellow said, he refused to believe Lydia gave herself to Zach willingly. That was like saying apples fell upward or rivers flowed backward. Not his Lydia.

Nonetheless, he rode back to Zach's house and banged on the door, but there was no answer. He tried again that evening with no better luck. Finally, a neighbor told him that Zach had left town, destination unknown.

After a sleepless night, Sebastian realized there was nothing more he could do here. At least Zach had given him one precious, if tainted, gift: Henry and Lydia were alive. He yet might hold his wife in his arms, work side by side with her on the farm, talk about simple things like how the crops were growing in the evening by lamplight.. As he began the long trip back to Round Top, the idea lifted his spirits a little, despite the painful conversation with Faith that lay ahead.

Jane stood in the woods near her grandparents' farmhouse and hugged herself. It was a frosty spring morning, barely above freezing, but she wanted to be alone. Her breath made little puffs of steam in the cold air. Around her, wooden buckets hung from maple trees tapped for the spring sugaring. Mama is alive, she thought. It was the most wonderful news in the world. Arms flung wide, she whirled around and around, screaming the news to the trees, until she collapsed in a heap on the frozen ground.

Then she sat, breathless, and leaned against a tree. She hugged her knees close to her to keep warm and thought about the other, not-so-wonderful things that were happening. A whirlpool in the Susquehanna is calmer than this farm, she thought. Papa had returned from Stroudsburg with the news that Mama and Henry were alive. He was happy about it, but he seemed worried, too. The next day he rode into town to see Faith. When he came back, he said the wedding was off. That was good, even if it was hard on Faith. Wilhelm had smiled at the news and Papa had started chopping firewood like he wanted to turn it to splinters.

Jane shivered a little in the cold, then gave a little shrug. She was sorry about everyone's problems, but only one thing mattered. Mama and Henry were alive.

A sudden thought struck her. First, Papa had been sure Mama was dead. Now he was sure she was alive. What if he were wrong again? Once Jane would have said that life couldn't be that cruel. Now, she wasn't so sure.

Chapter Twenty Six

May 1779

The shad were running on the Hudson River near Round Top. Jane waded barefoot into the water with the other children, grabbing the fish caught in the net stretched across a channel and throwing them on the bank to twist and jump like silver in the sun. All around her other men, women and children were doing the same. Luther Vanderhook splashed water on her, grinning, and she splashed back. Life seemed better these days. Even Papa smiled as a particularly big shad dashed past him, jumped high in the air and escaped the net, flashing away to safety.

"He deserves to live for a leap like that," he said. Wilhelm beside him nodded, then glanced toward the bank where Faith, along with other women from the area, was setting out food under the trees for a community picnic. Jane watched as her father followed his brother's glance and lost his smile.

Love was so strange. It seemed as if it could make you happy and sad and angry and calm. She wondered what it would be like to love a young man. Lately, she'd been having thoughts like that more often. Another year and a half and she'd be sixteen and of an age to consider marriage.

"Hey, Red. Watch out," Luther called, and splashed her again.

"Watch out yourself," she said, splashing back.

Later, as she sat on the bank in the sun letting her skirts dry, she saw Luther talking to her father. In a few minutes, Luther came over.

"There's a pretty patch of wild phlox in bloom along the creek," he said. "All white and purple and kind of a deep blue. Smells real pretty. Want to go see it? Your father says it's all right as long as we stay in shouting distance." He smiled and lifted his eyebrows inquiringly.

"Um. Fine," she said.

As they approached the creek, she could smell the phlox perfuming the air. Dogwood blossoms burst forth where openings in the trees provided dappled shade. Dogwood had been in bloom a year ago when the Indians swooped down on the farm in Wysox and everyone's world changed.

"Here now, why so serious?" Luther said.

"It's nothing," she said, although it was everything. She cast about for something to say, but conversation had deserted her. They stood awkwardly on the bank of the creek. Here and there purple and white violets still bloomed. She was intensely conscious of his presence, the way sunlight lit his curly, brown hair, the faint heat she felt or imagined radiating off his body.

"The creek sounds nice, doesn't it?" she said when the silence stretched on.

"Sure does," he said. "I like sometimes to just sit and listen to it."

She looked at him with fresh interest. "So do I," she said. "It makes me feel peaceful inside."

"Wanna sit?"

They sank down beside the water and watched it flow. Tentatively, he reached out and put his hand over hers. Startled, she resisted the impulse to pull her hand away. After a moment, he curled his fingers around hers.

"Do you like dogs?" she asked.

"Sure."

"I have a little dog named Gertie that I got at Forty Fort."

"Yeah? We've got a big farm dog, the same as everybody does. She's pretty old now and starting to go blind and deaf. I kind of watch out for her as best I can." They sat quietly a little longer.

"I thought I might come visiting Saturday night," he said at last. He let the sentence hang there as if half afraid to make it a question or request.

A faint, pleasant heat rose in her cheeks. "That would be nice," she said.

"Good."

His grip tightened on her hand and they sat a while longer until she heard her father calling her.

In the cool of Saturday evening, Sebastian sat on a bench outside the kitchen door and watched Luther and Jane stroll around the farmhouse yard. The boy had been quiet at supper, and the young people didn't seem to talk much, but they walked close together and looked at each other often. It was hard to believe his little girl was old enough to attract boys. If only Lydia were here to see it.

He listened to the sound of crickets and the rustle of the breeze in the trees. Wilhelm had gone to see Faith, and everyone else was inside. It was left to him to play chaperone. He welcomed the isolation and the time to think. It still hurt to lose Faith, even while he tried to be glad for his brother. But most of all, it hurt to think about what Zach said. He refused to believe Lydia had slept with Zach willingly, but something had happened between them. Otherwise, how would he know about the scar? He must have forced her. The thought made Sebastian sick. Zach kissing her, caressing her thigh, entering her. Sebastian shook his head back and forth like a bull getting ready to charge. He knew it wasn't her fault, and yet…true, he'd lain with Faith, but that was different, wasn't it? They were engaged and he thought Lydia was dead.

Then there was Kathleen. Jane had asked him if Kathleen could come back to the farm in Wysox with them when the war was over. "She might want to be with her mother's people," he'd told her. "Folks won't look too kindly on Indians after all that's happened."

Jane hadn't raised the subject again. But he knew what she hoped.

I've treated Kathleen kindly, he thought. She's an innocent child. But every time I look at her I see double: a sweet little girl and a symbol of everything the Indians have done to me and my family.

He straightened on the bench. A man couldn't help what he thought, only what he did.

The figures of Jane and Luther were cast in shadow as the sun dipped behind the hills. He started to call to them. Luther needed to start the long ride home. Movement in the field caught his attention. He rose to his feet and called to Jane.

A figure staggered toward him across the yard. He wished he had his rifle until he recognized Scarred Fox, a local Indian. So the old drunk was back, probably wanting a handout. He hadn't been around for a while. Sebastian had hoped he was gone for good. Some people became amorous or maudlin or playful when they drank. Scarred Fox became mean.

Sebastian rose to his feet as Luther and Jane came up. Scarred Fox mumbled a greeting. Dirt stained his breechclout. The scars on his chest and arms that gave him his name, souvenirs of burns from a campfire in childhood, shone palely in the fading light.

"Bastian, I heard you are back." He peered at Jane. "All grown up now."

She nodded uncertainly.

"Go in the house, Jane," Sebastian said. Luther moved to his side. "You, too, Luther. I'll handle this."

Luther glanced at Jane. "I want to stay."

"Inside," Sebastian repeated.

Luther frowned, but he and Jane went in the house.

Once they were gone, Sebastian turned to Scarred Fox. "What do you want?"

"Tobacco. Whiskey."

"Tobacco I've got. You've had enough whiskey."

Scarred Fox scowled. "Always you white men know what's best for Indians. Give me whiskey now. I will give you a nice fur later."

"No whiskey," Sebastian said. "Stay here and I'll get you some tobacco. Then be on your way."

Scarred Fox poked a finger in Sebastian's chest. "Whiskey."

Sebastian pushed the hand away. Scarred Fox poked him again and giggled.

The whirlpool of anger that had swirled in Sebastian for months swept away any semblance of calm and he knocked Scarred Fox to the ground, then stepped back, fists clenched.

Scarred Fox touched his jaw where Sebastian had struck him and staggered to his feet.

"Big mistake," Scarred Fox mumbled and lurched off into the darkness.

Sebastian stared after him. What was happening to him? He never would have struck a man in anger before all this happened. I need to get away, he thought. A sergeant had come to the village last week asking for volunteers to join General Sullivan's march on the Indian villages in upper New York state, Indians friendly to the British like Queen Esther.

He thought of the Hartley expedition he'd gone on the previous year that had led to the discovery of Lydia's Bible. Maybe this new expedition would let him find fresh news of his family. He yearned for news, especially after his encounter with that bastard Zach. He clenched his jaw at thought of Zach, then forced himself to breathe deeply. He'd volunteer in the morning. Maybe fighting in a good cause would cleanse him. He didn't like the man he was becoming.

Chapter Twenty Seven

August 1779

S ebastian stared across the Susquehanna River at the Standing Stone. The late summer sun beat down and he sweated beneath his linen shirt. Around him, soldiers under the command of General John Sullivan moved about as they prepared to bivouac for the night. Three months ago, when he'd agreed to help shepherd the packhorses for Sullivan's campaign, he'd thought he was getting away for a while. Now, as he looked at Standing Stone and remembered the day Gideon drowned here and the morning more than a year ago that he had halted here on his way to seek help for his family, he realized he'd wandered deeper into the swamp of his unresolved grief and anger. Regardless, it was better to be busy than sitting at home brooding and striking out at innocent people.

He turned to tend to the horses. They'd lost several when they tumbled off the paths along the cliffs and fell on the rocks hundreds of feet below. Still more rugged trails lay ahead. So far, there had been no sign of the enemy, unless you counted a paddle floating down the river, an empty canoe on the bank and a few moccasin prints.

Waterfowl skimmed low over the river and he heard wild turkeys calling in the woods. Behind him, Darius Jones, the soldier he'd met on the earlier Hartley expedition, grumbled. "I'd give a lot if they'd let us shoot some of them for supper. I'm tempted to do it anyway. I'm so damned tired of chewin' on beef. I bet there's not an Indian for miles around to hear a rifle shot. And even if there is, one of us is worth ten of them Indians in a fight."

"Some venison would be a welcome change," Sebastian said. He was getting tired of Darius' complaining, but Darius, oblivious, acted as if the two were close friends.

Tomorrow, the men would spend the night on the banks of Wysox creek near his old farm. The spreading flats made it ideal for an army of several thousand. He wondered how much the wilderness had claimed since his visit last year.

The farm, when they reached it, looked even more decrepit. Some fences had fallen, weeds were taller, poking up between the blackened remains of the house and covering the yard and fields. The springhouse still stood and Lydia's roses were in bloom. The mint in her garden had multiplied, spreading wildly. He picked a leaf, crushed it and smelled it, then threw it to the ground, missing Lydia afresh.

The next day, under threatening skies, they burned an Indian settlement. Fresh tracks showed the inhabitants had fled hours earlier. Sebastian joined the cheers of the men as the flames crackled and smoke billowed.

"Serves them right, don't it?" Darius said.

Sebastian looked at the smoldering timber and remembered the sick feeling he'd had when he first saw the still-smoking ruins of his own farm.

Instead of responding, he squinted up at the thunderheads forming. "Looks like a storm brewing. I need to tend to the horses. Lightning might spook them."

Darius shrugged and stared at the flames.

A few days later, the troops entered Queen Esther's destroyed village with drums beating and fifes playing.

"Hey," one of the men exclaimed as they fanned out, "here's an Indian graveyard. There might be something here worth digging for." He grabbed a shovel, scattering dirt and bones as he dug.

Darius and some of the other men joined him. "Look at this. It has a nice, sharp edge," Darius said. He brandished a tomahawk he'd looted from a grave. "And lookit here. Some mighty pretty beads." He swung a necklace from one finger. "You want it? Maybe for your daughter."

Sebastian looked at the necklace. Maybe it had belonged to some little girl like Kathleen. "No," he said. "You keep it."

Darius stuck the beads in his pocket and fastened the tomahawk to his belt, then wandered away.

At Chemung, in morning fog, they descended on an empty village and burned fifty more houses. "Save some food for the army, then destroy all the rest," an officer ordered. "Let them starve this winter." The men fanned out over the acres of grain and vegetables, slashing at crops with their swords.

"Come on," Darius said. Sebastian plucked a ripe ear from the stalk and pulled back the silk tassel. The full, juicy kernels shone in the sun. It seemed a shame to destroy such a fine crop. But it was a shame for the Indians to destroy settlers' crops too. He picked up a handful of dirt, letting it sift through his fingers. Good rich soil. The kind a farmer wished for.

Dropping the ear, he left the corn field and stamped pumpkin and cucumber vines underfoot until his boots were slick with pulp. More destruction, even if it was necessary in the fight for independence. He watched with mixed emotions while soldiers ran from field to field setting them ablaze. Clouds of dense smoke rose over the valley.

The days melted into each other as the army marched west across the state, burning homes and destroying crops. Occasionally they found a white dog hung in a village as an ineffectual sacrifice to prevent the ongoing rampage.

At night, Sebastian began to dream of flaming homes and awaken thinking he smelled smoke.

Over the rough terrain, packhorses lost their loads and supplies dwindled. Meat and flour rations were cut, and still they marched on.

They awoke one September morning to a dusting of frost. Sebastian and Darius huddled together for warmth at night since they had no blankets. At least, Sebastian thought, his snoring is keeping me from dreaming about things I can't change.

Fodder for nightmares was everywhere. In the woods near Chemussio, they discovered the remains of two American officers who'd been tortured. Their noses, ears and tongues had been cut off, their severed genitals hung from a nearby limb.

"Jesus, " Darius said. "Those damn savages aren't even human."

Sebastian, struggling not to vomit, nodded in agreement.

Then, one morning, they stumbled on two Indians, recently shot to death. Two of the officers skinned the bodies from their hips down.

"For boot legs," Darius said. "Nobody will have a pair like that."

Sebastian turned away, sickened. "We're no better than they are," he muttered.

"Hey," Darius said, "At least they were dead first."

At Kanadasag, they found a naked, emaciated six-year-old white captive. The boy had forgotten most of his English and didn't know his parents' names. Is that what's happening to Isaac? Sebastian wondered. All night, he thought about the boy they'd rescued, and in the morning he asked if he could take the boy home with him. Too late, he was told. An officer had already adopted him. Something good at last, Sebastian thought.

He began to long for home. The anger that had sustained him was replaced by a vast weariness and a yearning for family and the familiar chores of tilling the soil, creating instead of destroying, tending the animals, who at least did not torture each other.

Finally, at the Genesee River, they burned their last village and turned back. Sebastian still had no fresh news about his family. As he stared at still another plume of smoke rising from burning crops and homes, he thought of a verse in Isaiah, one Lydia had quoted on occasion. "They shall beat their swords into plowshares and their spears into pruning hooks."

If only that could be so.

Sebastian sat on his horse looking down at the farmhouse and fields at Round Top, tired from his long journey back to his parents' farm. He had pushed himself, eager to be home with those he loved, in a place where no one was trying to kill anyone.

But how good it would be to see Jane and Faith, his parents and sister and even prickly Wilhelm. He thought of the time when he had stood in this spot with Faith after the massacre at Forty Fort. Now here he was back again, only this time he had been part of the destruction wrought on the Indians. It didn't feel like revenge or even justice. Necessary, he supposed, but it left a sour taste in a man's mouth. He was more than sated with killing, the anger burned out of him.

October was just touching the hills with color. The hay lay in golden stacks in the field, lit by the setting sun. Tomorrow, he would wake up to the sound of roosters crowing instead of the cannon fire that had greeted him many mornings as Sullivan announced his advance. And the only smoke would be from the wood stove as the women prepared food and from the giant chimney that warmed the main room.

He saw cows moving toward the barn. A shift in the wind brought the faint clanking of their bells and he started down. If he hurried, he'd be in time to help with milking.

October 1779

Lydia spooned honey into her red clover tea and sat down heavily at the table in their dwelling at Fort Niagara. Her monthly courses were upon her and the tea would help with cramps. Lydia wondered about Jane. Had her daughter entered her womanhood yet? Had there been a woman there to help her understand what was happening to her body or had she been like Lydia, terrified she was bleeding to death because no one had prepared her?

She looked up to see Margaretha coming toward her.

"Why so pensive, sister?" Margaretha asked, standing in front of her.

"I was thinking of Jane, wondering what is happening with her."

"I know you miss her." Margaretha patted her shoulder. "Such thoughts are fruitless. Thinking of the past only makes us unhappy. Doesn't the Good Book say "Sufficient unto the day is the trouble thereof?""

Lydia nodded. "You're right." She took another sip of tea. "We should count our blessings."

"Indeed. I'm cooking lunch for the officers again today. At least we are here in the fort and not living in an Indian village as servants like so many others."

Margaretha reached behind Lydia and picked up her apron. "I must be off now."

Lydia looked after her sister fondly, glad she wasn't bearing her captivity alone.

She thought back over the past few months. They were a mixture of blessings and hardships.

Her hopes of finding a way to be with Isaac had dimmed. She saw him occasionally, but almost always from a distance. Supported by the recommendation of the fort's surgeon, Dr. Kingsley, she and Margaretha had made several welcome forays to the woods to gather herbs, starting with bloodroot in spring to alleviate the cough that so many soldiers had acquired over the winter. But always guards accompanied them, and none of her wild schemes of escape or a visit to the Indian village where Isaac lived bore fruit.

Still, she had made friends among the other women, exchanged remedies, minded their children, taught a few young ones their alphabet, worshipped at Sabbath services. Sunrise this morning had been glorious and she had stood for a few moments drinking it in, letting nature fill her soul with calm. Yes, she felt she had learned some patience as the routine days drifted by.

She put down her cup. Time to mend for the third time what was left of Henry's ragged shirt. Somehow she would have to find new shoes for him, although with the way he mostly ran barefoot, the soles of his feet were like leather.

She sat down again, needle and shirt in hand, only to see Margaretha hurrying toward her.

"I just heard," Margaretha said. "They're moving some prisoners to LaChine."

Oh no, Lydia thought. Not LaChine. It was hundreds of miles away on the other side of Canada near Montreal. She might lose track of Isaac forever.

If she and Henry were moved, would Margaretha, Elisha and John go with them, or would the officers decide they didn't want to lose their cook?

And would Rebecca or Queen Esther use whatever influence they might have to send her away from Isaac?

"Do we know how they're choosing who goes?" she asked.

"I have no idea. The news just came."

"I pray we can stay here," Lydia said. "I pray we can."

December 1779

Another Christmas, another birthday, her fifteenth and this one happier than the last, Jane thought. She looked around the table at the family and guests beaming at her, then removed the colored paper from the present on her plate.

It was a pair of leather gloves, dyed red.

"It's beautiful, Papa," she said, throwing her arms around him. He smiled fondly. Papa had been different since he came back from fighting the Indians. He wouldn't talk about what he'd seen or done, but he didn't seem as irritable and he was quieter. Even the fact Wilhelm and Faith were seeing each other steadily didn't seem to bother him that much. Sometimes at night, she heard him cry out and knew he was having a bad dream, but outwardly he seemed more like her old Papa. As long as she didn't mention Mama. That always made him tighten his lips, then talk about something else. It worried her. Did he know something about Mama that he was afraid to tell her?

Now Faith pulled out a package and handed it to Jane. It was a pair of intricately embroidered linen pillowcases. "For your hope chest," Faith said. All eyes turned to Luther, who was sitting to Jane's right, a visitor for this special occasion. He ducked his head and Jane blushed. Now that she was fifteen it was high time to be collecting items for the day she'd have a home of her own. Luther was still courting her, and she was enjoying the attention.

"It's lovely," Jane said. "Thank you."

"I saw old Scarred Fox the other day," Johann said. "Drunk as usual. He was looking for a handout, and it being Yuletide and all, I gave him some tobacco and food. He asked if you were here, Sebastian, and I told him you were working in the barn with Jacob and Wilhelm. Did you see him?"

"No. I can't say as I did," Sebastian said. "That suits me. Last time, he created a ruckus and I was stern with him. Too stern, I realize looking back."

"Well," Maria said, "maybe we've seen the last of him. How about some dessert?" She sat a cobbler made with dried apples on the table.

When everyone had finished the last crumbs, Faith turned to Jane. "Wilhelm and I are going over to see the Ridenhours. I hear they have a litter of puppies. Would you like to come with us?"

Luther laughed. "A litter of puppies. You know she would."

Wilhelm drove the sleigh with reckless abandon. It careened over the snow, throwing Faith against him, and Jane against Luther in the back seat. Maybe that was the idea, Jane thought. The wind nipped at her nose. She put her hands, clad in her new gloves, over her nose to warm it, but soon the cold penetrated even the gloves.

"Here, cover your head with the blanket," Luther said, and pulled it over them.

She giggled as he reached over and kissed her in the darkness. She liked his kisses. They made her stomach feel funny.

"Isn't this better?" he said.

"Yes," she whispered.

After a few more kisses, he reached out and put his hand on her breast, fumbling with the fastenings on her coat. This was new. She pushed his hand away. He waited a few seconds, then put it back again, cupping her breast in his hands through the cloth and breathing heavily.

"Stop that," she said.

"What's the harm?" he asked. "No one can see us and we can't do anything we shouldn't with them here."

"I just…" She felt confused at the feelings sweeping over her and sat up straight, uncovering her head.

Luther made one more try under the blanket.

"I said stop it," she said more loudly than she intended.

Faith looked back at them.

"Is everything all right?" she asked.

"Oh, they're just having fun," Wilhelm said. "Boys will be boys when girls are girls."

"Sometimes girls don't want boys to be boys," Faith said, her tone so serious Wilhelm turned his head to look at her.

"What do you mean?" he asked.

"Nothing," she said. "Forget it."

On the way back home, tired after the visit but delighted to have gotten a chance to play with the puppies, Jane watched the snow reflect the moonlight and leaned her head back against the seat. A long day, but a good one. The wind had moderated and the cold no longer bit at them. Wilhelm drove more slowly and she felt herself getting sleepy. Beside her, Luther had drifted off.

She closed her eyes. In a few minutes, Wilhelm spoke to Faith. "Is Jane asleep?"

"It looks like they both are," she said.

"Good. Now, what did you mean when you said that about sometimes girls don't want boys to be boys? Has someone been bothering you? Was it Sebastian?"

"Sebastian would never do anything against a woman's will," she said. "I was thinking of my late husband. He, you know, he would drink and then he wanted…" Her voice trailed off.

"I know what he wanted. Don't say any more," Wilhelm said, his voice tight. For a few minutes the only sound was the clop of the horses' hooves, the swish of the runners over snow and the gentle snoring of Luther.

"So did Sebastian do something that wasn't against your will?" Wilhelm asked.

"Stop it," Faith said. "You're always too suspicious. You think the gentlemen who come into the shop with their wives are trying to flirt with me. No, you think I'm trying to flirt with them. You have to trust me or this can't work between us."

"I do trust you," he said. "It's other men I don't trust. But you didn't answer me. Did Sebastian do something he shouldn't?"

Jane kept her eyes closed and tried to block out the idea that Papa might have slept with Faith. The idea made her uncomfortable. Mama would be furious if she knew.

"What I did or didn't do with Sebastian has nothing to do with us," Faith said.

"So you say. I'll…" His voice sank and Jane missed the last few words.

"Please don't, Wilhelm," Faith said.

Scared, although she wasn't sure of what, Jane coughed loudly. Faith jerked and Wilhelm cracked the whip over the horses' backs, urging them on until the sleigh swayed from side to side the rest of the ride home.

Chapter Twenty Eight

January, 1780

As the line of Indians and captives moved across the frozen landscape, headed for the camp at LaChine near Montreal, the cold seemed to penetrate to Lydia's bones. Henry coughed as they stumbled across the snow, walking in the footsteps of the person ahead of them. This was the most terrible winter anyone could remember. Every day brought freezing temperatures and more snow until the world seemed made only of white snow and the black skeletons of trees. Even the trees are suffering, she thought, staring at an elm stripped of bark by hungry moose. She didn't even turn her head away as they passed still another deer dead of starvation, lying half covered by the snow and gnawed by animals.

"Mama, I'm cold," Henry said.

"I know, son. Hang on. We'll be there soon."

The evening before, wandering with the Indian women in search of elm bark and acorns to make a thin soup, they'd slept beside a stream in a bed of hemlock boughs. Lydia didn't know a person could shiver that much. Starving wolves, thin gray wraiths, had howled around the campfire in a ghostly circle, their eyes glowing by the firelight. If only the sun would come out and warm them. It would be worth being half blinded by the glare off the snow.

Ahead of her an Indian woman slipped and fell. Lydia reached down to help her, and the woman nodded in appreciation. The Indians are in no better shape than we are, Lydia thought. The crops that would have fed everyone through the winter had gone up in smoke when Sullivan marched across upstate New York.

"I'm hungry," Henry said.

Like all of them, he was thin to the point of emaciation. It made the cold that much harder to bear. And walking became such an effort.

Lydia sighed. "I know, son," she said. It seemed to be the only answer she could give these days. When the winter began, they'd reveled in all the snow, catching it on their tongues and laughing, sweeping out snow angels in the drifts, tromping a circle to play the game of Fox Chases Geese. Now winter seemed like a living thing, a malevolent white giant, strong and unyielding. She hoped Margaretha and Elisha were faring better back at Fort Niagara.

"My feet are cold," Henry said. Their shoes had worn out. Now, like the Indians, they wore high-topped moccasins waterproofed with beeswax and tallow, but snow kept getting inside and melting.

"Henry," Lydia admonished, "stop complaining. Everyone is tired and hungry and cold. Nothing can be done about it."

He looked at her with eyes welling with tears, tears that froze on his cheeks.

"I'm sorry," she said. "I'll tell you what. Let's remember funny things. You start."

"All right. Umm, catching fireflies and putting one down Jane's back."

Lydia smiled. "That's a good one. Let's see. The time the pig put its nose in the grain bucket and got stuck and ran around with the bucket on its head."

Henry laughed. "How about the Christmas when Papa was pretending to be Der Belsnickel and his beard fell off. He picked it up and held it on with his hand, but I knew who he was."

I don't even know if Sebastian is alive or dead, Lydia thought.

"Yes, that was funny," she said, with a catch in her voice. "That's enough remembering for now."

Sunday service was over. Jane stood outside the church stamping her chilled feet and hoping her grandparents would stop socializing soon so they could go home to Round Top where it was warm.

Luther walked up beside her. She hadn't seen him since the night they'd ridden back in the sleigh from the Ridenhours. Now she nodded tentatively.

"I'm sorry about what happened in the sleigh," Luther blurted. "When I'm close to you like that it's hard to stop."

She thought of Faith, who usually bent herself into a pretzel to do whatever Wilhelm wanted. She never wanted to be like that.

"You better stop when I say stop or I'm not seeing you any more," Jane said.

He lowered his voice as more people came out of the church. "But you like it when we kiss," he said.

"Yes, I do, but Grandmama says girls need to be careful about some things."

"You talked to your grandmother about me?" He reddened and his voice, which had deepened in the past year, cracked.

"Not exactly you, but in general."

"Now I'll be embarrassed to face her."

"Well, don't be. She won't think a thing about it."

More and more people emerged. "I'd like to see you again," Luther said. "I promise to behave."

"All right then. I'll ask Papa if you can come to Sunday dinner with us."

"Maybe we can go ice skating, afterward, if it doesn't snow," he said.

"That would be fun."

He smiled and she smiled back.

"I missed you," she said.

Wilhelm threw a final pitchfork of hay from the loft to land at Sebastian's feet, then stared down at him. Wilhelm's face was grim.

What now? Sebastian wondered. He had hoped when he left the way clear for Wilhelm with Faith that he and his brother would return to their old camaraderie. But the last few weeks, it was clear something was bothering Wilhelm.

Sebastian picked up another pitchfork and began distributing the hay to the cows' stalls. A low shuffling and munching filled the barn as the cattle began to feed.

"You couldn't wait, could you?" Wilhelm burst out.

"What?"

"You know what I mean. You forced yourself on Faith, didn't you?" Wilhelm scrambled down the ladder.

Startled, Sebastian hesitated before replying, and Wilhelm's face darkened.

Sebastian thought of Faith's invitation that first night at Widow Bowman's. "I've never forced myself on a woman in my life," he said.

"So you're blaming it on Faith. Watch what you insinuate about the woman I plan to marry."

"I'm not insinuating anything." Sebastian dropped the pitchfork and stood facing his brother.

Wilhelm's gaze slid to the pitchfork, then his hands bunched into fists. For a long moment he stared at Sebastian.

Sebastian was reminded of the many times they had clashed as boys. Once it was over some fancy marbles Wilhelm thought Sebastian had won unfairly. Another time it was a dispute over whose horse could run fastest, and Wilhelm had accused Sebastian of bumping his horse to win. When they'd grown up, the rivalry had seemed to subside. But I guess I never had anything else he wanted until now, Sebastian thought.

"Watch yourself, brother," Wilhelm said at last.

The urge to lash out was strong. But what good would that do? Wilhelm would think what he wanted, regardless.

"If you plan to wed, then I'm glad for you," Sebastian said.

"I appreciate that," Wilhelm said, but his voice lacked conviction.

February 1780

"Are you sure about this marriage?" Sebastian asked Faith, setting down the axe he'd been sharpening. Gratefully, he took the hot cider she'd brought him. Despite the closed barn doors and the heat from the animals, the air was cold. They were alone in the barn, the first time he'd had to talk to her freely since she and Wilhelm announced their engagement a week ago. He hoped Wilhelm wasn't wondering where Faith was.

"What do you mean?" Faith asked.

Sebastian took a long swig of the cider, delaying his answer. "Sometimes, a person can...oh, never mind." How did you find the words to say you feared a woman you cared about might be plunging into another bad relationship? To say more would be disloyal to Wilhelm, who deserved his chance at happiness, even if he could be impatient and possessive.

"No, don't say never mind. What is it?" Faith pushed.

"I just want you to be happy. I hope you're choosing the right person for the right reasons."

"The right person is already married," she said.

He dropped his eyes, feeling miserable. "Faith..."

"I'll be happy," she said quickly. "Wilhelm can be difficult, but he can also be sweet. I care for him and I know he would never get drunk and beat me the way my first husband did. Even when Wilhelm has gotten upset, he has never threatened me in any way. I'll be glad to leave that shop and stay home like a proper wife. That's all I've ever wanted."

She reached up and touched his cheek. "You're sweet to care about me."

"I do care about you," he said. He put his hand over hers, then dropped it. That door was closed. "I'd best get back to work," he said. He drained the cup of cider and handed it back to her.

"Yes," Faith said. "You'd best do that."

June 1780

Afternoon sunlight slanted through the plain windows of the Lutheran church near Round Top. Faith, clad in a yellow gown, and Wilhelm, in his Sunday suit, stood in front of the pastor while friends and family looked on from the pews. Haying season was a busy, inconvenient time for a wedding, but the bride was pregnant, a fact barely hidden by the full skirt of her dress.

You couldn't wait either, could you, Wilhelm, Sebastian thought. *But who am I to judge?*

Wilhelm had spent most of the spring building a small house on land not far from the main farmhouse, and Maria had already given Faith a new broom, because it was bad luck to take an old broom into a new house.

Sebastian thought of the day he and Lydia stood in this same church and promised to love and honor each other. And the day a few years later when they'd loaded up their wagon, taken what stock they had and set off for the Pennsylvania wilderness. He realized the pangs he felt over losing Faith were nothing to compared to the absence of the woman who had stood by him during those hard years, the mother of his children, his lifelong companion. He blinked away moisture, hoping no one noticed. Beside Sebastian, Maria fumbled for her handkerchief as the vows were said and dabbed openly at tears.

Earlier, she had been concerned. She'd dreamed of eggs that morning, and that meant a quarrel by nightfall, she said.

"Maybe you were worried you didn't have enough eggs for the wedding feast," Sebastian told her. She laughed, yet she still looked worried. But the ceremony went smoothly.

Afterward, the guests adjourned to the farmhouse for the wedding dinner, where they exclaimed at the quantity and variety of food while Maria beamed.

Then everyone trooped out to the barn, where the dancing began. Lanterns strung from ropes lit the barn's interior. The guests filled the space and spilled out into the yard. In the darkness beyond the lanterns, fireflies flitted about, chased by eager children. Gertie jumped around and barked with excitement until Jane locked her in the house.

"Dance for flax," Maria called out. The fiddler and hammer dulcimer player struck up a fast tune and Wilhelm and Faith began to dance. Soon, other guests joined them.

Jane's pulse pounded as she raised her feet as high as she could. The higher the feet, the higher the crop of flax at the next harvest. Or so the saying went. Finally, panting and sweating, she moved over to stand in the shadows and watch.

Her eyes followed Faith, who had changed from her embroidered wedding gown to a simpler dress. The nipped-in waist and low, rounded neckline showed off her figure, made fuller by the pregnancy. Will I ever look like a woman? Jane wondered. Almost sixteen and she still hadn't filled out much. Not that Luther seemed to mind. At eighteen, he was ready to get serious. In the church, she had imagined herself standing at the altar with him. Her eyes had filled with tears as her uncle and new aunt said the vows. Marriage seemed like a wonderful idea.

Here and there, dancers tipsy from the liquor that had flowed freely all afternoon, weaved on their feet. Wilhelm, his face flushed, staggered against Faith and they both laughed. Jane looked at Papa. Sebastian's face was flushed, too, but his steps seemed sure as he danced with his sister, Anna.

A short, stocky young man with a blond cowlick walked across the barn floor toward Jane. His clothes were plain and he had a patch on one knee.

"Hello. I'm Hans Lingerfelt," he said. "Would you like to dance?"

"In just a minute," she said. "I need to catch my breath."

"Oh." He stood a moment as if unsure what to do next.

"Are you one of Hermann Lingerfelt's sons?" she asked.

"Yes. His sixth son. We don't get over this way much, but my father knows yours from the grist mill and my dad wouldn't miss a chance for a celebration."

A sixth son. Not much chance for a big farm of his own. She wondered if, like Papa, he planned to emigrate west in search of farmland. She cast about for something to say.

"Is your hay crop good this year?" she asked.

"Yes. It looks like a rich harvest."

"Good. Did you get through the winter all right?"

"It was hard on everyone, of course, but we managed." His toe tapped in time to the music as he talked.

"Good." Surely she could come up with another word than good. It was easier to talk to Luther, but then it had been difficult to talk to him, too, when they first met.

"What do you like to do when the chores are done?" she asked. There. That was better.

"Work with wood carving things. Play the fiddle."

"That sounds interesting. You should play for us," she said.

"No. I'm not that good yet. I don't get to practice much. Maybe someday."

"I'd like to hear you," she said. "I'm rested now and ready to dance if you are."

"Good."

He smiled and led her out on the floor. It was different to dance with someone who was almost the same height. She had to look up to Luther, which made her feel even smaller and feminine and like he would protect her. This made her feel more equal. She decided she liked it.

The musicians swung into "The Hay-Makers Dance," and people laughed or groaned. Tomorrow, they'd all be out working in the hayfields again. Papa whirled by with Faith, and Jane spotted Luther with a girl from church. At the end of "Hay-Makers," custom said the man stole a kiss from his partner. She turned her cheek as the music stopped and Hans planted a sweaty, gentle kiss. Out of the corner of her eye, she saw Luther kiss his partner firmly on the mouth. Darn him anyway. He didn't have to be so enthusiastic about it.

Behind her, someone shouted, making her jump. She turned to see Wilhelm shove her father away from Faith. "Leave her alone," Wilhelm said.

"What? I don't want to fight," Sebastian said, weaving on his feet.

Uncle Wilhelm laughed, weaving just as unsteadily. "Come on, be a man, brother," he said.

Anger surged through Jane. Papa was a man, a good one. He didn't swagger like some men, but he was kind and loving and he worked hard to provide for them.

A group of spectators gathered around the two men. Wilhelm's gaze swept the guests and he grinned, then again shoved Sebastian, who dropped to his knees. Suddenly, Wilhelm jumped on top of Sebastian, his smile gone, and the two tussled. Faith and the other women called for them to stop, but the men watching laughed and cheered them on, until Wilhelm groped for the pitchfork leaning against one wall, raised it high and brought it down.

Chapter Twenty Nine

Jane shrieked as the pitchfork descended. At the last second, Sebastian rolled away. Johann and Anna's husband, Jacob, rushed forward and pulled the two to their feet, holding them apart.

"Here now," Johann said. "That's enough. Wilhelm, go to the house and sober up. Sebastian, step outside and clear your head."

Wilhelm seemed dazed. "I didn't...I wouldn't..." he said. He spotted Faith standing whitefaced. "Come with me," he mumbled.

Lips tight and face impassive, she hesitated.

"Please," he said.

She put her arm around him and helped him stumble toward the house. The guests, silent now, stared after them, then murmured to each other.

"Just a little too much too drink, friends," Johann said. "Fiddler, play us a tune."

Jane walked out of the barn. Luther started to follow her, but she shook her head,

Her father stood bent over, hands on his knees. His face was sweaty and white and his breath came in gasps.

"Are you all right, Papa?"

"I'm fine."

Jane looked at him doubtfully.

Maria came up beside them. "What was that all about?" she asked. "I thought you two had mended your fences."

"I did, too, Mama, but he saw me kissing Faith when the dance ended, and I guess he imagined things that weren't so."

"Did he?"

Sebastian straightened. "Yes, he did. But it's not his fault. He had too much to drink. We both did."

"Don't make excuses for him. And you, you should have known better." She sighed deeply. "I thought I'd raised my sons better than that. Well, maybe with them in the new house things will improve."

"I hope so," Sebastian said.

Uncle Wilhelm and Papa would have to work together in the fields, Jane thought. They didn't have enough farmhands without them. Surely, once Uncle Wilhelm sobered up, everything would be all right.

Maria rounded on Sebastian. "I told you it meant something when I dreamed of eggs this morning." Then she turned her attention to Jane. "Go back to the dance, child. Enjoy yourself."

Dutifully, Jane reentered the barn. Luther stood just inside the doorway, face concerned.

"Is everything all right?" he asked.

"I suppose so," she said. She was embarrassed this had happened in front of Luther and their neighbors. Still unsettled, she thought about complaining about the hearty kiss Luther gave his dance partner. But that was exactly the way Uncle Wilhelm reacted. I won't be like that, she thought.

After another dance, the guests began going to their horses. Hans took Jane aside. "They say you're keeping company with Luther Vanderhook."

"That's right."

"If that changes, I'd like to see you again."

"Thank you," she said. "But I don't think it will."

August 1780

Lydia wiped sweat from her face and stared down from Fort Howe at the narrows of Canada's St. John River. A flock of honking geese swooped low and settled on the river with a flurry of wings.

The granite hill gave a spectacular view as sunset turned the water to ripples of gold. In the spring, after that terrible winter, when she learned the prisoners were being moved from LaChine to St. John, her spirit had quailed at the prospect. Another new place to adjust to and one even farther from Fort Niagara.

But she'd found the area beautiful, a balm to her spirit and a reminder of God the Creator. She gazed down with quiet eyes. The way the tide swept up the narrow gorge from the Bay of Fundy, lifting the water level, fascinated her. She'd made some friends. One of them was watching Henry so she could have a few minutes alone. But she was lonely. Rumor had it new prisoners were coming in tonight from Fort Niagara. Maybe they would have news of her family.

A bugle sounded in the distance, heralding the latest arrivals. With a last look at the river, she hurried back toward the fort to see a bedraggled line of men, women and children marching through the gates with British soldiers keeping watch. One man towered over the rest. Big John. And there beside him was Margaretha, carrying Elisha.

She ran toward them, only to be stopped by a soldier.

"Stay back, ma'am," he said. "We have to process them. Then you can talk to whoever you want."

All I do is wait, she thought. If patience is a virtue, I'm becoming a saint.

A crescent moon shone in the sky by the time the new captives were allowed to mingle. Lydia waited outside the processing office with a sleepy Henry as her sister and family emerged.

"Lydia," Margaretha exclaimed, throwing her arms around her. "I hoped we'd find you here." Big John, still thin and with even more scars, swept up Henry. "Look how you've grown, little man," he said. "Have you been taking good care of your mother?"

Henry, eyes big, nodded.

Later, they sat in a bunkhouse and talked while Henry and Elisha sprawled on a bed asleep.

"Thank God you're here and safe," Lydia said. "What news is there?"

"The winter was horrible," Big John said. "With their crops burnt, so many Indians starved to death outside the fort I almost felt sorry for them."

"It was the same with us," Lydia said. "But now that I've gotten enough food and some rest, I'm more like my old self, however that was."

"I just hope this will be over soon," Margaretha said. "Any news about the war?"

"You overhear bits and pieces," he said. "I know they're fighting in the South but that's about all."

"What about Isaac? Any news?" Lydia asked. She clasped her hands together tightly.

Margaretha shook her head. "Not really. We saw him once or twice at the fort and he seemed healthy, considering the winter."

"And Sebastian? Any word?" Lydia asked.

Margaretha shook her head. "I'm sorry. We've heard he's dead, killed in battle."

Lydia stared at the ground. She'd feared as much, but with conflicting reports it was possible to keep hope alive. "Are you sure?"

"Who knows? That's what the Indians say."

"But they might lie," Lydia said. With so much taken from her, she clung to the belief that somewhere her husband was alive and well. "They've lied before," she said fiercely.

Margaretha shook her head. "Yes, they might have lied. I hope they did. It's in God's hands."

Sebastian and Wilhelm rinsed their whetstones in the water horn they each carried and began stropping their scythes. Around them in the field, the other men gathered to help with the second haying of the season were doing the same. Women chatted, cooked food, prepared switchel, the cold vinegar and molasses drink served at haying time.

In the months since the wedding, the two brothers had spoken only when necessary, maintaining a frosty truce. Faith, when Wilhelm was around, kept her eyes averted from Sebastian and seemed to shrink into herself, careful to give no cause for jealousy.

Johann began a swath six feet wide on the left edge of the field, and Wilhelm began his swath fifteen feet behind him. Sebastian followed, then Jacob and another man and another. Sebastian swung the scythe in a steady rhythm, bending over to cut level to the ground; the motion felt good as the sun warmed his muscles. Soon he became aware of Wilhelm moving faster and faster. He speeded up to match. Wilhelm moved more quickly.

"A contest," someone called. Another man picked up the cry. "A contest between Wilhelm and Sebastian." Everyone stopped. The two looked at each other.

Johann walked back to where they were standing. "Ach. It's too hot," he said. "Let's just cut."

"I don't mind if Sebastian's willing," Wilhelm said.

Sebastian hesitated. Maybe this would be a way to work off some of the antagonism between them. He laughed, trying to make it light-hearted. "First man to finish gets an extra portion of whiskey," he said. Immediately, amid laughter, the betting began with the bets split evenly on the brothers.

"Three rows apiece," Sebastian said. It was a big field and the August sun was beating down.

Wilhelm nodded. "Three rows."

Johann shrugged. "All right," he said. "It will give the rest of us a break. Position yourselves and start when I say 'go'. Clean rows now; no sloppy cutting."

The two were even at the end of the first row. Sweat ran down Sebastian's face; he wiped his eyes. Chaff stung them, and he blinked to clear his vision. By the end of the second row, Wilhelm was ahead. Their linen shirts were soaked with sweat, but their pace never slowed. Sebastian felt a blister forming where he held the handle. His hands were calloused from farm work, but this was a different, repetitive action. He speeded up and pulled ahead as they started the third row. His back ached from the constant bending, Wilhelm must be in the same shape. Around them the men were shouting and egging them on. Wilhelm cursed as he swung too low and his blade hit a rock. Ordinarily, he would have stopped to examine it, but he kept swinging, faster and more wildly.

"Clean rows," Johann called. "Clean rows."

Sebastian, at the limit of endurance, put on a final burst of speed, but it wasn't enough. With one final swing, Wilhelm finished the third row, dropped the scythe and leaned forward with his hands on his knees panting. The men cheered him.

Sebastian stood for a few seconds, head hanging, while his breathing slowed, then walked over to his brother and held out his hand.

"Good job," Sebastian said. "You won fair and square."

Wilhelm looked at him for a long moment, his face impassive, then took his hand in a firm, sweaty grip.

"I did indeed."

Jane passed down the line of reapers with a pail of switchel, spooning out dippersful. Luther smiled at her, and she playfully splashed a few drops at him.

"Now I'll smell like molasses and vinegar," he said.

"Sweet and sour," she said with a laugh. "A good combination."

At the end of the line, she found Hans. His unruly hair was full of chaff and stuck out so much he looked like a hedgehog.

"Hello there," he said as he took the dipper from her.

"Hans, you came all this way to help?" she asked in surprise. He'd been showing up at church now and then, exchanging a few words with her, but this was the first time he'd been back since the ill-fated wedding party.

"Neighbors should help neighbors," he said. He lowered his voice. "Listen, I brought my fiddle. I've been practicing. I wondered if after haying was over you'd listen to me play. You'd be the first to listen outside my family."

"You should play for everybody," she said. "They'd enjoy it after working so hard."

"No. Just for you. I want your opinion first." He looked at her appealingly. "Please. We could go up Shingle Kill to where the rapids are and no one could hear me. It wouldn't take long."

"I don't know," she said.

Jacob set down his scythe and called to her. "How about a cold drink over here, please, Jane."

"If you decide you want to, I'll be waiting at the rapids," Hans said. "An hour after we finish haying. That will give time to eat and get cleaned up."

The rest of the afternoon, she thought about his invitation. There was no harm to it, and she did want to hear him play. If he was too shy to let other people listen, why not give him his first live audience? But how would Luther react to her slipping away? He didn't like Hans. She thought of the way Aunt Faith acted so meek around Uncle Wilhelm, so careful not to upset him. I'm not doing anything wrong and Luther can't tell me who my friends are, she thought. He doesn't own me. I'll do it.

Jane could hear the faint sounds of music as she picked her way through the woods toward the rapids. The woods seemed dim and cool after the blaze of sun in the hayfield.

Hans stopped playing when he saw her.

"I'm glad you came," he said.

"Is this your fiddle?" she asked, then winced. Of course it was his fiddle. He would think her witless.

"Yes," he said, holding the instrument out for her to examine. The wood, somewhat scratched, shone dully under the green light filtering through the trees. "It's not new," he said. "I'm saving to buy a new one."

She brushed dirt off a rock beside the creek and sat down. Now that she was here, she felt excited and a little nervous.

"Play for me," she said. "It will be dark soon and we need to get back."

"What would you like? Something lively or something quiet?"

"Quiet, I guess. It's been a lively day."

He picked up the bow, tucked the fiddle under his chin and began to play. He closed his eyes as the sweet, mournful sound mingled with the rushing water of Shingle Kill. His face was calm. He looked like someone who had entered another world. His playing was halting at times and some of the notes seemed slightly off, but it moved her nonetheless. It was a little like the feeling she had when she sat motionless near the stream bank and a fawn came to drink. Or when she lay spread-eagled under a maple tree in autumn and looked up through the leaves at shards of blue sky.

He stopped and opened his eyes.

"What do you think?" he asked.

"It was beautiful."

"Really?

"Really."

"I need more practice, and a better instrument. Maybe someday I'll learn how to make my own. Wouldn't that be something? Hans Lingerfelt, fiddle maker."

"It sounds wonderful," she said.

He shook his head. "Just a dream, probably. But it doesn't cost anything to dream. Now, here's how I play "Hay-Makers Dance.""

As he finished, she clapped her hands in delight. Again, it wasn't perfect, but she loved the way it make her feel and how he tapped his foot and bobbed his head in time to the music.

The woods were growing darker.

"I need to get back," she said.

"I know. I'll come with you."

When they entered the yard, most of the neighbors had gone. Luther sat talking with Sebastian on the bench outside.

"Where have you been?" Luther demanded. "It's getting dark. I was worried about you."

"I was safe. I was with Hans," she said.

"But I didn't know that."

Jane bit back a retort. "You're right. I'm sorry if I worried you," she said. "I should have told someone where I was."

"I'd best be going," Hans said, raising a hand in farewell. "Thanks again."

Luther watched as Hans walked to his horse, cradling his fiddle.

"I don't think you should be alone with that Hans boy," he said.

Chapter Thirty

April 1781

Sunday dinner was over, the dishes cleared, the men smoking their pipes while the women chatted. Luther stood in the doorway of the farmhouse's living room and cleared his throat.

"If I might speak to you alone, Jane," he said, his voice stilted and tense. "Outside."

"Of course." She sat down the stockings she'd been mending and walked outside with him. The spring air was chill and she wrapped her shawl closer around her shoulders.

"What is it?" she asked. "Is anything wrong?"

"I hope not. Your father has given me permission to speak to you, now that you're sixteen," Luther said. "Jane, will you marry me?"

She had half expected this, yet it still caught her by surprise.

"I don't know. That is, I thought I would wait to wed until my mother was free so she could be there. Can I give you my answer later?"

"No one knows how long this war will last," he said. "Your mother would want you to be happy. Anyway, what is there to think about? I love you and you love me. You have to marry sometime, and we get on well together. Maybe I should have been more romantic, brought flowers or gotten down on one knee, but I thought you felt the same way I do."

"I do care for you," Jane said. "It's just…"

"Is it that Hans boy? Are you spending time with him when I'm not around?"

He always calls him "that Hans boy," she thought. He's jealous. It must show he cares. But still, she didn't want anyone telling her who she could spend time with.

"You mean Hans Lingerfelt? We talk now and then, but I hardly know him. I just need more time."

"All right," he said. "As long as there's hope, I can wait."

He reached out, hugged her and kissed her. She returned the kiss half heartedly, wishing she felt more excitement at this, one of the biggest moments in a young woman's life.

It had been two weeks since Luther had asked Jane to marry him and he was becoming impatient, even hurt at the delay. "Am I so bad," he'd asked after church last Sunday.

I have to make up my mind, Jane thought. It's wrong to leave him dangling. She was unsure why she hesitated. When she'd mentioned the proposal to her father, he'd said only that he wanted her to be happy and that he thought Luther would be a good provider.

It was foolish, perhaps, to wish for more than a good provider, which every woman wanted, but she did wish for more. Still, he was a good man and a good farmer. She thought of the pleasant times she and Luther had together, the picnics, the walks and talks. And he was good looking. I'll do it, she thought. I'll tell Papa tonight and Luther at church on Sunday.

"Are you sure?" her father said when she told him. They sat alone on the benches outside the kitchen door as the sun dropped behind the mountain. The trees were starting to leaf out in the fresh green of spring. "You're young yet. There's time."

"That's true," she said. But it would be difficult to meet someone once they returned to the frontier, and she would have to marry eventually. Why not choose a man who loved her and that she felt comfortable with and cared about?

"How did you feel when you asked Mama to marry you?" she asked.

"It was different for us. It felt natural, right. We'd known each other since we were children. Everyone assumed we would marry, and we assumed that, too. And we were blessed that our love grew roots as deep, oh, I don't know, I guess as deep as that big old elm tree in our side yard at home." He stopped and cleared his throat. "The important thing isn't what I felt. It's what you feel. Love isn't necessary for marriage. But respect and liking are. And a willingness to work hard together to build a future."

"I respect Luther and I like him and we're both willing to work hard," she said, reassured. They sat together without talking for a few more minutes. Finally, she spoke. "I'm telling him yes."

"If that's what you want. He has a few acres of his own, but he'll need time to build a house, to provide for you properly. There's no rush to get married."

"I know. I thought I'd wait until Mama comes home."

"That's a nice thought. Of course, none of us knows when that will be. Soon, God willing." He reached over and kissed her on the cheek. "Well, little girl, I guess you're not so little any more."

Two days later, when Jane gave Luther her answer, he crushed her close, then stepped back and looked at her with such joy on his face that her heart filled with happiness, too.

May 1781

Lydia settled their few belongings in their new home at Three Rivers Point near the confluence of the Oneida and Seneca rivers. Once again they'd been moved, this time back to New York state. We're always near water, she mused, as she sat on the bed and picked up the worn Bible a British soldier had given her. It felt good to have a Bible to read again. Memory had sustained her a long time, but there was something special about touching the pages, seeing the words.

She opened the book to Psalm 19: "By the rivers of Babylon, there we sat down, yea, we wept, when we remembered Zion. We hanged our harps upon the willows in the midst thereof. For there they that carried us away captive required of us a song and they that wasted us required mirth, saying, 'Sing us one of the songs of Zion.' How shall we sing the Lord's song in a strange land?"

She closed the Bible and sat quietly with it on her lap. Wysox and the farm were like Zion, but still she was required to sing the Lord's song, hard as it might be. Sometimes, she got tired, yet underneath, she thought, the music was always there. And Margaretha had finally ceased to reproach her about Zach, whatever she might think privately.

Lydia prayed that Jane was safe at her grandparents' home. Did she know her father was probably dead? It he was alive, what joy. If he wasn't, how could they return to Wysox and farm the land without a man to help them? We'll find a way somehow, she thought. If we can get through this captivity, we can get through anything. She opened her eyes just as Henry rushed inside.

"Come see the frog I caught," he cried. "It's huge, Mama."

She smiled at his excitement and put the Bible down. Captivity taught some terrible lessons about powerlessness and cruelty, but it also made you cherish the tiny joys that came your way.

"My goodness," she said. "Let's see that big, old frog."

June 1781

"Be quiet, Bear," Jane said. "Stop barking. You, too, Gertie. What's the matter with you?" She stood outside the entrance to the cellar surveying the first rays of sun peeking over the hills surrounding Round Top. Kathleen stood beside her. Jane could see Aunt Anna with her two children already out in the field of rye. Suddenly Bear and Gertie darted off toward the woods and Anna screamed, then ran toward the opposite meadow, urging her children ahead of her.

Jane could barely make out three Indians in what looked like war paint approaching. Please let them be friendly, she thought. There's no man here to help us except Grandpapa, and he's out in the field. Papa had gone to Wynkoop's Mill on Kiskatom Creek along with Wilhelm and Jacob. Luther planned to stop by on his way to buy a pig from a neighbor. But that was no help now.

Maria peered out the door, saw Jane and Kathleen and motioned them to hide. But there was no place to go without being seen except the cellar under the house.

"Come on, Kathleen," Jane whispered. "Let's be quiet, like little mice."

Obediently, Kathleen scooted inside the cellar. Jane followed her, carefully pulling the door closed and plunging them into an earthy darkness relieved only by rays of light shining through the sides of the door. Crouching, they listened while her grandmother greeted the Indians.

"How do, how do" one said.

"Just fine," her grandmother said, her voice loud and cheerful.

Maybe everything would be all right. Then Jane heard the guttural voice of Scarred Fox. "Where Sebastian?" he asked.

Instantly, she was swept back to that dreadful day in May when Indians had come to ask for her father, then burned the farm and taken her mother and brothers captive. She felt dizzy and spots swam before her eyes. Kathleen clutched her hand in the darkness and Jane took a deep breath to steady herself.

"He's not here," Grandmama said. Then her voice rose. "What are you doing? Leave my husband's gun alone." Silence, then the voice of her grandmother again. "Get out of my linen chest. Nein. Nein. That's Sebastian's good shirt."

The Indian muttered something Jane couldn't hear.

"Why is she yelling?" Kathleen whispered. Jane put her finger to Kathleen's lips to signal her to silence.

Above them, she heard Grandmama's firm voice. "They'll not take my good linens."

Oh Grandmama, don't be stubborn now, of all times, Jane thought.

She heard a thunk and a scream, cut off abruptly as her grandfather charged through the kitchen door. "God Almighty," he exclaimed. A gun boomed in the kitchen, followed by a groan and silence. Jane's eyes, adjusted now to the dim light, looked around for a weapon. An axe with a broken handle lay in one corner. She pulled Kathleen over to the corner with her and grabbed the axe, not sure what she would do with it. Together they crouched in the darkest corner of the cellar.

What if they burn the house over our heads? Jane thought. She waited for the sound of flames, the smell of smoke. Instead, she heard someone at the cellar door. She stood up, clutching the axe and pressed closer against the dirt wall. An Indian was outlined in the doorway, sunlight bright behind him. We're not here, Jane thought. No one is here. The Indian swung his head from side to side, searching. Kathleen gasped, a tiny sound but enough.

Chapter Thirty One

No, Jane thought. I'm not sitting here waiting to die. Never again. As the Indian stepped inside, Jane rushed crazily at him, swinging the axe straight at his head. Caught off guard, he stepped back, stumbled and fell. As he lay stunned for a second, Jane brought the axe down with all her strength on the center of his head. He grabbed for her leg, tried to rise, then fell back with a groan, blood streaming from his forehead. She lifted the axe and slammed it down again. His skull made a sickening cracking sound. He twitched convulsively, then lay still, breathing shallowly.

"Don't look," she whispered to Kathleen. But Kathleen stared, frozen. Grabbing the Indian's legs, she tried to drag him the rest of the way inside the cellar. They were bound to notice he was missing. What would happen then? Had she just made things worse? But how could they be worse?

Nothing happened. No flames, no one calling the Indian's name. Gertie barked shrilly. Run away, Jane thought. They'll kill you, just like they did the other Gertie. Blood still flowed from the gash on the intruder's head, making a dark stain on the dirt floor, but he didn't move. So much blood. Almost she felt an urge to staunch the wound, to help others as she'd been taught to do until she learned that life wasn't that simple, that sometimes you had to make hard choices.

There had been three Indians. She'd killed one. The others could show up at any second. Or maybe they had fled. Let it be so, she prayed.

Kathleen crouched on the floor, arms wrapped around herself. "I was a bad girl," she whispered. "I wet my dress."

"It's all right, honey. No one will be mad at you. Now just stay quiet."

They sat in a silence broken only by the sound of their rapid breathing. She could no longer hear any sounds from the Indian and she averted her face from his body.

"Jane," a male voice called at last. "Where are you? Jane?"

She rushed to the open cellar door and she and Kathleen stepped out into the sunlight.

"Thank God," Luther said. "Are you all right?"

She swayed on her feet. "I think so. What about Grandmama and Grandpapa?"

He evaded a direct answer. "I just got here. When I rode up, an Indian looked out the door, saw me and ran across the yard." He grabbed her arm. "Jane, don't go in the kitchen."

Terrible news then. "I have to know," Jane said, pulling free. She bent down and looked Kathleen in the eyes. "Stay here and we'll be right back. All right?"

Kathleen nodded. Tears ran down her cheeks.

Jane stood by Luther's side outside the kitchen for a moment, bracing herself for what she might see. "Don't go in," Luther repeated.

"I have to," she said. "I have to see." Her legs trembled and she took a deep breath. Bad news didn't go away because you avoided it.

Luther reached out and took her hand. Together, they entered the house. Maria lay dead on the floor, her head split open, one of Sebastian's linen shirts in her hand covered with blood. Her scalp was partly severed as if the Indian had been interrupted at his work. Scarred Fox lay beside Maria unmoving. His face and neck bore huge gashes, apparently from the scythe beside him. Johann slumped against a wall, eyes blank, with a gunshot wound in his chest. Maybe he was alive.

Jane rushed to him, falling to her knees beside him. "Grandpapa, talk to me," she begged. His head lolled sideways. She felt for his pulse, put her face close to his mouth. Nothing.

"He's dead, too," Luther said in a shaky voice.

Jane burst into tears. "No, he can't be," she said. "He can't be." She dared another look at the scene, turned her head to one side and vomited on her grandmother's clean floor.

"I'm sorry," she said, as if Grandmama could hear and reproach her.

She straightened and put her hand to her mouth, struggling with her heaving stomach.

"It's all right. It's all right," Luther said. He held her while she sobbed against his chest.

Anna walked in, screamed and turned to her two children. "Don't look," she said. "Come outside."

"Come on, Jane," Luther said. "Let's go outside, too."

Jane pulled away. "I forgot," she said. "There's an Indian in the cellar."

"What?"

"He's hurt," she said. "I don't know how bad. We have to tie him up."

"Hurt?" Luther looked confused.

"He tried to come in and there was an old axe there, so I hit him in the head with it. Twice." The words came out jerkily.

Luther's eyes widened. "Oh," he said. "Oh."

"Come on." She pulled at his arm, anxious to restrain the injured Indian. She shouldn't have left Kathleen alone. What if he wasn't dead?

But the Indian lay unmoving, staring into nothingness. Kathleen stood frozen outside the cellar, crying softly.

"It's all right. The bad people are dead," Jane said, stroking her hair. "Go sit under the maple tree in the front yard. Do **not** go in the house. We have to take care of some things."

Kathleen walked over to the tree, crying softly. Jane wondered fleetingly how it felt to be part Indian and witness this. She stared at the dead Indian, hands falling to her side.

"Let's leave him here for now and get some help," Luther said.

A fly buzzed toward the man's bloody head. Jane brushed it away and swayed on her feet. "I need to sit down," she said, and slumped to the ground.

She looked at Luther. "I killed him," she said. "I killed another person."

"And he would have killed you and Kathleen if you hadn't."

"I know," she said, "I had to do it. But it's hard to take in just the same. I never killed anyone before."

"You picked the right time to start."

How could there be a right time? she wondered.

Everyone wore black for the Stropes' funeral: black bombazine dresses, black gloves, black suits. Even little Kathleen, who seemed to have recovered better than Jane, wore black. The tables at the Round Top farm groaned under the weight of the raisin pie, the cakes, apple cider, beer brought by neighbors from miles around as each mourner told those at the next farm in a chain of invitation. The best silver plate, used only on special occasions, gleamed. Mama would have loved this, Sebastian thought. She so enjoyed talking with neighbors over good food. He took a last sip of cider and mounted his horse, ready to follow the wagon with the two coffins to the church for the funeral service.

At the church, Jane sat beside him in the pew, staring blankly ahead. Since the night of the massacre, she'd slept badly. He'd heard her crying out in her sleep at times. He wished he knew how to help. But time likely was the only cure. He put his arm around her, but she remained stiffly upright. Only once did her expression vary. When a visibly nervous Hans Lingerfelt rose and played an uncertain, poignant hymn on his fiddle, tears pricked Jane's eyes.

I didn't realize the boy could play, Sebastian thought. He pulled out his handkerchief and handed it to Jane. "Thank you," she whispered and dabbed at bloodshot, haunted eyes before she passed it back.

How many blows can one person take? Sebastian wondered, unsure if he meant himself or Jane or both. As many as he has to, I suppose.

Last night Jane had asked him why people killed other people. He'd fumbled for answers. Power, fear, anger, a cause, to defend themselves or their families. He could tell she wasn't satisfied. Who would be? It was a conversation he couldn't imagine having three years ago. He felt far removed from his life on the farm when his days moved from dawn to dusk in a steady flow of chores and taming the wilderness. When the weather was his most important concern. Now it was as if a flood had raged through his orderly existence and created deeper, more twisted channels for his thoughts. Why were his parents dead? You could say it was because the Indians killed them. But if his mother had not resisted giving up her prized linens, would they have attacked? Would Scarred Fox have come looking for him if he hadn't lashed out in anger earlier over Zach and Lydia? Maybe if settlers hadn't traded rum for pelts, Scarred Fox wouldn't have become a drunk. It seemed everyone was to blame and no one was to blame.

He sighed. All a man could do was his best. He looked over at Wilhelm sitting solemnly with Faith, who cradled her infant daughter. There was one thing he could do.

The last clods of dirt covered the double graves in the family cemetery on the hill. Sebastian nodded and Jane stepped forward and placed dogwood branches, symbol of resurrection, on the mounds. The pastor read the final words of consolation from "Der Sanger Am Grabe." Wilhelm and Faith turned to go. The time had come to speak to his brother. He touched Wilhelm on the arm. His brother started and turned to stare at him.

"Our parents never wanted us to be at odds. And I don't want us to be at odds either."

Unexpectedly, tears sprang to Wilhelm's eyes. "You're right. Mama and Papa, God rest their souls, would want us to be friends again." He hesitated. "I was at fault, too. And…I'm sorry."

Sebastian reached out and clasped his brother's arms. Wilhelm returned the pressure for long seconds, then released him. Together they walked out past the rock wall enclosing the cemetery and down the hill to the farmhouse.

Rumors swept the prison at Montreal, the latest home for the captives.

"Do you think it's true?" Lydia asked Margaretha. "They say the British are going to free some of the prisoners."

"Best not to hope," Margaretha said. "This place breeds rumors like blackflies in summer. We'll find out when we find out."

"True," Lydia said. But she refused to extinguish the spark of hope at the thought of going home after all these years. Without hope, who could go on?

The next day it was confirmed: The rumors were true. They were to be freed in an exchange of prisoners, all except the able-bodied men, including John.

For once, she didn't mind moving again, although it seemed strange to have British soldiers as escorts now, instead of as their captors. As they trudged along with three hundred other women, children and old men toward Whitehall, New York, Margaretha raised the question that had been on Lydia's mind since she got the news.

"Where will you go if Sebastian's dead?" Margaretha asked. "You're welcome to come back to Wysox and live with John and me when they free him. Surely that will be soon. You can't farm the land alone and even though Henry's 11 now, he's not big or strong enough yet. We'd be glad to take you in."

"Thank you," Lydia said. "I appreciate the offer. You're a good sister." But she wasn't sure how well it would work to share a house with Margaretha.

"I think I'll go to Round Top first," Lydia said. "Sebastian's family is there. They'll make room for me. And I pray God that Jane and Sebastian are with them. After that, I don't know."

Hans rode into the yard at Round Top at a full trot and jumped off his bay horse almost before it stopped. It had been a long ride and the sun had set before he arrived. He rushed to the kitchen and pounded on the door.

Jane, settling the fire for the night, looked up in alarm as Sebastian slid the bolt and stared at Hans, gun in hand.

"What is it, Hans," he asked. "Indians?"

"No. Great news."

Jane appeared behind Sebastian, clad in a linen night wrapper. Hans spared her an appreciative glance and a smile. She blushed, embarrassed but enjoying his regard.

"What's happening, Papa?" she asked.

"Good news, apparently," he said. "Come on in, Hans."

"The British have freed three hundred prisoners," Hans blurted. "They're sending them home by way of Skeensborough. There's a list at Albany of who's being exchanged. I heard it at the mill and I wanted to be the first to tell you." He beamed with delight.

Jane and Sebastian looked at each other.

"Do you think Mama and the boys are on the list?" she asked.

"I don't know," Sebastian said. "I'll set out for Albany in the morning and find out."

"I want to come with you," Jane said.

"No. You stay here. It's better that way. We don't know what I'll find. It could be a big disappointment."

"But Papa, I can't stand to wait."

"I'm afraid you'll have to," he said.

"All right." I wonder if he'd be too angry if I snuck out and caught up with him down the trail, she thought.

He eyed her suspiciously.

Hans looked from one to the other. "I thought you'd both be happier," he said.

"We are," Sebastian said. "It's just that…"

"It's just that it hurts to hope," Jane finished. "It hurts to hope."

Nonetheless, she lay awake long into the night, hoping, dreaming, imagining what it would be like to see her mother again.

Sebastian left at dawn and Hans, who had spent the night, returned to his home. Jane slipped out moments later and stood irresolute in the stable looking at the mare in the stall. Should she go after her father? She turned to get the saddle and saw Uncle Wilhelm, arms folded, standing in the doorway.

"Your dad said you might not take no for an answer," he said. "Now, just march right back in the house and have some breakfast."

Sighing with exasperation, she turned and went inside. It was going to be a long wait.

Chapter Thirty Two

Sebastian ran his finger down the list of captives to be exchanged. Suddenly he stopped. There it was: "Lydia Strope and son; Margaretha Strope and son." Only one son. Had Zach told the truth about the Indians taking Isaac? The thought dampened the joy starting to swell in him.

And there was no mention of his brother John. But then, word was that no men under the age of 55 were being released yet.

Behind him, another man waited to examine the list. "Bad news?" he asked, seeing Sebastian's stunned expression and motionless body.

"Yes and no," Sebastian said, straightening. "At least some of my family is coming home. So good news, I suppose."

I can't wait for them to arrive, Sebastian thought, striding toward his horse. I'll go to meet them. He set off at once and found the road near Saratoga crowded with carts, wagons, every kind of vehicle filled with returning captives. Those able to walked on foot. He scanned the faces eagerly. So many people, their clothing worn, most of them thin and tired.

The line marched by with no sign of his family. Then he straightened in the saddle. There they were, all four of them, riding in a cart. His pulse raced as he pulled his horse up beside his wife.

"Lydia," he shouted. "Henry."

Lydia looked up and her face turned white. "Sebastian," she said. "Oh my God. Oh my God. We feared you were dead."

"Papa?" Henry whispered.

The driver pulled the cart to a stop at the side of the trail. Sebastian jumped from his horse as they piled out and grabbed his wife with one arm and his son with the other.

"It's really you," Lydia said. "Oh Sebastian." Her voice cracked and tears rolled down her face. Sebastian held her close, unable to speak. Around them people smiled and wiped their eyes.

"Let me look at you both," Sebastian said, stepping back. "You're thin.

Are you well?"

"Well enough now. I can hardly believe this is happening." Her voice trembled and she stared at his face.

"Believe it." He ruffled his son's hair. "Why, Henry, you're not a little boy anymore."

Henry, who had seemed on the verge of tears himself, grinned at his father. "No," he said. "I'm a big boy now."

Lydia continued to stare at Sebastian as if expecting him to disappear.

"And Isaac?" he asked.

"With the Indians," Lydia said. "I couldn't stop them." She looked at him, then burst into wracking sobs, the sobs of someone who has been brave for too many years while grief piled deep as winter snow inside her.

Sebastian swallowed hard. His son gone, perhaps forever. No, he wouldn't dwell on that now, not with Lydia and Henry here in front of him. He hugged Lydia again, reveling in being able to touch her. "Tell me later," he said. "When we're alone."

She nodded. "What about Jane?" she asked. "Is she with you? Is she well? And how is everyone else?"

Sebastian hesitated. Let no bad news mar this moment. Later would be time enough to tell her about the murder of his parents.

"Jane is fine," he said. "She'll be so glad to see you. Let's go home."

Keeping pace with the cart, he started toward Round Top with his wife and son beside him.

Jane couldn't stop looking at her mother. Mama was so thin. Her face had more lines, and her hair had grayed at the temples. But she was here where Jane could touch her, listen to her voice. After the first ecstatic reunion, Jane dreamed of pouring out everything that had happened. Instead, she contented herself with looking and looking and looking.

Now she listened as her father and mother sat around the table and talked about Isaac.

"Maybe we can redeem him," Sebastian said. "The Indians are letting some captives go if they're willing."

Jane wondered how much money it would take. Papa had gotten a little money from Grandpapa's death, but the Round Top farm, of course, went to Wilhelm.

"I hope we can buy his freedom," Lydia said. "But you don't know Rebecca." She gave a pained laugh. "She's as determined as I am."

"That's mighty determined," Sebastian said. "Just the same, I'll see what

I can find out. If he can be ransomed, we'll scrape together the money somehow, whatever it takes to get our son back."

Jane watched as her mother reached over, took her father's callused palm and smiled at him with glistening eyes. She tried to think if Luther had ever looked at her the way her mother looked at her father now. Maybe it took a long time for that to happen.

Lydia lay in bed with Sebastian beside her. She'd almost forgotten what it was like, the way the bed sagged toward his heavier weight, the warmth radiating from his body, the comforting sound of his breathing, the feel of the hair on his arms as he brushed against her.

She'd been at Round Top for three days now, resting and eating, absorbing the sad news of Maria's and Johann's deaths, learning a little of what had passed in her absence. She knew there was more to learn and that Jane ached to tell her about this young man, Luther, and so much more. She had met Faith, Wilhelm's new bride, and their young daughter. And Kathleen. What were they to do with this little half-Indian girl? Soon, she thought, soon I'll pay attention to the problems ahead. I may be selfish, but I want a little more time without burdens. I want to go where I want, do what I want and not be responsible for anyone.

Sebastian had fussed over her but made no move toward physical intimacy, even though they had the luxury of a bedroom to themselves. Tonight, she felt the first surge of desire in a long time. She let her hand rest on his arm. She felt his breathing quicken, then he reached over tentatively and touched her breast through her shift, waited a moment, then worked his hand under the cloth to touch her bare flesh.

She kept her breathing even, belying the emotions sweeping through her. The last time she'd been with a man had been the sordid bargain she'd made with Zach. And before that, the night before her capture when she had lain there stiffly beside Sebastian, still blaming him for their son's drowning. How useless blaming him had been. He was a good man and she was blessed to have him. But what would he say if he knew about Zach? Would he still want to touch her? Would he turn away in revulsion? Despite herself, she froze for a minute thinking of Zach's fumbling hands and thrusting body. In a few seconds when Sebastian got no further response, he took his hand away, sighed and turned on his side.

Was this the way it was to be, Sebastian wondered as he stared into the darkness. Would Lydia turn from him forever? That bastard Zach could only have made things worse. She was a virtuous woman. Zach must have forced her. Should he tell her that he knew or let her handle it her own way? Thank God she didn't know about Faith. Maybe it will be better when we're back at the farm in Wysox working together side by side, he thought. Maybe we just need more time.

There's no reason he need ever know about Zach, Lydia thought, acutely conscious of Sebastian's sigh and turned back. After all this time apart, I'm not going to let anything keep me from my husband. With a touch as tentative as Sebastian's had been, she slid her hand over his chest, then ran it lower down his body. He gasped, then turned toward her. He raised up on one elbow and stared at her, his form a dark outline in the room. She reached up with her other hand and drew his head down toward her mouth. His breath went out in an explosive sigh as he leaned closer. "I love you," he said before he kissed her. She kissed him with fervor, moved. He rarely spoke of love. His actions spoke for him. It was doubly sweet to hear it now.

"I love you, too," she said, and he bent and kissed her again.

Afterward, she snuggled against him content. She hadn't attained the ultimate release that used to happen often before Gideon's death, but the renewed closeness was enough for now. At the end, she had pretended a peak of passion that wasn't there. She had never discussed this deception with other women. But, she thought, I can't be the only one. And it makes both of us happy. She closed her eyes and soon fell asleep.

"Whoa," Luther said, pulling the reins on the buggy and guiding his horse to a stop in a meadow near the farmhouse. He lifted Jane down and handed her the picnic basket. It was the Sabbath and a rare free day before Jane and her family returned to Wysox.

"You don't need to go back with them," Luther said. "I'm sure Wilhelm would be happy to have you live here until we marry."

"I want to help Mama and Papa get reestablished first," she said, busying herself with spreading a blanket on the ground and setting out food. "There's a lot to do to rebuild, from what Papa says. And winter will be here before you know it, so we have to work quickly while the weather holds. It's only for a little while."

"I see," he said, his voice flat. "I thought you cared for me more than that."

"I do care for you. But I won't be gone that long." She reached out and touched his cheek. "Let's eat," she said. "Then we can talk about the future. Things go better when you're not hungry."

After they'd eaten, they sat together looking at wildflowers and basking in the summer sun. Somewhere in the distance, a bullfrog sounded a bass note, counterpoint to the buzzing of insects. "That was a great meal. I'm plumb sleepy," Luther said. "Aren't you?" He patted the blanket. "Lie down and get comfortable."

She laughed. "You have to promise to behave."

He smiled lazily. "I promise I won't do anything you don't want," he said.

"Hmm. All right." She adjusted her skirt, stretched out beside him. and closed her eyes. In the silence, she heard bees buzzing around the daisies and a bird warbling in the trees.

"You look good enough to eat lying there," Luther said. She popped her eyes open. His face was inches from hers. "How about a kiss?" he said. "Something for me to remember you by until we can be together again." Without waiting for a reply, he pressed his lips gently against hers. She returned the pressure and his kiss grew more intense. Her pulse quickened as she responded, then she pushed him away and sat up.

"I think we should stop, before something happens."

"But we're engaged. It's all right now."

"I know. But I don't want to be like Faith, pregnant at my wedding."

"Some women are pregnant at their wedding," he said. "People don't say anything."

"Not out loud. But they think things. Anyway, I don't want to start something I don't intend to finish, especially when I'm going away soon. It's not right for you or for me."

"Aw, Jane," he said. "Just a few kisses." He reached down to kiss her again. She kissed him back. His hand strayed to her leg and began to work the cloth of her skirt upward.

"No. Stop," she said.

"I thought you were enjoying it?"

"I was enjoying it. I do." She blushed. Women weren't supposed to admit that, but truth was truth, as her mother said. "That's not the point. I'm not ready, and you promised."

He removed his hand with a scowl. "I wish I hadn't."

"But you did."

"All right." He sighed, lay back and closed his eyes. She felt a surge of affection. He didn't want to stop, but he'd done it, for her. The engagement was a good decision, she thought, even if she felt uncertain at times. She just knew they could be happy together.

Chapter Thirty Three

October 1781

Jane looked at the note from Hans. She'd written to tell him she was leaving and wish him luck with his fiddle playing. He'd responded by saying he was moving to Lancaster to apprentice as a cabinet maker. Lancaster, he reminded her, was no more than a hundred miles from Wysox. Maybe I'll get up to see you sometime before you go back to Round Top for your wedding, he wrote.

It was a nice letter and brought back pleasant memories of when he played for her in the woods. She tucked it away with the other things she was packing for the move. Wilhelm and Faith had been generous with gifts of tools and household goods and even an extra horse to carry everything back to Wysox. It had been a strange few months, what with Mama still not knowing that Papa had proposed to Faith at one time. While no one said anything, Jane had caught Faith staring at her mother. If Mama noticed, she didn't show it.

Soon we'll be home again, Jane thought, then realized she should stop thinking of Wysox as home when she would be coming back to Round Top before long to start a new life with Luther.

The homestead in Wysox had changed. Bushes and weeds covered the clearing that had once been the front yard of the farmhouse. Traces of the fences remained; a pile of burned timbers still reached up like long, black fingers from the wreckage of the barn and house. A rattlesnake, startled by their approach, slithered away, scales gleaming in the sun until it disappeared into the brush.

Sebastian surveyed the scene. So much needed to be done. It was late in the year to plant crops. They would have to depend on the food they'd brought with them, plus the game he shot and what nuts and apples they found. No matter. What they'd done once, they could do again. The war wasn't officially over, but with the surrender of that British general, Cornwallis, it looked as if things were winding down. John had been freed at last and journeyed back to Wysox with them.

We're as safe here as at Round Top, Sebastian thought, and at last I'm on my own land where I belong. He looked at the mountains rising across the Susquehanna River, still unchanged, and a feeling of peace stole over him.

"We can clean out the springhouse and all sleep there tonight," he said. "Tomorrow, I'll start felling logs for the house."

He turned to John with a smile. Sebastian had been shocked at the scars covering John's body, but John's spirit seemed unbowed. So far, though, he'd been less combative, less sure he knew what was right for other people.

"You and Margaretha and the baby can share the springhouse with us if you need to," Sebastian told him. "Your springhouse was intact last time I was here, but if it's not, we'll all manage."

"Thanks," John rumbled. "Let me go look at my property, and we'll come back to help you."

Lydia turned to Jane. "Let's cut branches and sweep the springhouse floor," she said. Jane moved off with Kathleen and Gertie. The dog sniffed excitedly at the new smells. Sebastian stared after them. I never dreamed I'd end up with a half Indian to raise after everything the Indians have done to us, he thought. I lost my parents because of them. But Kathleen has nowhere else to go, and Jane loves her so much.

Kathleen tugged at a branch too strong for her to break and Sebastian smiled. She is a bright, pretty little thing, he thought. I can't blame her for what other people did. Maybe there's a certain balancing of the scales. She's not Isaac and never can be. But he's gone to the Indians and now here is this half Indian girl with us. Since the Indians had murdered his parents, Kathleen had insisted she wasn't Indian, that she was all Irish like her father. Indians were bad, she said. There was healing to be done there for both of them, he thought.

Enough musing. There was work aplenty waiting. He turned to Henry. "Give me a hand, son," he said, and they began unloading supplies.

Could you die of excitement? Lydia felt it was possible as she stood once again at Tioga Point, where Queen Esther was rebuilding her village with a remnant of her tribe.

Sebastian put his arm around her. "Stay calm," he said. But his voice shook.

"How can I stay calm?" she asked. "We're going to see Isaac at last. After all this time."

"Yes," he said, "but they refused our ransom offer and if not for Queen Esther's intercession, his Indian mother wouldn't have let us see him at all. Don't get your hopes up."

"She's not his mother," Lydia said. "I am."

"I know," he said. "I just meant..." He broke off as Queen Esther and an unsmiling Rebecca approached.

Lydia looked around. Where was Isaac? Had Rebecca changed her mind? Lydia had dreamed of this moment, and now surely God wouldn't be so cruel as to keep her from seeing her son.

Rebecca spoke first. "I am against this meeting," she said, "but Queen Esther says it may get you to give up this quest for your son that is unsettling us all."

Nothing can do that, Lydia thought.

"When can we see him?" she asked.

"Queen Esther says you have promised not to act rashly or call him your son. Does that promise still hold?"

I can do it, Lydia thought. "It does."

"Very well," Rebecca said. "He is happy with us. It's been more than three years and he knows very little English. I doubt he remembers you."

"He wouldn't forget his mother," Lydia said.

"See for yourself," Rebecca said. She turned, walked a few steps to one side and gestured.

A tall, slender man led a boy of eight clad in deerskin toward them. And there was Isaac in front of her. His tanned face still had a youthful roundness, but his frame was slim and he looked tall for his age. Like his father, Lydia thought. She felt like a starving person thrown a crumb of food. Fighting faintness, she took a deep breath.

"Hello, Isaac," she said.

He looked at her, plainly puzzled. For a second she thought she saw a spark of recognition in his eyes, but then it faded.

"Do you remember me?" she asked in English.

He turned toward Rebecca who spoke a few words in Seneca while Queen Esther watched impassively.

Isaac turned back to Lydia and shook his head. "I'm not sure," he said.

I promised not to call him my son, she thought. I didn't promise not to say I was his mother.

"I'm your real mother," she said. "Don't you remember? You have a sister named Jane and a brother named Henry. And here is your papa."

She gestured toward Sebastian, who gazed at Isaac with greedy eyes.

"Hello, son," he said. Rebecca frowned and he looked at her defiantly.

Isaac stared at him uncertainly, then turned again to Rebecca and said something in Seneca.

"He wants to know if he can leave," Rebecca said.

"No. Not so soon. Just a little longer," Lydia cried. "Can't I touch him?"

Rebecca frowned, then her face cleared. "Try it," she said.

Lydia wrapped her arms around Isaac in a fierce embrace and Sebastian stepped forward and ruffled his hair. Lydia burst into tears and Isaac pulled back alarmed.

"No," he said. "Stop."

"That's enough," Rebecca said. "There's no need to upset him further. You see that I speak the truth."

"No. It's my fault. I should have been more gentle. Let him stay," Lydia said.

"This was a mistake," Rebecca said. She looked at Queen Esther, who nodded. Rebecca spoke to Isaac in Seneca again. He began to walk away, casting glances backward. Lydia sobbed as she watched him go. Rebecca turned to leave, then looked back at them. "Oh, that fellow Zach, the trader who tried to steal Joshua from me. He got caught a few months ago." Her voice was rich with satisfaction. "He's a slave now at a village over Niagara way."

Sebastian clenched his fist. "Good," he muttered.

Lydia flinched in horror. He knows, she thought. He knows.

Chapter Thirty Four

The path from Tioga Point back to Wysox was too narrow for two horses to ride abreast. Lydia rode behind Sebastian, staring at his back as he guided his sorrel mare through the woods.

Sebastian had said nothing of consequence since they left the village. That's for the best, Lydia thought. They were both emotionally and physically exhausted. By mutual consent, they'd abandoned their plan to spend the night at Queen Esther's home and instead started for Wysox, even though it meant they'd have to camp in the woods at night.

An autumn chill filled the air, but the sky, glimpsed through the branches, was a brilliant blue. Around them, the trees blazed forth in unheeded October glory.

As darkness fell and the footing became too chancy, Sebastian called a halt. He tied his mare to a tree and helped Lydia down from the saddle without a word. She looked at him appealingly as he set her on her feet. They needed to turn toward each other now, not away.

"We can make a fire and camp here," he said, rummaging in the saddlebags.

"All right," Lydia said. She began gathering fallen wood and breaking off dead branches, feeling her dreams crumble.

The meal was a silent affair. Lydia was thrown back to the May evening when she had camped along this same trail as a captive. So much had happened to both of them since then. I made the best decisions I could at the time, she thought. Not always wise ones, perhaps, but the best I could for who I was then. We all did.

By the light of the fire, she looked at Sebastian. Still he said nothing, only stared into the flames. What was he thinking? The piercing pain over Isaac and now this new estrangement swept over her. I can't stand this, she thought. We have to talk about it, even if he despises me.

"I need to tell you something," she said.

He reached out and grabbed her wrist. "No. You don't," he said, looking at her for the first time, his gaze steady. "It's all right."

The temptation to let that be the end of it tugged at her like a whirlpool in the river. But whirlpools led down and down and few who were caught in them emerged unscathed.

"What do you know?" she asked.

"I met Zach at Stroudsburg and he told me he had lain with you. I fought with him because he said you were willing and I knew that couldn't be true."

She continued to look away. "He promised he would take Isaac to a safe place where I could be with him later if I...you know." She raised her head and she looked straight at him. "So I did."

His hand tightened on her wrist with an almost painful pressure, but she refused to pull away.

"Well," he said, his voice gentle, "you did what you thought you had to. I can't say what I wouldn't do to save our son. I didn't save Gideon."

"Don't," she said. "Let that go. I have."

He twisted his hand to turn the grip on her wrist into a handclasp. His throat moved as he swallowed hard. "While we're confessing things, when I thought you were dead, I laid with a woman I...fancied."

A swift pain pricked her, like a wasp stinging and flying away. She hated to think of Sebastian with another woman — who was it, she wondered — but she could understand. "I wouldn't want you to live your life alone," she said.

"Thank you," he said. "Not would I want you to be alone if something happened to me."

"Don't say that."

He pulled her closer. "About Isaac," he said, "while we're clearing the air. We can ask Queen Esther to help us keep up with him. Someday when he's older, we can try again. He may want to know his white parents then, even if he never comes back to us."

That wound was still too fresh. Lydia nodded, unable to speak.

"Let's get some sleep," he said. "We're both exhausted and tomorrow we'll be back at the farm. There's a lot to do. Thank God we're here together to start over."

A lot of people had died, and she wasn't sure God had a hand in that. But they were together, and that was, indeed, what mattered.

"Yes," she said. "Thank God."

Jane sat in the newly hollowed-out thicket and fingered her fossil shells.

They'd lain here untouched, waiting for her return. Through the dim green light filtering in, she examined a fragment of gray shale containing a tiny, fan-shaped shell with ridged edges. She wondered what kind it was. She felt more peaceful than she had in years. A lot had happened, much of it terrible, but not all of it bad. Mama and Papa had come back yesterday without Isaac, something they were all sad about. But things were different between them, in a good way. Papa had whistled while he milked the cows. Mama. even though she had had dark circles under her eyes in the morning, as if she'd slept badly, laughed with Papa at breakfast. Their love really was like that sturdy old oak tree Papa had mentioned.

Jane probed at her feelings for Luther. I should never have said I'd marry him, she thought. I knew that deep inside, but I didn't listen to myself. He was nice, and I was afraid of not finding someone I liked back on the frontier, I guess. I'll tell him as soon as I can. She felt sorry for the hurt it would cause. But it would be a worse hurt to marry him.

She thought of the note from Hans that she kept among her things. If he knew she was free, he would want to see her. The possibility pleased her, even if it was too soon for that. She wanted to go slower this time. All she really knew was that he was a nice boy who liked to work with wood and play the fiddle.

There's time to find out more, she thought. Time to find out more about a lot of things.

For the true story of the captivity of my ancestors, the Stropes, see the next page.

The True Story

On May 19, 1778, *during the Revolutionary War, a friendly Indian stayed at the Strope farm on Wysox Creek near the Susquehanna River in Bradford County. He warned the Stropes that Indians friendly to the British might raid the farm.*

Living there were Sebastian and Lydia Strope and their six children, along with Big John and Marytje (also known in historical records as Margaretha) Strope and their children, plus the parents of Lydia and Marytje VanValkenburg. The sisters had married the Strope brothers.

Sebastian set off for Forty Fort near Scranton for help, which arrived too late. On May 20, a group of Seneca Indians captured everyone, including Jane, burned the farms and drove off the livestock. It was probably Mr. VanValkenburg who pulled the Bible from the flames, although at least one account attributes the rescue to Lydia Strope. (The Bible survived and is on display in a museum in Towanda, Pa.)

The captives were taken to Tioga Point, Pa., to the settlement of Queen Esther, a part-Indian friend, where John was spared running the gauntlet through her intercession.

When the Hartley and Sullivan military expeditions came through, Tioga Point was destroyed. The captives were moved to various points in New York and Canada, including Niagara Falls and LaChine. The trader Zach is fictional, but Lazarus Stewart, Zeb Butler and Col. Denison were historical figures. Some of the dialogue I gave them at Forty Fort are words that history records they actually spoke.

Sebastian fought at the massacre at Forty Fort and escaped by hiding in either a gorse bush or near a stack of lumber. Queen Esther, enraged by the slaying of her son, apparently was there, although accounts differ about her presence.

At some point Sebastian made his way to the farm of his parents, Johann and Maria Strope, at Round Top, N.Y., on the Hudson River near present-

day Cairo. (*Faith and Wilhelm are fictional.*) In 1780, irate Indians came seeking Sebastian, who was away. His parents were killed after Maria resisted letting Indians take her son's shirts and her linens.

In the fall of 1781, the families were freed and Sebastian was reunited with his wife and all his children at Whitehall. They returned to Wysox to resume farming. Sebastian, Lydia, Big John and Margaretha and some of their children spent their lives in the Wysox area and died there.

In later life, Jane married twice and died in her eighties in 1852 in Toulon, Ill., at the home of a son after a short illness.

See next page for book club questions.

For an account of Jane Strope's captivity in her own words visit www.joycetice.com/families/janestro.htm

Discussion Questions

1. Did Lydia make the right decision by agreeing to have sex with Zach in exchange for his promise to rescue her son Isaac?
2. Much of the novel is about decisions and their consequences. Which decisions were good ones in your opinion and which ones were not?
3. Who is your favorite character? Least favorite? Why?
4. As a captive, Lydia had little control over her fate. What did she have control over? What are the lessons from that, if any, for us today?
5. If you were continuing the story, what future would you envision for Kathleen, the half Indian/ half white daughter of One Eye? For Jane?
6. Which of the three main characters do you think grew or changed the most during the novel? Why do you say that?

If you enjoyed this book, you might also enjoy Sandy Hill's novel "Tangled Threads," set in a North Carolina cotton mill village in the 1890s and 1950s.

To contact the author, visit **www.tangledthreadsbook.com**

Made in the USA
Charleston, SC
17 September 2013